FOOD FOR THOUGHT

The house was large, and as Gaetano mixed him a drink from the wet bar, Lano looked around the room they were in. A den, maybe, or a study. A fireplace and several leather chairs. There was a large desk with three phones on top and nothing else visible. No papers or pencils or anything. Maybe the old guy couldn't read or write. Or maybe he just didn't trust Lano.

"Like what you see?"

"Yes, sir."

Buffo grunted, and he and his son shot each other a quick glance before the old man looked back at Lano. "You got respect. It'll be a pleasure to help you out while you're here. Funny thing though. Art always said you was a wiseass." Said derisively, Lano decided; a little dig to put the kid in his place.

"Only at home," Lano said.

"That's good, because this ain't Chicago. You're in Atlantic City now, and we got guys here, cut your heart out and mix it inna their spaghetti sauce, you say something they don't like. . . ."

Rex Stout

THE BLACK MOUNTAIN
BROKEN VASE
DEATH OF A DUDE
DEATH TIMES THREE
FER-DE-LANCE
THE FINAL DEDUCTION
GAMBIT
PLOT IT YOURSELF
THE RUBBER BAND
SOME BURIED CAESAR
THREE FOR THE CHAIR
TOO MANY COOKS

Max Allan Collins

THE DARK CITY
BULLET PROOF

A. E. Maxwell

JUST ANOTHER DAY IN PARADISE
GATSBY'S VINEYARD
THE FROG AND THE SCORPION
JUST ENOUGH LIGHT TO KILL

Loren Estleman

PEEPER

Dick Lupoff

THE COMIC BOOK KILLER

Randy Russell

HOT WIRE

V. S. Anderson

BLOOD LIES

William Murray

WHEN THE FAT MAN SINGS
THE KING OF THE NIGHTCAP

Eugene Izzi

KING OF THE HUSTLERS
THE PRIME ROLL

Gloria Dank

FRIENDS TILL THE END
GOING OUT IN STYLE

Jeffery Deaver

MANHATTAN IS MY BEAT

Robert Goldsborough

MURDER IN E MINOR
DEATH ON DEADLINE
THE BLOODIED IVY
THE LAST COINCIDENCE

Sue Grafton

"A" IS FOR ALIBI
"B" IS FOR BURGLAR
"C" IS FOR CORPSE
"D" IS FOR DEADBEAT
"E" IS FOR EVIDENCE

David Lindsey

IN THE LAKE OF THE MOON

Carolyn G. Hart

DESIGN FOR MURDER
DEATH ON DEMAND
SOMETHING WICKED
HONEYMOON WITH MURDER
A LITTLE CLASS ON MURDER

Annette Meyers

THE BIG KILLING

Rob Kantner

DIRTY WORK
THE BACK-DOOR MAN
HELL'S ONLY HALF FULL

Robert Crais

THE MONKEY'S RAINCOAT
STALKING THE ANGEL

Keith Peterson

THE TRAPDOOR
THERE FELL A SHADOW
THE RAIN
ROUGH JUSTICE

David Handler

THE MAN WHO DIED LAUGHING
THE MAN WHO LIVED BY NIGHT

Jerry Oster

CLUB DEAD
INTERNAL AFFAIRS

THE PRIME ROLL

by Eugene Izzi

BANTAM BOOKS
NEW YORK · TORONTO · LONDON · SYDNEY · AUCKLAND

THE PRIME ROLL

A Bantam Book / March 1990

ISBN 0-553-28376-6

Published simultaneously in the United States and Canada

Bantam Books are published by Bantam Books, a division of Bantam Doubleday
Dell Publishing Group, Inc. Its trademark, consisting of the words "Bantam
Books" and the portrayal of a rooster, is Registered in U.S. Patent and Trademark
Office and in other countries. Marca Registrada. Bantam Books, 666 Fifth Av-
enue, New York, New York 10103.

PRINTED IN THE UNITED STATES OF AMERICA

O 0 9 8 7 6 5 4 3 2 1

*This book is dedicated with love
to the patron saint of Chicago
writers, Mary McLaughlin.*

To her daughter, and my friend, Ellen.

To her son, the world class runner, Andrew.

1

Lester hated this cold-ass weather. He'd been born and raised right there in Atlantic City, and here he was now pushing forty, trying to remember a time when it had been this cold, and coming up short.

He had to meet the man, though, in a spot where the man would feel safe in his mind that the conversation wasn't being recorded, so that meant out here in the shell of the building that would soon be the Eighth Wonder Casino and Hotel, far down the north end of the Boardwalk, where the wind could get at you and tear your ass up.

Lester hadn't planned on this meeting taking place so soon. Had, in fact, figured that the man would hold out, look for a settlement through the courts, bide his time and let the men Lester represented begin to hate each other, fermenting seeds of mistrust and hate that would evolve finally into revolt. The mob would plan to either have Lester ousted, or, worse, break the union.

Which was a joke. As union president, he represented over a thousand men, all of them electricians. Lester smiled, feeling the icicles on his mustache crack and dribble down his chin. Atlantic City without electricians. He had to smile, thinking about that, in a town where neon was king.

This time, though, he would be tough with them. He had to get safer working conditions for his men, get the raise in pay, too, that was important, but he had to get language written into the next contract that firmly stated that there would be no more work done while hanging off goddamn catwalks, none of that stupid shit the casino bosses were telling them to do these days. Big men with connections, acting like the electricians were slaves because they worked hard for their money.

"Hey, Fincher, that you in there?" Lester could see the man's shape out there on the Boardwalk, a broad man with big shoulders, wearing a long overcoat, no hat. He'd bet the coat was made of camel's hair. These guineas were big on that kind of stuff.

"Who else you think stupid enough to be standing in here?"

"Well, hell, come on, man. I'm freezin'." The man spoke with the hard nasal sound of South Philly.

Lester said, "Where's the man? He with you?"

"I'm gonna take you to him, you ever get your ass out of the wind."

Lester began to walk quickly toward the Boardwalk, hunched against the wind. He stepped out into the bright lights that reflected down on them from Resorts International right next door. He could hear the ocean attacking the beach, roaring, could taste the salt water misting all around him.

The man was standing there watching Lester approach, smiling, stomping his feet and waving one gloved hand, urging him to hurry. Lester obliged.

Their car was down the stairway, at the edge of the street where usually only municipal vehicles were allowed. Inside, a man was sitting behind the wheel, his features in shadow because here, behind the casinos, there was no neon.

Lester got into the backseat, on the driver's side, settled in back there and began to feel uncomfortable. In the history of Atlantic City, no union leader had ever been murdered on her streets. Still, there was always a first time.

Lester said, "Where's the boss man?"

The South Philly flash was next to him, smiling, acting like a pimp talking to a reluctant john. When he spoke, the olive oil was in his voice, persuading and smarmy.

"We're goin' to his house, Lester. Gonna sit down with the big man himself, have a glass of wine, a meal."

"Yeah?" Lester said. "What's on the menu." He spoke without enthusiasm, turning to look at the man, seeing the smile gone now, a vicious grimace twisting the man's face. Saw, too, a pistol coming up quick, then felt the barrel screwing into his ear.

He heard the little South Philly flash next to him hiss, "Your brains," and he tried to react, get his arm up in time to deflect the barrel, but he wasn't fast enough, and he never did hear the report as the pistol blasted loud in the enclosed space, just jumped as the bullet entered his brain. He was dead by the time the flash pulled the trigger the second time, putting the security round through the back of Lester's head.

Mother Nature was going fifteen rounds with mankind and if it had been a real fight with a referee it would have been stopped. Winter this year was kicking ass. Brian O'Shea stood leaning against the stone wall of the balcony outside his penthouse suite, staring at the Atlantic Ocean. He was hoping that the bitch Nature was punching herself out, so he could get off the ropes, maybe score a late-round knockout.

The Atlantic wasn't playing around. High waves were

crashing against the beach, whipped into a frenzy by a thirty-mile-an-hour wind. Below, a few brave souls on the Boardwalk pulled themselves along on the rail hand over hand, their heads down, their hair and clothing caught in the wind. It seemed as if a giant magnet was pulling them into the casino.

He should be so lucky.

He sighed, squared his shoulders, and walked back into his luxurious apartment, wondering if today was the day that his luck would finally change; then felt it. Yes, it would be.

Brian went into a tile bathroom and used a clean towel to wipe the salt water from his face. He combed his hair in the steam-proof, full-length mirror. He smiled. Fifty-two and he still had it, the face jowly now, wattled around the neck, but hell, wattles hadn't seemed to hurt Ronald Reagan any. There were deep dimples on either side of the smile, and the light green eyes twinkled at him. His bushy red hair was combed to the right. His eyes dropped to the large belly that hung over his belt. On a shorter man it might look fat, but with his sixty-inch shoulders, the belly looked, at least to him, natural. All of this on a large-boned, six-foot-three-inch frame. He pulled on the lapels of his lucky green blazer, straightened the seam of his pressed white pants. He pulled himself up to his full height, smiled at himself again, saw himself grinning cockily back; the perfect image of confidence.

As he headed to his private elevator, which would take him down into his casino, he decided that as long as he maintained that image of confidence, he would have a chance.

He did his walkthrough, smiling as his heart broke at the sight of the mostly empty tables. There was no clanging of coins or ringing of bells coming from any slot machines because there *were* no slot machines in the Shamrock. The only batch he'd got in from Acey's Manufacturing—the largest maker of slots in the world—had been defective, had paid out at ninety-nine percent instead of raking it in for him, making him rich the way the slots did for all the rest of the casinos in Atlantic City. And now Acey's was dragging their feet, telling him that they were waiting to see if he would get his permanent license before committing themselves to giving him the thousands of slot machines that would put him over the top; Acey's knowing damn well that without slots he'd never get the license. Like everyone else in this goddamn town, Acey's, with their own casino on the Boardwalk a couple miles away, was stonewalling him, trying to run him out.

The dealers were standing smiling behind their green felt tables, nodding and saying hello as he passed. Their starched white shirts with the shamrocks all over them had no pockets, and were tightly buttoned at the cuff. No jewelry was allowed when they were working, not even earrings. During working hours the dealers weren't supposed to be individual people; they were supposed to be polite and respectful dealing machines, raking in the chips.

He smiled and nodded back, gave stern looks to the bolder dealers who called him Brian instead of Mr. O'Shea. He'd have to let Malcolm know which ones they were, so they could get the ax. The problem with that was, Malcolm would have a lot more on his mind when they met today than disrespectful dealers.

He stopped at Millie's table, which was full, standing room only as the players called her by name, told her to be kind and give them the card they needed to make twenty-one. He smiled at her, Millie working, looking only at the cards, the customers, not into the casino or off into space like a lot of dealers.

He liked her. Liked her a lot. Millie Swan with her head of black hair, processed into little waves that fell to her shoulders. Dark flashing eyes that laughed even when her mouth didn't. A strong chin, too, no fat underneath. Or anywhere else on that fine tight body. She was the only employee he had who didn't gamble, didn't drink, didn't hang out with anybody. Every day, though, she'd be in the hotel gym, working out. After work, it was always straight home, where she was rumored to have a young child. It was rumored, too, that she was a dyke, but that was probably just some bullshit started by a resentful dealer who figured himself for a playboy, whom she'd shot down. O'Shea watched her, liking her style. She was apologizing to a player who had tapped out.

"Maybe next time, huh, sir?"

The guy was shaking his head. "You're hot today, lady." He picked up his cigarettes and put them in his pocket, and O'Shea watched him walk off, still shaking his head.

"'Evening, Millie," O'Shea said, and she didn't miss a trick, dealt the cards out and didn't look up until the hand was completed, the money paid out, and the loose cards raked in.

"Hi, Mr. O'Shea!" She appeared happy to see him, and this he took as another good omen. He knew that Millie loved the job, loved to deal cards, and seemed to like the hell out of the customers, but she had made it clear right from the first day, she didn't mess around with the employees.

"Working till closing?"

"Yes, sir."

"Come on up and see me when you get done, Millie, in the needle. We're having a meeting and we want you to sit in." He spoke with respect, no hidden meaning there for any of the players to misunderstand. The only person who had to understand anything was Millie, and she would know this meant O'Shea had chosen her to deal blackjack tonight in his after-hours game.

Her face brightened, and she nodded her head. "I'll be there, sir." He'd bet she would. Five hundred a night and she got to keep all her tips, she'd be dumb to take a pass.

He nodded back, wished the players at her table good luck, turned and walked away.

He stopped at the main attraction and smiled with pride at the square bullet-proof glass display. This was his good-luck charm, and as long as it was there he would have hope.

Inside the glass, stacked in a pyramid, was a million dollars in hundred-dollar bills. At the apex of the pyramid was a picture of O'Shea, smiling and holding his arms out. Underneath the picture were the typed words: FOR YOU! ONE MILLION DOLLARS CASH TO THE HIGH ROLLER WHO ROLLS ELEVEN STRAIGHT SEVENS ON THE COME-OUT, OR THE LUCKY BLACKJACK PLAYER WHO PULLS ELEVEN STRAIGHT BLACKJACKS! There was an asterisk behind the last word, and in much smaller print the card gave out the qualifications. To win the money, you had to be betting a minimum five-hundred-dollar bet at either game. There was always a guard within three feet of the display, watching carefully, and a camera was always trained upon it.

Brian bounced on his toes a few times, staring at his lucky million. He knew that the dealers and the pit crew would be watching him; that they'd heard all the rumors and were wondering if he had what it took to make it. He leaned forward and kissed the glass, knocked on it seven times with the knuckles of his right hand, the smile never fading.

"Everybody's winning your money lately." He heard the soft voice behind him, sexy, a telephone voice if ever he'd heard one. The difference being that usually broads with voices that sexy were ugly with warts and a hundred pounds overweight. But not this one. He turned slowly, nodding.

"Conway. I heard you had a short string of luck last night."

"More than that, Brian. I cleaned up for over a hundred thousand, following a roller from Seattle was on a streak, at the crap table."

"Only into me for—what—three hundred now, is it? Tell you what. I got to go meet Malcolm. You come up to the suite in maybe an hour, give me a blow-job, okay? We'll take another grand off the tab."

She'd been looking at him with near-triumph in her eyes, the woman red-headed and green-eyed. On more than one occasion she'd been mistaken for his sister, the one who'd gotten all the good-looking genes. She was tall and very slim, almost skinny from behind, but up front, ah, what a rack there. He could see the tops of them now, Conway still in her evening gown from the night before, which he'd paid for. All fragile and delicate-looking, her eyes filling with hurt as she realized maybe for the first time that the hundred-grand win last night didn't change anything. There wasn't a casino in town Conway wasn't into for big green, and all the rest of them had cut her off. O'Shea kept her in a double room in the hotel and paid for her clothes, let her gamble and get further and further into his debt. She was twenty-three and belonged to him. She didn't realize it, not yet, but he owned her, body and soul.

She lowered her eyes now, submissive, the way he liked it. "An hour?"

"Give or take. If I'm not there, wait."

She nodded and walked away.

O'Shea watched as the woman glided away from him, her head now held high, the light red hair fine and clean, hanging straight down to the middle of her back. The few players at the five-dollar blackjack tables turned and gave her long looks, a couple of them saying something to her. She didn't even bother to acknowledge their presence. He wondered what the small-time players would say if they knew the sort of things he made her do for him. He watched her swing it into the bar, needing a few belts to anesthetize her. Well, that was all right, too. As long as she did the things he told her to do when he wanted her to do them.

Malcolm was pacing the office when O'Shea entered. Malcolm was the comptroller for the hotel casinos and was always nervous. Sometimes his pessimism would even catch hold of O'Shea, too. But he wouldn't let it today. Today, he felt lucky.

Malcolm looked his age. His hair was gone, his face lined. He jumped right in before O'Shea even settled into his chair. "The hearing's Tuesday. If we don't get the slots, we're dead."

"Never say die."

"Brian, without the slots, we're goners. It's as simple as that. Maybe even with them, the way things are going."

"The odds are with us, Malcolm. Calm down. It'll swing our way."

"Brian, there're a couple things you really don't understand. Number one, you got the worst location on the Boardwalk—"

"Yeah? Location, is it? Hey, people drive all day, get on buses in New York, Philly, Boston, Syracuse, to come to Atlantic City, do their gambling. We're on the far south side of the Boardwalk, a single mile from the last casino, and you're telling me that mile makes a difference?"

"All the difference in the world, when you add it with all the other stuff, mainly the fact that we have no slots.

"Brian, the other casinos, they're paying their bus drivers extra to tell the passengers that we're going under, that we're in bankruptcy. Then they tell them they better stay away from us, 'cause with our problems, we'll cheat them.

"Take a look around, Brian. See what you got here. The law says you got to have five hundred rooms, you build a thousand. All doubles or suites, all with the mirrors on the ceilings over the beds, big tubs, brass fixtures. Hell, the cable TV and heating bill *alone* is killing us. Then you charge only seventeen-fifty a night for the room. This ain't Vegas, Brian. You can't get away with that here."

"We got a full house every weekend, don't we?"

"Oh, yeah. They love to stay here. Get the room for next to nothing then go out back, get in a cab and go down to

Trump's or somewhere else. You got to raise the room rates, for one."

"All right," O'Shea said, then smiled at the shock on Malcolm's face. He never gave in this easy, and now he could see Malcolm wondering what this was going to cost him.

Cautiously, Malcolm said, "You pay the dealers too damn much, too. Twice what the other casinos pay. You say it's so they'll smile, be polite to the customers. Well, Steve Wynn has the friendliest dealers in town over at the Golden Nugget, and he isn't paying his help any extra money."

"They make good money, they don't try to steal."

"Yeah? Maybe you're right, but the payroll's killing us."

"It's deductible."

"I know what isn't deductible."

"Don't even say it, Malcolm. The after-hours game stays open, no matter how much we're losing."

"You got six penthouse suites up in the needle, Brian, and one of them becomes a crap game after four. It's eating us up. We're getting the high rollers from the other joints because they know the game's straight, but they been tearing us up for twelve straight days. You playing there's eating us alive. And if the Gaming Commission hears about it, it's good-bye license."

"The game stays open."

"Just close it for a couple of weeks. Until the hearings are over. Or at least, quit playing in the game yourself."

"No."

Malcolm's face flushed. He said, "You're the only guy on earth who could come to Atlantic City and open a casino that loses money. Here we're supposed to have everything. Christ, our Paradise Island casino, we got to pay a three-and-a-half-million-dollar annual fee, plus twenty-two and a half percent of the gross. And there, we're making a fortune. Here, the tax rate is eight percent, and we're getting killed. Not to mention, we got people staying in the casino suites for free. That fag, hit us for a hundred-thirty G's over New

Year? We fly him in here, not a month later, put him up in a suite, comp him and his boyfriend to the eyeballs. They're eating steak and lobster twice a day, room service. He's ordering champagne, the works. He's downstairs last night, I'm looking through the Eye, he's betting five-dollar chips at the blackjack tables, telling everyone how he won big here three weeks ago. Scimone's walking by, the pit boss, this fag calls out to him: 'Oh, Jimmy? Bring me a book of matches, will you?' Like Scimone gets paid to wait on him." Malcolm took a second to catch his breath and O'Shea jumped into the silence feetfirst.

"I'm glad you brought up the Bahamas club, Malcolm."

Malcolm raised his eyebrows now, shaking his head.

"The permanent-license hearing is Tuesday. Without slots, we don't get the license, right?" He didn't wait for a reply. "Get me the slots off Paradise Island. Bring them in here and have them set up while we're closed, tomorrow night, Saturday night, early Sunday morning. By Monday, they'll be fully operational. Fuck Acey's, fuck Bally's, fuck 'em all. We'll close the Bahamas casino down, bring everything over here."

"Gamble it all on one roll of the dice."

"That's right, Malcolm." Brian watched Malcolm's face twist, Malcolm working himself up for a speech he wasn't sure he should make.

"Brian, we been together—what—thirty years? I've been with you since you were shooting craps in alleys, looking for a stake to get into a Miami pro game. We been through Cuba together, through legal and illegal games. I stood by you when the feds offered me full immunity and whatever was left of the business after you took a fall, in return for my testimony against you. I never once went against you. Now you got a casino lost six million in two months, a pro game after hours that would maybe be making money if you didn't play in it. A hotel full of freeloaders who park here and gamble someplace else. And you want to close down the only profitable operation we got going, and throw everything into this joint. Brian, it's throwing good money after bad."

"Malcolm, are you gonna do what I told you, or aren't you?"

"You won't play the *game* here, goddamnit, Brian. You won't talk to the mob guys. You won't pay off the politicians. You make everyone else look cheap by paying the dealers too much money. You let fags do what they want—"

"The fag stays. He'll lose that money, sooner or later."

"That's not the point!"

O'Shea glared at him, then watched as Malcolm took long, slow deep breaths, controlling himself. At last, the accountant said, calmly, "You think you can pull it off, don't you? Beat the odds and make this place go. That's what you're planning, isn't it?

"But Brian, listen to me. They *hate* you out here. They're working together to make sure you don't get your license."

"There's a new game in town, Malcolm. There's a mayor now, and a city-council rule. Not like it was before, when gambling was first passed in referendum. The mayor doesn't want the mob in here because of all the shit the mob's pulled since A.C. opened up to gamblers. I've talked to him. He's on our side. We get the slots, we'll get the license."

"You still didn't answer my question, Brian."

O'Shea still didn't.

Malcolm said, "Brian?" thoughtfully, then said, softly, "You really do think you can pull it off, don't you? You never went with the percentages in your life, and you're not about to start now, are you, Brian?" There was surprise in his voice, wonder there, too. O'Shea softened his glare, shrugged his shoulders.

"I feel lucky," he said, and Malcolm surprised him; he grinned.

"OK, Brian. I wouldn't even be listening to this if it were another man talking. I'd'a pulled stakes and left a long time ago. But you, Brian, if anyone in the world can do this, you can."

"So get on the phone and call Riordon in the Bahamas, will you?" O'Shea checked his watch, started to get to his feet.

Malcolm said, "Wait, one more thing. There's some cop been coming around, asking questions about the union boss got hit last week—"

"You sure it's a cop? Not some goddamn hitter from Biari?"

Malcolm shook his head. "I checked his badge, called his home base. He's straight. The cop's from Akron, Ohio. On loan out here on account of the dead guy's his brother. All he wants to know is if we did business with his brother's union. I told him of course we did, shit, everyone in Atlantic City deals with the unions. Told him we know nothing about the dead guy, that you never talked to him. That's what we got casino managers for, to deal with that bullshit."

Brian pushed back his chair and got to his feet. "Tell this cop to go fuck with the Biari family. They're the only ones crazy enough to kill a union bigwig. Everyone else out here just pays. I'll be in my suite for about a half-hour, you need me."

Malcolm was already holding the phone receiver to his ear with his shoulder, tapping out the number of the Bahamas casino with the bottom of a pen. He said, "Speaking of which, there's that guy from Seattle, hit us for half a million last night. He wants Conway, comped, in his room." He saw the look on O'Shea's face, and hurriedly added, "I told him she's private stock, the boss's lady." He said it and watched as O'Shea surprised him again, this time by getting a thoughtful look on his face and nodding his head, then not saying anything as he walked out of the room.

2

His back was to her. He was watching the hometown Chicago Bulls play the Boston Celtics on the big-screen TV and cheering for the Bulls. Arliss Owen leaned against the doorframe of their near North apartment, looking at him almost wistfully. She had a decision to make here. She knew that it would be easier for her if she wasn't staring at him, but she couldn't help herself. In all her thirty-one years, he was the guy she'd come the closest to loving. Anyway, she really loved watching him gamble.

Arliss was an even six feet tall in her bare feet, and at sixteen her hair had turned from light blond to almost white. It was thin hair, but long and beautiful. She had a habit of grabbing a few strands of it and twisting it around in her fingers, then putting the hair in her mouth. She usually did this when she was thinking about something, like she was now.

Thinking about whether she should stay or leave. She was a gambler's woman and the man she was staring at, Juliano Branka—Lano to everyone who knew him—was indeed a gambler. All her life, Arliss had gone from gambler to gambler, following the odds and percentages, flitting from streak to streak. But she'd stayed with Lano six months, which was some kind of record. She wasn't thinking about leaving him because he was losing; if anything, the man was on the roll of his life, had won thousands and thousands of dollars in a lucky streak that had started right before Christmas and had lasted until today, January 27. In fact, he'd told her that he had seventeen dimes— thousands—on the Bulls tonight. They were 17½-point underdogs and he'd taken them against the Celtics at the Boston Garden. He'd told her that the smart money was riding on Boston but that no team in the Eastern Division was a goddamn seventeen-point favorite against any other Eastern team, and especially the Bulls. And it would appear now that he'd been right. With four minutes left in the game, the Bulls were down eleven and had the ball.

She listened to him talking to the television, her man being the single most intense individual she'd ever known; Arliss watching him and feeling tears in her eyes, that's how much she liked him and did not want to leave.

Lano's intensity was not limited to basketball games. He'd get her in bed and, God, it was the best. He would kiss her passionately, with his eyes open, staring at her like he was learning the meaning of life. And when he came he'd scream, sounding as if he were going to die. When he was talking to her about something he would shut the rest of the world out; the phone would ring and he'd let the machine answer. Early on, he'd been telling her about some conventioneer doctors he'd beaten out of three grand playing craps in a downtown hotel room and the phone had buzzed and she'd told him it was ringing, but he'd ignored it. Later, he'd told her, when he was with her, he was *with* her. That's why he'd gotten the answering machine.

And when he was gambling, he was *gambling*.

He would light up, there was no other way to describe what happened to him then. His black, wild eyes would shine, and his face would transform, and his arms would nearly burst from his shirt as he shook the dice or looked at his hole card or dealt a hand of poker. He'd talk to the tools of his trade, too, tell them what he wanted from them. His voice would caress the dice as he softly shook them, sometimes shooting them onto the crap table from behind his back. He was a card and he had a good sense of humor. Like the time they'd been walking together in downtown Chicago and some Jesus freak had asked him if he'd found Jesus and Lano had said, "Shit, I didn't know he was lost."

And he treated her better than any other gambler had; he never slapped her around or blamed her when things went bad. Lano was pretty much in control, always acted as if he knew the night's outcome before he'd left the house. He'd lose, smile, tell the players he'd get them next time, then he'd split, and another word was never spoken. Lano knew the percentages, he was their master. He knew when to quit.

Romantic. That was the word that described him, mostly, Arliss decided. Once they'd been eating in an Italian restaurant and he'd looked at her, staring at her hair, smiling, and when she'd asked him what was so amusing he told her that he'd never again be able to eat angel-hair spaghetti without thinking of her. She'd been so flattered and moved that she'd had to go to the little girls' room so he wouldn't see her cry. She was used to just being an adornment on someone's arm; more a possession than a person. Most gamblers weren't much in the sack, and when they were losing couldn't do it at all. Not Lano, though. He was the most confident man she'd ever met, he never showed fear or panic. He was himself, no matter how badly the dice were rolling.

She watched, smiling now, gnawing a strand of hair. There were two minutes left to play and the Bulls were down fifteen, someone had elbowed Larry Bird and he had two free throws. Lano was yelling at the guy who'd done the foul. "That's it, asshole, foul the best free-thrower in the league, Jesus!" She watched Bird swish one, get the ball from the ref and bounce it on the floor a few times, lift it and shoot the second shot. The ball rolled around the rim, then dropped through. The Boston crowd roared and Lano groaned, yelled to someone to give the ball to Jordan now.

If someone put a gun to her head and told her to tell the truth, she'd have to admit, the guy was a compulsive. It wasn't a business to Lano, like with some gamblers, it was his entire life. Arliss knew that all compulsive gamblers eventually went broke, wanted to lose, and that she should leave before he started his downward slide. But he was so cute . . . and he was winning.

His hair was as black as his eyes, longish and always wet-looking and combed straight back. He put some kind of stuff on it every afternoon after he showered, and the hair would stay in place until he washed it out during his before-bed shower, which was usually at dawn or later. He dressed well, and was very generous with her. He had a little bit of extra flesh at the sides and in the back, and he told her that he put on fifteen or twenty pounds every winter, would then work it off as soon as spring rolled around. Bike riding and jogging for a month would do it every time. The rest of him was big and muscular. He was a strong and emotional man who liked to use his mind and, when he had to, his fists. She'd seen him fight. Some gambler would lose and would accuse him of cheating, and Lano would freeze him with a glare, then ask the guy what he was doing there if he didn't know how to lose. Tell the guy he had no business gambling. Lano fought the way he gambled, full out, swinging his fists like windmills, tearing into people.

His voice, unless he was gambling, was usually low and even. He had a reputation as a stand-up guy who didn't take any shit from anybody.

The Bulls had kept even with the Celtics. There hadn't been a defensive stop in the last two minutes, and there were three seconds left and the Bulls were down seventeen.

The Celtics had the ball and someone she didn't recognize was throwing it in from half-court. Lano was yelling, "Dribble it out, dribble it out, goddamn you!" not wanting the Celtics to make another two points; put them nineteen points ahead. The guy threw the inbounds pass and some idiot took it, threw a shot from the time line and it bounced off the rim, went straight up in the air, rolled around the rim a second then fell to the floor without touching the net.

The buzzer sounded and the game was over and Lano Branka had won another seventeen thousand dollars and he was leaping into the air, punching at the ceiling. She went to him, now that the game was over and it was all right to do so, put her arms around him and he squeezed her, kissed her cheek. They watched as the Bulls, hanging their heads, walked off the court. She said, "Michael Jordan's got the nicest ass I've ever seen on a man, you know it?"

He said, "You never watched Bill Chamberlain," then said, "I won seventeen dimes by half a point." Then he said to her, "I think I'm on the roll." She could feel he was shaking, his fingers and arm trembling.

She knew he'd won fifty-six grand last week, which he'd collect tonight, Friday, payoff day, at the casino game run by his uncle Artie. The new gambling week had begun on Wednesday, the bookie Lano bet with had two days to play with the winner's money before having to pay off, and in the two days past Lano had won seventeen grand. He'd bet it all on the Bulls tonight, and had won, so he was already thirty-four thousand to the good for a week that was really only three days old.

Thinking of the bookie made her shiver a little bit herself. The man Lano bet with was the man she'd left six months before for Lano, a married son of a bitch who was a degenerate gambler and liked to beat her up when he lost. His name was Tough Tony Tomase, and he was the worst bastard she'd ever known.

The decision she had to make about leaving Lano—and

make soon—had everything to do with Tough Tony. Although he was much shorter and fatter and uglier—but richer—than Lano, he was a made member of the mob, and he liked to flaunt it. She'd heard Lano talking on the phone to his uncle Artie just last night, telling him that Tony had fucking well better have his money tonight. She wondered then if maybe Lano was getting in a little over his head, was letting his successful month-long high roll get to him, because nobody ever, ever told Tough Tony what he'd better fucking well do. The problem was, if Tough Tony came after Lano with intent to commit bodily harm, he wouldn't wait until Lano was alone. He'd send that monster bodyguard, Virgil, out, and maybe even give him orders to mess up Arliss's face some, teach her a lesson about loyalty. Tony was real big on "teaching" people things. He would think that Lano, who was only twenty-eight, would have a lot to learn. She shivered and pulled away, grabbing Lano's hand, leading him into the bedroom slowly. She turned to him, a seductive smile on her face.

"Hey, big spender," Arliss Owen sang, "spe-e-e-nd a little time with me!"

She lay there later, naked and sweating. He was smoking, there right beside her in the bed. As he took a drag of his cigarette he checked his watch. "Time to go," he said.

"Why won't Artie let women into the game, hon?"

"It ain't a game. Art runs a casino. For pros and high rollers and conventioneers can be proven to be all right. Women distract them."

He got up and began to putter around, pulling clothes from the dresser and draping them over his valet chair. "You got to understand something, Arliss. It's a business for him. He treats people well and pretends they're his friends, but when it comes down to it, all Art wants is their dough. Say someone that can get past the door into the casino every week decides to sponsor someone else, and that second guy turns out to be a rat. Art would have the guy who sponsored him shot." He shrugged. "It's the way it's done.

"All he needs is for someone's old lady to be there at the guy's side, bitching and crying about the money the guy's spending. Art's liable to slap her one to shut her up. Or what happens if the old lady gets pissed off about the guy losing all his dough, and figures she'll be a genius and call the cops, get the casino shut down?"

"He pays the cops, doesn't he?"

Lano chose a pair of gray socks, held them up to the light, nodded and added them to the small pile of underwear. "Not for complaints. They know he operates and he gives them ten or twenty points a week to stay off his ass, but if there's a complaint, the law got to check it out. Then Art gotta waste time, finding out whose old lady beefed, got to spend money to have the guy's legs broke for not being able to control her, shit like that."

Lano went into the shower, came out with a towel wrapped around his waist. He lit a cigarette and kept it in the corner of his mouth, let the smoke curl up into his face as he dressed in a pearl-gray suit over a white pullover shirt. He had a topcoat that looked to be made of the same material the suit was cut from. He got it out of the closet, looking at her, smiling at the pout on her face.

"Tomorrow night, you feel like gambling, I'll take you to the South Side. We'll do some rolling with the brothers down at the gym. Tonight I got to collect, and run over to Balmoral racetrack. There's a horse in the last race called Bucking Bronco N."

"Artie's mean."

Lano kissed her on the cheek, told her he'd see her later, then walked out of the room just as the phone rang. He hollered to her that he'd get it, and in a couple of minutes she heard him hollering and shouting, calling Tough Tony all kinds of names, telling someone what he was going to do to him, and it almost broke her heart to hear it because it was at that moment that Lano himself made her decision for her.

Millie Swan felt the tap on her shoulder and nodded, but kept dealing. When the hand was done she put the used cards in the clear plastic shoe, tapped her knuckles on the felt, opened them palm outward for the camera's sake, then walked away from the table. The man who had tapped her shoulder would take her place, dealing while she took her break. Several of the players at her table made remarks when she left, telling her to hurry back, stuff like that. She liked that, knew it invoked jealousy in a lot of the other dealers, but what did they expect? God, treat tourists, who should be the kings and *queens* of this town, like shit, the way most of the dealers did, and the gamblers had a right not to want to be around them, to be happy and ready to blow their money when they finally found a pleasant dealer.

The break room was full, people on breaks watching the Nets game on the wide-screen projection TV O'Shea had popped for. She said hi to several of them, ignored others. She walked to the refrigerator and got a Pepsi, popped the top and took a long drink, then sat down at the desk in the corner of the room, grabbed the phone, dialed nine to get an outside line, then punched out a number.

"Hi, Stevie? It's Mom, hon, where's Mrs. Tyler? Would you ask her to come to the phone, please, baby?" Millie waited, tapping her foot impatiently. It was after eight, past time for the child to be in bed, but there wasn't much she could say to Mrs. Tyler. She was going to have enough trouble as it was, getting her to stay over.

"Mrs. Tyler, hi, it's Millie."

"Working over, Millie, that why you called?"

"I know I'm supposed to work tomorrow night, but the boss just told me he wanted me tonight, too, Mrs. Tyler, so it'll be a little later than usual . . ."

"Millie, six o'clock's late enough. I'm here fifty hours a

week, every week, and fifty hours is enough. There just ain't no way—"

"A hundred if you stay until seven, and fifty an hour after that."

"Well . . ."

"Mrs. Tyler, that's as high as I can go."

"Well, all right." Mrs. Tyler paused, and Millie sighed. She wanted to hang up before the woman could make some dumb remark, but didn't want to alienate her. A good baby-sitter was hard to find in this town.

"Do you think it's good for your son to see his mother as little as Stevie does, Millie?"

The words said and hanging in the air, Mrs. Tyler hung up, her mission fulfilled. She'd given Millie a little more guilt to carry, over her usual heavy load.

Millie sighed again, hung up the phone. She swigged at the pop, her eyes closed, felt a shadow fall upon her.

Calo again, that ignorant geek. Standing there looking at her as if he was shopping at the 7-Eleven, checking out a piece of meat.

"Working for the man again tonight, sweetie?"

"Calo, go away . . ."

"*I* was supposed to work tonight, you tomorrow. Wanna tell me how you got the extra shift?"

"Talk to Mr. O'Shea."

"Would it do me any good?" He spoke low. The other dealers weren't supposed to be aware of the after-hours game. There were only a couple dozen of them who worked it, who Malcolm or O'Shea trusted.

"I suppose not."

"Maybe I should find a job where the boss's a broad. Hop in the sack with her, work all the hours I want."

"What makes you think that would get you anything but fired?"

"One way to find out, little lady."

"Calo, I'll call you when I get desperate, all right? When every other man in town dies of the Black Plague, after all the goddamn cucumbers go rotten, and when they close every porno shop around this stinking place that sells marital aids, then I'll look you up, all right? Until then, just fuck off, Calo."

She looked him in the eye when she spoke, her voice soft but venomous. He turned red, his forehead crinkling, his face getting all mean around the mouth. She could paint him, call it *Macho Man in Shock*. He opened his mouth, was about to say something, but shut it quick, his lips in a tight line. He spun on his heel and marched away, his head high, probably about to go spread the word again, tell everyone she was a bull-dagger.

Millie finished her Pepsi, wondering when she had turned so cold inside, but not wondering for long. She knew the answer. It had happened right after she had left Chicago, when she'd gone to Las Vegas on the recommendation of Art Pella, when he'd pulled strings and had gotten her a job dealing out West.

Remembering, Millie thought of him, of the man who'd put her in this position in the first place, and she had to pull her mind off it, had to get right back to the here and now because she might have turned cold, might have become a bitch, but in the environment in which she lived and worked it was better to be a bitch than to be a quivery, weak, crying little girl, which was what she would become if she let her mind wander back to the man she'd loved, the man she'd run away from, pregnant and alone. If she thought too long about Lano.

3

At about the time that Lano was eating a half-time sandwich, his "uncle" Artie (The Arm) Pella was sitting behind his desk counting the early receipts from the tables. He nodded, grunted in satisfaction. It was going to be a good weekend. He locked the money in the walk-in safe behind him, sat behind his desk, put his hands behind his head. He put his feet up and stared at the many twelve-inch TV screens mounted along the far wall.

Closed-circuit cameras showed the action at all eight tables; four blackjack tables, three for poker, and the craps table. Another camera was pointed at the door, where Elihue Roosevelt Baker was standing, staring at the parking-lot camera. All six feet, eight inches and three hundred and twelve pounds of him. Nobody came through the steel front door without Elihue first checking them out, then collecting the hundred cover charge to enter. Artie had to keep an eye on Elihue, because the man was a stone compulsive. Reliable and dependable, he'd be there every week on time, take speed to get him through the weekend, then take the money Art paid him and head out to the track or to another card game somewhere, and would usually wind up broke by Tuesday.

But he was a trip, this big bouncer.

For a while Art had toyed with video poker, which paid off in dollars instead of quarters the way the taverns did. He'd had one Ms. Pac-Man game installed with the poker machines, just for the hell of it, let the gamblers take a break from the action and test their reflexes against the ghost monsters that would chase their little yellow Pac-girl through her maze.

Elihue loved that game. He'd talk to it, unknowingly entertaining the customers better than a Vegas lounge act, yelling at the attacking ghosts: "Get your orange ass the fuck *away* from me, motherfucker!" Using body language, shifting as he moved the stick. "Come *here*, fruit, god-damn!" or, "*Jump* back, you brown ghost lick-a-dick!" The big bodyguard would ignore his work, lost in the maze.

A lot of the big spenders had complained about the noise the machines made. Artie had decided video poker wasn't worth the trouble. Ms. Pac-Man had been the first game to go. Elihue had been sad.

The gamblers drank and ate for free in Artie's place, and paid the hundred-dollar cover charge to Elihue so that Art wouldn't have to go into his own pocket for anything.

It was a gold mine, was what it was, just as he'd predicted when he'd proposed it to his bosses.

The game was in the basement of a gun shop on the North Side of Chicago Art owned through a cover, a tailor-made front for a casino. The walls were six inches thick and lined with lead; the windows all heavy and secure cinder block. If the cops ever decided to ignore the twenty percent he threw them every Monday, or figured it wasn't enough, there was a tunnel leading from the casino into a building next door that Artie also owned. The tables would be converted, run against the rails at the front of the range, the felt covers ripped off and thrown into a vat of acid in one of the offices. Guns would be laid upon the tables, and the dealers and the others who worked for Artie would begin shooting at the targets hanging against the far wall. By the time the cops got inside, it would be too late.

One of the cameras was aimed at the parking lot, mounted on the roof of the building. Artie was looking at it when he saw Tough Tony pull up, Virgil driving him around in a brand-new gleaming black Cadillac Seville. Artie chuckled. The guy was losing his ass to Lano for what—a month now? And here he was playing the big shot, driving a new car.

"Hello, sucker," Artie said, and swung his feet off the desk.

He walked to the bathroom and checked his appearance. He was a vain man, and he colored his hair to mask the gray. He'd had a small perm to cover a bald spot that was growing in the back, and now he fluffed that part of his hair out. His face was still firm but now, at forty-seven, it was lined and creased. He was tall, slender, and always spent the casino weekends in a tuxedo, which he would change every eight hours or so. When he went back into his office and answered the knock at his door, he was smiling.

Tough Tony was all business tonight. Artie sat back, let him talk, enjoying it for a while, his gaze just atop the little guy's head so he could see one of the TV screens behind him, watching Elihue and Tony's hatchet man, Virgil, standing by the door and shooting the breeze, looking like a couple of Italian Alps with faces. It was hard for him, trying to keep the smile off his face.

"Fifty-six motherfucking dimes, Artie. What is it, is this kid on a prime roll, or what? He's *breaking* me. Wednesday, I figure, it can't last. It's the fourth week in a row, he's took me for double dimes. The last two days, he's betting five hundred here, five hundred there, a dime now, two dimes later. Eleven games and he's up seventeen dimes, which he drops tonight on the Bulls. If the Bulls win, Artie, I owe him thirty-four K for three days this week."

Artie picked up a remote control from atop his desk and hit a button. The camera from the crap table began to roll left, toward the TV screens mounted on the casino wall, near the bar. The satellite dishes on the roof brought in any basketball games being played anywhere in the country, and roving handbooks worked the crowd, taking the action. The middle screen showed the third quarter just beginning. The Bulls were trailing by twenty-two points.

"Looks like you got a safe bet on that one, Tony," Artie said. His voice was dry, but he couldn't keep the pleasure from creeping in.

"You think this is funny, Art? Let me tell you something. That kid wins tonight, then for the first time in twenty-eight years of booking, I'm gonna get broke."

"Tonight? What's tonight got to do with you might have to pay him next week?" Artie sat back in his chair, giving Tony a glare. "What you're saying, is, you ain't got Lano's fifty-six."

"He got to wait for that, until maybe Tuesday, Art," Tony said, and Artie shook his head.

"You remember here, what, last September? The kid dropped forty-two in two weeks, and you made him pay six for five every week until he made it up. You think he's forgot about that? Shit, he was hanging out at hotels, hustling conventioneers into games, working around the clock to pay you back."

Tony spat dryly at the floor. "You want to know something, Artie? Sometimes, like now, you got a way about you that pisses me off. Me and you, we're supposed to be blood, mister. We took the *oath* together. I don't take no North Side pro action on anything on the weekends, because you got this going here. I lose a ton every weekend, doing you a favor, and now, you back this kid up over me." Tony leaned back in his chair, pouting, then said, "Besides, six to five's the going rate."

Art sighed. He himself was hard on the kid, Lano, but for a reason. This little prick was going hard just to prove he was a badass. It was time, he figured, to clue Tough Tony in on some of the facts of life.

"I'll tell you something, Tony. That kid's old man was my partner, and died jumping on a fucking grenade was meant to blow the entire foxhole to bits. I come home a few years later, took him under my wing to save him from a crazy mother was always trying to cut his balls off. He moved in with us, he was maybe eleven years old.

"He always liked to gamble, hang around me and the guys, before I got the button. We'd let him hang out, run for sandwiches and coffee. That guy, Johnny Peaches, had the bad kidneys? He paid the kid five an hour to stand behind him and hold a bag of ice against his back, so it wouldn't bother him in big games." Art sat back, wondering if he was getting through. Tomase was looking at him in a funny way. The way he'd maybe watch his old lady when she was emotionally involved in an afternoon soap opera. Okay. He'd try another tack.

"Remember Jimmy the Weasel, he was booking on the South Side? Back in seventy-nine, eighty?"

"I remember the Weasel, that piece of shit."

"Yeah, well, he remembers Lano, too, I'll bet. Lano took him for three hundred, on the double out at Balmoral. Comes time to pay up, Weasel says, sue me. It's illegal for a kid your age to gamble." Artie opened his desk drawer, took out a bottle of Fernet-Branca. He poured two small shots and pushed one across toward Tony. "Settles the stomach," he said, then drank a small sip.

"So the Weasel, he's bragging about it around town, and I go looking for him, but Lano finds him first."

"He's the guy, broke the Weasel's leg for him?"

"With a baseball bat. Both legs, and then he come over

to the house, waited for me. I come home, my wife, she's got him in the kitchen eating fucking peppers-and-tomato sandwiches, drinking dago red. I says, seeing the look on his face when he spots me, I goes, 'What happened to the Weasel?' and the kid, he brings out a roll of hundreds, choke a horse. He hands it to me, says if I would give this to whoever it goes to, he'd appreciate it. He'd already dragged his three hundred."

"Yeah, well I ain't no Jimmy the Weasel."

"Don't make no difference. Same story, different ending. See, what I did, I took the money to Mad Mike. You got to remember, this was when Campo and Paterro were still running things, and everything was smooth. Mike thanks me, tells me he'd heard what had happened, and he was about to send some guys out, do a number on the kid, get the rest of the money back. He tells me to tell the kid thanks, he got one coming, and to tell him he don't blame him a fucking bit, busting up a welsher. 'As long as I'm in charge of this fucking game,' Mike tells me, 'ain't no book ever gonna welsh.' "

Artie sipped his Fernet, looking at Tony over the rim of the shot glass. He said, "Campo and Paterro's gone. But Mad Mike, he's *still* in charge of this fucking game. Mine, yours, and everyone else who takes a nickel in any gambling action in this city."

Artie gave Tony a few seconds to let his words sink in. "A couple of years ago, it looked as if our thing was dead. Guys were rolling over like whores, spilling their guts to the Gee. Mad Mike and the rest, they hung tough, and now it looks like things might work out. The niggers, the beaners, they made big inroads in gambling, and it cost Mike plenty to get them in line. Took a couple of years, too, just to get things almost back to where they were before." Artie stood up and leaned on the desk, his fists holding him up. He leaned way over, until he was almost eye to eye with Tony.

"You think, Tony, for one fucking minute, that Mike's

gonna let one of his books welsh *now*, after all he's done to try and keep the gambling in the family?"

Tony's face was purple with rage. "And you'd tell him, right? Is that it, you'd go against a blood oath for that kid?"

Artie sat down and stared at him. "I wouldn't have to. The kid would go to him himself. Remember, ten, eleven years ago? What I told you? Mad Mike owes him one."

Artie watched the TV screens, watching Tough Tony, too, out of the corner of his eye. He could almost hear the wheels spinning in the fat little guy's head. At last Tony grunted, seemed to come to a decision.

"Hey Artie? Front me—what—" Tony rolled his eyes to the ceiling and his lips moved as he added figures, "ninety dimes."

"Ninety dimes? What the fuck for?"

"I'm paying the kid off. Right now. Tonight. He gets no more action from me, or any of my people. All he'll get from now on is the independents, let him bet a hundred, tops."

"He ain't gonna like that."

"Hey, fuck what he likes, all right? I got a right to restrict my clientele, just like any business. Mad Mike says one fucking word about it, I'll tell him a story, say that I heard the kid's been talking to the Gee. Mike won't like that."

Artie sat back, wanting to push it but knowing it would cause too much trouble. The guy was within his rights. If push came to shove, Tony could not pay the kid at all and then take his chances with Mad Mike's wrath. Maybe he even had more pull with Mike than he himself had; maybe Mike would believe his story about Lano; maybe a lot of things. Artie got up, walked to the safe, turned his back to Tony and as he spun the dial he said, "Ninety dimes, Tony, at six to five, weekly, right?"

"Come *on*, Artie, Jesus Christ!"

Artie, who had watched Lano's father get blown to bits

while the guy saved his life, stopped spinning the dial and turned into a stare-down with Tony. When he wanted to, he could be a pretty tough guy himself. "Hey," he said, "six to five's the going rate."

This time, Tony didn't answer, just sat there staring at him, so Artie winked at him and turned back to the safe. He pulled open the heavy door, and entered. Ninety would leave him short, but the way things were going this weekend, he'd be all right. He stacked the bills on one side and walked out of the safe. He said, "It's in here, when you need it," then made a big deal out of locking the safe behind him, adding insult to injury.

Tony wasn't out of the room five seconds when Artie reached for the phone.

Tommy (The Tomato) Gambesi watched Tough Tony stomp out of the office. From the look on the man's face, this wasn't the time to approach him. For the last six months, since Tommy got out of jail, he'd been running errands for the man through Virgil. Making a few hundred a week and an occasional thousand dollars bonus for a job well done. Chicken feed, really, considering. He wanted to approach the man himself, let him know he was available for anything the man might need. Virgil, who was maybe jealous of Tommy, was keeping him down, holding him back. Even though he'd proved himself to be stand-up by serving eleven months in the Metropolitan Correctional Center for refusing to talk to a federal grand jury about gambling in Chicago. They'd given him immunity and he'd still told them to get laid. Tommy figured that a guy who would do time rather than tell things to a grand jury that wouldn't hurt anyone anyway—when was the last time a gambler had gone to jail in Chicago, for Christ's sake— deserved better than he was getting.

He leaned against the back of the blackjack table, heard the dealer tell him, "Turn around and play, or step aside," and turned to the man, tried to level him with a glare. But the guy was ignoring him, dealing the cards. Slowly, so the dealer would know he wasn't intimidated, Tommy pushed his hips off the table and took a couple steps away, staring at Tough Tony's back. Tony now at the crap table, shouting to the shooter to move it or lose it.

Tommy tried to figure what it was with the man, what was in his ass tonight. If he could figure that, then he could maybe find a way to solve the problem for him, show Tough Tony how valuable he was to have around.

It came to him in a burst of brilliant thought. Virgil had been telling him things, man to man, the big prick figuring that if he talked business to Tommy then maybe he'd feel like an equal and stay in his place. Virgil had told him about this guy Branka, who was killing Tony's book.

Tommy knew Branka from seeing him around. The guy was a gambling fool who thought he was a hardass. Lived somewhere on the Northwest Side and had stolen Tony's woman from him. If he could be sure that it was this Branka character who was pissing Tony off, then he could whack the guy, put him in the lake, and drop a hint to Tony in passing, let him know he'd done the job.

But no, if the guy was into Tony for a ton of money, then Tony wouldn't want him dead. He'd want a chance to get his money back. Even busting the guy's hump for him wouldn't help Tommy's cause. If the guy was in the hospital, he wouldn't be gambling.

Tommy fumed, wondering how he could get in the boss man's good graces, resenting Virgil because the big dummy wasn't helping him any. He looked at Virgil, standing there shooting the shit with the big jig by the door, the two of them staring at the two cameras mounted on the wall. The two of them were acting as if they didn't have a care in the world. Elihue, Tommy could understand. Jigs weren't ever worried about anything but getting laid. But Virgil should have known better, acting carefree when the boss was upset about something. Maybe there was a way he could do the boss a big one, maybe even take Virgil's place. But for the time being, he had paid the big jig a C to walk through the door. He turned back to the blackjack table, dropped a ten-dollar bill on an open spot. It was time he started getting some of it back.

4

As soon as Lano heard the phone ring, he knew it was going to be bad news. He couldn't say how he knew, any more than he could say how he'd known that the Bulls would cover against the Celtics. Or that the Bears would win the Super Bowl against Miami last Sunday, against a fourteen-point spread. But for the last month, he'd been able to feel things and know things and he wasn't complaining. He picked up the phone and once again he was proved right.

"That asshole, Artie I swear to Christ, I'll kill him."

"Grow up, Lano. You mess with Tony, even I can't help you. Just take the money and lay low, give me the bets you want to make and I'll see they get laid at the right spread."

"That ain't the point." Lano was starting to calm down but he was still shaking, thinking of the nerve of Tough Tony, shutting him out when he was winning.

"It's the only point that matters right now. And you get this straight, Lano. If you're planning on coming into the casino and making a scene, just stay the fuck away, because if it comes down to a public thing, I got no choice but to side with Tony. Play it like I tell you and you can take the guy for his new Cadillac. Do it your way, kid, and you'll wind up in a place you don't want to be. Like for instance, the bottom of the lake."

Lano checked his watch, saw that it was almost nine. The horse he wanted to bet heavy on would be racing in the tenth at Balmoral, and it would go off at close to or right after midnight. He had more than enough time to pick up his money and get out to the track, maybe even lay a few bets with Artie for tomorrow's basketball games.

He said, "I'm on my way," and Artie said, "Take your time. Walk around in the cold air, cool off. Remember what I told you," and hung up.

Walk around in the cold air. Sometimes, Artie could be a real pain in the ass. Lano's goal was to never be cold or hot if he could help it. He'd done a little brig time when he was in the Marines, then later a short stretch in the County waiting on a hearing for assault and battery. He knew about heat and cold and didn't like to be in either of them anymore if he could help it, which for the most part he could.

He got into his car, which had been parked in the heated garage of the apartment building his home was in; shit, two bills a month to park the damn thing out of the elements. The car was a two-year-old Ford LTD Crown Victoria, black with the half-vinyl roof. A luxury car with the climate-control deal that kept it at seventy-two degrees year-round. He pulled out of his slot, out into the Chicago streets, hit the button that would bring the garage door back down, and headed for the North Side, to Artie's gun shop, thinking and for maybe the millionth time wondering about the man who had damn near raised him.

Artie always kept him at a distance, at arm's length. He'd

taken him in when he'd seen what the old lady was doing to him, seen to it that Lano had gotten educated and had food in his belly, clothes on his back, a roof over his head.

It had been infinitely better than it had been at home.

When Lano's dad had caught his lunch, his ma had gone over the edge. For a time she'd done some drinking, trying to kill the pain, then had turned to bringing home strange men to try and lose herself in them. She'd been losing it a little more each day and Lano watched, hating the guys she brought home, too little and frightened to say or do anything.

One guy, Ray, Jesus, what a jag in the bag. He was the type who would turn off his lights when he backed into their driveway, not wanting to have his headlights shine into the picture window of the neighbor across the street. He'd come over with his half-pints and offer Lano a shot when the old lady was out of the room, trying to be buddies. Or want to wrestle, the fat dago son of a bitch showing off and rubbing Lano's nose into the carpet, show him how tough he was. Every time you said something to him he didn't like he'd say, "Oh, *real*ly," staring at you like you were an asshole for doubting him. He worried about the neighbors all the time, what they thought of him, until he got a few drinks in him, then he'd call Lano's mother a whore and a bitch and Lano would attack him. When Ray stopped coming around, Lano's ma had blamed him.

"Every man that likes me hates you," she'd tell him. "I could be a married woman today, with my own house, it wasn't for you." She'd get mad at him and tell him, "That's it, pack your bags, you're going to the goddamn orphanage." He'd tremble with terror until he got big enough to call her bluff, understand she was just screwing around with his head.

She'd dress like her idol, Marilyn Monroe, would use eyeliner to draw a little mole on the right side of her mouth, and it was sad, seeing her stuffing her fleshy body into a low-cut cocktail dress and then leaving him alone while she was out looking for a replacement for his father. She was proud of the fact that she wasn't a hooker, it was her claim to fame. It was an admirable achievement, but not the way she put it to him.

"I get plenty of offers, you know," she would tell Lano. "I tell them, what kind of girl do you think I am?" She'd say this and Lano would think: A stupid one. Giving away what she could have been selling.

By the time Artie came along and rescued him it was almost too late. Art kept his distance, but it was a better deal than the one he'd had.

He gave Lano spending money and took him to ball-games; football, basketball, baseball, and even soccer games, but Lano always got the impression that Artie was watching him, observing, maybe measuring him against something only Artie knew about. He never felt close to the man, never went to him with his adolescent problems. They never talked about girls, or school problems. Artie never took him aside and told him about sex or venereal disease or masturbation. He always seemed to be some-where way above him, looking down.

On the other hand, Lano couldn't remember Artie ever raising his voice at him and he'd never even come close to punching him out. That counted for something. Artie mostly left Lano's raising to his wife Louisa, who'd died here two years back. At the wake, Artie's eyes had been dry.

It seemed that after his wife's death, Artie had loosened up some. He started wearing nicer clothes, with a stylish cut to them. He'd had his hair done and it was all Lano could do not to say something cute about it—an Italian man of respect in his late forties getting a perm, for Christ's sake—but Artie wasn't much of a guy for kidding around. He was a grown-up, a heavyweight, and he never let you forget it.

For instance, once, when he'd got in trouble, Lano had come to him and had walked into his house, Lano grown now and out on his own, but still having a key to Artie's home. Artie had been at the living-room table, on the phone, talking a mile a minute, papers spread all around the table, a cup of coffee steaming in one hand, the phone held in the other. He'd cut the conversation short when he'd spotted Lano, had hung up and had raised his eyebrows. Making Lano feel, as he always did in Artie's presence, somehow left out. Here the guy had been laughing and joking around on the phone with someone he probably didn't much care for, and the second he spotted a guy whose life and sanity he'd more than likely saved, he clammed.

Lano had said, "Art, I need a favor," and Artie had said, straight-faced and immediately, "I don't do favors," so Lano had shrugged, turned right around, and walked out of the house. He'd used his key and had come right back inside, walked up to Artie, waiting behind his desk, sipping the coffee now, and he'd said, "Art, I need your *help*," and Artie had favored Lano with a rare smile. He'd lowered the coffee cup and said, "What do you need?" He'd helped him out, too.

That time. But last autumn, when the chips were down and Lano was into that fatass Tony for forty-two dimes, he'd gone to Artie and Artie had shrugged, told him that a man took care of his own problems, and he'd give him the money but Lano would have to pay the same rate to him as he had to pay Tony. Business was business. Lano had busted his hump to get the dough, the juice eating him alive, and it had taken him until after Thanksgiving to get right.

But now all that had changed. He was doing good and was rolling like a champ. Changed, too—and for the better, it seemed—was his relationship with Artie.

In New York, where Lano had been several times when on the circuit, learning the games, they had athletic clubs where the mob guys held the card games, fleeced the suckers out of their paychecks. In Cleveland (Lano shivered thinking about it, he hated the entire fucking *state* of Ohio) they played in private games behind the locked doors of private homes, the guys running the games either taking a fat fee at the front door or a percentage of each winning pot. In Miami, it was in the bowels of sports arenas; in Alabama, in tents that could be folded up and carted off with ten minutes' notice; in New Orleans they played in the alleys, or in the lobbies of funny-looking, public-housing apartment buildings built in tiers, the rollers shooting on the tile floors while little ghetto kids from the tiny apartments scurried past so as not to anger the white men playing.

In Chicago, you played in the taverns. Every mob gambler had his place, either in the back room or upstairs or in the basement, where a sucker could come in and lay down his hard-earned dollars and try to beat the house. In a mob game, you were assured of a solid chance, which in itself was a sucker bet, but at least you knew the game was clean. They couldn't stay open if word got around that the game was rigged or the dice were loaded or shaved. The odds were the best you could find, not as good as Vegas or Atlantic City, but still, action was action and if you were on a roll you could clean up. If a shooter was caught cheating, the management would tear up his money, give him a good beating, make him eat the remains of the dough, and then throw him into the street.

Lano didn't play strictly in the mob joints. He knew, like every other heads-up gambler, what conventions were going on at any given time, where they were, and what the climate of the place was like. He'd play the conventioneers in the rooms of the downtown hotels and loved it because they were the biggest suckers, didn't know the true odds and would roll a five on the come-out and offer you even money that they could come right back. Lano and the rest of the gambling hustlers got fat off these games, and never had to cheat. It was at such a game that he'd begun the roll that had been sustaining him for the past month.

Even during the best of times, against men who had no idea what the true odds were, you had your moments. Your fortunes would rise or fall on the whim of the fickle bitch Luck, and you passed the dice or kept them at her convenience. Losing in one of these games never bothered Lano, because the doctor or lawyer or dentist or plumber or whatever would be there tomorrow, after spending the night in wonder at how easy it was, the conventioneer counting his money on the hotel bed over and over, amazed at the fact that he'd won so much, wondering how soon he could sneak away from the next day's festivities so he could wander on down to the bar, see if any of the gamblers were around. Lano was used to losing at these games at Luck's leisure, and he was patient. He'd had good rolls and bad rolls before.

But he'd never had a roll like he'd had this past month.

Now he drove through the night streets slowly, the streets slick with patches of ice everywhere and mounds of snow at the curbs. He passed several bars where he knew there were games, and maybe he'd come back later, after watching the last race at Balmoral. Thinking about his roll made him almost horny, and he smiled. Wondering what a shrink would make of that.

It had begun after he'd paid Tony off completely. He had retired for two weeks, vowing to lay low, not do any sport book betting until after the holidays, until after he put a good stake together. To a gambler, his roll was just as important as his dice, and it was going to be hard, he knew, to keep Arliss happy. She liked to live well and he liked having her around, even if there was nothing there emotionally for either of them. But you never knew when your last ten-dollar bill would be the one that put you on the way to your fortune.

He'd gone into a dentists' convention hotel at around nine on a Sunday night in December. He'd been holding his own lately, doing all right, everything working out just about to the proper mathematical probabilities. He had a stake, a bankroll, of forty-seven hundred dollars. His bills were paid until the first of January. If he really had to, he could always beat the black brohams at the gym on the South Side anytime he needed grub money, they didn't know shit about the odds and looked upon him as a challenge. So he went into the game feeling pretty good. He'd been away for a while and craved the action. He was a little nervous, thinking that the bankroll was pretty thin, but he was used to that. He'd been down before and would be again. The burning his fingers had taken from Tough Tony was right in the front of his mind.

Right away Lano knew there was going to be trouble. One of the dentists in the game had been drunk, was shooting his mouth off about the dice, about the big-city Chicago gamblers thinking that they were all hicks, and how did he know that the game wasn't rigged? Lano had the urge to leave, right now. Get the hell·out before the guy lost the last dollar his old lady had allowed him for the week in the big city and maybe then called the cops in his bitterness. Guys who thought like that had no business in a heads-up game. There were always a couple of pros in the game and as long as there were, it would be honest. What the drunk did was, he reached a compromise. He said that he'd go into the nearest drugstore, buy two pair of dice, and if the players wouldn't shoot with them then he wouldn't risk his money.

Which was all right with everyone in the game. The dentist left and Lano hoped that he'd find a hooker on a corner somewhere, maybe keep him away for the rest of the night. He got down on his knees there on the floor and when the dice came around he shot them.

Seven.

He'd laid down ten and had been faded by the dentist next to him, and he let it ride. Lano shook the dice, feeling the familiar sense of warmth in his gut that risk always brought, felt the heat in his arm and shook the dice, letting the heat work its way down into his hand and from there

into the dice themselves. He shook them, then pulled his
hand back and whispered "Come to me," and let them go
against the wall of the rented room.

Eleven.

There were two other pros in the game, and he knew
them both by sight as they knew him. They were staring
at him, their money held lengthwise in their hands, making
side bets with each roll. The bets were small, tens and
twenties, and one of the pros, looking at Lano, threw a
hundred on the floor and looked at the other, told him a C
that the shooter passed. The other pro smiled at the man,
then covered the bill with one of his own. Lano let the forty
at his knees ride, and the dentist next to him, seeing the
large bills there across the semicircle, was shamed into
covering it all.

Lano took the dice into his hand and closed his eyes,
spoke aloud but softly to the Lucky Lady on his shoulder,
a soft smile transforming his face into something that appeared to the other players as almost spiritual. He rolled,
shook, threw, and by the time the drunken dentist with
the big mouth came back with his two pair of newly bought
store dice Lano was up almost three thousand dollars. He
smiled at the man, took the dice from his hand, checked
them out to make sure the guy wasn't trying a hustle, and
by the time the dentist dropped his last convention dollar
on the carpet, Lano had won a total of seven grand and
change.

He didn't stop there. After the dentists gave up he went
to a tavern where there was a game, brought a beer with
him into the back room and tried his luck, see if he really
had it. It was one thing to go up against dentists with forty-
seven hundred and come away with twelve; it was another
thing completely to play against pros who knew the odds
as well as he did and who wouldn't give quarter.

Before the night was over, he'd won eighteen grand.

From that night on, everything he touched turned to
gold. Basketball, the football playoffs, he'd beat the spread

twice as often as he lost. Dice, cards, he couldn't seem to lose and on the rare occasions when he did he'd leave early, go home to bed.

But he'd always go back, insecure with the belief that he'd lost it, that luck had abandoned him, that the bitch had flown to someone else's shoulder. He'd come back and win and rest easy in bed that night.

As he pulled into Artie's parking lot—passing the gleaming black new Seville at the front of the place, what had Artie said about winning Tough Tony's new car?—he decided that Artie was right. He was doing too good to fuck around and lose it all by getting hot over Tony's decision. He pulled into a back parking slot where no one was likely to park next to him, open the car door into his vehicle and ding it, thinking that he maybe couldn't even blame Tony much.

Since December seventeenth, he'd beaten Tony out of more than thirty grand, which, along with the other twenty grand he'd won elsewhere, was in his safe spot hidden under the closet rug in the bedroom. He had three grand in his pocket tonight, and would be picking up ninety grand from Artie right now. Lano smiled, took the keys out of the ignition. Shit, maybe he was even on the prime roll.

5

Conway Mallory sat on the bed in her private suite in the needle of O'Shea's casino, naked, looking at her dressing room. The room was filled with gowns, not your run-of-the-mill bridesmaid bullshit but designer stuff, as nice as the things Mrs. Reagan used to wear when she and Ronnie were in the White House. Conway was aware of the fact that she was beautiful, young and sexy with a way of turning a man's head, make him want to comfort her. Her vulnerability. It was one of the things she had spent her life perfecting.

She looked at the gowns, at the row of pressed designer jeans, most of them from France. She would have to lie down on the bed to zip them up, and when she stood and looked in the mirrors in the bathroom, the wall mirror in front of her and the door mirror behind her, she could see the crack of her backside, the pants molded to her like an apple's skin.

There were cowboy boots in there that had cost O'Shea a thousand dollars a pair, a couple of furs, too. The time had been when he would tell her, Doll up, honey, we're doing the town, and she would, proceed from the Shamrock with her high-rolling lover boy to do the town, paint it red. She'd wear the jewelry he'd paid for, do her hair up, hold his arm with the top of her head barely reaching his shoulder, and be his lady. They'd sit ringside at heavyweight-championship fights, and after it was over they'd be invited to the winner's dressing room. Conway had met Mike Tyson, and before him, Larry Holmes. She liked Holmes better. He didn't make wise remarks and stare at her tits.

Sometimes O'Shea would have to go to the islands on business and he'd take her along, on a private jet he'd either charted or owned, she wasn't sure. He didn't like for her to ask about his business. She'd go and lie on the black-sand beach, swim in the ocean and love every second.

They had been good times, back then.

Now, though, it was: Be in the room in an hour, give him a blow-job, and he'd knock a grand off the bill.

She let her eyes wander around the rest of the suite. Five, six hundred a night, easy, she'd bet. Satin sheets on a king-size bed she'd never made, there was help for that. When she was hungry she went down to one of the seven restaurants, or ordered room service up. There was a well-stocked bar in the corner of the living room, but she couldn't see that from where she was, seated on the edge of the bed, lost in reflection.

Or rationalization. Trying to reason out a way to do the things he wanted, because if she didn't, all this was history.

Oh, my God, when had it gone bad?

She felt the sheet beneath her bare thigh, elegant and sensual. There was a strong Scotch on the rocks in a glass on the nightstand, and she drained it, threw herself back and stared at her reflection in the mirror above the bed. The headboard had a mirror in it, too, built in.

It wasn't a bad life.

Now she was trying to figure out how far she was willing to go to keep it.

There was that high roller from Seattle, the one she'd followed on her streak last night, when she thought that she might just break even. O'Shea had told her that the gambler wanted her, now, in his suite, for a little fun and games before he embarked on his nightly gambling business.

She was trying to figure out if she should keep the date.

Conway stared at herself, a beautiful woman lying naked on a bed, atop satin sheets. Soft and curvy.

"A drink and a 'lude, and it'll be like a dream." She said this, staring at herself, then fought the sudden strong urge to close her eyes. It would be easier than giving up the designer gowns and the jewelry and the life to which she'd grown accustomed.

Virgil was standing by the door with Elihue, discussing Lano in easy tones, goofing on the man because he wasn't there yet, and trying to keep things light. They both liked the man because he was fun and easy to be around, didn't get into that shit respect game most of the high-rolling dagos played, nor did he talk down to them, treat them like the help. Sometimes people tried that. Once.

Elihue could stand flat and look Virgil in the eye. The white man was tall, but there the resemblance ended. Virgil was one of those freaks who worked out every day at some karate gym for three hours, could break boards with his hands and shit, which impressed Elihue some but not a whole lot. Elihue figured that as long as he was in possession of his pistol, he could handle Virgil. He had yet to meet the man bullets bounced off of. 'Course, that would be a bad time to hear the click of a misfire.

"Man got Tony shitting in his pants." Virgil spoke slowly, out of the corner of his mouth. Elihue stood with his hands behind his back looking as if he were comfortable in silence, but not missing a word. The scar down Virgil's right cheek, from the bottom of his eyeball to his chin, moved more when he spoke than his lips did. Virgil and Elihue had both done time, and knew how to play the game.

"Gots to be careful, else the man walk up to him, kill him a couple of times right in his head." Elihue bounced on his toes twice. He hadn't been in a gym since he'd dropped out of college and entered himself into the NFL alternative draft, where no pro team had drafted him. There had been rumors even then that he had problems with bookies. He flexed his muscles when he was talking to Virgil, so as not to feel inadequate.

"Worse yet, tell *me* to kill him," Virgil said. "Shit, I really like the kid."

"He a good man," Elihue agreed. Then waited before adding, "Too, the man inside find out that Tough Tony has his boy killed, he gonna want to respond in a like manner."

"Worst part about this job, you know it?" Virgil's eyes scanned the room, and he sneered unconsciously as he saw Tommy the Tomato, old puss-face himself, sitting at a blackjack table acting like he knew the game. Dumb shit. Virgil personally never gambled. Didn't believe in it. He was watching his boss right now losing his ass to a bunch of gamblers on a lucky streak. No, he was a working stiff and money was too tight to blow at a blackjack table. He said to Elihue, "Having to do things you know can cause wars, or worse, get you your own ass killed. I can see it now, Tough Tony in a sitdown with Artie and Mad Mike, the three of them kissing each other on the cheeks, then coming to a decision. Tony gets to live on account of he's such a big moneymaker, but the guy who pulled the trigger on Lano, he got to go, to die young. Eye for an eye."

"Well, it comes to that, why'n't you tell that pizza-faced little cocksucker you staring at to do it?"

Virgil grunted. His hair was buzzed short in a crew cut, and his ears stuck out. He had scar tissue around his eyes, and his nose was mostly flat. He would say things to Elihue on Friday and Saturday night that he wouldn't even say to his wife. It was as if they were each other's confessor or something. They could blow off steam together. Elihue was cool and would keep his mouth shut, could, even, come up with some pretty good ideas from time to time. Virgil weighed Elihue's words and grunted again, disdainfully.

"Lano'd tear that kid a new asshole. Even if Tommy had his knife in his hand."

Elihue said, "There it is, Virgil. Solve all the problems. Man tell you, kill Lano's head, you send out Contadina-skin. Lano kill him instead, come back and tell Art the score, Art go to Mad Mike and everybody kisses everybody else on the cheek and on the asshole, and it's all solved. Lano lives, the punk dies. Everybody happy." He was wearing a self-satisfied smirk now because Virgil was looking at him with respect, realizing that Elihue had set him up right from the beginning to save his pal Lano. Seeing the way out of a potential mess for all of them and laying it on Virgil in a gentle manner. Elihue bounced on his toes and his belly shook. He said, "Now, tells me the truth, Virgil. That sweet little thing Tommy any good at running the head job?"

Virgil smiled easily and was about to reply in kind when he saw the topic of their conversation walking around on one of the two little TV screens mounted on the wall there over Elihue's head. Lano walked around Tony's new car, stopped to shoot a devilish look at the camera. He winked, then quickly mimed the act of urination before turning into the doorway.

The second TV screen showed the hallway leading to the casino's door. The two of them watched Lano strut confidently down the hallway, his lips together, pursed. He appeared to be whistling. Elihue said, " 'Nother thing I likes about the boy, got himself a lot of cool."

As Elihue pulled the door open and walked into the hallway to meet Lano, he heard Virgil mutter, "Sometimes, that can backfire. Freeze your ass to death," and Elihue couldn't agree with him more.

Elihue had seen them come and had seen them go. He'd

been working for Artie now for what, eleven, twelve years? And what he hadn't seen! The kids who came into town thinking that because they could outshoot every sissy in their little hometown they could do the same thing here. He'd seen the tough guys try to will the dice to fall their way. And the players who knew all the odds, who got carried away while on a hot streak and who put their entire stake on one roll of the dice. Elihue had sat back and watched the kids learn just how good they really were, then ushered them into a cab after giving them broke money; enough to get them to the bus station. He'd seen the tough guys, angry when they lost, who accused the casino of rigging the game and then finding out that they weren't really so tough after all. He'd seen the heads-up gamblers lose their entire stake and sometimes walk out like men, and he'd seen others break right down and cry.

But he'd never seen a dude like Lano before.

Lano, who could lose his stake and thank the players for the action before leaving with his head held high. The boy, he was an inspiration. All guts and balls, with some brains thrown in for good measure. He had a way of saying things to piss you off on purpose, but he'd have that harmless little smile on his face while he spoke, told you he was only jiving. Sometimes it was enough. Other times—well, Lano wasn't afraid to mix it up a little when he had to, either.

Elihue walked up to him, this man who seemed to be on the prime roll, and watched as Lano stopped, realizing why Elihue was coming away from his post to greet him and showing no anger. Elihue appreciated that.

Lano said, "Got to pat me down, right?" and leaned himself against the wall, hands high and wide. He looked over his shoulder at the camera and winked. "Virgil inside, Elihue, watching?"

"No need for the procedure, Lano. Just open the coat and let me feel the pockets, that about do it. Man don't want you going inside, causing a scene with no big bad ma-fi-o-so."

Lano turned and stood holding his topcoat wide open, the suit jacket too. He was mugging for the camera again. He mouthed the words "Your mamma" a couple of times, pointed his head at Elihue, who was dutifully patting his pockets.

Lano said, "Not too hard right there, okay? We don't know each other that well, Elihue."

Elihue finished patting him down and stood back, nodding. He said, "I know you well enough to tell you feeling mighty chipper tonight."

"There's a horse in the tenth out at Balmoral. Named Bucking Bronco N. Bet your lungs, Elihue."

"The fix in?"

"Naw. I just like the name."

"Way you going, Lano, that mean the fix is in." Elihue stepped back and opened the door, ushered Lano in with a flourish. He appreciated the fact that the man held no grudge about the patdown. Knew that he was just doing his job. But still, he had a job to do, and as Lano sauntered through the door and nodded smiling at Virgil, he said, "Got the C, Lano?" and watched Lano grin.

"Can't fool you, can I, Elihue?" He pulled a very large round roll out of his pocket, opened it so both men could see that it was all hundreds, and whipped one off, handed it to Elihue, then made a big thing out of folding the bundle and replacing it.

"Feel lucky tonight, kid?" Virgil said.

"Oh, yeah," Lano said. He began to walk into the casino as eyes turned and whispers began—*here was the man who was tearing the city a new asshole*—then said over his shoulder, "Get on me, Virgil, the boss lets you play instead of stand here by the door. I got a feeling I'm about to break the bank."

Softly, but loud enough so Lano could hear him, Virgil said, "Just make sure it ain't your legs get broke," and he watched as Lano nodded, but didn't say anything wiseass to that one.

*   *   *

Lano didn't even look at the gaming tables. He could hear Tough Tony yelling something at whoever the poor chump was rolling on the crap table, the little fat Hitler ordering the guy to quit fucking around, roll the dice or pass them. He wondered why Artie put up with the man. He knocked twice and walked on into Artie's office, cockily.

The thing that puzzled him was, their relationship had seemed to change for the better right when Lano's lucky streak began. Artie would talk to him more than he was used to, telling him things. Telling him about the prime roll and all that was supposed to go along with it. There were times, like earlier this evening when the Bulls covered, when Lano was sure he was on it; when the adrenaline was rushing and the blood was racing and his head was light. And there were other times when he was not so sure.

Such as now. Artie had told him that almost every professional gambler had one prime roll in his life, when everything went his way and he couldn't lose. One of the symptoms of it was a surge in ego; the gambler knew he just could not lose; it was as if God himself was rolling the dice. He could call what was going to come up before the dice hit the backboard. A feeling of serenity and all-knowing would fill the gambler, a warmth engulfing him with each throw of the dice, every flip of the cards. It was, Artie had told him, a nearly sexual feeling. Lano had never felt that, and didn't know if that was good or bad. He enjoyed the slight feeling of dread that filled him with every roll, and the rush of knowing that he'd beaten the odds. He'd told Artie over and over again that he didn't think he was on a prime roll, but whatever he was on, he wasn't complaining.

Now, as he closed the door behind him, he smiled widely. "Man chickened out, did he, Art?"

Artie smiled and nodded, rising and holding out his hand. "Good to see you, Lano. In this frame of mind, too."

"The fucking guy, his problem is, he gambles for money. He don't give a shit about anything else but trying to make a buck."

"That'll be his downfall." Artie sat down behind his desk and poured himself another shot of Fernet, offered the bottle to Lano, who shook his head. He never drank when he was working.

"You'll get the bets in for me?"

Artie didn't bother to answer him. He'd already said he would, and he wasn't in the habit of saying something more than once just to reassure people.

Lano said, "There's a horse in the tenth out at Balmoral. Bucking Bronco N. I want two dimes to win, two dimes to place."

"You give the bet to Elihue?" Artie said, and Lano nodded. Artie said, "I figured as much. Look."

Lano turned his head and looked at the camera pointed at the two men by the front entrance. Elihue was pleading his case with one of the roving handbooks, to no avail. The rule was, Elihue did no gambling on duty. Lano knew that Artie would say something to him for trying to break it. He saw Virgil grab the money angrily from Elihue's hand, thrust it into the face of the book, and point at his own chest. Virgil's face was a mask of intimidation and Lano could almost hear him saying, "You take the bet from *me*, motherfucker?" He watched the little bookie nodding again and again, writing something down in his black notebook, and as soon as the sweating man turned his back Elihue and Virgil slapped palms.

"Now, I won't place this bet myself," Artie was saying. "Can't, when I got the books out there taking them, and especially not when you're on a streak like this. What's the horse going off at?"

"Won his qualifying heat, then died last six times out. Program got him at twenty-to-one."

Artie grunted. "I had any sense, I'd book it myself. But my man out there, he just gave me an idea." He reached under his desk and pressed a button and Lano turned his head quickly to the screen, saw Elihue lose all of his infamous cool as the thing rang at his ear. Saw Elihue stare guiltily at the camera, then shrug fatalistically and begin walking toward the office. Artie grunted again and told Lano to keep his mouth shut.

When Elihue walked in he reminded Lano of nothing as much as the old cartoon character Baby Huey. The giant black dude who broke heads on command was dragging his feet, his eyes rolled up in their sockets. Artie didn't let him say a word. He handed him a banded stack of money, then said, "Next time Tony goes to the toilet, slip this to him. Tell him you want two dimes to win and place on—" Artie opened the desk drawer and pulled out a racing program for Balmoral Park, turned the pages to the tenth race, then said, "the six horse, tenth race. Get a receipt so you can show Mad Mike if you got to. He gives you any shit, don't worry about it. I'll get Virgil to handle it."

Elihue looked relieved. He shoved the money into his inner jacket pocket, and began to walk out. Artie said, "And Elihue?" and the man froze in his tracks in mid-stride. He turned.

"Yeah, Art?"

"You know, right?"

"Yeah, Art. Won't happen again."

Artie nodded and Elihue walked out of the door. Artie turned his attention back to Lano. He said, "You're down, I'll take the four out of your ninety," and Lano thanked him.

"So, you heading out to the track to watch the race?"

Lano said, smiling his wiseass smile, "In a while. First, though, I think I'll wander over to the crap table, see if my luck's still holding."

"Lano . . ."

"I'll be cool."

Artie sighed. "Tony don't know you know about the deal he made. Let him tell you in his own time. Remember who he is. Take it the right way, you can even rub it in, act like he's backing down. Just so you don't get tough with him. You go ahead and be cool. Just make sure you don't be so cool, you wind up getting chilled." He said the words and Lano nodded, wondering why all of a sudden everyone was being so goddamn free with the helpful advice.

6

He walked to the crap table, feeling good. Artie was right. He had won, and there was nothing that this useless little piece of shit could do about it. Lano had backed him down; had put him against the wall, and the man's worship of the dollar had caused him to blink first.

This was okay, now that Lano had a chance to think about it. He was way ahead, and even if he shot the limit every night at every crap table in the city it would take a month of solid losses to take away what he had won. Most of the money had come from the football playoffs and basketball games. Now he wondered if he would get the same thrill of risk by betting only a hundred here and there. He doubted it. But then again, if he wanted heavier action, Artie would somehow get it down for him with Tony.

Which would be a funny thing. Artie would have to go through Elihue or somebody else, like Virgil, because everybody knew that Artie did not gamble. He had had his prime roll, years before, and had made a couple of million. He'd tried to explain to Lano about quitting and getting out when you were ahead but Lano wasn't listening. At least not yet.

Artie would tell him about guys like Nick the Greek who had found themselves on a dozen prime rolls over their lifetimes; guys who made and lost millions, living in tall cotton when they were doing good and on the street when they weren't. Horror stories. He'd told Lano that the time to quit was now, when the getting was good, when he was way ahead, because otherwise he would spend the rest of his life chasing his losses. Losses that would have to come, eventually. Nobody stayed lucky forever.

Lano elbowed his way into a spot at the table, looking around, not seeing Tony for a minute, then catching sight of the fat man walking out of the bathroom, Elihue right behind him, stuffing a piece of paper into his pants pocket. So he was down. He had a total of four grand bet on a horse he'd never heard of before seeing his name in the program today. Quit? No, not yet. Not when the feeling of power was so strong. When the time came, when his losses began to outweigh his winnings, he would. He figured himself to have the inner strength to give it all up when the time was right. He wasn't a compulsive.

Tony took his place across the table from Lano, ignoring him as the man who'd stepped in to fill the vacant space nearly leaped away because here was Tough Tony, a real-live mafioso, in the flesh. Asshole. He probably took the horse bet to spite Artie, dealing on him in his own casino. The dice were two men away from Lano, and he reached into his pocket, removed his stake, smoothed it out and held the pile of hundreds tightly in his left fist. Directly, the dice were his.

As he began to shake them Tony started in. He said to the crap dealer, the dealer all wide-eyed and interested, such a big shot taking the time to talk to him intimately, "I used to shack with this bitch, Arliss?" Lano tried to ignore him. He put the hundred-dollar bill on the line and rattled the dice in his fist.

Tony said, "I always had this fantasy, something I wanted to do to a bitch, but it wasn't right, being a Catholic and all, to want the wife to do it, and even hookers sometimes balk at really kinky shit."

Lano rolled the dice. Seven. "Let it ride," he said.

Tony said, "Well Arliss, I says to her one night, honey, let's try something really novel, you know, out of the ordinary. Let's expand our horizons." He stopped long enough to throw two hundred at the dealer and say, "Against the roller."

Lano shot. Eleven. Again, he said, "Let it ride."

Tony said, "I tell her what I want to do, the thing that even nigger street hookers don't think is moral, and when I'm done she says to me, 'Novel?' the bitch all surprised. 'Honey,' she says, 'that's not novel. Hell, I been doing that since I was eleven years old!' " He dropped five hundred, the house limit, on the felt, and said to the dealer, "Against."

Lano said, "I got—what—thirty-three hundred total in my hand, Tony." He dropped it on the felt and stared at the little man. "You got the balls to cover it all?" He knew as he spoke the words that he was wrong, but enough was e-goddamn-nough.

All conversation stopped. Tony and Lano stared at each other. Players began to drift away from the table, and the pit boss began to sweat in his Johnny Carson suit, his head swiveling back and forth between the two. Softly, between clenched teeth, Tony said, "You're covered, punk."

The pit boss said, "Sir? Gentlemen? The limit's five hundred and there's no private betting, the house covers all—"

"Shut the fuck up." Tony was still staring at Lano, and for a second Lano felt fear race up his spine, tingling deliciously. He fought it off. Tony couldn't do anything here, and if he did anything on the street he'd be finished in Chicago. A bookie couldn't just kill a guy because he was winning. Tony would be signing his own death warrant.

Behind him, he heard someone say, "Just walk away, now, homes, pick up your money and stroll out the place, and everything be cool." He didn't have to turn his head to know that it was Elihue. He sensed Virgil on his other side. Flanked now by maybe six hundred pounds of human, Lano felt his confidence rise. Fuck them.

He said to the pit boss, "Stay out of this," and picked up the dice.

Artie heard the gentle burr of the buzzer and his eyes shot up to the cameras, looking for trouble. He saw Tony and Lano facing off on opposite sides of the crap table, the pit boss and two dealers standing there scared, the pit boss wringing his hands and staring pleadingly at the closed-circuit camera. Softly, Artie said, "You dumb fucking punk," and ran to the office door.

He crossed the casino floor quickly, watching as Lano shook the dice in his right hand, his fist now above his head, giving them the juju South Side shake. His entire body seemed to be into the shake, except for his head, which was pointed in Tony's direction. As Artie neared, he saw Elihue notice him and step aside, but he didn't stand in the vacated spot, he elbowed his way past Virgil—where the trouble would come from if it came—and stood next to Lano, between him and Virgil, heard Lano say softly, nearly a whisper, "Come to me," and watched as Lano flipped the dice almost casually at the backboard, his eyes never leaving Tough Tony's face.

Artie had to hand it to the kid, he won the staredown. As the dice hit the board and bounced back to the felt, Tony tore his eyes away and watched them dance. The expression in Tony's eyes let Lano and Artie know the decision a second before the stunned voice of the dealer said,

"Eleven," followed immediately by Lano's voice saying, "Roll it all."

Tony's head came up as if from an uppercut to the chin, he stared venomously at Lano, was opening his mouth to speak when Artie said, in a normal tone of voice, "What seems to be the problem here?"

"The problem?" Tony said it in the office, the only words he'd spoken since Lano had rolled his eleven. When Artie had asked the question it had been answered by three voices at once—the pit boss and the two dealers began to jabber excitedly, and for that Artie was grateful; it gave him the opportunity to get the principals in the little play the hell away from the table, and, more importantly, away from the other players.

As Tony spoke now Artie looked up at the television screens and nearly sighed with relief at the sight of the crowded crap table. The scene hadn't scared anyone off, because it hadn't come to violence. Men were shooting, talking rapidly about what had just occurred. Elihue was back at the door. It was just the four of them because it was unthinkable that violence would occur in Artie's office. Shit, the casino was mob-protected.

Tony said, "The problem is, this punk here, he challenges me to a high roll almost ten times more than your maximum bet, and what am I supposed to do, back down? Lose face in front of everybody? Shit, I know the rules, never bet over five hundred, house covers the bets. But hardass here, he's gonna teach me a lesson in front of everybody. The maximum's five, Artie. And that's what I figured I lost."

Lano said, "I got your thirty-three hundred in my pocket, Tony. You got the balls to take it?"

Tony stared at him, and Virgil, standing behind Lano, breathed in quickly.

Tony said, "That's the second time tonight this punk

questioned my balls. He know who he's fucking with?" This directed almost pleadingly at Artie, who was beginning to get the picture.

Artie said, very softly, "Lano, you know the rules here. The maximum bet is five hundred. No personal bets. You broke the rules, not Tony. He couldn't back down after you challenged his manhood. Who the fuck you think you are, kid? A tough guy? Come in my place and start trouble with one of my own people? Get that fucking money up, now. Hand Mr. Tomase his twenty-eight hundred, you win the five hundred. You want to play no limit with him, go out into the goddamn alley."

Lano was looking at Artie with a question in his eyes, Lano beginning to see things and figure them out. Without hesitation, he reached into his pocket, grabbed five hundreds off the second roll, that he'd taken off the table, and handed the rest to Virgil.

"Give it to Mr. Tomase, Lano." Artie's voice was soft, but it conveyed deadly intentions. Lano stood, walked to the man. Fighting the urge to throw the money into his fat face, he held it out to him. Tony let him stand there for a few seconds, relishing his victory. Then, smirking, he finally took the money. Lano turned to sit down, but Artie's voice stopped him cold.

"Get out of here, this minute. Wait by the office door until I call you back in. You drop one nickel on any of my tables, I'll break your arms. And from now on, kid, you are barred from this joint." Artie sat behind his desk, his hands knotted into fists. He said, "Go ahead, what are you waiting for?" and Lano, filled with anger, did as he was told, hearing Virgil sigh his relief as he reached for the doorknob.

All eyes were upon him. As he stood there, feeling like a little kid outside the principal's office, the other gamblers stared, some discreetly, others openly, at the guy they all figured would be found in the river before morning. He avoided their eyes, looked at Elihue, who was studiously ignoring him.

He thought, for a fleeting moment, that if he got out of this, he would never gamble again. The thought passed quickly. He would get out of this. He had to.

He shifted his stance, stared away over toward the large screens where the late basketball games were just getting under way. The Lakers were killing the New York Knicks. It almost made him smile. Arliss thought that the Knicks' center, Patrick Ewing, was the ugliest man alive. He wondered if it was too late to get a few dimes down on them, thought that the Lakers over the Knicks would be a safe bet if L.A. were a forty-point favorite, thought anything at all to take his mind off his recent humiliation and the distinct possibility that he had maybe ten minutes to live if Artie didn't come up with something, quick.

Although he was expecting it and had tried to prepare himself for it, when the door opened he still jumped. Tough Tony Tomase swaggered past him without a glance, but Virgil stopped next to him, said in his jailhouse out-of-the-side-of-his-mouth style, "Fuck's wrong with you, Lano? Christ Almighty. Go on in there, your uncle wants to talk to you."

Artie told him to sit down and poured him a rock glass full of Fernet. "Drink it," he ordered. Lano did not think that this was the proper time to argue with him.

"You know what saved your life tonight, so far, kid?"

"Keeping my mouth shut."

"And paying him off. Now, see, the little asshole is out there at the crap table telling everyone how he got his money back, how you begged for mercy, how he never wanted a problem with some punk civilian, wasn't worth his time and trouble. In here, earlier? That act he put on? You got any idea what he was doing? Let me spell it out to you. He was pleading his case. Not before me, but for Mad Mike, acting it out. He was gonna go to Mike, I can see him now, telling the guy, 'I done everything I could. Talked to the kid, to Art, they both shot me down, wouldn't give me relief. The kid questioned my manhood twice in ten minutes, what was I supposed to do?' And you know something, Lano? He'da been within his rights. He could have walked out of here and had you killed and there wouldn't have been a fucking thing I could do about it because you had to play it tough."

Lano squirmed in his seat. His defense was going to be that Tony had insulted Arliss, but he knew what Artie's reaction to that would be. He said nothing. Artie continued.

"You know how things work in this town? Or are you just stupid? Me and Tony, we're bound by a vow, Lano, deeper than any blood bond. We're together in a thing bigger than any industry in the world. Anyone who breaks the vow, the rules, got to go. Being raised by me, you should have known that. If Tony wants *me* hit, he got to go to Mike, get the okay, Mike's the boss. He wants to hit *you*, he don't got to do a fucking thing but tell Virgil to take you somewhere and put you to sleep. I beef, and Tony's got a righteous reason, I could get whacked for going against the vow, taking sides against him. That's what that little farce was about earlier.

"The reason you ain't dead right this minute is sitting in my vault, and wherever you got the rest of the money you won off Tony this past month. He wants it back. He'll wait until the odds catch up to you and you start to lose, then he'll take your action again. When he gets the money back, and more, you're dead. It's simple as that." Artie held up his hand and brought it down hard on the desk.

"Unless," Artie said, "he decides to just cut his losses and whack you the hell out tonight. That's up to him. And you know something, Lano? There won't be a fucking thing I can do about that, either." He flipped the shot glass to his lips, downed the entire glass of Fernet in one swallow. Lano knew that it hurt Artie to say these things to him; not because he loved him so much, but because he'd made a vow to Lano's dead father to always look after the family. But it was the way things were. Still, Lano sat silently.

"I got your bet down for the race, kid, and I suggest you go out there, to the track, watch your horse run, then go home and pack your clothes, take a little trip. There's a two-o'clock flight East. I got pieces of two hotels in Atlantic City."

"Atlantic *City*—"

"Shut up. You do what you want, but A.C.'s the only place where I can halfway guarantee your safety, and that's only because Angelo Biari's only son made it through the Nam because of me. He'll watch out for you. You go out there, stay clear of my casinos, and any of them we got a piece of. That's the first place Tony'll look, he decides you got to go. Which he will as soon as he figures out you ain't gonna give him back his dough. And besides, the way you're gambling, we can't afford the losses."

Lano didn't know if Artie was kidding or not, so stayed silent.

Artie said, "And one other joint, too. Stay the hell out of the Shamrock, Lano. You stay at the Palermo Hotel. I'll make a call later, tell my people you're coming." Artie rose and went to his vault, opened it, and entered. When he came out he had a canvas money sack in his hands, the money inside in hundreds, the bag folded over onto itself several times. He handed the bag to Lano, who stuffed it down the waistband of his pants, then buttoned his suit jacket and coat over it.

"Why I got to stay out of the Shamrock?"

"Because I told you to."

"Art, come on. You said to stay out of the mob joints, then told me to stay out of the Shamrock, too. You got to have a reason."

Art sat back down at his desk, staring hard at Lano, who was feeling fear running up and down his spine. Art was not a man to play games with, but still . . .

"You stay out of the Shamrock on account of Millie Swan's working there, buddy, and I don't want you anywhere near her."

Lano's head jerked up and his hands stopped patting the money bag at his waist. His jaw fell, and he stared at Art. "You said she dumped me for another man, Art. You keeping tabs on her, too?"

"You better hope," Artie said, "that Tony don't decide to take the eighty-six and call it quits." Subject dropped.

"Palermo Hotel, Atlantic City, right?" Lano said, afraid to say anything else. He had already angered one man tonight who thought nothing of castration; he didn't need Artie on his ass. Artie ignored him. Lano said, "Thanks, Art."

"Don't thank me. Thank the memory of your father. Wasn't for him, I might have killed you myself, you make a scene in my place of business."

Lano headed for the door, then stopped with his hand on the knob.

He turned and was about to say something else, not knowing fully what feelings he wanted to express but desperately wanting to say something. The way Artie was staring at him made his mind a blank. Without another word he opened the door and stepped out into the casino.

Directly into the chest of Tommy the Tomato. Jesus, he looked like he hadn't ever washed his face. It was red and splotchy, covered with deep acne scars and some kind of big round pimples, had hair in the middle of them.

Lano said, "Excuse me," but the Tomato didn't move. He stepped around him and felt the guy following him. There'd been enough trouble in here already tonight, and Lano couldn't do anything more, not even if the Tomato decided to slap him in the face.

But in the parking lot, now, that was another story.

7

Elihue stood with his hands behind his back, belly jutting out before him, a hint of a smile on his lips. He watched Virgil standing next to his boss, nodding seriously as Tony spoke rapidly and with much hand movement. What was the old joke—how do you render a dago mute, tie his hands up? Fit that ignorant little man to a tee. Look there, the man waving and whispering, jabbing fingers into Virgil's chest. Thank God Elihue had found Art. He might have to take the supreme risk, he had to work for a man like Tomase. Take the chance he could get away with killing the fucker.

He saw Lano coming toward him, stepping around the other resident ignorant little man, what was his name? Tomato. That was it. Only he didn't like being called that, on account of he was sensitive about his complexion. Virgil had told him that the man liked to cut people, and Elihue had always wondered why on earth someone would prefer doing that to taking out a pistol—bang—it was all over, nice and clean. The boy had to be lacking character.

He nodded at Lano, thinking, my, my. Maybe we'll see

if Virgil was right. Find out if maybe Lano could indeed eat this little scab-face for lunch.

He closed the door behind Lano and said to the man, "We ain't got no rubber stamp to press on your wrist here, Tomato man. You go out, it's another C to get back in."

"What did you call me?"

See that? Lord, some people were plain stupid. The dude was squinching up his face, staring at Elihue menacingly. Like he was bad. And reaching without thinking about it for his back pocket.

"You got something in that back pocket, white boy?" Elihue decided to stir him up some, see what happened. "You forget about the rules? No women, no drugs, and no weapons allowed on the premises. Your master, he get a mite upset I tell him, you breaking the rules. Not to mention, you pull something on me, I be liable to slap the taste out your mouth."

"Get outta my way, ni— Just get the fuck out of my way."

Elihue smiled lazily. The man had almost called him a nigger. He couldn't remember the last time anyone had said that up close. Sometimes a white man would yell it at him, driving down the Dan Ryan Expressway, the man all safe and fearless in his vehicle. Using his car as an extension of his wee white dick. But it had to be when he was in prison, last time someone called him nigger face-to-face. Yes, he believed it was.

Elihue said, "Doin' you a favor, son. Lano there going on an errand for Mr. Art. You don't want to bother him now. Mr. Art, he might get pissed. He got to walk on over North for the man, do some business. Then he be coming back." It was off the top of his head, the best he could do at the moment. Elihue knew that Lano would not be back, and believed that he was carrying the money Virgil had told him Tony had decided to pay Lano. The last thing Elihue wanted was to see this little sissy here maybe get lucky, stab Lano in the back when his mind was elsewhere, take the man's hard-earned money. And besides, Lano had given him a horse tonight.

The Tomato said, "What's he driving?" and Elihue saw his shot.

The thing was, did scab-face come in before or after Tomase and Virgil? Before, yes, because he remembered the kid peeling the hundred off his roll, the only large bill there. It had been wrapped around a bunch of fives and tens; what gamblers call a Philadelphia roll. The Tomato had been there long before Virgil and Tough Tony arrived.

Elihue said, "That brand new Cadillac Seville, sitting right out front." Then stepped aside as the ugly one grunted his thanks and made for the door.

Elihue smiled, positioned himself in front of the camera, looked up—

And, sure enough, there was dumb old Lano, leaning against the fender of the damn Seville, his face all scrunched up in thought. After Elihue had gone ahead and saved him once tonight. He crossed his own arms, thinking that it would take a better mind than his to figure out white folks, and settled back against the door. Whatever happened now, it would at least be fun to watch.

He watched as the Tomato stepped out into the night and looked around furtively. Then stooped next to the Seville and said a few words to Lano, who ignored him. When the little man reached into his pocket and brought out the switch, Lano uncrossed his arms and stepped back. Elihue smiled, seeing Lano quickly glance at the camera, figuring things out. Lano took a few steps back, as if in fear. Shit, look at that crazy kid, winking at the camera and saying "No, please," then scurrying away, trying like hell not to bust a gut as that dumb little Tomato bent down and thrust that skinny sharp blade right into the Cadillac's right-front tire. When he stood, Elihue could see the knife gleaming in the dim light of the parking-lot vapor lamp. He could see something else, too. He saw that he might have stepped on his own black dick a little bit. Tough Tony sees his car, right away blames Lano, and there goes the ballgame. Elihue could see that, but he sure couldn't see Lano. Man may be crazy, but he ain't stupid. Soon as the little man with his switch cut the tire, he hauled ass. Probably figured old Tough Tony might kill Tomato for cutting the tire and Lano, too, for not stopping him. Elihue knew that he had to get a witness to this before the Tomato-man made his escape. He waited until the boy had slashed three of the tires, then signaled to one of the roving waiters, told him to get Virgil over by him, quick.

What made him go a little overboard was, the nigger had called him Tomato-man. For as long as Tommy Gambesi could remember, some son of a bitch somewhere figured he was being real original calling him something like that. Figured themselves to be Milton Berle, calling a man with a skin problem Pizza-face. In high school, where the real problems had begun, he'd been forced to take it. He was little and weak and there was nothing he could do. Out on the street one night, in Hegewisch, some punk had gone too far while Tommy had been drinking beer with him, and he'd gone home, gotten a butcher knife, and had stabbed the guy twice in the back before the other kids pulled him away. After that, nobody ever made fun of him to his face.

Until this nigger. Tommy hated them bad enough already, stinking up places with the shit they put on their hair, fucking up the city with their thirst for power. Since Daley croaked, Chicago had really been a shitty town to live in, a day never went by where some jig wasn't calling a white guy a racist and getting money from the white man with their bogus lawsuits. He was carrying racial and personal resentment at the insult when he'd gone out to face Mr. Big Shot Tough Guy Lano Branka.

Tommy had been having fun. His original plan was to flatten two of the tires, make the asshole have to call a tow truck. Inconvenience him. When Tough Tony decided to have Lano hit, Tommy would ask Virgil for the job, let the man know that to him, the tires were just an appetizer.

But once he got going, he just couldn't seem to stop himself. Especially after the punk ran in terror. His cowardice fueled Tommy's mean streak. He'd always been that way, even as a kid. On the rare occasion that he'd won a childhood fight, before he began carrying a knife for respect, he would stomp the guy to death the second he had him down, when the kid was screaming "I give," or "Uncle." Tommy had no use for cowards. Hell, he'd taken enough solid ass-kickings himself and had never once asked for a break. So once he heard Lano running away, he went ahead and carved all four of the tires. He was running the razor-sharp edge of the knife across the highly polished finish of the car's paint job, drawing swastikas and happy faces there, digging it in deep, wishing it was the fat belly of the overfed nigger at the door that he was cutting, when he heard a bellow come from the front of the building and jumped, frightened, before seeing that it was only Virgil, with Tough Tony right behind him. He folded the knife, was reaching to put it back into his pocket when the thought struck him: Why are they running at me? The thought struck him and then Virgil struck him and then Tough Tony himself was striking him and Tommy Gambesi struck the ground before he could think straight enough to figure out that he'd been set up.

Lano entered the apartment in a hurry, wanting to break the news of his impending trip to Arliss before he went to the track. The apartment wasn't out of his way, he told himself. Then told himself that there was no sense in dragging it out. He told himself these things, then did his best to believe them. The thing of it was, he was coming home to tell Arliss now, before the race, so she would maybe take the hint, be packed and out before he returned. And because he didn't want to be around to listen to her song and dance while she packed.

He looked around. The TV was on with the sound turned off. Images flickered in the darkness of the room, casting shadows. A teeny man was screaming into a teeny woman's face, the scene on the television bizarre without sound. He turned his head away and saw the light coming from the bedroom, heard a low voice speaking rapidly.

Lano thought, Aw, shit. Here he was, about to break the bad news to Arliss, she had to get out, and there she was, in the bedroom talking to somebody. Then he smiled. If she was in there with another man, it would make his task smoother to perform.

He winced when he saw that she was just on the phone. He tried to cover it up with a smile but that too faded when he saw the packed suitcases on the bed.

"Going somewhere?"

Arliss looked at him, caught in the act. She hung up the phone, cast him a guilty glance, then turned her eyes to her lap.

"I was going to leave you a note."

Over his shoulder, as he turned to walk from the room, Lano said, "The key, Arliss. That's all you got to leave." And as he walked out of the apartment he wondered why he felt so relieved.

Driving to the track, he tried to figure it out. For months, he'd felt more like a six-foot dildo than a lover; just scratching the girl's itches. He knew that Arliss was crass and ignorant. Uneducated, but he didn't hold that against her. He'd barely gotten his high-school diploma himself. She had never acted on him, run a game. Had never pretended that it was more than it was. Although he had wondered, last fall, why she had stayed when he'd been down over forty grand. No, Arliss had always been up-front and real about their having nothing special, and had never played as if she wasn't the type to run when a better offer came around. Instead of the way Millie had done him, acting like she loved him, then running off on him.

Still, it confused him, the fact that he felt nothing when a six-month-long affair ended. When Millie had disappeared, four years ago, it had nearly killed him. They'd been living together, the two of them partying all night, Lano taking her with him on his junkets, expecting to marry her someday. After Millie, no woman seemed to matter anymore. He'd been cold to Arliss mainly for her sake, so she could make herself believe that she'd broken his heart. Then she could act as if she still had it, was still a heart-breaker, instead of a soon-to-be over-the-hill, rapidly aging sex toy. She was getting soft around the middle, spreading a little in the hips. Tits starting to sag. How long could she play the game, sucking on strands of her hair and acting like a teenager?

And how long could he?

That thought hit him with the strength of a hammer blow. He'd skated by for years, talking trash, fighting when he had a mind to, then hiding behind Artie's button when heat came down around him.

It had almost come to a head tonight, he knew damn well. He'd felt real fear outside Artie's door, knowing that his future existence was being discussed a few feet away by men to whom the taking of life was part of the daily routine.

What bothered him the most was, why had he risen to the bait, looked for a problem with a guy who had already probably killed a couple of dozen people, merely because the guy was talking trash about a woman Lano didn't care about? For instance, Lano knew that if the man had merely mentioned Millie's name, he would have jumped the table, sucked his eyeballs out of his head for him. But he'd bad-mouthed *Arliss*, for Christ's sake. Was it ego that had made him act as he had, was that it?

Or did it go deeper? Was he turning into one of the gamblers he'd seen and heard about his entire life, one of the compulsives who couldn't stand to win? Who took their winnings and put them in their pockets and then went home and blew their brains all over their garages?

Lano pulled into the parking lot of Balmoral Park, handed the parking attendant the two-buck fee, and added a dollar tip. "What race we got?" he asked, and the attendant told him, "Ninth coming up."

Lano parked as far away from the other cars as he could—he hated to get his car marked up—and hurried into the grandstand. The attendance was free now, after the sixth race had run.

Millie Swan, in Atlantic City, working at—where?—the Shamrock. Jesus Christ, and how did Art know?

The track was half-empty, most of the bettors men like him, coming late to bet the trifecta. Lano shouldered his way up to the second floor, thinking. As he walked toward the betting windows he shook off the cold, and on a conscious level was glad that he was inside the park on a Friday night and that the place was half-packed with gamblers, because now he didn't have to think about things that frightened him.

Tommy was wiping the blood off his face, in the can inside the casino. He was smiling because the big jig, even though he'd set him up, had been true to his word. He'd made Tough Tony pay three hundred dollars for all of them to have the privilege of coming back inside. The jig was the enemy but now Tommy liked him; at least he hadn't kicked Tommy's ass, like Virgil and Tony had. Tommy looked in the mirror. Blood dribbled back out of his nose, the inside of his mouth was cut. At least two teeth were goners, missing completely, and there was another one there loose as hell. It had been driven through his lower lip. Goddamn, that Virgil could hit.

By contrast, the punches Tomase had thrown had done no damage. The man was fat and old, slow. He slapped his fists at you without causing any pain. So Virgil could hit like a mule kicking downhill and his boss was a sissy when it came to fighting. Wiping the blood off his face, Tommy filed these facts away in his memory for future reference. He'd pull them out again and remember to shoot Virgil first when the time came that he felt secure in the knowledge that he could get away with killing those two pricks.

Tough Tony and Virgil had a meet in Art's office, Art right there behind his desk, watching the two of them speaking of killing a young man who was like a son to him. He didn't like it, but there was nothing he could do about it. Tony was, after all, blood, and if what he was saying was true, then Lano had finally gone too far.

Virgil said, "He'll be at the track, Tony, for the tenth race. Told me and Elihue as much. Said he was gonna bet a horse, and gave it to Elihue."

"Elihue bet four grand on a horse tonight. Sixth horse, tenth race. Two dimes to win, two to place." Tony turned to Art. "You know your boy's gambling on the job?" Acting like he was doing Artie a favor. Just one of the boys helping another out. Artie fought the urge to go up into the gun shop, get a piece, and shoot the fucker.

"I'll talk to him," Art said, wishing these two would get out of his office so he could call Elihue in and get the real lowdown.

There was no doubt in his mind that Lano would never play with a man's car. If the kid had a problem with a man that could only be solved through violence, Lano would take care of it face-to-face, no matter who the man was. Artie looked at his camera, listening as the two men set Lano up. He wished that he'd stayed in the office after Lano had stalked out, had watched him drive off. But he hadn't, he'd made the rounds, seen to it that the gamblers were safe and happy, had enough to drink, had forgotten all about the ugly little scene earlier. If they were happy, they'd stay, and drop their money at his tables. He'd gone out into his casino and hadn't even thought that Tony would be stupid enough to have one of his men follow Lano out, do damage to him or lay the groundwork for potential damage. Maybe waylay him later, outside his home, that was one thing. Which was why Art had told Lano to go to the track first, see his horse race before going home to pack. That would give Art time to check Tony out, make sure he wasn't planning on whacking Lano tonight. If Tomase did plan to kill the boy, Artie would have Kenny the Mons, who owed him a big one, get over to the track and tell him to get the hell out, now.

But something didn't ring true. Artie had been out on the casino floor and hadn't seen what happened, but he had seen Virgil and Tony walking toward Elihue, while Elihue hurried them on. He'd seen Elihue point at the camera, and had watched as the two men had gone flying out the door. He'd been so preoccupied that he'd only thought, Good riddance, knowing Lano wasn't stupid enough to be the cause of this problem, whatever it was. The kid had been scared enough to follow orders for a change.

Then they'd come back in, with that vile little idiot who thought he was a tough guy, Artie couldn't even remember his name. The ugly kid was all beat to shit and they'd dragged him into the toilet, violently, causing heads to turn. Art had looked at Elihue, who'd shrugged and held his huge hands out, looking sheepish. Big dumb bastard probably thought he'd gotten into enough trouble for one night.

Then they'd come out, Tony and Virgil, and had told him that Lano had cut Tony's car all to shit and had then beaten the ugly one half to death when he'd—Tommy, that was his name—when Tommy'd tried to stop him.

No, that wasn't Lano's style. But Art couldn't call Tony Tomase a liar. Not without proof.

It was with a sinking feeling that he came to the realization that he couldn't even call Tony a liar *with* proof, not if all the proof he had was the word of a gambling compulsive who was also black, and known to be fiercely loyal to both Art and Lano.

So he listened, and when the soft knock came at the door he opened it and let Tommy in, then went back and sat down in his chair, watching and listening. He would have to go along with it, on the surface, at least for now. After he knew their plan, well, anything could happen.

But one thing was certain in his mind. Although he would never admit it, least of all to Lano, he loved that boy like the son he'd never had, and he'd be goddamned if he would allow this fat piece of shit to kill him without a fight. The way it looked now, it would all work out in the short run and he wouldn't have to take any foolish chances this evening. They were planning to send Tommy out to take care of Lano. As they discussed it, a funny thing happened.

Virgil looked at Artie, just as Tony was telling the kid to take no chances, stab Lano in the back and leave him in the parking lot of the track. Looked at him with relief in his eyes, and winked.

Well, well, Artie thought. He tried desperately to hide his smile. He was grateful, because throughout the years he'd made an effort to go out of his way to be nice to the people around him, especially the people who could some-day hurt him. And now, it appeared, he had a confederate in the enemy camp.

Between the two of them, they'd find a way to save Lano. There was no real problem tonight. Lano would be on his guard and would almost deserve to die if he let this ugly young amateur take him. But to cover it just in case, Artie would get the word to him through Kenny the Mons, who lived less than a mile from the track. The Mons would get to Lano long before Tommy hit the track. And by tomorrow Lano should be in Atlantic City, under the protection of Angelo Biari and his son, Gaetano. There would be time enough then to figure a way to get Mad Mike to call off his maddest dog.

And if he couldn't, then Artie would have to kill the man

himself. Not just because he loved the kid, but because he'd made a vow many years before, standing over the body of Lano's dead father, to look out for his family, and Artie planned on keeping that vow. He would keep it because he and Lano's old man had been bound by a tie stronger than a spoiled, drunken, self-absorbed gangster like Tomase could ever understand. They were partners in a war, tested and true, who'd depended on each other every day to stay alive. Artie had made it home and had right away begun to honor his promise, and would continue to do so now.

Even if it killed him.

8

Lano was waiting in line before the ninth race, craning his head every minute or so to check the posted odds on the tote board outside. A light snow had begun falling, and he blessed it. Between the snow and the icy cold, there would be few long-shot bettors here waiting for a horse to come along and make them rich. He scanned the crowd. A lot of people, still, but they had their heads buried in the *Racing Form* or the *Green Sheet*. These were serious bettors, not folks looking to get rich, out on a lark. Good. Two minutes before the ninth race ran, the next-race tote board showed the odds on Bucking Bronco N. to be ninety-nine to one. As high as the board could gō. The horse could conceivably pay a couple of hundred dollars for a two-dollar bet.

His game plan was: Make a heavy trifecta bet and get the hell out. The track had computer betting now, and you could come in for the first race, make all your bets for the night and go on home, listen to the racing wrap-up program on the radio at midnight, see how you made out. So although the ninth race hadn't run yet, Lano could bet on the tenth.

He'd make his bet, leave, head to the empty apartment and pack. Art had said there was a plane East leaving tonight, and he planned to be on it. He hoped it would be a direct flight. He hated traveling by bus from Pittsburgh to Atlantic City. Maybe, if he had to get off at Pittsburgh, he'd rent a limo.

The more he thought about it, the better he liked it. What better way to test the prime roll, if that's what he was on, than in a casino with the odds dead against you? Hell, any two-bit hustler could make a good living suckering the convention crowds. He'd go to A.C., let Artie smooth over things out here. Maybe make his fortune and go away for a long time. Maybe even head somewhere where winter was kind.

A hand grabbed his forearm and he tensed, was swinging with his left hand when he spotted the cowboy hat high atop the sandy head. He pulled the punch, his fist just bouncing off the crown of the hat, tearing off the multicolored peacock feather that had been placed in the headband. The hat flew directly into the face of the short, cigar-chomping bettor behind Lano, a guy who'd been bitching at the long line since he'd gotten into it. He glared at Lano, and Lano figured he didn't have to apologize, because Mons was here, and if the guy said a word to the Mons, then the Mons might feel obliged to tear the guy's head clean off at the shoulders.

Mons was looking hurt, bending over and trying to stick the feather back into the hat, jeans tight across a cowboy ass that had no hips. He straightened, and his broad shoulders were where they usually were, right about at Lano's eye level.

"Hey big guy." Lano smiled. Behind them, someone shouted, "Hey, no cutting in the fucking line," angrily. Mons stood next to Lano, making it clear that he wasn't betting, just talking. A voice over the loudspeaker announced that there was now one minute to post.

"Got a message for you from your uncle." Mons said it softly out of the side of his mouth, and Lano smiled. Mons was enjoying this, being a conspirator. Lano waited patiently while the man in front of him, who was now at the betting window, placed a couple dozen two-dollar bets. Unobtrusively, he slipped his hand into his right front pocket, pulled out his wad.

"Wait for me in the bar," he told the Mons, and moved up to the window.

Mons walked away—looking even more hurt—and Lano said to the poker-faced woman, "Wheel the six horse with everything in the tenth, trifecta."

"Two-dollar bet?" The woman sounding pissed that she had to ask. Lano smiled at her.

He said, "Two-*hundred*-dollar bet, sweetheart." There. That got her attention.

The Mons was a barber and a good one, but he was an even better cowboy. He had three horses of his own and he'd ride them every morning, summer and winter, spend hours grooming them, talking to them, treating them the way other men his age treated their children. When he used to gamble he booked horses on the side for Artie. He'd call them in for his customers and Artie would give him ten percent of the customers' losses, which worked out pretty well, because when the customers won they would usually give Mons ten percent of their earnings for a tip.

It was a no-lose situation, as long as the Mons didn't bet personally. Unfortunately for him, he acquired a taste for the wager.

He'd taken a bet for a guy he'd hardly known, a twenty-dollar daily-double bet on a couple of horses that were one race away from the bubble-gum factory, and he'd gone to buy hay that evening and had forgotten to call in the bet.

The double had paid $158.70.

In remorse—it had been an honest mistake, and Mons, when he remembered the bet early the next morning, was glad he would be able to give the guy his money back, knowing the guy didn't have a winner because the horses were so bad—the barber had offered to pay the guy off, fifty a week, until the debt was fulfilled.

The guy had refused, had gotten drunk, then had come to the shop and had shot Mons through the right hand, successfully taking away Mons's earning ability.

The bullet had torn ligaments, ripped veins, and broken bones, but the doctor had assured Mons that he would cut hair again, after therapy, maybe six months down the road. By that time, Mons knew, his customers would all have gone elsewhere.

He was surprised to be visited in the hospital by Artie himself, who inquired about the insurance (which, thank God, was paid up). Safe in the knowledge that he would earn his base pay even while laid up, Artie had slipped him a sheaf of bills, and Mons had seen that the top one was a hundred and had no reason to doubt that the rest were of the same denomination. He'd thanked Artie over and over, then apologized for the error.

"What error?" Artie had said, then had looked shocked. "The punk, you mean? The one who laid the bet would have cost me fifteen hundred? Oh, that was no error," and that had been that until the Mons had gone home and learned that Artie had had his crew cut off both of the guy's trigger fingers right down to the hand.

It was then that Mons decided to quit gambling and booking. Artie had understood. But when he'd called that night, asking for a small favor, Mons had been more than happy to oblige. He'd seen how Artie treated people who displeased him.

He was sipping an Old Style from the bottle, another one right there on the little table for Lano, the houselights dimmed, feeling a little antsy because the horses were taking off from the post now for the ninth race, and he was getting the urge to bet some money on the last race. He looked at the little pink star right in the middle of his palm, a constant reminder of the error of his past ways, and the urge left him. He took a long drink of the beer, burped, placed it on the table as Lano came into the bar, making a big thing out of looking around, as if he couldn't see him. Clown son of a bitch, he hadn't changed a bit.

Lano said, "How's the hand?" and Mons wiggled it back and forth.

"It cuts hair, but it's still, even now, pretty stiff. What, you have a hard time finding me here?"

Lano had been waiting for this. "Some. You gotta learn to dress so you stand out, Mons. I mean, you blend into the crowd so much, the way you dress now." Mons was wearing the tall hat with the feather, jeans over orange ostrich-skin boots, and a big Marlboro-man leather jacket with a fur collar. "What's my uncle want now?"

"Wants you to get up, right now, and run, don't walk, the hell out of here. There's a guy named Tommy on his way here to hurt you, paybacks for you cutting up someone's car. Artie didn't say too much and I didn't want to know. Just said to tell you to do what he told you to do earlier tonight. I been running around here for a half-hour looking for you. Thought maybe the guy had caught up to you. Then I spot you and you swing on me. Jesus." Mons got the last in to show his hurt, but Lano wasn't paying attention.

Lano forgot about the way Mons was dressed, about the plane to A.C.; he forgot about Arliss leaving. He even forgot about the horse in the tenth race, because over the brim of the Mons's hat, through the bar window, he could see Tommy the Tomato Gambesi working his way through the crowd, his head on a swivel, searching.

He slipped the tickets into his wallet, swiveled on the stool as he put it back into his pocket. He grabbed his beer and, with his back now to the window, began guzzling it.

Without turning, he took it away from his lips and said to Mons, "That's him, right outside, the ugly jag in the bag with the black hair and the boils all over his face. He spot me?"

Mons put his chin in his hand and gazed through the window. The man—Christ, was he ugly or what?—was looking at him now, no, at the back of Lano's head. Mons looked back, challenging him. Trying to act the innocent bettor outraged at the scrutiny he was getting. It wasn't working. The light dawned in Tommy's eyes, and he began to walk urgently toward the bar entrance. It was the only way in or out of the bar.

"Here he comes," Mons said, but the warning wasn't needed, because Lano had already turned and risen from the table, the beer bottle in his right hand, running for the bar entrance as Tommy entered with his hand coming out of his coat pocket.

Tommy walked into the bar with the switch coming out, his finger on the button, pushing it open as he spotted Lano racing toward him. He'd gone against Tony's orders and had decided to kill Lano here and now, the ignorant-looking goof with him, too, if he had to. He was filled with so much pent-up hatred that somebody had to die, and right away, or he might just explode on the spot. It would be safe; the lights had gone out and a bell had rung when the race had begun, so the place was as dark as a movie theater. The other three dozen or so men in the bar were staring intently at the TV screen mounted on the wall, shouting now for their horse of choice, paying them no attention. He stepped back, not expecting an assault, felt better as he felt the knife buck in his hand as the spring snapped and the blade came out, and he was swinging it at Lano underhanded, going to gut him, when the beer bottle split the top of his skull nearly to the bone.

* * *

Lano hit Tommy a solid shot in the head, and the knife swished through the air an inch from his stomach as he dropped the bottle and began to run for the exit. Behind him he heard some surprised grunts and a single shout— "*Whaaa!?*"—but no one accosted him on the way out, nor even looked his way.

He shoved his shaking hands into his coat pockets, and had the terrifying thought that maybe Tommy was just the lead-off man. If Virgil was waiting for him somewhere outside, he was dead, and that's all there was to it.

He ran through the doors, banging into people arriving late to bet on the trifecta, and raced into the parking lot, skidding a little on the snow, searching for his car, for Virgil, his head swiveling around the way Tommy's had been moments before. He cursed himself for caring so much about his car. Out here, at the end of the lot, it stuck out like a beacon, calling Virgil to him. He said a silent prayer, breathed thanks as he got to his car unmolested.

The snow was coming down harder. As he raced out onto Goodenow Road without looking for traffic, he heard the announcer over the outside speaker call the horses to post for the tenth and final race.

He drove quickly, hands shaking but under control now, out of danger. Feeling safe enough to think.

Virgil not being in the parking lot, what about that? He'd been sure that Virgil had sent Tommy in as a decoy; Virgil would know full well that Tommy with a knife in each hand and one between his teeth would be no match for Lano.

Maybe Virgil was waiting at the apartment.

The thought struck him hard. Yes, Virgil would know right off that Lano would head for home, to see about Arliss, check her safety. He made up his mind swiftly and without condition that if Virgil or any other of Tony's mad dogs had harmed Arliss, he would kill them, starting with Tough Tony himself. He hadn't been raised by one of the shrewdest and most cunning mobsters in the city without picking up some sense of honor.

The decision made him feel good, more mature. Lately he'd been feeling like a little kid playing a man's game, and he didn't know why.

He circled his apartment house casually, slowly, seeing nothing out of place, knowing inside himself that nothing would seem out of place. These were professionals and would act as such. He left the Crown Vic on the street in front of the apartment house and walked boldly right up the front stairs, to the elevator. If they were waiting for him, he was going to die anyway, so why act like a skulking coward?

Feeling better and better with each decision, Lano stepped out of the elevator and entered his apartment.

To find the only thing waiting for him to be a message from Arliss, on the answering machine. He dragged a single suitcase from the closet—thankfully, she'd left him one— and listened to the message as he quickly packed some clothes.

"I hate writing letters, you know it?" Arliss began. "The past six months have been fun, Lano, but honest to God, you've been acting like such a baby since you've been on this winning streak. You're always gonna kill someone, always gonna do this, do that. You got to learn to grow up, Lano, get some character. Because you as a winner are starting to remind me of Tough Tony when he was losing, so does that make you a loser, or what?" Her voice droned on. Lano frowned. Stupid illiterate little hustler, listen to her talk down at him. He wondered where she'd have spent the past six months if it hadn't been for him. Then decided that she would have made out.

At the closet again now, Lano turned back the wall-to-wall carpeting inside and lifted up the false cedar floor.

Inside, covering the concrete floor—that would be the ceiling of the closet in the apartment downstairs—to a depth of two inches, were tightly banded and stacked bundles of hundred-dollar bills. Fifty thousand dollars' worth. All of his net worth; his liquid assets. He stuffed his inside suit-jacket pockets with the money, surprised at what a small bundle so much money made when it was ironed, the way this cash was. Didn't even make a bulge. He patted the cash, touched the bank bag still safely tucked down the front of his pants, grabbed the suitcase, and left the apartment, with Arliss's voice still giving him a load of shit, coming out of the little plastic-and-electronic device sitting there next to the phone.

For some reason, the sound of her voice on the machine reassured him.

He called Mons from the airport.

"Goddamnit, Lano, what the hell's *wrong* with you? Shit, I got a wife, a kid, three horses, you think I got time for this in my life?" He rattled on and Lano let him go. Suddenly everyone was giving him static over the telephone lines. When Mons paused for breath, he cut in.

"How'd we do?"

"The trifecta? You mean the two grand worth of trifecta bets you laid? I ought to give you some shit, I ought to say that I ran out, like you did, I might add, when I saw the man with the switch." Mons's voice was heavy with accusation. In the phone booth, in spite of himself, Lano smiled. He could picture Mons, at home, his hands still trembling with fear, maybe looking at the scar on his right palm and wondering how close he'd come to getting a matching one, in his belly this time.

"I ought to tell you that," Mons was saying, "but I wouldn't lie, even to you, a so-called friend runs out on a guy, leaves me holding the bag. The fact is, security grabbed me. Hustled me off to their office. Someone at the bar remembered me sitting with the guy who coldcocked the ugly guy. By the time security got there, the switch was nowhere to be found. They bundled the guy up, took him away, probably to the hospital. I told them you were just some asshole, sat down next to me touting horses."

"Well?" Lano said, then heard the woman's voice come over the speakers in the ceiling of Midway Airport, announcing the boarding of his flight to Atlantic City. She was telling the crowded terminal that the plane would be leaving on time, in spite of the weather.

"Well, what?" Mons said.

"Did the horse win?"

"Win? How the hell would *I* know if the horse won? You smashed the guy and I tried to walk away, walked right by him as he was sitting up, groaning. Bar full of people and they're all nudging each other, going, 'Looky there, shit,' not one of them coming around to see if the guy was all right. Soon as the men with guns show up, everyone clams up except for this one dumb son of a bitch—"

"Mons!"

"What!"

"Did the fucking horse *win*?"

"How the hell would I know? Time the race went off, I'm down in security, wondering if I should tell them the truth and what Art would do to me if I did."

Without answering—he felt that he had been handed more than his fair share of garbage for one night—Lano hung up the phone and grabbed his bag. He made it to the gate just as the last call for boarding was going out over the loudspeaker.

"Would you like a drink?" the stewardess asked, and Lano told her he'd love one. He was sitting in first class, with plenty of leg room, looking down at the lights of Chicago, wondering how a city that looked so beautiful from ten thousand feet could be so ugly up close and real.

Thinking, too, about Mons. Thinking that maybe he shouldn't have hung up on him. The bettors at Balmoral would have put the six horse in their trifectas, a lot of them, just to increase the payoff if they won. But hardly any of them, if any at all, would have put it on top, to win. If the horse won, he had it wheeled with everything else. If it came in first, he'd win, no matter what came in second and third. Then he could take the payoff for a two-dollar bet, which would be gigantic, and multiply it by a hundred to get his winnings. There would be a couple of hundred grand there for him. Serious money. The man who had helped make that possible was not to be alienated.

The stewardess brought his drink and smiled, and he downed it, ordered another. When it came he sipped it slowly and sat back, deciding that it wasn't worth thinking about anymore. At ninety-nine to one on the tote board, there wasn't a hope in hell that the horse would win. He finished the drink and the stewardess took the glass away, and he slipped into a restless sleep, dreaming of Millie, and of what might have been.

9

He awoke with a start and was surprised to be where he was, in an airplane high above the ground, the plane descending. The No Smoking and Fasten Seat Belts signs were on. Lano looked out the window, craning his neck, staring out at the gaudy neon lights of Atlantic City.

He'd been here before, twice, with Artie for the fights. The first time, he'd paid five hundred dollars a copy for six tickets to the Holmes-Tyson match. A group of them had flown in and it was only on fight night that they'd learned that Donald Trump had about seventeen thousand seats he considered to be ringside. They were in a bad spot; the two hundred and fifty true ringside seats had been fenced off for the celebrities. The HBO cameramen stood with the tools of their trade on the ring's apron, blocking their view for most of the fight. The fighters looked like little black Tonka trucks from where they were sitting. When Tyson hit Holmes the knockout punch in the fourth round, though, they'd heard it well enough. It had sounded like Kevin Butler kicking a fifty-yard field-goal shot.

The second time they came was when Tyson fought Spinks, and this time Art took care of things. They'd been put up in a suite at the Trump Plaza, the two of them having their own bedrooms and private bathrooms with gold-plated faucets. The night of the fight they'd been escorted to ringside, and Lano had sat three seats down from Jack Nicholson, right next to Warren Beatty. When he'd asked Artie, after the ninety-second fight, how he had promoted the tickets, Art had just smiled at him, a little sadly.

Lano did not have happy memories of Atlantic City.

The plane was buffeted by a fierce wind on the way down and had to go back up twice before finally landing roughly on the runway. Lano sat, calming down, as the other passengers disembarked, in a hurry to get to the casinos. The casinos would be closing at four and it was after three now. He wondered if he'd have time to get into the action, check his luck.

There was a vaguely familiar-looking guy standing outside of the Continental Airlines terminal, a tall, older man, dressed in a coat that had a thick wide fur collar. He wore a funny Russian-looking black fur hat. Lano could see the tight knot of a red silk tie at his throat. The guy had a twitch in his face, a slight tic that seemed to pulse with his heartbeat. He spotted Lano and smiled. Lano walked up to him, a confused grin twisting his own mouth, feeling slightly embarrassed and oddly uneasy at the man's appearance. Was he with Tough Tony? Was that why he recognized him? Were they on to him already?

"Lano," the man said, reaching out to shake his hand. Lano squeezed back, looking around. "Good to see you again." As Lano heard his voice he placed him. He'd been introduced to him once before, on the second trip here for the Spinks-Tyson fight. His father ran the mob action in the town, and this guy—Gaetano, that was his name—was his right-hand man.

"Mr. Biari," Lano said. "Good to see you again." He

looked around again, surprised. "Why you come out to pick me up personally?"

Gaetano held on to Lano's arm and guided him toward the exit. "There's a guy picking up your luggage. He'll take it to your room."

They walked out into a ferocious wind that was coming off the ocean. Biari held on to his fur hat with one gloved hand and held Lano's arm with the other. He walked Lano to a maroon Lincoln Town Car, this year's model. They got into the backseat together and Lano leaned back, enjoying the smell and feel of leather, glad to be in out of the frigid salt-smelling night air. From somewhere nearby, he could hear the roar of the ocean, even through the tightly shut windows.

Gaetano said, "Your father, he saved my life, you know that? You think I could ever forget that? Why you think I got Art high-roller ringside for Spinks-Tyson?" Lano looked at him sharply but kept quiet. "I didn't have time to stick around, get to know you better then. I was busy running things with the old man away for a while. But if it hadn't been for your father, I wouldn't be here. That's one reason I come out myself. The other is, Art the Arm called my father tonight, he was worried about your safety, and my father called me. When he told me who it was and to send some people over to make sure you got in okay, I decided to come myself."

A young man, hatless, wearing what looked like a silk topcoat, got into the car on the driver's side, and Lano heard the trunk slam shut and a second later another young man, also hatless, slid into the passenger seat. The kid driving started the car and pulled it smoothly from the curb.

"Where to, Mr. Biari?" he asked.

"To the house first, then after Mr. Branka talks to my father, you'll take him to the Palermo." He turned to Lano.

"The old man was doing three years for refusing to speak to a federal grand jury when you were down here last. He's dying to meet you. Heard a lot about you from Art."

"He did?"

"Art ain't got no sons."

"He's made that clear."

"Don't take it personal. The guy, he'd die for you. Told me when you was here last, your only problem is, you don't want to grow up."

Lano said, "Everyone's been telling me that lately," then said, "Listen, Mr. Biari? Would you tell me about my father?"

He'd always been compared to the man, mostly unfavorably. Art would just have to look at him and without a word being spoken Lano would know: he was being sized up and rejected. As Gaetano spoke, Lano listened intently and began to dislike the man. He spoke of his father as if he were a saint; that wasn't the problem, but there was something about him that didn't sit right, as if the whole thing, picking him up personally, taking him to a command audience with the great Angelo Biari, having him delivered to his hotel in a brand-new Lincoln, was part of some scam. Lano began to believe that these guys needed Art for something, and were laying the groundwork for it by their behavior toward him. He began to feel guilty with the knowledge, knowing now that this was going to cost Art, that no one here was going to be doing him any free favors. It would be a matter of one hand washing the other.

Too, there was the way the guy treated him. The crack about growing up, he shouldn't have said that. That should have stayed between Art and Gaetano. It was an offhand insult, intended to put Lano in his place right from the beginning. As the man talked on, Lano could feel him staring at him, another mob wise guy sizing him up once again, another one telling him by the subtle change in the tone of his voice that he just didn't quite stack up.

Well, Lano could do some comparing of his own.

For one thing, Art was the only one of these so-called

men of respect who didn't seem to be cut from the same mold. They wore their gold jewelry and their thousand-dollar suits and their five-hundred-dollar shoes, and they spoke of "class" and bought for themselves only the most beautiful women. They drove the Lincolns and the Cadillacs and they wore the expensive colognes, and at home they relaxed in five-hundred-dollar jogging suits, but it didn't change a thing. Five minutes into the conversation, Lano would know he was speaking to a guy who was interchange-able with Tough Tony. They took their expressions from TV shows or from what they heard someone in the New York mob was saying. For years, it was, "*What* are you, nuts?" every other sentence. Then it became, "Get the fuck *outta* here," said derisively. These days, it was "*Forget* about it." Gaetano must have said that one twenty times on the drive from the Atlantic City airport to his father's estate in Longport.

And the old man was no different. Angelo Biari was wear-ing a white jogging suit with his name stitched in gold thread across the shirt pocket. He was much older than Gaetano, who must have either been a late child or an accident. Lano put Gaetano at about thirty-six or so, and the old man close to eighty.

His hair was white and thick, combed straight back in the Old-Country style. He was a lot shorter than Lano, and stood far back from him as he spoke so he would not have to look up. He did not offer to shake hands.

The house was large, and as Gaetano mixed him a drink from the wet bar, Lano looked around the room they were in. A den, maybe, or a study. A fireplace and several leather chairs. There was a big desk with three phones on top and nothing else visible. No papers or pencils or anything. Maybe the old guy couldn't read or write. Or maybe he just didn't trust Lano.

"Like what you see?"

"Yes, sir."

Biari grunted, and he and his son shot each other a quick

glance before the old man looked back at Lano. "You got respect. It'll be a pleasure to help you out while you're here. Funny thing though. Art always said you was a wise-ass." Said derisively, Lano decided; a little dig to put the kid in his place.

"Only at home," Lano said.

"That's good, because this ain't Chicago. We got guys here, cut your heart out and mix it inna their spaghetti sauce, you say something they don't like."

"I'll watch my step." Lano watched as the two Biaris once again glanced at each other. He wondered if they were stupid or just figured him to be.

"I want to thank you, both, for doing this," Lano said, finishing his drink and placing the glass atop the desk. He hadn't been asked to sit down, and so it was easy to move toward the door, smiling softly. "I appreciate it, you doing this for Art."

"Wait a minute—shit, what's the hurry?" And they did the look again. As the old man spoke, Gaetano hurriedly moved to a chair near the fire, patted the back of it, smiling.

"Come on, sit down, have another drink."

"I don't want to impose . . ." Lano looked at the old man, wondering how to play it. If he said the guy might need his sleep, he'd take it as an insult. Maybe put Lano's heart in some lasagna, have a late-night snack. And if he just walked out, he'd be nearly slapping them in the face. Whatever it was they were selling, he didn't want to buy, but he had no choice now but to listen to the pitch. He settled into the chair and accepted another drink from Gaetano with a smile and a thank-you, then sat quietly, watching the two of them smile at him.

At last, the old man said, "Art tell you where you can and can't play?"

Lano decided it would be best to keep the answers short and to keep smiling. He'd rather they thought him to be stupid than to be too smart, and, besides, when he was nervous he had a habit of talking too much and too fast.

And right now, he was for some reason quite nervous. He took it as an omen.

"Yes, sir. Gave me the names, yes, sir."

Straight-faced, in a man-to-man tone, Angelo Biari said, "He tell you we're having a few problems with one of the casino owners?"

Smiling Lano said, "No, sir, he didn't mention it."

"Well, we sure the hell are. Guy named O'Shea, owns the Shamrock at the far end of the Boardwalk. Stay away from there, too, if Art didn't mention it. Guy's gonna have a heart attack or a stroke here before Tuesday. Some kind of accident." Biari winked. "You understand what I'm saying."

Lano's smile was failing him now, the muscles in his face crying for relief. These two bozos were sitting here telling a complete stranger about a hit in their town. He said, "I'll do that, Mr. Biari."

"Hey," Angelo Biari said, all smiles himself now, "call me Ange, eh? Any member of Art Pella's crew is a friend of mine." The smile dropped and he turned to his son. "Get him the piece, 'Tan."

With a growing sense of dread Lano watched Gaetano walk over to the wall, swing a painting of a sheepdog away from it and twist dials on a safe. As he stared, his sudden good buddy Ange kept up a line of chatter, and Lano was instantly on his guard.

"You never know about a psycho cocksucker like Tomase. He might come out here in the dead of night, whack you in the hotel like a thief while you sleep. He's a goon, is what Tony is. A throwback." Lano tore his eyes away from Gaetano's back and stared incredulously at Ange. He was being used here, he could sense that, could nearly taste betrayal in his mouth. What he couldn't figure out was why.

"Him or that piece-of-shit monster he got hanging around him, what's his name, Virgin?" Ange laughed and Gaetano joined in, now close to Lano, holding a pistol by the grip and extending it. Lano just looked at it.

Ange ignored Lano ignoring Gaetano and suddenly Lano began to feel very afraid. The old man took the gun away from Gaetano and stared hard at Lano, offering the pistol, thrusting it at him with his own gnarled hand around the barrel.

"You see either one of them come up to you, in the street, in your hotel, anywhere, you use this, you understand?" It was a command instead of a question, and Lano knew better than to argue. Biari's reputation was national, and it was frightening.

He reached out and quickly took the pistol, pointing it away from Ange, and he stood, stuck it down the front of his pants; felt it rustle there atop the money.

"And don't you hesitate," Ange said. He looked at his son. "See that the kid gets a ride home," he said, then turned back to Lano and said, "Good meeting you, kid." But this time Lano forgot his respect and his manners and just walked shakily from the room.

The Palermo was an old hotel on South Illinois Avenue, less than a block from the Boardwalk and directly across the street from the Sands Hotel and Casino. Butted up against the building was the five-story parking lot for the Sands, with a glass-covered walkway high above the street so the players would never have to step out onto the mean streets of Atlantic City.

It had been more fun riding back into A.C. than it had been riding out. For one thing, Gaetano didn't come along, and the driver was more loose, talkative. He kept a conversation going and Lano thought he was just being friendly until later, when he figured out that the chatter was just a diversion.

Lano was disappointed in himself. Brooding over the way he had acted at the house in front of the two mobsters, he listened to the driver with half an ear, wondering why the man had told him to sit in the back of the car.

"The niggers," the driver said, "got Atlantic City by the ears, and they're trying to ram their tools down her throat."

Headlights poured through the back window. Lano craned his head, turned in his seat, and stared out at the car behind them. The lights were blinding. He couldn't tell the make or color of the car. He turned back ahead and stared through the windshield. There was little traffic on the road at this time of night, and the idiot behind them could pass anytime he wanted. But he stayed right on their ass and kept the brights on.

Lano decided it wasn't his problem. The driver was ignoring the other car, and if it didn't bother him, why should it bother Lano?

The driver was saying, "You got Trump Plaza, you take the garbage out the back door at night and see the tenements, burnt-out, half of them, but the jigs, they're like cockroaches, once they get in, man, that's it. Stick to the Boardwalk, in broad daylight, and you'll be all right. Walk through town, even at high noon, you're taking your life in your hands. You smoke?"

It took Lano a second for the question to register in his mind. The car was still behind them, almost crawling up the Lincoln's bumper. He said, "Two packs a day."

"Don't. Shines see you smoke, they come strutting up, looking for a light. They don't outright mug you, they'll lift your wallet while you're standing there holding out a match, trying to show how liberal and unafraid you are.

"Yeah," the driver said, "stick to the Boardwalk, you'll be all right."

"The casinos safe?"

"You shitting me?"

They were pulling onto Illinois Avenue off Pacific, the front of the Claridge Casino right there, bright and pretty. Across the street, Lano could see the Sands, and next door, on the other side, Bally's. People were walking the streets, in droves, and Lano couldn't understand why. The gambling houses were supposed to close at four in the morning. In spite of himself he felt a little shiver of excitement, and he wished that the casinos didn't close for six hours a night. He wanted some action, now.

"The safest place in the world for you is inside one of the casinos. When they first opened up, a couple of niggers tried to rob an old couple in the elevator of Resorts? Got maybe thirty bucks. The city sent the jigs a message right away, sentenced them to sixty years in Rahway. Ain't been much of a problem since." They were there, the bright neon lights of the Palermo spilling into the car. Coupled with the lights of the car still behind them, pulling in to the curb, it gave the interior of the car the illusion of daylight.

Lano turned in his seat, tried to see the driver of the car behind them, then turned to the front again. Biari's driver was reaching into the glove box to push the button that would pop the trunk.

"How come there're so many people out this time of night?"

"It's Friday night, Saturday morning. Casinos stay open till six."

"What time is it?" There was an excitement in his voice he wished wasn't there, and the driver turned in his seat, giving him the sort of grin Lano guessed he'd give to a wino who saw what he thought to be a half-bottle of wine floating far out in the ocean surf, wondering if he could get at it and get back out before he drowned.

"Four-fifteen," the man said, gleefully.

Lano got out of the car and dragged his suitcase from the trunk, venting his anger on the driver of the car behind him. He was either a tall man or a short man who kept his seat all the way up and in. His head reached the car's top and he had a broad, dark face, with wide-apart eyes that were holding Lano's steadily. Lano stepped to the curb, about to shout something to the guy, when the Lincoln pulled from the curb with a squeal of rubber. He turned his head to look at it and when he turned back he noticed the car now instead of the man.

It was a dark blue Plymouth, a few years old, and the front and rear tires that Lano could see had no whitewalls. There was a little skinny antenna sticking out of the middle of the trunk. In Chicago, Atlantic City, or anywhere else in the country, an unmarked squad was easy to spot.

Lano turned, fast, and entered the hotel, feeling the gun there down his pants, the knowledge of it making the barrel burn into his belly.

It was hard, getting away from the desk clerk. He was told that he was registered as Jules Pella, and was shown to a suite facing the ocean. Lano would have preferred one facing the street, so he could see if the cop was still out there, but he didn't say anything. After the clerk told him to see him personally if there was anything he could do for him, Lano closed and locked the door and sat down on the edge of the bed without removing his coat.

So that was why the driver had kept jabbering away, trying to draw his attention away from the cop. And why he'd ignored the solitary vehicle riding their bumper all the way in. Maybe, too, why he had insisted that Lano sit in the backseat, so the cop could get a good look at him.

Which Lano'd given him, first by turning around and staring at him, and then by getting out of the car and facing off with him. He wondered if the cop had a camera with him.

Then wondered if he was being paranoid. No, shit, nothing was too outrageous when you were dealing with Sicilians like the Biaris. The thought struck him hard, and he shivered. Sicilians like the Biaris—and Tough Tony Tomase.

Lano reached for the phone and dialed the desk, told the guy who he was and that he wanted a large, heavy-duty economy size Baggie from the restaurant, large enough to maybe freeze a five-pound roast. The guy was so intimidated by the guest he thought to be the son of the owner that he didn't ask any questions, told him that a bellhop would have it up to him right away.

While he waited, Lano thought.

What was going on? He was here to get out of one bit of trouble, and it looked as if he'd stepped into one even worse.

The gun, that was a key to something. Maybe it had been used in a mob hit for which the Biaris were drawing heat, and they'd given it to him and then tipped off the cops that the killer was staying at the Palermo.

Jesus Christ. That was just one of a thousand scenarios that passed through his mind as he waited. Another was that maybe Artie had underestimated Tomase, maybe he had more pull out here than Art had figured him to, maybe, maybe—

When the knock came at the door he jumped, nearly ran to it, peeked through the peephole and sighed his relief when he saw the round red cap of the bellboy. He opened the door, took the bag, tipped him and asked him if they had a safe. The bellhop thanked him and assured him that they did, that the desk clerk would be more than happy to—

Lano shut the door in his face while the kid was still talking. He sat down on the bed again, took out the pistol and, holding it by the grip, dropped it into the huge Baggie. There was plenty of room to spare.

He dropped it on the bed and then removed the money bag, emptied his pockets, too. Over a hundred and thirty grand. He stacked it up, removed the black plastic bag from the small wastebasket next to the bed, and placed the money inside. He wrapped the plastic around the money, then stuck the pistol back down his pants, buttoned his coat, held the money in his left hand and left the room.

The clerk had gasped and gone pale when he saw the money. He gave Lano a receipt without counting it, which

Lano appreciated. He was nervous already, his head swiveling around, trying to see through the double glass doors to the curb. All he could see was a cab parked there, idling.

As he waited for the clerk to come back from the safe room, he noticed a small lounge across from the elevators, sounds of laughter and warmth there inside. A jukebox played something country that was familiar and made him sad, a little homesick. He looked at the clock mounted on the wall behind the clerk's desk, saw that it was four-thirty. Saturday morning, the twenty-eighth of January. The crowd inside was probably part of a convention, drinking now that they'd lost the fifty or hundred dollars they allowed themselves to blow each day. He looked outside the door again, and saw that a steady, heavy snow had begun to fall.

Conway was a woman who prided herself on always knowing the score, even if it took her a little while to figure things out. She would hesitate and think things through.

Which was what she had done tonight. She'd kept delaying, putting it off, but when O'Shea called from the casino floor and told her that her high-roller date was getting antsy, she knew exactly what it was she would have to do.

She dressed, carefully, in a light gown, shivering at the thought of having to slip it off, drop it to the floor while that big ugly bastard groped at her body . . .

She forced the thought from her mind as she slipped on her pumps, hurriedly ran a brush through her hair. She was Conway Mallory, named that way, her mother had told her, because she'd been conceived in a motel room after her parents had attended a Conway Twitty concert.

Conway hummed softly, thinking of her mother. She was flying, almost in a dream state from the two half 'ludes she'd dropped, on top of the Scotch. It would be a dream, the entire episode. Get down there and get it over with and then get home, pretend it was all a dream when she woke up tomorrow.

She left her suite, floated to the elevator, still humming vaguely, feeling lost, as if someone else was inside her head, and she was watching that person go down the road to whoredom. Poor little girl, doing something like that.

She rode down in silence, alone, feeling sorry for the girl whom she now felt totally detached from, and when the elevator doors opened onto the casino she stepped out, gloriously, her head held high, Conway gliding over to the table where the pretty black-haired woman with the beautiful body was dealing cards, three hands of blackjack, to the high roller Conway was planning on watching the little girl inside of her head fuck tonight.

She stood next to the man, close, then moved in closer until her breasts brushed his broad back. His hair, she could tell from here, was greased, and she could smell a cheap musk cologne which he must have thought was sexy. She could smell, too, his stale sweat. His nerves must not be as strong as he thought.

He turned to her when he felt her touch him, and his face, which had been grim, broke into a smile.

"Hey, little lucky lady. Are those chips in your bra or are you just glad to see me?"

Conway allowed the poor girl inside her head to giggle, while she fought the urge to groan. She wasn't at all sure anymore that she was willing to go through with this.

10

Tommy the Tomato didn't get back to the game until nearly dawn, and by then Art was getting a little tired of Tough Tony. Here was the guy, rubbing it in. Now and then Elihue would stick his head in, see what was going on and ask Art if there was anything he could do for him. He would glance at Art strangely, as if he were trying to silently tell him something. Art liked the fact that Elihue did this, liked, too, the fact that Elihue would skin Tomase alive if Art gave the nod, take his chances with Virgil later, if it came down to it. But each time he'd shake his head, finally told him they had a business to run and he should be out there doing what he was getting paid to do.

The two of them had been gone long enough to learn that Tommy's car was a fifteen-year-old Buick, and Tomase wouldn't be caught dead in a car that had no class. He said they'd stick around until Tommy did the job, then take a cab home. Art offered his car and Tony had thanked him but refused it, enjoying sitting behind the desk while Art did his job outside in the casino. At one point Artie had even offered to leave and drive them home himself, and Tony had merely smiled.

Outside of that, though, it was a good night. He'd had enough time to call Mons and tell him the score, and to get ahold of Ange Biari and the manager of the Palermo. He'd just been hanging up with the hotel and was watching Elihue step lively toward his office door when the outside buzzer had sounded and Tony and Virgil had come back into the casino. Strange, that. As he'd been talking on the phone he'd seen Elihue staring at the office door, watched on his television screen as the big black man squirmed, as if with an inner pain. Art'd been angry when Tony had buzzed. He was interested to know what had been bothering Elihue. Then Elihue had been forgotten as Art watched, seething, as Tony acted like he owned the place. Well, Art would be speaking with Mad Mike very soon, like later today, and he'd get more than a few things straight about this jagoff.

But for now there was nothing he could do. Except count his money, which was coming in in droves. It was going to be one of his best weekends ever. The place was packed and more than half the players were well lubricated and betting the limit.

There was also the embarrassment on Virgil's face, that was something worth seeing. And remembering. It never hurt to have an ally in the enemy's camp. Art would look at Virgil and the man would look right back at him, once even shrugging his shoulders in a what-can-I-do gesture. He had balls, doing that in front of Tony, Art had to hand him that.

He locked the safe every time he walked out of it, and he knew that was pissing Tony off. It was a small victory in a night of large battles.

Nor was he worried about Lano. The kid should have been able to handle an idiot like Tommy without a lot of trouble, even without fair warning, but with Mons giving him the word, it had all worked out. The night clerk at the

Palermo had phoned him as soon as Lano had checked in, and he'd, thank God, been in the office at the time, had thanked the man and had told him he'd be talking to him soon. Tony hadn't asked who it was who'd called and Art didn't offer the information. So Lano was safe, Tommy the Tomato had been stymied, and in a couple of hours he'd sit down with Mad Mike, see just how far his pull went around here.

It had to go further than Tony's. Hell, the man, he covered any and all bets, taking wagers on things he was supposedly forbidden to touch, like the fights and wrestling matches. Kickboxing contests, for Christ's sake. Mad Mike let him go and didn't say much. The mob had just recently gotten into the dope business and that was bringing in a ton. Mike would let the bets slide for now, knowing that sooner or later they'd make it all back up, as long as no one was stealing. The odds would make it so. Tony was expected to skim some of the cream, but to bet and to lose too much too regularly was to incur the wrath of Mad Mike and the other bosses, and that was something no living man in Chicago was tough enough to do, no matter what his nickname was. Artie wondered how much Mike knew, then smiled inwardly at the thought of being the one to tell him. He'd never in his life beefed to any of the bosses about a made member of the mob, and was sure that his doing so now would carry great weight. Some guys, like Tony, beefed everyone every chance they got, looking to further their own ambitions through malicious gossip and jealous backstabbing, never aware of how they were making themselves look when they did such things. No, Art decided, if Tony weren't usually such a good moneymaker, he'd have gone swimming a long time ago.

But he wasn't doing so hot these days, was he? No, Mad Mike wouldn't be aware of how much he'd been losing, nor about how he had almost tried to beat Lano out of his money tonight. Lano was safe for the night, at least, and Mike would be learning, soon, the real reason that Tony had put the hit out on the kid. He should then be justifiably outraged, and, when given all the rest of the damning evidence, should give the hit order on Tony.

There was one thing he was worried about, though, and had been since his call out East.

Angelo Biari had been too goddamn nice.

You call a man in the middle of the night and you have to expect him to be a little upset. Artie had called Angelo instead of Gaetano to impress upon the man the importance of this matter, and he'd been prepared to take a little static before calming him down.

But Biari had been awakened from his sleep and had been immediately jovial. Artie thought about that. They had enjoyed a good working relationship, and Angelo would never forget the fact that without Art and Juliano Sr., Gaetano would have been history twenty-five years back. He'd even opened up a little one night with the old man, two heavyweights together drinking wine late at night in front of the fire in the Longport estate; had told him about his feelings for Lano and his disappointment in the kid, wanting to be a player when he could be anything he wanted, at Artie's expense. He was worried now that maybe he'd said too much to a Sicilian.

Being from Naples, Art knew the differences between regions. Had in fact known men to die because they were far too loyal to their own area of the country and far too free in expressing their negative view of the regions of others. Art had been raised in America, and considered himself to be an American. He never played the guinea game, had never, even as a young man, spoken the Italian language outside of his home. But he knew that a Sicilian —fifty generations removed from the Old Country and living in New World sophistication—would always consider himself a Sicilian first.

Which worried him. Sicilians would use others, even

other Italians, without the slightest hesitation, to protect a fellow islander. Would turn on their closest friend, kill him, to save a Sicilian they hardly even knew.

Angelo Biari had been overjoyed to hear from him that night and there had been obvious relief in the old man's voice when he'd been told what was going on. He'd expressed gratitude that he had the chance to help out. He had offered Lano protection and safety without hesitation, and this bothered Art. Was there something going on that he didn't know about? Had his talking about Lano in a derogatory manner in front of Angelo years ago been a mistake? Had it given the man the impression that he didn't love Lano like a son? Would Angelo dare use Lano as a pawn in one of his constant and varied Byzantine plots, thinking that Art wouldn't mind, since the boy was a disappointment to him anyway?

Well, there was nothing he could do about that tonight. He would worry about it in the morning, after he straightened things out with Mike. Lano couldn't get into too much trouble in a few short hours, could he? No, he'd be safe, and tomorrow, things would be okay. Lano would be safe, and Tony would be dead or on the way to it.

Thinking this made Artie the Arm Pella smile, and he walked out of his safe, leaving the door open this time. In a friendly voice he asked Tony if he would maybe like a little shot of Fernet.

Tommy the Tomato came in with a tale of woe.

"There was someone else with him. I had the punk, cold, in the shitter like you said, when someone came up behind me, spun me around and coldcocked me."

He was standing in front of Artie's desk, Tony sitting there regally, staring at him coldly. Virgil was perched on the edge of the chair, shaking his head sadly. Art stood and watched, suddenly an outsider in his own place of business. For a second, he wanted to walk upstairs into the gun shop, get a piece, load it, then come on back down and solve his problem with Tony personally, right on the spot. He forced himself to calm down. It would be taken care of soon enough.

Tony said, "Tommy? You want to know something? The tow-truck guy had to float my brand-new fucking car onto a semi, haul it away. You know what that's gonna cost me?"

"I'll pay for that—"

"Shut up!" Tony pounded his open hand on the desktop and leaped to his feet, staring hotly at Tommy. Art wondered if he practiced the move in front of the mirror.

"You stupid fuck!" Tony shouted. "I take you on because Virgil says you're all right, I pay you every week, and what do you do? How do you pay me back? You fuck up my car, knife it. Then you can't even do a simple fucking thing like whack out a piece-of-shit, punk-degenerate gambler like Branka, that's how you pay me back." Tony walked around the desk now, eyes ablaze, the eyes never coming off Tommy. Art had the urge to quietly push the wastebasket in his way, watch the fat little shit fall on his face, see how much of a Sicilian don he felt like lying on the carpet. He was beginning to feel a cold fury rise up from deep down in his belly.

Tony stood directly in front of Tommy, breathing hard. He said, softly, "And then you fucking *lie* to me? You expect me to believe that you had the punk cornered in the shithouse with a knife, someone spun you around and you didn't gut the fucker on the spin? What do you got, shit in your head?" He made a disgusted noise and turned to Virgil, who was staring at Art, seeing things Tony hadn't yet noticed.

"Catch a ride home with this punk. Straighten him out about the way things are done in Chicago. I'll get a ride with Art." He turned to Art. "Okay?" Art smiled and nodded, thinking about how much fun it was going to be, explaining this scene to Mad Mike. He watched as Tommy and Virgil left the office.

Tony said, "Where's Lano live?" and Art shook his head firmly, back and forth, once.

"Bullshit. You had your chance." Art settled down in his chair and spun it halfway to stare hard at Tony. When he spoke his voice was cold and hard.

"You set it up, tried to pull it off and there wasn't a thing I could do because I couldn't take sides against you. Elihue watched it all, and he's been trying to tell me about it all night. You were going to kill Lano for wrecking your car, and now you admit right here in front of me that this little punk on your payroll did it all along." He was speaking softly, not slapping the top of his desk or jumping to his feet, but his words were carrying a lot more weight and darkness than Tony's ever could. The thought of going upstairs for a piece was now right there in the front of his mind.

"Elihue had been coming toward me, I was watching it on the TV screen, when you guys came back in and buzzed. He walked away. If he'd told me then, I could have gotten it all taken care of with one phone call. You, too, Tony. I could have had you taken care of.

"Mad Mike isn't gonna like this. Not one fucking bit. You were gonna kill a guy who's like a son to me because he beat you out of a few bucks. You said it yourself, Tony, the punk Tommy wrecked your car, not Lano. It slipped out when you were busting your ass, trying to show the punk how tough you are. You got no leg to stand on before the bosses.

"But I'll tell you something. Mad Mike doesn't have to hear about this. You're a liar and a goddamn sneak, but you're blood and your word is gold. You call off the hit, take the heat off the kid, and I'll forget what you did, what you tried to do, and how you acted tonight. But you stay the hell clear of my casino from now on, and believe me, if Lano dies of AIDS, you'll get blamed."

Tony had been standing on the carpet, in shock, obviously not believing he'd been stupid enough to say what he had in front of Art. Now he tried to control himself, not knowing his face had drained of blood, that he was staring wide-eyed and white-faced at Art, but Art didn't miss it, in fact, he enjoyed it.

Enjoyed, too, the sight of the fat piece of shit trying to save face, pulling himself up to his full height, sticking his chest out and saying, "I never said *shit*. Whatever I said was in front of my two men and you, and it'll be your word against mine. Mad Mike'll believe me."

"Get the fuck out of my office, asshole."

Art would never keep a pistol in his home, on his person, or in any place where it could be directly traced to him. He had a rap sheet with two convictions for felonious crimes, and if the Gee ever somehow lucked onto the casino through one of their stool pigeons and they busted the place, he would do two years without parole in a federal pen for being a convicted felon in direct possession of a firearm. The gun shop was in his brother's name. Elihue carried, as did two of the pit bosses, in case there was trouble, but that was not Art's problem if the Gee came calling. Now he thanked God that he didn't have a gun in his desk, because if he did, he might follow Tony out into the night and blow his Sicilian head off his shoulders.

He took deep breaths and checked his watch. Dawn would be outside, rising. Soon, most of the players would go home to rest before coming back this evening. Only the compulsives would be left. He would be able to leave Elihue and the pit people in charge and leave for a while, go see Mad Mike. It wouldn't be a good idea to wake him up, but if he called, say, at eight, Mike would respect that. And would see him. Two short hours and it would all be over.

He took the marker for the ninety thousand dollars that he'd made Tony sign out of his inside breast pocket and looked at it, then got up and locked it in the safe. Two hours. He checked his cameras, decided time would go by faster if he was in the casino, talking to the customers, being their friend. Checks had been getting cashed all night, as the players ran out of money, and cash advances given on MasterCards and Visas. Soon, it would be time for the heavy losers to resort to a loan from him, paid back at the going rate of six for five. He had to get out there and mingle, let the losers know that he was on their side.

And once out there, he could have a little talk with Elihue. Maybe even take him along later to the sitdown with Mad Mike.

Virgil was in the passenger seat, fuming. Not only did dumbass Tough Tony set up a bogus hit on Lano, he shot his mouth off about Tommy being the guy responsible for the damage to his car right there in front of Art. Stupid, is what it was. A dumbass thing to do simply because the kid had been hitting him heavy for the past few weeks. And Arliss, too, her leaving Tony for Lano figured into it.

Virgil waited, thinking and smiling, waiting for this stupid sad goof driving to be far enough away from the casino, yet not close enough to Virgil's home to draw any heat. The midway point would be fine. Maybe three more blocks, and he'd be okay.

He thought about what he was going to do if he was called on the carpet by Mad Mike. Mike would say, What happened? And that would be it. Tough Tony could not only be a made man but could have seventeen *brothers* who were made, and it wouldn't mean a thing. Virgil would not lie to Mad Mike. You might get away with getting your boss in trouble, although that was the exception to the rule. Usually, since the big mob shake-up a few years back, when a boss caught his lunch, so did his three or four closest associates. Keep peace in the family and keep what happened before from ever happening again. Yeah, he guessed that he might get away with telling on Tony, how he set up Lano for no good reason, but he knew that he would never get away with lying to Mad Mike. Mad Mike killed people who told him a truth he disliked; imagine what he did to suckers who lied to him face-to-face.

What a position to be in. Forty-two years old, a loyal soldier for near twenty years, suddenly his boss goes stupid and he faces the option of maybe swimming in Lake Michigan chained to a bunch of steam irons with him, or trying to cover for the man by lying to Mad Mike and letting that big fool use his personal built-in never-fail lie detector on you.

The choice was clear. If he had to go down, Tony was going, too. One way or the other.

Virgil wished there was someone he could talk to about it, other than Elihue. Elihue would juke and jive and play silly, making jokes, but he had never been, was not now, and would never be in the position to give advice on this level. Art, now, he'd be perfect. And Art liked him, too, Virgil was sure of it. But if Tony caught Virgil speaking to Art about him, even suspected him of it, he'd kill him himself.

Jesus Christ, Virgil thought, Papa was right: I shoulda stayed in school.

Tommy the Tomato Gambesi pulled over to the curb at a stoplight, his right directional signal going, waiting for a guy creeping by with the right-of-way, driving an old station wagon, to get through the intersection so he could run the light. "Goddamn working stiffs," Tommy said. "Man, I hate 'em. Drive like fucking old ladies," and that was the last thing he ever said because Virgil put a pistol to his head, pulled the trigger twice, then used his other hand to slam the gearshift into park. He stuffed the gun back into his clamshell shoulder holster, opened the passenger-side door and stepped out into the street, looking left and right. Nothing moving at all. Good.

He walked away from the car, moving quickly but not running, his head down. The falling snow muffled his footsteps. He heard the beat-up old Buick idling, wondered how long it would be before someone came along and stopped next to it, glanced over casually and saw the goof sitting there with the top of his head gone. The thought made Virgil smile, then he frowned.

It was just like that piece of shit Tony, send him out alone on a hit in the winter, knowing full well that he'd have to walk a long way home in the fucking cold.

11

Millie Swan knew who the woman was, had even said hello to her a few times. She didn't seem to act like a snotty bitch or anything, the way other kept women of rich men sometimes did. Millie knew about kept women because she'd met her share of them, knocking around this town and Vegas. Still, something wasn't right, the woman coming on to this lucky bastard. She wondered if Brian O'Shea knew what was going on. Then wondered if this was his idea.

The man had been tearing them up for days now, playing the limit at three table spots and winning most of his plays. Millie knew it would have to turn, had expected it to last night when the woman—Conway—had been following him on the crap table. For the last six weeks or so, Conway had been death in the casino, and from the few rumors Millie heard, her luck hadn't been any better anywhere else in town. Word was, in fact, she was barred from the other joints.

Millie was dealing at the table nearest to the north casino

entrance. A sucker would walk in, step down three carpeted steps, and bang, he'd be right at her table. So she couldn't see the elevator on the other side of the casino, unless she stopped dealing and craned her neck, and anyway, it wasn't that big a deal. The man had collected his large stack of hundred-dollar bills and had put his arms around the red-head's waist, and they'd staggered together, away from the table, the guy tipping Millie a hundred, which she appreciated.

She wondered, though, if they had just gone in for a drink, or if they headed for the elevators, to the suite the man was surely comped for.

He was comped for everything else, that's for sure. Big dumb animal, he'd been hitting on her all night, bragging about all his winnings, as if the casino employees weren't briefed every day on who had won big, so they could keep their eyes on the winners, see if they could spot them cheating. The camera upstairs would snap their photo, and the pit bosses would show it around before the start of every shift, tell the employees to keep an eye out.

The man had told her that his dear friend Brian O'Shea had said he could have anything he wanted, all he had to do was ask. Then he'd nailed her with a hard look and he'd said, Well? She'd pretended not to notice, ignored him and had kept dealing the cards, pleased that her fingers weren't trembling. She'd seen more than a few women fired from casino jobs for refusing a "favor" for a special guest, and if that had to be the way it went, well, so be it. Millie had been in Vegas and Atlantic City, and if she had to, she could go to Puerto Rico, try dealing out there in the sun. Anyway, it appeared now that he'd gotten a better offer.

The hell with it. It was none of her business. She dealt the cards, wishing for six, so she could get upstairs, make her real money for the night, and when the woman Conway flew past her in tears Millie was so shocked that she could just stare after her.

* * *

As Lano walked out of the hotel the wind drove the snow into his face, so he ducked down into his topcoat, turned the collar up. Man, it was cold.

Lano's eyes searched the street but he did not see the unmarked squad anywhere, which didn't mean much. Hell, there was a five-story indoor parking garage right next door, if the cop wanted to keep warm. Just flash the badge and tell the attendant you wanted some free parking time. Then watch in the large round mirrors mounted just outside the building's entrance, so people leaving wouldn't smash into street traffic. Stand there, protected from the snow and cold, and watch for Lano to come out into the street with a gun in his possession that had maybe killed ten people.

Lano forced himself to get his mind off it, and he stared hard into the darkness of the parking garage as he passed it. Nothing. So far, so good.

Stooped against the slashing wind, he walked the block to the stairway leading up to the Boardwalk and mounted it. The pounding of the vicious surf was now nearly a living thing surrounding him.

At the top of the stairs he couldn't help himself, he simply stood there and stared.

White-capped waves crashed into the sandy shore maybe a hundred yards from where he stood, the broad expanse of beach taking it and spitting it right back. The sun was just about to rise, and in the early-morning pinkness he looked at wild churning water for as far as the eye could see.

It took his breath away.

This ocean, which had been here for millions of years, seemed to be rebelling at the glitter and neon just out of reach, as if maybe it were trying to vomit onto the casinos that were stealing its thunder. Suck the casinos up, the entire city of Atlantic City while it was at it, and civilization could start again.

The ocean had always been here, and Lano wondered what all it had seen, the secrets it could tell.

He stared at the ocean for a very long time, taking deep breaths of the freezing air, not feeling the icy sting of the snowflakes attacking his cheeks.

Then he turned and faced the casinos, stared at them for a long time, at their glitter and neon brightly flashing.

And decided that it was a shallow, shabby little town.

He turned back, walked south down the Boardwalk, looking out to sea, lost in thought.

Maybe Artie had been right all along. Arliss, too, for that matter. He had no character, wasn't a mature adult. Maybe he had to grow up. Hell, the Marines had kicked him out, called him a "subversive influence" because everywhere he was, he started big-time games going. Too many leathernecks had bitched about losing their money to him on payday. Too many of their wives, too, for that matter. The brass refused to believe that any one man was that lucky, although he'd tell the ones who would listen that it was just a matter of knowing the odds.

All these years, he'd prided himself on his heart, on the fact that he had balls. And what did he do the first time they were truly tested on unfamiliar territory? He choked, that's what he did.

It was one thing to prance around Chicago and challenge the manhood of mobsters, or to hit people in the legs with baseball bats, when you knew good and well that one of the most respected men in the mob was right behind you. Other things, too. The fights with gamblers who had no clout, didn't know anyone. That didn't take a lot of heart or balls. Or character. It was another thing altogether to stand up in front of not only a couple of made guys, but the chief made guys of the entire *city*, and refuse a gun, as he should have done, if he had any real heart.

It had all begun there in Artie's office, hours ago, when he felt the terror fill him when the thought struck him that maybe he had gotten himself into the one jam that Art couldn't fix. And it had been downhill from there.

The sun came up as he walked and Lano watched it, feeling better and better as it arose. The sun, too, had always been there, and had always had the power to drive away man's worst fears.

So, okay. The balls aren't there. He'd been deluding himself for so long that when the realization hit him he felt nearly relieved. He wasn't what he thought he was. All right. That wasn't so bad, because how many men were?

The problem he was wrestling with now was: If he had no character, how did he go about getting some?

Well, a good start would be ditching the gun, and the hell with the Biaris. Another thing he could do was to start taking responsibility for his actions. No more calling Art every time he put himself into a jackpot. If he could get himself into those situations, he would have to find a way to get himself out. And if the Biaris asked about the gun, he'd tell them that he'd thrown it into the ocean, that he hadn't felt good about carrying it around on unfamiliar turf.

He stopped at the edge of the original Boardwalk, out past Ridgeway Avenue, and looked around. There was a tall building blocking his view of the rest of the beach, a big steel thing that extended out into the ocean, built on a long, wide pier. He turned around.

There it was, the place he'd been told to stay away from. Isolated out here, miles from the last casino. Lano wished he wore a watch, as he'd lost track of time, but he was a professional gambler and watches were liabilities to men who might look at them and wonder if they'd been playing twelve hours or twenty-four. It had taken some time to walk this far, though, that was for sure. His face was numb from the icy wind and the snow, and his feet felt frozen. The front of his topcoat was soaking wet. He looked at the front of O'Shea's Shamrock Hotel and Casino, the name written in cursive in neon, standing up there ten stories high, and wondered what the big deal was.

There was a giant green iron shamrock built around the entrance, with a doorway cut into it so people could enter and exit. He wondered what the back of the place looked like. The part facing the slums his mob driver had warned him away from. Funny, he must have walked for an hour, and he hadn't run into any marauding gangs of blacks trying to molest him.

The place was tall, it looked bigger even than Trump's. Long and stylish, with towers on each corner, like the castles had in the olden days.

A gaudy casino owned and run by an Irish guy whom the Biaris were planning to murder. A place where he'd been warned not to go. Lano was glad it was open, decided to go on in, maybe learn a few things about character that way. No, disobeying was half the reason he was in the bind he was in now. The hell with it. His immediate problem was to get rid of the gun.

He walked down the stairway to the sand, ducked under the Boardwalk. He counted the pillars from the stairway, one, two, three, then got down on his knees and began to dig. If the Biaris got hard, didn't buy his story, he could give them their piece back, but that didn't mean he was going to take a fall for carrying the son of a bitch.

He dug down to his elbow, then dropped the gun in, covered it with sand. He patted the hole until he couldn't tell where it had been. The only way he could find it again was to come down the stairway, walk to the third pillar, get down on the south side of the thing and commence digging. That was good, because if he couldn't find it, neither could the Biaris. Or the cop who'd been following him.

There was a noise directly above his head, on the wood, someone walking. Jesus Christ, don't let it be the cops.

* * *

It wasn't. It was a woman in an evening gown who came down the stairway and made her way slowly to the ocean. Lano stood under the Boardwalk, out of sight, wondering if she was on angel dust or crack or something. She had long, fine red hair that was whipping around her face in the wind, and it didn't take long for the ocean spray to soak through her thin green strapless gown. Lano watched the curve of her ass, thinking that it was a hell of a waste, a fine young thing like this being a compulsive gambler.

It was obvious to him that that's what she was. He'd seen it before in Vegas, a chick dressed to kill losing it all at the tables, going a little wild, being politely and quietly hustled away by the security guys. Usually, you left them alone for a while and they got ashamed of the way they'd acted, got their dignity back and walked out of the place, already scheming how they would get enough dough to come back.

So that's what this broad was doing. She would walk to the edge of the ocean, oblivious to the cold and the snow, the wetness in the air, and sit on the edge of the world here and think for a time. Then she'd head back in as soon as her sense came back and she realized that she was freezing. He decided that as soon as she was far enough away so she wouldn't hear him, he would sneak up the steps and find a cab somewhere. He didn't want her to see him and maybe think it was okay to strike up a conversation. He'd watch her for now, though. Man, what a body there was there under that flimsy material.

She didn't seem to be walking, now that he thought of it. It was like she was floating, no, it was more like he was watching a blind person walk around their house. They knew where everything was but there was still that slight hesitation in their step, a sense of unease as they sightlessly made their way around. She walked that way, to the edge of the ocean, and her feet were in the white surf before Lano figured out that she wasn't planning on stopping.

"Hey," he yelled. He took a few tentative steps out onto

the sand, out of the protection of the Boardwalk. He cupped his hands around his mouth. "HEY!"

The woman kept walking.

Lano began to run after her, stripping off his topcoat and kicking off his shoes, his mind made up that he'd kick her right in that fine little ass the second he dragged her out of the water.

She was almost to her waist when he reached her, still walking forward with dogged determination, her hands up now out of the surf so she could keep her balance, get the job done right. The current tore at him, tried to take him off his feet, he was moving a lot faster than she was, calling after her every couple of seconds, but the wind was driving west, ripped the breath from his mouth, and it was with a sudden shock that Lano thought for the first time that he, too, might die out here. The thought spurred him on.

He caught her around the shoulders and she turned limply in his arms, gazed blankly at him, not fighting at all. "That's better," Lano said. His teeth were chattering and he could see that his hands on her naked skin were already half-blue. He could barely feel his legs. "Let's go."

"No!"

Lano wasn't about to stand out there and argue. He drew back his hand and slapped her once, hard, then grabbed her arm and began to drag her quickly from the ocean.

He saw three men in business suits racing on the sand, coming toward them, and thought: Thank God. His legs were leaden and although she wasn't fighting him, she wasn't helping much, either. Every step was an ordeal. He was breathing in huge quick gasps. He was shivering terribly, his suit coat plastered to him, trying to drag him down. The three men didn't come into the surf, just stood there yelling at him to hurry up. One of them held a blanket, and Lano focused on it, thought of nothing but the warmth he could draw from it, if he could make it, saw nothing else but that blanket, and then he was there, his feet hitting wet sand, being held back by nothing.

He wanted to collapse onto the sand, but he knew that if he did he would never get up. The men ignored him, wrapped the woman in the blanket and started to hustle her away. They were to the steps leading up to the Board-walk by the time Lano retrieved his topcoat, shivered him-self into it. He wouldn't even try to put his shoes on yet. He wasn't even sure right then if he had any feet left to put shoes on.

"Hey," he said. The men continued to ignore him. He sloshed after them, moving slowly, and he wouldn't have made it if the woman hadn't decided that it was time to fight.

She lashed out at the man holding her in the blanket, managed to get free, threw the blanket over his head, and began to run back down the stairs just as Lano reached the bottom step. She fell into him, hugged him, staring right into his eyes. Hers were very green and desperate.

"Help me," she pleaded, so softly that he could barely hear her. But by then they were right there, all three of them, dragging her away. Lano tried to hold on to her but one of them hit him, hard, right on the button, and he felt his jaw-hinge crack with the blow, his unsteady feet gave way beneath him, and he toppled to the sand, cursing.

By the time he got to his feet they were at the door of O'Shea's Shamrock, dragging the woman through the iron-arched green-shamrock doorway. A very tall fat man was standing just inside, staring at him. He grabbed one of the three by the arm, said something to him, pointed at Lano. Lano shivered and watched, waiting. He was too cold and tired to run. If he were to die, man, he was ready. He sat down on the top step and tried to fit his feet into his shoes. His mind was muddy, befuddled, and by the time he was inspired by the thought of the gun buried so near to him it was too late. A heavy hand fell on his shoulder, and a heavy man with black hair parted in the middle was squatting down next to him.

"You didn't see nothing, you didn't hear nothing. You report this, son, there ain't no place in New Jersey you can hide. Before the cops leave the casino, you'll be out there," the man pointed with his chin toward the Atlantic. He squeezed Lano's shoulder for emphasis, then reached down, shoved a sheaf of bills into Lano's hand. "Now get a cab down the road there, on Ridgeway, and go on home."

Lano turned his head and watched him leave, the man running across the street now. He let the bills flutter to the sand. The man never gave him a second look, but the big heavy man was staring at him through the glass doors. As soon as the other man was inside, though, the big guy turned, and the two of them walked away into the darkened casino. Lano, shivering mightily, could not find his tongue. He simply stared at the man's back, incredulously, until he was gone.

Then got mad. Something had happened here, something major. A woman had tried to kill herself and he'd saved her. She'd begged for help, and these jag in the bags thought he'd just walk away from it with a few bucks in his hand? Well, fuck them, it wasn't going to happen.

Lano collected the bills, stuffed them into his pants pocket and began to slosh across the street. He figured that in the past twelve hours he'd taken all the shit he was about to take. It was way past time for him to start fighting back.

12

Lano hurried across the street, stomping mad, working himself up for a fight.

A scene from the past flashed into his mind as he half-ran: the last time he had helped someone out.

It had been in a joint in Chicago called George's which had later been ashed, killing seven, by a madman with an attitude problem, pissed because he'd been kicked out of the bar the night before. A big biker type had been shooting pool in a joint that didn't come alive until the millworkers got off the night shift. Lano was waiting for them, patiently. It was Thursday night, payday, and on any given Thursday he could find maybe ten compulsives who'd want to roll some dice in the alley after closing. Easy pickings. There was Lano, George, the biker, his old lady and maybe three other guys, regulars, nursing beers and listening to the jukebox, when the biker began slapping his girlfriend around.

Lano'd slid off the stool, grabbed the guy, spun him around and hustled him outside, kicked the shit out of him

123

just as the millworkers began to drive into the lot. The biker had split (the disease-farm old lady hugging his belly hard, shooting Lano the finger as they tore away from the place), and as he sat back down at the bar, Lano'd noticed that his new LED watch had popped off his wrist during the fight.

One of the steelworkers told him he'd seen the biker babe grab it before jumping on the bike with her boyfriend.

Lano remembered this and tried to smile, but it wouldn't come. He was having trouble feeling his legs below the knees, and he made squishy noises with each step. The snow stung his face. His teeth were chattering. All he hoped for was the strength to give a little back to them, show them he had character, wasn't some punk from New York who quivered when an A.C. badass spoke. And maybe even not get his ass killed in the process, as Atlantic City had just showed him how it treated people who tried to cultivate the asset.

He pushed through the hotel doors, into the bright glare of the lobby, ignoring the stares of the women at the desk. He walked into the relatively dark casino, his fists balled up, his eyes bulging, ready.

The first thing he saw was Millie Swan, dealing cards at the table right there down the steps, looking at him as if he'd just crawled out of her worst nightmare.

Millie had watched the men run after Conway, but had kept dealing, had even begun bantering with the customers, trying to keep them at the table. "There goes another lucky winner," she'd said, trying for levity, but the words spoken without much heart.

The funny thing was, except for O'Shea's goons and then the great man himself, nobody seemed to care much one way or the other. They watched, then turned back to their cards. Great group of people, gamblers. She'd once seen a woman go into an epileptic fit at the Stardust in Vegas, and all anyone seemed to want to do was giggle until the security people dragged her away, a belt stuck halfway down her throat so she wouldn't bite off her tongue.

Millie dealt the cards, coolly, a professional, but her mind was racing. Where was the woman going? The front desk was there, but the elevators to any of the rooms were the other way, there was nothing out there but a tunnel leading to some washrooms, some pay phones . . .

And the doors outside.

She began to worry about Conway. In this weather, good God, it would take maybe two minutes out there to catch hypothermia, then freeze to death. Especially in a damn-near-see-through gown.

She tried to tell herself that it was none of her business, tried to put it out of her mind, but it wouldn't go away. That was another human being out there, a compulsive who was being shafted around by the big shots, by the men . . .

The way Millie herself had been shafted by them. She was about to call the pit boss over and tell him she needed an emergency break when the goons came back, two of them, dragging a drenched, sobbing Conway all the way through the casino.

That got even the gamblers' close attention. They watched, as Millie did, the trio stumbling down the main aisle, Conway putting up a fight, but not much of one. It was an event, something to talk about back home. Maybe be a little proud that they themselves had been man or woman enough to not break down like that after they lost all of their money.

Filled with contempt, Millie decided to go ahead with her original plan. Take the emergency break and go see if she could help the woman. If the bosses didn't like it, then screw 'em, she'd go to Puerto Rico. She was sick of this town, anyway.

She was speaking to Frank, the pit boss—the big dago idiot giving her a hard time, telling her not to make waves, the gamblers watching them argue—when Brian O'Shea came back with his other goon, the two of them conferring, deep in conversation.

"I'm going to help her, Frank, and if you don't like it—"

She stopped, her mouth open in mid-sentence, staring at a dripping Lano Branka who was standing at the top of the stairway, looking as insane as she'd ever seen him.

A security guard was walking toward Lano, and Millie saw him coming out of the corner of her eye but didn't turn her eyes away from Lano's. He seemed to notice the guard, too, though, and O'Shea, who was walking back toward Lano. He turned his head away from her, stepped toward the guard, and pulled his hand back to swing . . .

Millie did the unthinkable: she abandoned her post without relief. She was running toward Lano, who was swinging, smacking the guard on the chin and moving in, going for O'Shea, when she reached him, threw her arms around his chest, and shouted his name in his face.

"Lano! Don't! *Stop* it!" He tried to push her away but she held tight, the hours in the gym doing their stuff, Lano reluctant to hurt her and not putting much effort into fighting her off.

"Where's the girl?" Lano shouted at O'Shea, who was right there, a foot from Millie's back. The loud voice in her ear made her wince, and she pulled back, looked into Lano's face.

"They'll kill you," she said, softly.

He ignored her. "Where's the *girl*, you son of a bitch!"

The security guard had picked himself up off the floor, had pulled his gun. He was aiming it at them both. O'Shea turned and patted his arm down as he stepped closer to them, within reach, and Lano struck out at him, caught him with a punch that barely landed, bounced off the top of O'Shea's head, and then she couldn't hold him any longer, he was a man possessed, rushing O'Shea, who stepped back in fear, letting the security guard and his bodyguard handle him. They dragged Lano, punching and kicking him, out of the casino. Millie watched, torn between running after them and letting them go. The hell with him, she'd done what she could, and besides, what had he ever done for her?

O'Shea was touching her, leaning down into her face, and when he spoke it was in a whisper.

"You know that guy?" His face was intense, worried. Millie was amazed. She'd seen the man lose millions and stand there like a rock, congratulating the winner. She tried to speak but couldn't. She nodded.

"Go out there, now, with me," O'Shea said. "We'll wait with him while you get your car. Take him home and get him to keep his fucking mouth shut about this and there's two grand in it for you."

The guard was holding Lano at gunpoint when she pulled her car to the front of the casino. Standing there away from the green-shamrock entranceway, so the gamblers leaving now that it was six in the morning would not be too afraid to come back in when the place reopened in four hours. He stood there silently, staring at the men, shivering in the freezing morning air. The sight nearly broke her heart.

They bundled him into the car and the first thing he said to her was, "Why'd you leave me?"

Millie turned the heater on high, sitting close to the wheel in the driver's seat of her year-old Mustang. "Lano, you have to understand something. This isn't Chicago. Uncle Artie isn't here to help you. These men out here don't allow anyone to put a dent in their operations, and you, buddy, are putting dents in an already seriously dented operation. You're just lucky Brian O'Shea isn't one of the mobbed-up guys in this town, or you'd be out there in the Atlantic already, with chains wrapped around your feet. I don't know why you're here or what you want, but do yourself a favor, go on home, now, tonight. And if you stay, don't come into the Shamrock again."

"Why'd you leave me!" The shout made her jump. She wanted to tell him, tell him everything. Remind him of a few things he'd said then tell him all about his wonderful uncle Artie, what he'd ordered her to do.

But she didn't. It was history, and whatever he had to say held no concern for her anymore. But still, he was soaking wet, it was obvious he'd gone into the ocean to help Conway. Maybe he'd changed . . .

No! She fought the urge to be gentle, to ask him what had happened. She'd gone to his defense and maybe saved his life tonight, might even have lost her job in the process. She owed him nothing.

Millie said, going for a tone of resignation, "Lano, where are you staying? . . ."

He was thinking, as he entered the Palermo, that if one of the bellhops made any cracks, he would crush his windpipe. He breathed a sigh of thanks as he got into the elevator unmolested.

A hot shower helped, then another one after picking up the phone and ordering a jug of Haig & Haig Pinch from room service, and a plate of a half-dozen eggs, scrambled, with bacon. There were no numb white patches, so he figured he'd beaten frostbite this time.

As far as he was concerned, there wouldn't be a next time to worry about. As he answered the door to let in the kid with the booze and breakfast, he solemnly vowed that his mother could be wading into the ocean, and he'd let her go. No more trying to stop mature adults in the midst of carrying out their personal choices.

But Millie, shit, how about her? He'd asked her a simple question and she'd shot him down, had let him know in no uncertain terms that she had no interest in speaking to him. She'd sat there like an iceberg, not even glancing his way the whole time, had let him out in front of the Palermo and had driven away slowly, not even spinning the tires or anything.

What had happened, why had she left? He'd loved her and she'd left him and he'd cried, then gone on with life, although with a colder side to him, harder than before he'd met her.

For instance, he never went to sad movies anymore, never watched Bogart and Bacall on late-night television. Nor did he go to the restaurants they'd made their own. He'd changed, after Millie.

He thought about it, saw that he really cut his life into two parts, B.M. and A.M. Before Millie, After Millie.

She'd told him to stay out of it, that it was none of his business.

The hell it wasn't. He knew that fighting with the guard after they threw him out of the Shamrock would only get him arrested or shot, so he'd stayed cool, kept his mouth shut and waited for his ride home.

But he'd be back. O'Shea or whoever the hell it was who'd been there watching him so dispassionately as he'd shivered, would see him again.

The first shot helped, and the second one spread the welcome warmth he'd usually get from the first. He ate the eggs, had another drink. Lano put the empty tray in the hallway, feeling pretty good now, on top of things. He lay in bed, under the covers, holding a glass of Scotch, warm, listening to the wind batter something besides himself, smiling at the consolation. Kicked its ass. Nature herself couldn't stop him, so who was O'Shea? Or Biari? Or, for that matter, the cop who'd been following him?

Each sip of the Scotch made him feel more in control. A day, maybe two, and he'd have things together again back home. He'd put Millie back in the compartment of his mind where she belonged, straighten out the problem with O'Shea, even help the woman who'd asked for help. Every shot made him feel more secure, in charge of his life and capable. For now, though, he had to get some rest, but man, it was hard, closing your eyes when you felt as mellow as he did now.

But he would have to, because he would have to get up in time to study the papers, make his basketball bets before the first games went off, and he'd lost an hour coming East. On top of which, he was dead tired, drained from the early-morning swim and the fight, the shock of seeing Millie again.

Lano began to laugh, the Scotch catching in his throat and coming back up into his nose, dripping onto the covers. He began to laugh harder, thinking that it was a good thing he wasn't smoking just then, or *whoosh*, he'd have gone up in smoke as the booze hit the cigarette, done a Richard Pryor on the Boardwalk. He laughed harder as he thought of the good job he was doing, keeping a low profile here, just as Art had ordered.

He stopped laughing when he saw that the bottle was nearly empty and a foul thought struck him hard, and Lano began wondering if he'd need a fifth of Scotch in his gut from now on in order to not be afraid.

Mad Mike was sixty-two and looked fifteen years younger, testimony to the fact that crime did indeed pay. He was big, strong, and when he wanted to be, kind. Usually his kindness was limited to his two grandchildren, on Sunday afternoon, when his daughter the lawyer and his son-in-law the trader would bring them to play and collect the little sacks of quarters Grampy Mike would hand out to each of them. He would be kind to his family, sometimes, on Sunday, but early on a Saturday morning, the one day a week he slept late, was not the best of times for an employee to catch him in a benevolent mood.

Still, Art figured he was doing all right by the man, because Mike was listening, paying strict attention, not cutting in. Sitting behind his desk in the enormous den in the house on the Southeast Side. Someone had lit a fire for them and it was almost cozy, eight in the morning on a late-January Saturday, Mad Mike in his pajamas and robe, a cup of coffee in his hands. He held it tightly, sitting straight up, his dark eyes piercing, trying to penetrate Art's skull.

"So that's it," Art said, and now Mike began with the questions, short and to the point.

"Elihue saw all this, you say, no one else?"

"Well, Lano, naturally." Without thinking, Art's eyes moved to rest on the large, black wooden chair with all the fancy carving on the legs, over there right next to the desk. Thankfully, he hadn't been ordered to sit in it. At least not yet. He sat comfortably, knowing that nerves meant weakness, secure in the knowledge that in Mike's eyes, he was confident and unafraid. What was going on inside him was another matter altogether.

"And how far is Tony in the hole to you?"

"Ninety grand."

Mike sat back and spoke aloud, but not to Art. "And that's not to mention how far he is in to other people, shit we don't know about." He stared at the ceiling thoughtfully, and Art waited, in a big room in a big house in an old neighborhood that had at one time been full of big houses, before the geniuses who ran U.S. Steel let the Japanese and the Germans kick their asses for them, stealing away all the customers. These days the large homes had been cut up into apartment houses, with more people living in each apartment than used to live in the houses when they were single-family dwellings.

Mad Mike was crazy, but like a fox, and, Art knew, sentimental. Which was why he was still here, in a faded shabby neighborhood, one of the last white guys left. He'd never move, any more than he'd ever go soft.

Mad Mike said, "All right. Thanks for filling me in," breaking into Art's thoughts, almost catching him off base and making him smile with relief. He was off the hook and Tony was on it, not knowing it yet but squirming, about to be devoured.

Art said, "Thanks, Mike," keeping his face straight. There were hundreds of thousands of dollars in jeopardy here, either way Mike went, and it wasn't the time to grin over a personal victory, make the man think he was rubbing it in.

Before he made it to the door of the den, he heard Mike speaking into the telephone, telling Virgil's wife that he didn't give a fuck *what* time the guy had gotten in, put him on the phone, *now*. With the door closing behind him, and none of the guards in sight, Art figured that now was the time to go ahead and smile a little, surprised at how good it felt and at the relief he felt, leaving Mad Mike behind him.

Mad Mike said to Virgil, who was standing tough in front of the desk, "You see that chair there? The black one?" and smiled inside when Virgil swallowed before saying, "Yeah, Mike." It was good to keep a little fear in the troops. That had been one of the mistakes the Old Guard had made, which had nearly caused the mob to get busted in half a few years back. Not enough discipline. They'd allowed their underbosses to run free, make too much money, and the bosses hadn't kept the underlings in fear. They'd allowed them to get greedy and fat, which had made them complacent, which had nearly brought about their doom.

Mike believed in an iron fist inside the velvet glove. Didn't want his men to be too afraid of him, because then they might rebel, whack him out in fear of what he might do next, like they had Anastasia in New York years ago, the guy getting a shave and ba-boom, all over.

No, Mike would put the fear of God in them, then let them know that he was thoughtful, fair, would never kill anyone without thinking it over for a long time, checking with his advisers. So speaking to Virgil, letting him sweat while Mike gave him the glare, was part of the routine, the tough but fair coach letting one of his players know he was on the edge of getting cut from the squad.

"Eleven men been invited to sit down in that chair." Mike said the words then lit a smoke, slowly, taking his eyes from Virgil, knowing the big man would be staring at the chair, waiting for the punch line. He blew out the match, dropped it in the ashtray, turned his attention casually back to Virgil and said, "Eight of them died, suddenly, within twelve hours." He grinned, staring at the chair, as if he enjoyed the idea of having his own Seat of Death in his den.

"Sit down, Virgil," Mike said, watching the man start, showing up-front fear for the first time, before adding, "In the *leather* chair, not the black one."

As Virgil sat, Mike began to ask him questions, secure in the knowledge that he'd get nothing but the truth from the man.

As Virgil was getting up to leave, Mad Mike said to him, "How loyal are you to Tony, Virgil?" giving him pause for thought.

If he said the guy was a piece of shit who deserved to sit in the black wooden chair, Mike would whack him out for being a wiseass without the guts to speak his mind. On the other hand, if Virgil responded in a manner that left any room in Mike's mind about his keeping his mouth shut, he'd get whacked for that. Virgil rose, stood as straight as he could, squared his shoulders and said, "Loyal? I'm so loyal that I drove thousands and thousands of miles when other guys, they fly, on business with their boss, because Tony's scared of heights. So loyal that I slept in chairs outside doors to luxury sleeper cars on the Amtrak trains, so the boss could get a good night's rest. I never went behind his back, never stole a dime I wasn't expected to, never spoke bad about him to a living soul. The last few months, shit, all I've stuck *around* for is loyalty. Knowing if I come to you I'm ratting out my boss, knowing if I don't then he's hurting you, me, our families, and knowing, too, that if he goes down I'll probably go down with him." He spread his hands, palms up, helplessly. "He's my boss, you're his boss. I got to do what's best for my wife and kids. You tell me, Mike, what to do, it's done."

Mad Mike puffed on his cigar. "First off," he said, "you are out of touch until this whole thing's taken care of. Don't talk on the phone, don't go out at night. Lock yourself up in your house and don't come out until you read in the paper or hear on the TV that Tony's history. You want me to tell you what to do? For now, what you do, you get another phone installed with a private number, one for your bedroom, that no one but you ever uses. I ever get a load of shit from your old lady again about 'He's sleeping,' you're gonna hear about it in a way ain't as nice as this one."

As Virgil nodded, over and over again, reassuring Mike that he'd have the phone installed Monday, sliding out the door and shutting it behind him, Mike smiled, outwardly this time. The iron fist in the velvet glove worked every time.

He picked up the phone, punched out a number, and grunted into it when Tough Tony's wife told him in a bitchy tone that her husband hadn't come home all night. "Tell him to call Mike the second he comes in, you got it?" and his good humor returned as she said, "Oh, yes, sir, I didn't know it was you, sir." Mad Mike was smiling until he hung up the phone, until he remembered about the quarter-million a week that Tony Tomase appeared to be losing.

The son of a bitch, he was telling Mike that things were bad, he was getting beat, being honest up to a point but never telling him the entire truth. At least not the way Virgil had told it.

It appeared to Mike that Lano Branka wasn't the only guy, beating the odds regular. Lano he was sure of, because Art the Arm, who was as solid as they came, told him it was so. But Virgil had told him that Tony had been losing, desperately, and was a couple of million in the hole, with markers out for the money, since before Thanksgiving. Eight weeks ago. That son of a bitch.

Mike called in a couple of the bodyguards, told them to get out there this minute and not to come back unless they had Tough Tony Tomase with them. They left, and Mike sighed heavily, got up to go and shower, get dressed, have the maid cook up some breakfast. It was an unpleasantness that had to be dealt with, and immediately, because he himself had invoked stringent rules when he'd taken over; protocols that had to be met before a man of Tomase's stature could be whacked. His entire board would have to vote on it, and would have to decide how much would come from each boss to pay back the losses Tony had incurred. There was no doubt that the markers would be paid; they'd be out of business in a week if their street bosses could get away with beating the gamblers out of their hard-earned dough, even through death. No, the markers would all get paid, and Tony, if what Mike had been told today was true, would die, probably tonight.

Mike wanted the entire matter cleared up today for two reasons. First, Tomase was deep in the hole for money he himself would have to go into his pocket for, and he wanted the guy whacked before he got any further into debt. And second, because tomorrow was Sunday, and the last thing Mike wanted if he could help it was any loose ends floating around, wrecking his day with the grandkids.

So he'd give Tony his chance. Sit him down in the Seat of Death and see what he had to say for himself. If there was any investigating to do, any facts that had to be checked out, he would have it done, but these would be done at his discretion, only if he wanted them. He didn't think that it would come down to that. Art was a hundred percent solid, and Mike had had his eye on Virgil for years, looking to move him up when the time came.

Well, it looked like the time was here. Virgil had given him a good answer to the loyalty question, Mike had to hand that to him. Maybe bring him into the house, make him chief of security now that Albert was making noises about retiring. Hell, Virgil'd somehow managed to keep Tomase alive all this time, while the guy lost millions of dollars, didn't belong to him.

Mad Mike showered, sat down to breakfast, with another pot of coffee brewing, when he decided, for the hundredth time, that it was lonely at the top. He took a cup into the den with him, made the calls he had to make to set up his full council meeting, get the matter settled. Then, with the afternoon to kill, at least until someone rounded up Tough Tony Tomase and brought him over, Mike lifted the phone and called his mistress, a sweet little Mexican was Miss South Chicago in '85. Yeah, he figured, it was lonely at the top, but it had its perks, too, being the top dog.

13

Lano had tried to sleep, but as soon as the effects of the booze had worn off he was wide-awake, in a town that was built around gambling. A man on a roll like the one he was on couldn't afford the luxury of too much sleep. When the odds turned against him, he could sleep twelve hours a day to catch up.

The hangover was slight, thank God. Booze had never hurt him too much the day after. After a shave and a hot shower it was almost gone.

Now it was time to work, the woman from last night in the back of his mind, there to be called forth later, when he made his way down to O'Shea's.

There was one thing he had to do before he left the room, though.

He took the phone book out of the nightstand, wondering if Millie had gotten married, pleased to see the name: Swan, M., with a number and a Margate address. He dialed the number, waited a few rings then nearly hung up when a child answered.

What the hell was this, did Millie have a kid these days?

"Who is this?" he asked.

The kid said, "Stevie."

"Stevie Swan?"

"Yep."

It was a young child, barely old enough to form sentences. There was a slight lisp in his voice. Maybe four, five years old, getting off on answering the phone. He'd said his last name was Swan, though, so it was a safe bet that Millie hadn't gotten married.

"Is your mother there?"

"She's sleeping." The kid speaking in whispers.

"Good-bye, Stevie."

"Bye-bye," the kid said.

A kid. How about that. Lano wanted to put the episode out of his mind, forget her for good, four years gone and the hell with it.

But he couldn't. He pulled the phone book to him, grabbed some of the Palermo stationery and jotted her address down on an envelope. Stared at a blank sheet of paper, the pen poised in his hand. All right. Just write what comes naturally.

> *Dear Millie:*
>
> *I don't know why you left me for someone else. All I know is that my life's been empty ever since. I never stopped loving you, caring for you. I dream about you still even now, still love you. Like I said, I don't know what got into you, but I can figure it out. Your other boyfriend knocked you up and you didn't want to face me. Right, huh? But I'm going to tell you something. Anytime you want to come home, come back, I'll be waiting, 'cause it ain't worth it without you, and I don't care if you have five kids.*

He signed it with love, read it back to himself, then almost tore it up. Decided not to. He meant what he'd written, it felt good reading the words, even if they were mushy.

He stuck the letter in the envelope, sealed it and put it in his inside suit-jacket pocket. He'd mail it on his way out of Atlantic City.

He left the room with a hint of swagger in his step, putting his mind at ease, letting go of the Biaris and the redhead in the gown who'd tried to do the Dutch in the Atlantic, forgetting even about the guys who'd belted him around. And about Millie. The five hundred the big goof on the beach had slipped him was in his left-hand pocket, separate from his own money. He would find a way to get it back to its proper owner, when the time was right. As the elevator doors opened, he remembered that he could, with very little trouble, dig up a gun to use if push came to shove.

He was here, in Atlantic City, feeling better than he had in a very long time, wondering about the cause.

Decided that maybe, after last night, after doing what he'd done, he was finally starting to respect himself.

He leaned on the desk counter, wondering what the right amount of money to take with him would be. The day clerk, an older guy with a bald head and a wispy mustache, showed him respect. Lano could picture him, when he was off duty, using his most recent strategy, his new system, to beat the casinos at blackjack. When the guy brought him his money bag, Lano walked away from the desk, into the lounge, to the public bathroom. He locked himself in a stall, smelling disinfectant trying hard to cover up the smell of vomit.

He sat on the toilet seat and riffled through the money, nodded, it was all there. The people here thought he was the hotel owner's son, and even the worst of compulsives would have to think twice before trying to sneak some of the money away.

How much should he take, though? It was early, just noon. He had eighteen hours left before the casinos closed. In some of them, he would only stay a few minutes, in others, well, probably hours. He knew that if he walked straight outside the front door of the Palermo he would be directly across the street from the Sands. He could walk out the Sands' south doors and enter the north doors of Claridge's, walk straight through the casino and out the east doors and across the street to the western entrance of Bally's Park Place. After those three, it would take a short hike to get to the next casino, Caesars, then: Trump's, the Atlantis, the Tropicana and the Golden Nugget. Eight casinos within walking distance to the south of the hotel, four more to the east, but spread out a little more. From where he was he could go to, in order: Resorts International, Resorts International 2, then way the hell west and a ways north to Trump's Castle, then Harrah's Marina a little further north and west, across the Brigantine Bridge. No, for changing games and casinos quickly, he would have to head south on the Boardwalk. Maybe tomorrow he'd head down to the others, taking cabs.

So, eight casinos. Nine, if he went all the way past the Nugget, a mile or so to the Shamrock.

And why the hell not? Who the hell were they, that he had to stay away from the place? Who was Angelo Biari to tell him where he could and could not go?

Okay, a grand at each place, stay an hour if things looked good, longer if he was hot, less if he was dying. Eight casinos, nine counting the Shamrock. He'd eat for nothing at any casino in town, the way he would be betting. Get laid and see shows, too, if he felt like it. So take a grand for a buffer, make it an even ten grand.

He removed the money from the bag and smiled, staring down into it. It didn't look any less full than it had before he had removed the cash. Ten grand and well over a hundred and twenty more to fall back on; not too shabby for a kid born and raised in the shadows of the El, on the poor side of the Loop. He gave the rest of the money to the old guy behind the desk, asking for a receipt, making the guy count it. Lano feeling confidence growing stronger and filling him more and more with each passing second.

It had been a bad day, breaking up with the woman, getting screwed by Tomase. Yesterday had shaken his confidence, that was all. By the time he'd left the Biaris', he had been ready to call it quits, give it up and do whatever he was told. Frightened due to lack of sleep and the close call in Chicago hours earlier.

Now, in the shadows inside the Palermo, looking at the midday sun, things were different. No longer was he worried or afraid. He was a guest of the Biaris and would show them respect, but he didn't take orders from them. In fact doing so would be a direct slap in the face to Art, since he was, in Biari's own words, "a member of Art's crew."

Fuck 'em.

He wasn't made, and he wasn't in their debt. He was paying his own way, a full-grown man with cash in his pockets that he'd earned with his superior knowledge of the odds. And whatever the Biaris wanted from him (if he hadn't just been paranoid from lack of sleep, maybe they didn't want shit from him), he would just tell them no. Besides, no one punched him in the side of his face and got away with it. No one. If he ever let that happen, he would deserve to be pushed around and bullied by people like the Biaris.

It was strange, the way a little sleep and some sun could change your mind about things.

As soon as he walked through the door of the hotel the wind whipped at him, ripping at his topcoat, his hair. He smiled into it, feeling the spine-climbing tingle of the excitement of the hunt, the gambler with money in his pocket and casinos facing him.

He crossed the street, smiling, seeing the posters encased in shatter-proof plastic spread out along the wall of the Sands, pictures of Billy Crystal and George Burns, Susan Anton and Ben Vereen, a bunch of other people he didn't recognize. There was a very fat guy with oily hair, standing in front of the picture of Jackie Mason, hunched against the wind, beating his fist into his palm over and over again. He was saying, in a conversational tone, "I will *not* go home fucking broke again today. I just will *not*." The guy building his confidence up, standing there in checkered pants that made him look like a cook in a Greek joint, oily hair being tossed by the wind. Lano gave him a wide berth, passed him, pulled open the doors to the casino—

And stepped into another world. One without wind or cold, or clocks either. There was no time in Atlantic City casinos. It was supposed to stand still until you either busted out or the place closed down. As soon as he entered the place the sound of the clanging machines assaulted him, thousands of people dropping thousands of quarters into thousands of slot machines. The floors carpeted and the walls mirrored, all muted lighting and warmth and sounds of happy gamblers winning.

Lano took a deep breath and held it, drinking it all in. Heaven. He removed his coat, laid it across his arm so the cut of his pearl-gray suit would show, and sauntered down the three entranceway steps into the casino proper.

He would watch a game before he entered it, see what he thought of the dealer, the other players. The sorry part was when he found a dealer who seemed agreeable enough, there would be some goof sitting at the table hitting with seventeen when the dealer showed a six. He didn't even look over at the crap tables yet, that would be for later, into the evening. For now he would play blackjack, with the dealer's built-in edge against him. He was standing at a table, thinking of getting in, when the little blond-haired Barbie doll dealing leaned over right into the face of a player and said, loudly, "I'm only gonna say this once: You don't touch the cards, and you don't touch the chips, you got it?" And the guy, bald-headed and half in the bag already, nodded meekly. Lano looked at her directly, her eyes meeting his, challengingly. Snotty little chippy with her Bronx accent and her East Coast attitude of superiority. Lano figured that if he sat down, he could maybe last five minutes before slapping her one. He saw the pit boss watching him, a young guy with a plastic-coated badge telling the world he was Sal, and he smiled, nodded at Sal, sat down at the next table, the last seat before the dealer. There were two other players at the table, a twenty-five-dollar minimum table with a five-hundred-dollar maximum. Times were changing: this was a No Smoking table.

The dealer eyed him, bored, a big guy named Bruno with light brown hair combed straight back. Lano spread ten hundred-dollar bills on the green felt in front of him, rested his feet on the indoor-outdoor carpeting, squared his shoulders and said, "Half green, half black," wanting twenty-five-dollar and hundred-dollar chips. When the dealer set the chips in front of him, Lano took one of the greens, dropped it in front of the dealer and said, "For you, Bruno, for luck." Bruno's eyes widened and he said, "Thank you, sir," and Lano could feel the little blond girl at the next table staring daggers at him, knowing her little show of prissiness had cost her a big tipper. He smiled, put a green chip in his gambling circle, and started to play blackjack.

Some people make the mistake of thinking that blackjack is a near-even-odds game, them against the house, whoever gets closest to twenty-one wins. If the dealer is showing a ten and they have eighteen, some people react to instinct and hit, having seen Burt Reynolds or someone do it in a movie and draw a three. To Lano and men like him, this was bullshit. They knew the rules, they knew the odds, and they played the game accordingly.

For instance: In Atlantic City the player isn't allowed to touch his cards. He has to tap the felt with a finger to tell the dealer to hit him. The dealer's first card is dealt down, giving him the built-in advantage of knowing what you have while you had to guess what he had.

For instance: You are dealt two cards. The count of those cards could be anywhere from two to twenty-one. There is, then, a total of 1,326 ways for those two cards to fall, per deck. With a four-deck stack, dealt from a shoe, the number of ways increase astronomically, lowering the chances that you can count the cards already used.

For instance: There is an automatic 8.27 hidden percentage built in for the house. There is no way, without a lucky streak, that the average player can come away ahead.

But Lano was not an average player. With his knowledge of the odds and probability, which means exactly what it says, *probability*, not guarantee, he could cut that edge down to 2.37 percent. There were men writing books that came out every month, bragging that they had been barred from the world's casinos, and telling the reader that they could learn the secrets of their success for $19.95 plus postage and handling. These books would teach you to be an adequate player, a thing you could become with a library card and a couple of hours studying *Scarne's Complete Guide to Gambling*. The only people who got rich from those books were the guys who wrote them. What Lano knew, the things he had learned over the years, made it not an even game, because he would always have to play before the dealer, but a game in which he had an honest chance. There were certain rules for gambling at blackjack, which were never to be overlooked. When to hit and when to stand, when to double down and when to split pairs.

Lano's knowledge of these things and his built-in radar

for sensing when the cards were about to turn earned him seven wins in the first eight hands, a good run of luck, and when Sal the pit boss came over with an index card and asked him if he wanted to be rated, Lano told him, "I'm a ten wherever I go, Ace," and smiled back when he got a laugh out of the usually reserved Bruno.

He never counted his chips until right before he checked out, although they were always stacked in neat piles, in front of him, by denomination. As he threw Bruno a black chip and walked away from the table, he began to count, knowing the total was going to be high because Sal and then Sal's boss, Jake, followed him from the table.

"You're leaving us?" Sal asked. Jake said, "Where you staying? We got a suite, empty, waiting on you. How about a little dinner?" Lano shook his head and they took offense, hurt, a couple of tough guys not understanding how a gambler wasn't ready to roll over and spread his legs in gratitude because they'd acknowledged the fact that he was alive.

Eleven thousand, seven hundred and fifteen dollars. He left it with the cashier and took a marker, which he stuffed into his left-hand pocket next to the five hundred he owed someone over at the Shamrock.

At Claridge's, an hour later, he had a hard time finding the cashier's booth because it was downstairs, hidden away in the hope that maybe a winner would lose his way, find a nice comfortable table to rest at while he figured out where it was. His marker there was for four thousand, even. He'd left the change for the dealer.

At Bally's he ate a steak, compliments of the house, with a glass of milk, after depositing seven grand in the vault.

Walking through the casino to leave Bally's, Lano was nearly laughing. He saw the greasy-haired guy in the cook's pants at the crap table, with a pile of chips before him. He hoped that the guy had been right, that he wouldn't be going home broke again. Lano felt the eyes of the gamblers on him, enjoying his status; they were staring at the high roller who had just torn the blackjack table a new rear end. He smiled, stepping right out, walked out of Bally's on a cloud, his right palm nearly burning with the desire to get a pair of dice in them, itching with the need.

His spine was tingling and his head was light, he was getting there, to the prime roll, a near-sexual thing now but not enough to make him stay in one place and go for it all at one casino. When it came, he'd know it, and bet accordingly. It was coming, he'd do it, soon, but not with blackjack. The sun was on the other side of the casinos now, and he guessed it to be nearly five, nighttime on the way. He'd spent almost twice as much time in each casino as he'd planned. Well, he'd have a nice walk down to Caesars, stretch the legs and clear the head, a hundred hundreds still folded into his right-front pants pocket. He would look at the pretty girls dressed like slaves, maybe watch them for a while before going all the way, breaking the goddamn bank.

He had the feeling, strong within him, that the prime roll would come along at the very next casino he entered.

He was thinking such thoughts, floating along, when a large form drifted up on either side of him, hands grasped his biceps firmly, and a deep voice said softly, "Mr. Pella? You want to come along with us please? We got a few questions we got to ask you."

Stevie told her some man had called, and she thought nothing of it. Men from the casino were calling all the time, wanting her to cover their shifts when they found some chicky or whatever. It was noon when she awakened, Stevie already fed and cleaned up before the babysitter left, the child having spent four hours or so watching cartoons, used to Mommy's schedule. She would spend the day with her kid, the way mothers were supposed to spend Saturdays. And if she had to go to work at eleven, so what? Did that make her less of a mother? A lot of single mothers, waitresses for instance, worked the midnight shift. That was nothing to be ashamed of.

She made Stevie lunch, played games with him throughout the day. During the week she would come home from work and sleep two hours, then get up, feed him, and drop him off at a day-care center at seven, so she could get a little more sleep, then work out, never picking him up later than one or two in the afternoon. Stevie was better off than most of the kids in the center, whose mothers didn't pick them up until five or six. She spent all of her days off with him, loving him and feeling his love for her coming right back at her.

She was a good mother.

The problem was, last night she'd run into Stevie's father.

She had spent years trying to keep it down deep, but it was never far from the surface. Lano had told her that he hated kids, would never have one. They were a drag, cried all the time, and what man in his right mind would want one of them around? She'd listened, and when she'd found she was pregnant she'd turned to Art.

"Responsibility? Lano?" Art had made her feel puny, like a whore. "Hey, kid, you got yourself knocked up, you better look for a daddy somewhere else, Lano ain't gonna play that shit with you or anyone else."

She'd been devastated. Art had always seemed so nice to her. Like the father she'd never known. Her mother— well, she'd kicked her out when Millie had been seventeen, and they hadn't spoken since.

It was only later that she figured it out, Art had gone hard and cold for her sake, not Lano's, knowing that his nephew could never be a decent father or husband. Art had given her ten thousand dollars, told her to use part of it for an abortion, and had set her up through a connection he had in Vegas, got her started as a dealer.

Which she did for seven months, until it was time to have the baby.

She'd told Art, over the phone long distance. He'd been surprised to hear that she'd decided to keep the baby. She told him that she only was calling to tell him thanks for helping her when she needed it, that she had moved to Atlantic City and was going to work at Trump's. That's what she'd said to Art, but she was still sore from having Stevie and she was lonely, frightened, and had said a prayer before calling, petitioned God that Art would tell Lano he had a son, so Lano would change, act like a man, quit gambling and come to her, love her, marry her . . .

All Art had told her was to forget about Lano, he wasn't for her, find a nice understanding guy and settle down.

When she'd tried again, telling him she had moved to O'Shea's, he'd been brusque, hadn't even asked about Stevie. She'd finally plucked up her courage and asked him straight out: had he ever talked to Lano about her?

Sure he had, Art had told her. Lano was living with some chick but was still single, and when Art had told him that Millie had been pregnant he'd laughed and asked Art who the father was.

She always wondered if she should have gone to Lano, confronted him and laid her cards on the table. Today, now, that's exactly what she would do. Then again, today, the last thing she would do was get herself pregnant by Lano or any other gambler. Or, for that matter, by anyone. She didn't spend all those hours in a gym just to build muscle. She worked off her need, her desire, determined to never fall into that trap again.

God, how she'd wanted Art to tell her that Lano had changed, that he had quit gambling and was trying to straighten out his life.

She'd felt the child inside her belly, four years ago, had listened to Art and had known he was right.

Lano had been a fool, romantic and headstrong. He would have married her, but that would have been the end of their love, of their ever having anything special between them. He would resent her, hate the child, and he would cheat on her, making their lives hell.

Being in gambling towns these past four years had convinced her that she'd made the right decision. She saw the way compulsives treated their women, how little respect they had for anything but their bankrolls, the next game, chasing the prime roll. The thing was, very few of them ever got one in the first place. They just sadly stalked the elusive dream, the long-term winning streak, and went after it with tunnel vision, resenting then getting rid of anything that stood in their way.

No, she'd made the right choice, and had learned to live with it.

Then he'd walked in last night, looking as handsome as ever, something else there in his face, too. What was it? A determination, that was sure. He had jumped into the ocean after Conway and had been insulted when Brian had offered him money in return. At least, that's what Brian had told her, when she'd reported back.

Did that sound like the Lano she knew? Millie had to pause and think. Not the Lano she wanted him to be—the one who had quit gambling and had come racing after her on his white horse—but the real Lano, the man she used to live with?

No, it didn't. He would have taken O'Shea's money and gone off to find the next game.

Had he changed? She couldn't dare hope. He hadn't come hunting her, that was for sure. He'd been in O'Shea's for other reasons.

No, Lano had been a foolish mistake. A youthful error she'd made. Having been brought up with nothing, with no one to love her, she'd gone and moved in with the first good-looking guy who'd come along, who'd been willing to take care of her and show her a good time.

She wasn't looking for that kind of action, these days.

No matter what, though, she could never hate the man. He'd given her the most precious thing she'd ever had.

"Honey?" Millie said. "After we finish this game, you want to go for a ride to the museum?"

He looked up at her with puppy-dog eyes, Lano's eyes, filled now with joy.

"Can we, Mommy, please?" Stevie said, and the yearning in his little voice was enough to break your heart.

14

From the moment he'd opened his mouth back there in Art the Arm's office, Tough Tony Tomase had been aware that he'd made a major mistake. He figured out just how major it was now as he hung up the phone on Loretta, wife of Virgil.

"He's not in, Tony," Loretta had said, her feathers all ruffled. The daughter of a small-time hustler who used to fence for Tommy Campo, she figured she was above Mad Mike coming over, pulling her out of her safe suburban kitchen, and putting her out on the street for twenty bucks a shot, if he felt the urge. "Mr. Big Shot Mike called, made me wake him up. Demanded a command performance," she told Tony.

"Hey," Loretta said, surprised, "how come you're not there?" Which was when he'd hung up on her.

What a night, shit, and now this.

First he'd gotten home, after stepping on his shlong over at the casino, letting the cat out of the bag in front of Art, had to take a cab home, and his wife, God bless her fat

Irish ass, laying a load of shit on him about Arliss Owen calling, and who in the hell is Arliss Owen? Christ, standing there with her arms crossed under her cow tits. The only thing missing was the rolling pin in her hand, maybe tapping her right foot angrily.

He'd almost whacked her, just to put her in line, but he'd been so happy, hearing about Arliss, that he didn't, simply turned around without a word, got his other car from the garage and went to the old place, the apartment he kept for his outside activities.

And there she'd been, as if she'd never left, sitting on the couch fully clothed, eating a strand of her hair.

"I kept the key, I didn't think—" was all she'd had time for, before Tony was on her, ripping at her clothes.

Later, she'd told him the reasons she'd left Lano. Because he was always acting tough suddenly, saying bad things about her Tony, Arliss knowing full well that Lano was no match for Tony.

Tony would say, "He talked bad about me?" Or, "He said that, did he, that piece of shit?" His lips curled, his eyebrows raised, silently cursing Tommy Gambesi for not being man enough to put the punk to sleep.

God Almighty, he'd almost blown a five-million-dollar deal, trying to teach this broad a lesson, and now here she was, next to him naked, as if she'd never left. Well, it wasn't too late to call things off.

The first problem, right off, was Art wasn't around. Tony was going to apologize, maybe even kiss Art's ass, what did he care? Another week, maybe two, and the scam would be complete, he'd be out East, and Art would be sucking hind tit, with his hand on his ass waiting for Tony to come up with his ninety grand.

But Art wasn't around and it was like pulling teeth, trying to get information out of that nigger flunky Elihue. He'd told him not to get cute or he'd come down there, right now, and Elihue had told him, "Come on down, Mr. Tony, but you got to pay the hundred dollar at the door," and had hung up on him.

Then Virgil gone, too. And when Loretta told him where Virgil was, well, Tony could guess the rest.

Arliss was stroking his back, softly, with her fingernails, up and down, back and forth, making little patterns on his flesh. He liked that, but it stopped his thinking process. He turned around, slapped her once, not too hard, and watched her recoil.

"Don't you know better, goof with me when I'm on the phone? Shit." He got up from the bed and found a robe hanging on a peg in the closet, covered his short, fat body with it. There, that was better.

The thing was coming down around his ears, a five-million-dollar deal about to fall apart because he was going to get killed if he didn't move soon. All because of Arliss, too, that was the worst part. Especially seeing that she'd come back to him all on her own, without any prompting. He turned to her.

"Go make me some coffee."

"Don't you want to get some sleep, Daddy?"

He looked at her, letting her know what was gonna happen if she didn't do as she was told, and she was off the bed, running naked and without any self-consciousness into the kitchen. Okay. Now he could think clearly.

It had been so easy, and was working like a charm, until tonight. Until his passion for Arliss had caused him to fuck up, maybe too far to be saved.

For months, he'd been skimming. Which was no big thing. You were *supposed* to skim, it was expected. If a boss got too much money from you, he'd start to think there was no larceny in your heart, that you weren't playing by the rules. Next thing you knew, you were hanging from a hook in a meat factory, with one guy throwing buckets of water on you while another put a cattle prod to your balls, trying to find out if you were with the Gee. No, skimming was all right, as long as it was within reason. What he'd been doing, though, was winning, and big, for—what?—over four months now.

And telling Mad Mike that he was losing, heavily.

Even Virgil didn't know, and if Virgil couldn't find out, being closest to Tony, Mike never would. No, the bookies paid their handbook money directly to him (after skimming their own piece from it), he took their sheets, doctored them up right here in the apartment, turned them over to Mike with an apology and a sad shake of the head. What are you gonna do? There it is in black and white, Mike. We're down now a million for the football season, half-million on the basketball games, losing our ass with the hockey and soccer. It's getting so bad out there, Mike, jeez, I'm telling the boys, take the action on kickboxing, karate, any goddamn thing, just start recouping our losses.

And it had worked, too, because of greed.

If he'd tried it when Mad Mike had first taken over and had begun to straighten things out, it wouldn't have worked. He'd be dead by now. Mike ran things like a military general, giving no quarter to malcontents. The gambling, the women, these were their biggest moneymakers, until Mike got into something else.

Narcotics.

For many years, there was no mob action in Chicago when it came to narcotics. Oh, from time to time some idiot would make a run at it, do it on the side, and if the feds caught him he'd do fifteen in Atlanta and not get a dime from the mob while he was in, and if the mob caught him, well, he'd get a dime, all right. Copper, anyway, through the skull wrapped around a bullet. Along with some lead, wrapped around his legs, as he dropped from a boat into Lake Michigan. The Old Guard had been fanatic about this, and that's the way it had been until now.

Well, the Old Guard was gone, and the mob, fighting for its life in the city, had turned the reins over to Mad Mike and given him free run. He'd learned, quickly, that the quickest way to infuse some cash was through powder and pills.

To the best of Tony's knowledge, and he wasn't even sure about most of it, there was at the very least three million a day coming into the coffers through the noses, veins, and gullets of Chicago's drug abusers. From the junky in the street to the housewife in Winnetka who didn't want to pay for a doctor's visit and the charge of a prescription for her Valium and diet pills, to the high-dealing traders and brokers in the Financial Center, to the coke-snorting celebrities and teenyboppers in the elite and chic lounges, they all paid tribute, gladly, for the ability to swallow or snort and shoot and say, "Wow, good shit, man."

And it was good shit indeed.

Mad Mike wouldn't let the coke or smack get cut too far, and never with poisons. The pills weren't put together in Venezuela, and the PCP wasn't chemically compounded in a bikers' haven in the forest preserve. No, the mob pushers had the best shit, man, only grade-A stuff; the only way you'd OD or get sick was if you took too much on purpose or were allergic to it.

It kept the suckers coming back.

At three million a day, Mike wasn't going to get too worried about a few bucks here and there lost on wagers. Oh, eventually, he'd get his ass up, want to know what the hell was going on, but by the time he smelled a rat and got wise, Tony planned to be far away, set up in charge as the heir apparent to his good friend and paisan, Angelo Biari, in Atlantic City.

They'd been planning for months now, the takeover. Gaetano was too stupid to run things properly. He was all sophistication and education, no balls. The war had messed with his heart, left him a coward leaping at every car backfiring on the street. Angelo needed someone to keep the dynasty going after he died, and he would never turn it over to anyone but another Sicilian, who knew the old ways and would live, and die, by them.

Five million dollars, to buy his seat at the top of a multibillion-dollar industry.

And not even Mad Mike could do a damn thing about it, because A.C. was like Vegas, open territory, a safe haven. If bodies started turning up there due to a gang war, it would keep the suckers away, and then where would they be? Mike wouldn't kill the goose that was laying the golden egg over five million—well, four and a half now. Even if he wanted to, the other mob leaders in the country would have him whacked in a minute if he tried anything in Atlantic City. The other half a million would have to be forgotten. He had to leave, and quickly. Sure, Tony could never set foot in Chicago again, or anywhere else where Mike could make a move on him, but as long as he could find his way East, he would be safe. He would have a company of fifty guys working for him, and if they couldn't keep him safe, nobody could. Not to mention that when the old man died, it would all be his.

But he'd had to go and get cocky, as if ninety grand meant anything to him. Shit, with a million-five already hidden away in the safe spot in his house. The problem was that punk Lano. He'd taken away the only woman Tony had ever really loved, and that would have to be avenged. Even if Angelo found out about it, he would understand. Honor meant more to a Sicilian than money or even life itself, and his honor had to be avenged. He'd used the money and the cut-up Cadillac as his excuse, because Mike and Art, being from the Northland, would never understand about honor, but that's what it was all about.

And if he hadn't called Virgil's house, his honor would have cost him his life.

Jesus Christ, wasn't it funny, the way you sometimes got the breaks.

Arliss entered the room, making him start. "Coffee's ready, Daddy."

"Take a shower and get dressed, baby," Tough Tony said.

"Then call Union Station, get a luxury berth on the next *Broadway Special*. In your name."

"We taking a trip?" Arliss the middle-aged little girl said, her hands under her chin, bouncing up and down. Man, look at them titties, jiggling.

"Yeah, we are. A long, long trip."

He called the house first. "Anyone been around, asking about me?"

His wife, Evangeline, the cow, said, "Some people." Icily.

Tony sighed. "Listen, Evie? I want to tell you something. There's a fucking hit order out on me. This ain't no wrist-slapping here, we're talking about. There's guys, gonna *kill* me if they see me. You too, if you're with me. So quit the bitching and just answer my question."

She got immediately serious, fright in her tone. "Mike Tile called. He was mad about something. Then a couple of men came here, about an hour ago, one of them's walking around the sidewalk right now, freezing. The other one left, in the car." Spoken in a straight tone, after the initial sharp intake of breath. That was better. She hadn't been married to him thirty-two years for nothing.

"No one out back?"

"No, I looked. And have kept looking. Oh, Tony, am I gonna be all right?" Just like her to think only of herself.

In a soft, compassionate voice, he said, "Evie, you're gonna be just fine," before hanging up.

Okay, one in the front, the other gone somewhere, no one in back. He listened to Arliss, who was now making the train reservations on the living-room phone, went to the nightstand and got out his piece, a .44 Magnum Colt six-shot revolver. He checked the load, threw it on the bed, and got dressed.

When Arliss came into the room, she gasped, and he said, "What car you driving these days, baby?"

* * *

A piece-of-shit, baby-turd-brown Cordoba, that's what kind. He drove it now, slowly, obeying all the traffic laws. Mike had more than a couple cops on the payroll, and the last thing he needed was a traffic pinch getting him killed. As he turned into his alley, Arliss beside him, he said, "Just around the block, twice, slow. Then right back here."

"I know, I know . . ." Arliss nervous, able to get away with her mouthy tone this time because he needed her. He put the car into park, slipped out the driver's door, and hurried to his backyard, six houses down in the middle of the block.

Evie was there, by the back door, wringing her hands. "You gonna be all right, Mike, huh?" Now, suddenly, she was worried about his welfare. Probably remembered what she'd said on the phone, the selfish bitch, and wanted to make up for it.

He ignored her, locked the door and, hand on the butt of his pistol stuck down the left side of his pants, headed for the basement.

What they'd do, the Gee, was, they'd look for safes. Big walk-in suckers. Then they'd break in, take your dough, and make you prove in federal court that it was yours. They'd gotten a few of Tony's friends like that, before the friends got whacked for being so damn stupid, leaving millions lying around the house. But they wouldn't get him.

He protected his money.

The big old-time coal furnace had been replaced with a forced-air type, but had never been removed. It had asbestos-wrapped pipes sticking out of it everywhere, large pipes, as thick as a man's thigh. He went to these pipes, began to tear the wrapping from them, the tape dripping with condensation, green in places with mold and mildew. With nearly each foot of tape, another plastic-wrapped wad of hundred-dollar bills would fall. A hundred thousand in a bag, fifteen bags in all. When he was sure he had them all he stacked them in a small leather suitcase that had been placed under the workbench, the money fitting in there as if it had been custom-built around it. The bills had been individually ironed before they were shrink-wrapped. It was amazing to Tony, so much money in there, the suitcase only a little bigger than a briefcase. There was a handle, and a leash to pull it along with. Not that he'd be using that. This thing wouldn't be out of his sight, not even behind him, until it was transferred into hidden accounts in his own and Angelo Biari's names.

He went back to the workbench, opened the desk-size toolbox with all the drawers, got out another piece, this one a Baretta nine-millimeter. He checked the clip, slapped it back in, and put it in his right coat pocket. In his left coat pocket, he put a .38 Smith & Wesson, a Chief's Special with a four-inch barrel. He was ready.

He walked up the stairs, lugging the suitcase, made Evie look out the window to make sure no one had come back in a car, that there was still only one man outside. He walked to the back door, assuring her all the way that he'd call as soon as he got this mess straightened out.

He didn't kiss her good-bye.

In the car, Arliss said, "Where you been, Daddy? I been waiting and waiting," and Tony, not really needing her to stay alive anymore, his getaway money on his lap, both hands on top resting on it, said, "Shut the fuck up and drive, Arliss, will you?"

15

All right, it was time to do or die. The thought raced through Lano's head as the black Ford LTD tore through the streets of Atlantic City. The car was comfortable, reminded him of his own, and maybe that had something to do with his decision to stand up.

The thing of it was, he'd been humiliated last night, had felt the emotion fully for the first time in his life. Always before, in the brig in the Marines, in a street fight, whenever he'd been in the position to know fear, he'd stood up to it. Looked it in the eye and did what he had to do in spite of it. Even walking from a crap game, broke, after being taken for all he was worth, he'd never felt humiliated. Dejected, angry, hurt, but never humiliated, as he'd always given it his best shot.

Until last night, sitting in the den at the home of Angelo Biari. He'd backed down, without even an argument, taken a pistol which he was now sure had been used in a felony, had allowed himself to be set up simply because he was frightened.

He made the decision riding in the backseat of the car, no matter what, he would stand up, be a man. Then maybe, when he got out, he would call Gaetano Biari and tell him what he thought of him.

His confidence level hadn't sunk since being pinched. Maybe because the two coppers treated him with respect and the utmost courtesy. Back home, he was used to the heat throwing him up against a wall, telling him, "Freeze, asshole," using him and other players as pawns, trying to convince the guys who ran the gambling dens that they shouldn't be late with their payment anymore. That wasn't the case here. It had been Mr. Pella, this, and Mr. Pella, that, since they'd grabbed him on the Boardwalk, the two cops obviously having gotten his bogus name from the hotel register.

Neither one of these guys was the copper from last night, either, he was sure of it. As they drove him through the parts of Atlantic City that the tourists never got a chance to see, he wondered if he'd been under a roving surveillance since he got into town.

Things didn't change much at the station, either. The same drill, in a drab cramped office with a frosted-glass door that had the name Kenneth Daniels, Captain, Homicide, stenciled in block letters on the smudged glass. The two cops stood, hands in front of them, folded over their overcoats, which they were holding, since it was about a hundred and ten degrees in the room. Lano was seated in a wood chair directly across the desk from the captain, a curly-haired short guy who was smiling at him. Directly behind the man was a wide radiator that had recently been painted silver. The smell of paint was strong in the smoky room. The radiator hissed loud enough to notice, and to the left of it, on the far side of the window in the corner, stood the cop Lano had seen last night.

"Tough night, huh?" the captain said. Smiling widely.

"You've met officers Blake and Reynolds? Good. I'm Captain Daniels. Sorry to drag you in on a night like this, shit, the wind ain't never gonna die, huh?" He spoke with a casual authority that came easy to him, with a lot of body language. Daniels made the chair swivel a lot on its base, moving and talking with his hands, turning to look out the window as he mentioned the wind, the chair swiveling, pointing to the two cops standing at ease as he mentioned their names.

"There're a couple of things, Mr. Pella, we want to clear up with you before we take you back to whatever casino you'd like." He spread his hands as he said this, as if he was doing Lano a favor, bringing him in when he was on a roll.

"Who's that?" Lano said, using his own body language, pointing his chin at the man in the corner. Daniels sighed, looked around as if he didn't know the guy was back there, stared at him for a second and Lano saw his body stiffen, wondered if he were leveling the guy with a killer glare for some reason. The captain turned back, looking a little embarrassed.

"That's Percy Fincher. Now, Mr. Pella—"

"Wait a minute, wait a minute, who the hell is Percy Fincher? He one of yours?" As he asked it he saw Fincher stiffen, scowl, and take a step forward, a deeply tanned man with green eyes, staring menacingly. Lano smiled at him.

"He ain't even a cop, is he?"

"Mr. Pella, could we get on with this, please?"

"Nope." Lano was smiling, returning Fincher's stare. A big guy like this, tough as nails, it would be good to stand up to him right now, maybe get back some of what he'd lost last night. "We can't just get on with this. If you're gonna charge me, go ahead. You want to book me, I'm ready. I'll call my lawyer, see what he says. But if you aren't, then cut me loose, 'cause I ain't gonna say one more goddamn word to you or your buddies, or to this sucker here, standing around looking at me like I'm lunch."

Fincher said, "You were at Biari's house early this morning, left around three-forty. I want to know what you were doing there."

"I went over to visit your mother. She throws freebies at the Biaris' every Friday night." Lano said the words and that was all he had time for, Fincher was coming, the room was exploding into shouts and hollers as the two cops dropped their coats and Daniels leaped from his chair and Lano threw himself back just as Fincher's fist popped his right cheek. The force of the blow propelled him backward and he rolled with it, landing on his shoulder and popping to his feet, bringing his fist back as the two detectives got ahold of Fincher, one on either side of him. Fincher was yelling something in the captain's face as Lano hit him, hard, his fist twisting as it landed, hard, on the left side of his jaw. Fincher dropped in the detective's arms, limp, and Daniels turned quickly, reaching for the pistol on his belt, when Lano threw up his hands.

"Hey, fuck this," Lano said, "get me to a telephone, now, all right?"

Daniels was speaking soothingly and urgently, looking over his shoulder every few seconds, making Lano wonder if he was looking for someone with wings to pop up there at the glass, listening in. It wasn't body language, the guy had a nerve problem, but Lano liked what he was saying.

"He's a cop from *Akron*, for Christ's sake. That's in Ohio." Peek over the shoulder. "The guy's mother, she had three sons. His oldest brother was the union president of the IB of E, local seventy-six, here in Atlantic City, where the family was raised. His other brother, the middle one, he's the fucking coroner here. This guy, the youngest in the family, he turns drunk, gets in some trouble, goes to the Army, gets kicked out of there. He gets into AA, makes a pilgrimage to Akron, where the thing started there, winds up staying sober and getting on the force. He's been a cop maybe two years, a detective about three months. See, I've known him all his life. Hell, I've *pinched* him. I'm glad he's straight, even gladder he's out of town, but his brother's the coroner so he gets, let's say, some professional courtesies he otherwise wouldn't be entitled to." The man's nervous gestures were starting to bother Lano.

"Ange Biari's an old and dear friend of mine." Daniels leaned over the desk, then sat back, drumming his fingers on the blotter. He shook a cigarette out of a pack there on the desk, lit it, and let it hang out of the corner of his mouth and stared at Lano through the smoke. The butt jiggled up and down, making tiny smoke rings.

"We go back a long ways, if you get what I'm saying."

"What's this guy Fincher want with me?"

"He's conducting his own unauthorized investigation into his brother's death. He was watching the Biari mansion, figures the old man put out the order that killed his oldest brother—"

"What?"

"Lester Fincher was about to lead the Electrical Workers in Atlantic City out on strike for more dough. You got any idea what that would do to this town? Christ, it's all lights. Someone shot him, twice, with a thirty-eight, in the head, buried him in the sand across the Absecon Channel, next to the Brigantine Bridge. Shit, the government's investigating, seeing if they can maybe prove that someone violated Lester's right to strike by whacking him. They come into it, the last thing I need is some hotshot cop from Akron, saying I wouldn't cooperate with him, get them to give me a close look." Which told Lano why Daniels was so nervous. An old friend of Angelo Biari, a captain of homicide, probably couldn't stand too deep of a checking.

"So I let him use a car, as long as he doesn't harass any citizens without checking with us first."

"So where do I come into it?"

Daniels shrugged. "He saw you come out of the Biari house, figured you were mixed up in it somehow. He checked with someone he knows at the hotel—he grew up around here, remember—got your name, brought it over to us at about seven this morning. Shit, I wasn't even here yet, but someone told him, Look, leave the tourists alone, gave him a line of shit until I could get here, straighten things out. We told him first we had to let you get your eight hours, then clean up, then get a bite to eat." He shrugged. "Finally, I ran out of excuses."

"Doesn't he ever sleep?"

Another shrug. "Maybe not. Maybe he's gonna drop from exhaustion, have a stroke or something, I should be so lucky."

"Then I can go?"

Daniels checked his watch. "Yeah, we been talking long enough. I'll tell him I grilled you, you don't know nothing, you're a friend of Gaetano's from Vegas, okay?" Then added as Lano was walking toward the door, "And listen, I'd appreciate it if you wouldn't say anything about this to Ange, all right? And if you got to, tell him I cut you a break, will you?"

The man, Fincher, wasn't in the outer office, but one of the other cops was. Reynolds, that was his name. He was sitting there waiting for Lano, calmly, his coat over his lap, smiling.

"I think you broke his jaw."

"Good for him."

"Known him all my life, that guy, he always been a tough one."

"What're you trying to tell me?"

Reynolds shrugged. "I talked to him, me and Blake. Told him he had no clout out here, if he bothered you at all over this, we'd pinch him. We don't need guys, get called to early-morning meetings with Ange, getting harassed in our town. He listened and nodded his head, all the other bullshit, apologized even. Which tells me, he ain't gonna let this go so easy." Reynolds stood up, stretched, yawned, then said, "Where you want to go? I'll drop you off on my way home."

Without even thinking about it, Lano said, "How about the Shamrock?"

He stood outside on the Boardwalk, feeling good. His fist hurt a little, and his right cheek throbbed along with his heartbeat, but he'd stood up. He'd by God stood up and fought back even when he'd figured them all to be A.C. cops, about to stomp him into the ground. He hadn't given an inch and that made him feel good.

He didn't feel too good about what had happened last night, though. He was sure that the gun the Biaris had given him was the same one that had killed the union guy, Lester. So the Biaris were setting him up.

Which worked now in his favor. He'd gotten rid of the gun and now had no reason to respect Ange's orders concerning where to gamble. Hell, he hadn't been respecting their wishes since he'd arrived, but now, if he got called on the carpet, he'd be able to talk a good case, tell them about the girl in the ocean, about O'Shea's money.

Lano was under no illusions about A.C. Here, people didn't get killed, no matter what they did. Even cheats, they got barred from the casino and got a ride to the airport, and that was the end of it. The take was too lucrative to risk losing over any single person, no matter what he did. So he wouldn't get killed, not as long as he stayed in town. When he got home, he'd tell Art about the setup, see what he thought of it. Maybe it would even win him some points with Art, standing up to a couple of heavy hitters like Ange and Gaetano, after he'd figured out they were doing him wrong. The hell with them. He'd steer clear of them, maybe take one of the other hotels up on their offers to let him stay there. Use another name and the Biaris wouldn't even be able to find him. It was a good idea, but one he'd have to ponder later. Too, it might get Art to open up a little bit, tell him what he'd learned about Millie all those years ago, ask the questions he'd been afraid to ask since Art had said he'd looked into it. When Art told you something, you didn't question him.

His hand was on the ten grand wrapped in a big roll in his trouser pocket. It burned his palm. A warmth filled him, and he began to sweat, even with the bitter east wind trying to drive him off his feet. He took this as an omen.

For a moment he was rooted to the spot, suspended in time, as a hot flush filled him, beginning at his toes and spreading until he felt his forehead redden with the rush. He had to take deep breaths, and for a moment wondered with detachment if he was having a heart attack. The thing was sure pounding in his chest hard enough.

Lano laughed into the wind, and before he started the short walk into the casino he said to it, "I own you," softly and with conviction.

The first thing he noticed inside the Shamrock was the quiet. He hadn't noticed it last night because he'd been in neither the frame of mind nor the mood to pay attention, but now, after being in the other casinos, this place seemed liked a funeral parlor. He could see the doorway leading into the casino from where he stood facing the long registration desk, the desk packed with Saturday-evening check-ins, the reservations having been made at least a year ago. The people stood in line, used to the waiting, seasoned gamblers who knew the ropes. They weren't high rollers so they would have to wait until the clerk could get to them.

The quiet, though, coming from the casino, was eerie. He waited a second, then got it.

No sounds from slot machines. No screams from winners and groans from losers, no shouts for the third little glass window, "Come on, cherry, come on, you fucking bell!" Lano could hear, in the relative silence, the sounds of crap players shouting for their number to come up, but none of the sounds associated with casinos, especially here in Atlantic City, the nickels and dimes and quarters and half-dollar and dollar coins being shoved into one-arm bandits, and the rolling sound the machine makes as it spins toward another resolution. Confidently, curiously, he began to stroll toward the casino doorway.

Then stopped right in front. To his left was a tunnellike hallway. Back there, discreetly, would be bathrooms and telephones. The owners wouldn't want to give the impression that you could do anything besides check in without passing through the casino, so the phones and bathrooms here would be hidden, but there nevertheless. Lano stared at the dark entranceway. Like everything else he'd seen so far here at the Shamrock it was classy, with the deep blue carpet with little green clovers woven in every few inches. He entered the tunnel, with its scarlet-rose-papered walls, walking hesitantly, his heart wanting him to race for the gaming tables but his head telling him, Call Art. Which he did, collect.

Art said by way of greeting, "You tap out already?"

Lano said, "Up about twenty-three, twenty-four already, you want to know."

"Then what's on your mind?" Art's voice was cautious, yet impatient. He'd asked what was on Lano's mind and Lano was trying to think of a way to tell him that a guy named Lester Fincher was dead now, two in the head and buried in the sand across the Absecon Channel next to the Brigantine Bridge.

He wanted to tell Art this because all of a sudden he wasn't so sure that he was safe, no longer believed that as long as he stayed in Atlantic City he'd be all right. Lester had been in A.C., and look how he'd wound up.

Yet something held him back, and he was about to ask about the horse he'd bet on, make a feeble pass at conversation then hang up when Art said, "Hey, come clean, Lano.

What's wrong?" with something sounding close to concern in his voice.

Lano said, "I'm on a public phone in a casino in a joint called O'Shea's Shamrock Hotel and Casino. You think it's safe to talk?"

"My thing here scrambles both ways." Art telling him that his phone de-bugger would cover incoming calls, anyone listening in would hear nothing but disjointed gibberish.

With no excuse left not to, Lano told him everything.

"What you do is, right now, hang up the phone, turn around, get in a cab and go right to the airport. Leave the clothes, the money, everything. I'll get it for you later. Something ain't right, and I don't want you hanging around to find out what. The gun, it couldn't be the one used on the labor boss. Ange ever pulled a shot like that out there, the East Coast bosses would string him up by his balls from a lightpost as an example. It ain't what you think. Maybe even they told you the truth, they wanted you to have protection in case Tomase comes calling." Art hesitated, and Lano got the impression that he was about to say something else then changed his mind. "Blow town right now, kid. I mean it." There was an urgency in his voice that Lano had never heard before.

"You want me to run? They set me up, were gonna do me worse than Tomase could dream of, and you want me to take off?"

"What you planning on doing, fighting? You know who these guys are?"

"You said I could trust them."

"Maybe I was wrong." There was a pause, then Art said, "Look, things are wild back here. What you said put some things together for me. Now listen. Tomase disappeared, Mike went hard and talked to the other underbosses, just going through the motions before whacking him. Found out in passing that Tomase was doing a lot better than he was letting on. Juggling the books or something. He owes me ninety K, borrowed all over town from a lot of our other guys, felt sorry for him 'cause he was losing so bad. There was two, three million right there. And there's a few million missing from the handbooks. They're checking into it now, but it looks like the guy took off with five million or so."

"How you know he took off?"

"Some boys went into his house and braced his old lady. Searched the place and found a big coal furnace torn to hell in the basement. The thing of it was, it was a fluke, Mike finding out. One of the bosses asked him why he wanted to have a guy killed, was making them a ton in gambling. Mike questions him, the guy, he runs the barboot games directly for Tony, so even Tomase couldn't bullshit him. When Mike found out Tony was holding out, he sent some guys to guard the house around the clock, and talk to the wife. The old woman said he made a lot of noise down there, came up again carrying a little black leather satchel thing. Split out the back door so the guy out front wouldn't see him. At first they didn't know he was running, they just had a guy out front to tell Tony the word when he got in. The old lady, she said the only calls he got all day were from Mad Mike, and the one call late last night from a broad."

"Arliss?"

"Yeah. He came home, the wife told him she'd called, and he took off and she didn't see him again until he came home to pick up the satchel." Art paused, which was a good thing, as Lano's mind was racing. Jesus, Arliss and Tony, heading God knows where with a ton of money.

"Art, what's this got to do with me?"

"The boys checked Tony's back phone bills, the long distance. It seems that since last summer, the guy's been

THE PRIME ROLL · 171

burning up the wires between Chicago and Longport, New Jersey."

"Biari?"

"It stands to reason. They're both Sicilian, and you know how those people are."

"But why would Tony steal millions for Biari?"

"Hey, I don't know and I don't care. All I know is that piece of shit is probably on his way there, and Biari somehow mixed you up in it all. Hey, Lano?"

"What."

"I didn't tell you all this just to keep you updated. You got to understand that the way things were here for you last night when Tony had you shitting blood, was a walk on the beach, compared to what might be going on out there. I'm telling you for your own good, come on home, now. The heat's off. I been trying to call your hotel room since three, tell you to come back. So now you've heard. Get your ass home, now."

"Art?" Lano said, his head spinning. "How'd Bucking Bronco N. do over at Balmoral?" He barely got the words out of his mouth when Art slammed the phone down, which was all right with Lano. He'd been about to ask him what he really knew about Millie.

He sat on a padded leather backless bench next to the ladies' room, taking deep breaths. Art had almost had him convinced. He was about to say okay to everything and jump in a cab to the airport when Art had to go and spoil everything, bring up Lano's fear of the night before.

And Art wasn't even aware of the razor blades Lano'd been sitting on with Ange Biari.

Thank God Art hadn't asked the right questions. Lano didn't know what he would have said if Art had wanted to know why Lano took the gun in the first place. He grimaced, thinking of Art sneering into the phone if Lano said, "I was scared, Art." Lano would be telling this to a guy to whom fear was a foreign entity, something for someone else to experience. To be felt by lesser men, immature suckers who lacked character.

No, reminding Lano of his fear had torn it. He might still be able to squirm out of it, head home running, but he'd never be able to look Art in the face again without seeing the disappointment. He wondered if maybe Art had said it on purpose, to test him. Decided that it didn't matter. Lester didn't matter, none of it mattered anymore, because if a man couldn't handle what came up, no matter how bad it was, without help or without trying to squirm out of it, then he had never been a man in the first place.

He had been told that his father had died to preserve freedom in America. Had gladly given his life so that Lano and the other kids growing up in America could do so in a free world, without the threat of communism hanging over their heads. There had been a time when he had figured that his old man had volunteered for Nam the second time because he'd seen the Vietcong as tame when compared to his wife. But that argument didn't wash anymore.

Maybe, Lano thought, he'd gone back to exorcise demons. Maybe the man had faced death the first time and had come up wanting. Maybe he'd even questioned his own manhood. His character.

Yeah, and look how *he'd* wound up.

A woman came rushing through the hallway, breaking into Lano's thoughts. She was being followed by a very tall heavy man dressed in a security-guard outfit, pistol on the right, in a polished leather holster. She kept saying, "Oh, God, oh, God," over and over, in an anguished voice. The security guard looked bored and indifferent, detached. If there was any emotion there on his deadpan exterior, it was impatience.

"Come on, lady, you signed the marker," the guard said as the woman raced past Lano, into the rest room. He caught a quick glimpse of rich blond hair, could see a diamond pendant hanging from her left ear, big rings on her fingers. The guard said, "I'll wait as long as you're in there, there ain't no other way out." From inside the toilet, Lano heard wailing.

"All gone," then sobs, "God, all gone!"

"We'll make a phone call, get him to send you some more." The guard wheedling now, ignoring Lano, who sighed, rose, and, his decision made, headed for the casino.

16

The anxiety he'd been feeling left him as he entered the gambling casino, as did the self-doubt. The Biaris, Art, everyone faded to a less important back compartment of his mind as he wandered from table to table, watching the action, fingering the bills in his pocket, fighting now simply the desire to jump right in. It was a much easier battle than the one he'd been involved in minutes earlier.

He looked around, a little surprised that no one seemed to remember him. At the midpoint of the spacious casino he stopped and stared at stacks and stacks of bills, encased in glass. He bent down and peered at the small print, smiled at the sucker bets you'd have to make to win, then wondered if any high rollers ever tried, just for the hell of it. From his experience, he would have to assume that O'Shea had maybe had to replace this bundle a time or two, because the only strict scientific rule about gambling was that anything could happen and probably would if you played the game long enough.

Himself, he'd had a streak once, from two in the morning

until dawn, where every time he got his hands on the dice, he'd rolled craps. One, one. The laws of probability said that was impossible. Reality is always different from probability. He'd stayed in the game like a fool because he couldn't believe that the fates had abandoned him so cruelly; he'd figured that sooner or later, things would turn around, he'd start rolling those lucky sevens and break the bank. He'd been younger then. He knew better now.

The extraordinary quiet he'd noticed in the lobby now had a sound reason. The place was devoid of slot machines, another little detail he'd failed to notice last night, and Lano wondered how that was possible, a place of gambling in a town that thrived on slots, not having any at all. There were workmen, trying to be discreet but nevertheless noticeable, dressed in green pants and shirts with shamrocks on the back of them, swarming in recessed areas of the casino. Making ready for something, busting their asses, too, from the looks of them. An older shortish man supervised them, making frantic hand movements. There were seats and stools and stands for the machines, and it was a logical assumption that they were making ready for the coming of some one-arm bandits. Did the lack of them have anything to do with Biari's statements to Lano, about giving O'Shea a heart attack? If so, that wasn't Lano's problem. Shit, the guy deserved one. Lano's problem, as he now saw it, was to find a way to separate some of O'Shea's cash from him before his chest seized up on him, courtesy of Ange Biari.

The table he chose was half-full, as they all were, even in a hot town on a Saturday night. The surprising thing was that there were plenty of five-dollar tables, a rarity in this town after five in the afternoon, and an impossibility on a weekend evening. Still, here they were, a good many of them, too. For some reason, Lano appreciated that. He looked around at all the tables, trying to spot Millie. He couldn't find her. But he did spot someone else.

The girl he'd yanked out of the Atlantic was sitting at a blackjack table, a table with only one other player. He walked to it, sat next to her, smiled, said, "Remember me?" to her and then to the dealer, "What's the limit?"

He smiled at the dealer only after she welcomed him to the table with a warm smile herself. He spread half his roll, fifty hundred-dollar bills, on the felt, asked for five-hundred-dollar chips. As the dealer checked change with the pit boss, Lano decided that he would begin here, and if his luck was bearing up at all, he would stroll over to the crap table in maybe five minutes, the big chips already in his coat pockets so the crap dealers would have no idea as to the size of his bankroll. They'd see the five hundreds and become wary. It would be a small advantage.

He'd felt the redhead's eyes on him since he'd sat down and he'd stayed busy, playing with his money, looking around, acting casual as her stare bore into the side of his head. As he laid down the first five-hundred-dollar chip to begin gambling, he turned to her, smiled, and said, "You still looking for help?" But she didn't answer him.

"Stick around, Red," Lano said, remembering that half of all luck was being able to maintain the illusion of strict confidence, then said, "and watch me get us all the help we need."

The funny thing was that he'd always intended on winning big at craps. Blackjack was a good solid card game, one he enjoyed, and as he placed his first five-hundred-dollar bet on the felt then crossed his arms over his coat on his lap, he had no idea that he'd never get to the crap table tonight at all.

The cards came out of the shoe and he had a righteous blackjack, the jack and the ace of spades. The redhead gasped, looking at the big dark guy who'd pulled her out of the ocean and who'd bet the limit and blackjacked first time out of the shoe, but the dealer had an ace showing, and she asked if anybody wanted insurance against the possibility that she herself had a blackjack. When she got to Lano she said, "You sure?" smiling, looking at his bet, and Lano told her that he never bet against himself. She shrugged and gave a card to the woman next to him, who was tapping the table lightly with her index finger, ordering a six for her fifteen showing. She busted out. Casually, he said to Conway, "See? What'd I tell you."

He began to stare intently at the cards after the fifth blackjack, had to take controlled breaths after the sixth. By the time the young woman dealt him his tenth, he'd forgotten all about the redhead and he hadn't even noticed that a crowd had gathered around the table.

"I don't fucking understand it at all," Brian O'Shea said to Malcolm. It was maybe the hundredth time he'd said the words since they'd brought Conway in early that morning, soaking and freezing. "The woman's a compulsive, isn't she?" Brian would ask the rhetorical questions and Malcolm would nod his head, wishing the man would leave his office so he could get some work done. Somebody had to be on top of the business, and the slots from Paradise Island were already off-loading at the airport, almost ready for transport. He had to get back out there in the casino, make sure the workmen weren't slacking off now that he'd dared come back in here for a minute, and been buttonholed by O'Shea. He'd been here now a half-hour, and was getting tired of it.

"She wants, I mean, what's more important? Her goddamn virtue or her gambling bill? She owes us over three hundred, I offer to knock ten off the bill she's nice to this guy from Seattle, and how does she act? She tries to drown herself." O'Shea turned to Malcolm, his face imploring, his hands palm-up. "Now does that figure? I mean, what does she expect?"

Malcolm almost felt sorry for the man. Big giant pacing

back and forth, worried about a woman was a dime a dozen out here. He'd tried to tell him forget about it, let her go, but O'Shea was having none of it. At first Malcolm thought it was because of the money the woman owed, but the way the guy was acting, now he wasn't so sure. Maybe he was mellowing out, beginning to care about someone other than himself for the first time in his life. If that was the case, Malcolm decided, he was gone, and nothing O'Shea could say or do would make him stay. This was a cutthroat business and they'd survived all these years on courage and luck and a solid knowledge of the odds. There was no room in their world for sentiment.

The phone rang and Malcolm reached for it gratefully, half-listening to Brian rambling, something about she was already back out there, down on the floor, gambling for Chrissakes. What the pit boss was telling him though, made him forget all about O'Shea, all about Conway, all about the slots. Because some fool was down there on table fifty-six, about to win one million dollars, cash.

They held up play before the eleventh deal. The table was swamped now, people watching as the chips piled up in front of Lano, who was ignoring them and watching the shoe.

He had it and he knew it. In fact, he'd be willing to bet a million himself that the next two cards dealt to him would be a blackjack. He might even bet on which cards they would be, that's how good it felt.

What Art had told him about was happening. His blood was pounding, and Christ, he was half-erect. It was erotic, there was no way around it. His confidence was soaring to the ceiling, ready to spill over and out and infect the other gamblers with his overflow. He believed that he could take the dice and roll eleven sevens as soon as he left this table, was tempted to do so now, just to show his disdain for probabilities and to impress upon the people watching that he was embarked upon the gambler's dream, a prime roll.

But that would be showboating, not to mention foolish. No, he'd win here and quit. Take the million and go back to the hotel, check out. After having a little talk with O'Shea, letting him know the score. That would even things with the Biaris.

Lano thought these things in the seconds it took for the pit boss to whisper something to the dealer, and for her to step aside.

"Is there some problem?" Lano said, and the smiling pit boss assured him that there was not. They were just waiting for the photographer in case he hit his eleventh blackjack, so they could have a nice picture to hang on the wall for other hopeful gamblers to drool over.

The pit boss smiled and Lano told him, "Forget the picture. Let the woman deal." The pit boss was about to say something smart, Lano could tell, when he looked up. His expression changed, and he said, "Good evening, Mr. O'Shea, Mr. Lynch."

Lano didn't bother to even turn on his stool, never took his eyes from the pit boss. He said, softly, "You can change dealers, you can shuffle new decks, you can wait for picture-takers and you can wait, too, for hell to freeze over, because mister, my next hand is a blackjack and nothing's gonna stop it from coming." He turned now, stared hard at Brian O'Shea, felt a flicker of recognition—this was him all right, the son of a bitch from last night—before saying, "Tell the woman to deal, please," and heard O'Shea say, "Well, you heard the man, honey, deal them cards." Lano smiled, admiring the guy, about to lose a million and sounding like a cheerleader for him.

The dealer stepped back into her spot and a roar went up from the crowd as the other bettors around the table demurred, didn't bet. Then they fell silent as the game began. It was Lano and the dealer, the gambler on the roll against the house and the first card she dealt to Lano was the king of spades and then she dealt her first card down. When she slipped his second card from the shoe Lano said, "Come to me," softly but with emotion, now clenching a fist and holding it up and shouting "YEAH!" as she dealt him the ace of hearts and the casino went mad.

They were reaching over, touching his arms and shoulders, tearing at him in their zeal to grab some of his luck off for themselves. And he let them. It was a pleasure. Even O'Shea seemed pleased, towering over everyone and rubbing his hands, smiling. The other guy, what had the pit boss called him? Lynch. He didn't seem too happy with the deal. The pit boss tried to pull him away but Lano was having none of it just yet, turned to the dealer and stared at her left breast for a moment, read the name Donna on the ID card pinned there. He did a quick calculation in his head.

He'd laid out five grand, so he'd started with a total of ten five-hundred-dollar chips. At five hundred a bet, for eleven blackjacks, he'd have won a total of $8250.00 more. He grabbed a single chip off the top, flipped it in the air and caught it, put it in his shirt pocket. He said to Donna, "The rest's yours." He didn't hear her reply. It was drowned in the screaming of the crowd that followed his remark.

They were high above the Boardwalk, looking out, O'Shea and Lano, two big men who understood what it was all about. Through the sliding glass door way up there it looked as if the ocean was all there was, if you were careful to keep your eyes straight ahead. To look down would bring sight of the Boardwalk, the beach, and other sights that wrecked the illusion. Lano was thinking this, sipping the Scotch that O'Shea had poured him, when the man spoke, using the same word in Lano's mind.

"It's the illusion that separates the winners from the losers in the end, Lano. You and I, we understand that."

Lano turned from the window to give him a long slow look. The man here on top of the world speaking of illusions. "I'm still young enough to believe in luck."

O'Shea laughed. "Luck's a good thing, but the odds, Lano, they catch up to you every time. For instance, you told me your name here for a reason, right? Your real name. I know the odds, and I know, too, that you're registered at another hotel, under another name. That tells me that you're figuring now that someone, somewhere, is gonna find out that you're here, and you won a million. The question is, who are you trying to lure here?"

Lano looked at him, thinking that he'd underrated him. "I told you my real name so I could cash the check back home, but just for the hell of it, tell me, how'd you know about the hotel, the different name?"

The man shrugged. "I had someone look after you, this morning, after you fished Conway out of the water and Millie took you home. Followed you, in case you gave her a hard time. In the casino, we don't want trouble, but out there, well, let's just say, it's a good thing you showed her respect. 'Jules Pella.' Sounds a little faggy to me, anyway." He shrugged. "I like Lano better."

Lano stayed quiet, looking into O'Shea's knowing green eyes. The guy, he was likeable, managed to be that way without trying. He was trying to tell Lano one thing while mouthing another—the sparkle there in his eyes told Lano this. What they didn't tell him was what that something was.

"Why didn't you tell the guy to give me a ride?" Lano wasn't smiling now. It was time to get down to it.

"Because he didn't want to get his car seat wet on account of a stranger, and Millie said she knew you, that's why."

"I cost you more than the price of a rug shampoo now, though, didn't I Brian. Hadn't have been for that deal this morning, I wouldn't have ever come into the casino."

He was surprised when O'Shea brayed laughter. The guy either rich and confident enough not to care that his million was gone or good enough to act as if he didn't. Lano remembered the word O'Shea had used earlier. Illusion. Knowing that the illusion of confidence was often enough when it came to a heads-up game.

"Lano," O'Shea said, "don't you get it? Tonight, the slots come in. In another hour, the word will have passed around town. By midnight, the joint will be packed, people wanting to be where the action is. By tomorrow night at this time, I'll have made up that million and another to match it, just from the publicity of your roll. And the million, it'll be there, safe and sound, for others to look at, salivate over, try and win the same way you did."

"No, it won't."

"What?"

"The sign down below in the glass cage said that the million, *that* million, could be mine. I won it, I want it." Lano said it and enjoyed watching the man's face fall. He was likable, there was no doubt about it, but there was nothing wrong with keeping him on his toes. Also, Lano wasn't sure if he liked the man enough to tell him about Biari's plan for him. The jury was still out on that one. And what was his connection to the redheaded girl? No, better to keep him on his toes.

"You can put it in the cashier's safe for me, until I leave, but when I go I'm taking it the way it's stacked right there in the window." Lano smiled. "Now, if you could have somebody show me to my suite? It's been a long day."

He had to admit it, the guy didn't miss a beat. He bowed a little and regained his composure, smiled back at Lano.

"That works in my favor too, you know." O'Shea spoke as he walked toward the phone, hesitated with his hand on the receiver. "People come in, see the empty glass there, know it's not just a rumor. A check'd been better for us, but what the hell, the money wasn't in use anyway." He picked up the phone and dialed for a boy to show Lano to one of the needle suites, hung up and grinned at Lano, who couldn't help himself, found himself grinning right back.

"And there's someone maybe you want to talk to while you're here, enjoying our hospitality?"

"Who's that?"

"Conway Mallory. I could have her come up, thank you properly for this morning." There was no macho posturing here, no promise in his voice of sexual favors being offered, but still, there was that goddamn glint in his eyes . . .

"I'd like that," Lano said, trying to read what the guy was truly saying behind his words, worldly enough to know that there was plenty there that was not being stated.

He reached into his pocket, fingered the single five-hundred-dollar chip he retained.

"And that was a good touch," O'Shea said, "giving the dealer over ten grand. Shows you're a sport. That more's involved than counting money." He caught the chip when Lano tossed it at him. "What's this for?"

"Your goon, he gave me five hundred this morning when he sent me packing. I don't need it anymore." He remembered something, reached into his inside jacket pocket and pulled out the envelope. "And could you get this to Millie Swan, please? It's a thank-you note, for helping me out this morning."

O'Shea put the letter in his jacket pocket, then the token in his pocket, nodding his head, and said, "Why that son of a bitch, I gave him a grand for you."

17

O'Shea had said to him, "Who are you trying to lure?" and he hadn't answered. Lano thought about that now, in the suite right next to O'Shea's, staring out at a near-identical view. The drapes were opened wide, showing a large expanse of blue ocean, white-capped waves rolling in and pounding the surf. Someone had told him that the average daily temperature in Atlantic City was fifty-two degrees. It appeared that that person had lied.

Who was he trying to lure? Or was O'Shea all wrong? Lano tried to tell himself that it was a lapse, a momentary loss of cover as he spoke, caught 'up in the excitement of the climax of his lucky streak. He sipped Scotch slowly, not wanting to get drunk, drinking to come down a little so he could savor the moment without getting antsy, maybe get the desire to go down and double the million, take the immediate risk of losing it all.

Maybe later. Tomorrow. But for right now he wanted to enjoy the feeling of security for a while, the joy of being a millionaire. Christ, was it something, or what? He put his feet up on the leather hassock before the leather couch, staring at the ocean with the roaring fire in the fireplace casting shadows around him. The place was sure big enough. Three bedrooms, a sitting room, a wet bar and a spacious living room, decorated with taste, none of the glitz he'd expected. The tub in the john was the only exception, sunk down and big enough for three adults. The king-size bed looked inviting, but he had to talk to someone first. While he waited, he thought.

Was he trying to lure the Biaris here? Force a confrontation with them in what he thought to be the safety of this casino? Knowing full well that he was safe here, that O'Shea was the enemy of Angelo Biari and therefore to be trusted to some extent? Or had it just been a casual slip of the tongue?

He was hoping that it hadn't been, that he'd been forcing a confrontation, but didn't have time to dwell on it because as he was thinking it the doorbell chimed.

"Nice place," Conway said. "I got one just like it, down the hall and across the building. All six of the needle suites face the ocean. Cost him a fortune, but you have to know Brian, with him, it's first class or nothing." She was speaking from nervousness, uncomfortable with him in silence, this man who'd saved her life and was now sitting down the couch from her, watching intently.

"Thanks," she said, sipping her drink.

"The vodka was here," the man who called himself Lano said, and shrugged.

"I mean for this morning."

"Why'd you do it?" the man asked her, and she didn't know what to tell him, wasn't sure if he really wanted to know or was just talking himself, trying to keep the ball rolling.

It had worried her at first, when Malcolm had cornered her in the casino and had told her that the man who'd pulled her from the Atlantic was the one who'd won the million, and wanted to talk to her. She'd decided, too, that if she was supposed to be a comp for him, then she'd give in. Try it with him because he was young and good-looking and because she owed him. Try it and if it wasn't too bad, maybe go ahead and do what Brian wanted.

Thinking about it filled her with self-loathing. It would make her a whore. But on the other hand, what was she now? Brian had told her once during an argument that she was nothing but a chip-whore, and never to forget it. Later he'd apologized and she'd told him that she accepted his apology, but she knew that he'd meant it and believed it.

Why'd she do it? Did he really want to know? He was sitting there waiting for an answer, patiently, not acting nervous or anything. Kind of casual, looking at her with interest. She could see him looking at her breasts when he thought she wasn't looking, her lower legs showing from the hem of the gown she was wearing this evening, but that didn't mean much, in fact, she felt flattered that he was attracted to her, didn't pity her or think she was a self-destructive freak. No, he wasn't looking down on her or judging her. He seemed, if it was possible in this town, to care.

She said, "I did it because I've lived with Brian exclusively for some time, and he wanted to give me away to a high roller."

"Like a comp?"

"Exactly." She held her head up and tried for dignity, hoped she was making it. Why was she feeling ashamed? My God, did she care about what this man thought of her? Did it matter? It was with a sudden sinking feeling that she realized that it did. For the first time in a long time, it did.

It hadn't always been that way. Conway's story was:

The simple farm girl looking for a way out. With her fine red hair and slim build, she'd always felt too good for the

Minnesota town and the folks around it. Her dream was to be an actress, a great one, like Faye Dunaway or somebody, able to convey her displeasure with a mere glance.

It was a fantasy her mother would feed, at night alone with their father-husband in town, drinking with the boys. Her mother would tell her she was too good to stay, too beautiful. The prettiest girl in town, easy, and when she was eighteen, three days after her high-school graduation, she'd taken her savings and the two thousand Mom had squirreled away and she'd gone to California, to L.A.

And had found out that she suddenly wasn't the most beautiful girl in town anymore. Not even close.

In L.A. the beauties seemed to grow out of the palm trees, out of the sand on the beach. So many blonds with deep tans and doctored boobs, altered noses and raised cheekbones. Conway's beauty was natural but she burned easily, could not cultivate a tan, and looked almost freakish next to the tanned light-haired bunnies who were vying for every part.

Her vulnerability got her invited to the right social functions, but as the word got around that she was aloof, would not play the game and fuck for a bit part in a B movie, they left her alone. The only ones interested then were the sharks who were ready to capitalize on her lovely soft looks until they faded. She would have no part of them.

There was, however, a drug dealer who was truly interested. He never asked her to do anything perverted and treated her with respect. She moved in with him and spent his money, enjoying the trips to Rodeo Drive in his chauffeured Jag while he did his business, becoming friends with the driver and the other help around the large Spanish-style mansion in the Hills.

The trouble began when he'd taken her to Vegas and allowed her to gamble while he sat ringside at a fight.

God but it was good, risking money at a table with people who were there to make her rich in her own right. Before the bell had rung in the first preliminary bout, she'd lost thirty thousand dollars of the drug dealer's money. His line of credit was extensive, and as he watched the main event with interest, she lost fifty more. By the time he'd had a drink with some buddies in the bar of Caesars Palace and begun actively seeking her, she had dropped a quarter of a million of his hard-earned dollars.

He'd been furious, had threatened to put her out on the street to make it up, but she'd lowered her eyes and had begun to cry, and he'd given in. That was the first night she could remember feeling shame as she manipulated a man into forgiving her her transgressions.

But it wouldn't be the last. Here, five years later, no longer allowed to play in Vegas, Reno, or Tahoe, barred from all but one Atlantic City casino, she couldn't count the nights she'd fallen asleep crying in shame at having to lie and cheat and manipulate the feelings of a man who cared for her. It began to scare her, on a distant level, when the shame disappeared and such behavior became commonplace.

Brian O'Shea had been her savior. Some of the people out here were about to force her into prostitution to make her square up. She'd run the gamut of caring, loving men who were drawn to her soft light skin and her air of vulnerability. By the time she'd hit Atlantic City, the word was out on her and it wasn't good.

Which didn't seem to bother O'Shea too much. He'd been loving and attentive at first, although he'd told the casino workers that she wasn't allowed a line of more than three thousand a night. It had lasted for some time, too, his kindness, before it began to turn bad.

He wouldn't put her out but he stopped being so nice, would make cutting, rude remarks to her, always when they were alone, but still, the words hurt. Like yesterday, telling her to come up and blow him, he'd take a grand off the bill. A year ago, he'd have never been so crude.

Last night, though, had been more than she could stand. Brian telling her that he'd take ten grand off the tab if she'd "be good" to a friend of his. She'd been drinking throughout the day and drank more while Brian thought she was cleaning up for the date, dropping a full 'lude, too, to make it go away, the hurt she was feeling. Hurt not because of what Brian was requesting, but rather because she found the prospect rather attractive.

Ten grand a shot, and she'd only have to spend thirty nights with strangers to get off the hook. And as soon as she was, boy, she was gone, out of there. There were places now that would take you in if you admitted you had a gambling problem, free of charge, too, and help you break the pattern. She'd pay Brian off, go to one of those places and straighten her life out.

It was the thought of maybe being able to manipulate the high roller into a big tip that drove her over the edge.

He touched her arm. Where was she? Yeah, telling this stranger that she'd decided to kill herself when the realization struck that she was about to become a whore. A high-paid whore less than seven years after leaving the farm and heading for L.A. as the prettiest girl in town.

"So O'Shea wanted you to go with this guy to what, keep him in the casino?"

She nodded her head. She'd been under sedation most of the day and was riding the wave of a high as she spoke, mellowing out, feeling that the confession would be a good thing for her. He was so nice to talk to.

She cursed herself for ever making plans to screw him to see how bad it was, doing it for money. He wasn't that type and goddamnit, neither was she.

Was she?

She said, "It's more than that. Brian runs a game in one of the needle suites after the casino closes. The guy took him for a bundle the last few nights. Brian wanted me to go to him to get him the hell out of last night's regular casino game, let him cool off, figuring that by the time he got through with me, his luck would have run cold. The man, he took me to his suite the second I sat down next to him." She threw her hair back with a toss of her head. "I meant more to him, I guess, than winning more of Brian's money."

"I can see why."

Sudden tears filled her eyes. "Do you, really?" she said, then cursed herself again because of the desperation in her voice.

"What happened to the guy?" he asked her, and she was grateful that he hadn't seemed to notice her anguish.

"When I tried to . . . when I did that last night, he checked out. Pissed off, maybe, that I'd rather die than fuck him. Maybe mad at Brian for offering something that maybe wasn't his to give."

"You're not, you know."

"Not what?"

"His to give out."

"You're wrong there, my friend. Until the bill's paid off, he can do anything he wants, really." It was good, talking like this. Maybe she wouldn't have done it if she hadn't had the drugs to ease her inhibitions, but she was glad that she was opening up, being herself for a change instead of trying to act like she was enjoying sex with a fat pig like Brian O'Shea. It was kind of like the old days, in the kitchen with some of the drug dealer's servants, talking and laughing together, insiders, having fun while the master of the house did his dark dealings in cavernous rooms.

She kicked off her shoes and put her feet up on the hassock, right there next to his, rubbed his stockinged left foot with the toes of her right. Like buddies, that's all.

"He owns me," Conway said, without drama, stating a fact she'd accepted.

"Until you pay him off, is that it?"

"Probably with interest."

"Well then, it's easy, isn't it?"

"Sure it is." Conway said it and began to laugh. "All I have to do is win three hundred thousand dollars, some change. Pay him off and walk away." She began to laugh a little harder and found she couldn't stop, was laughing hysterically and with bitterness. Panic began to clutch at her, there she was out of control, laughing and sobbing and slobbering down her chin onto her gown, and she got up, began to pace aimlessly, without a destination in mind, just trying to get away from him so he would not witness her breakdown.

But he wouldn't allow it, caught her as she made her break, grabbed her and held her and didn't *that* feel good, strong arms around her squeezing gently. The man Lano now making shushing sounds in her ear, caressing her as one would a frightened child.

After a time, she began to relax, and the sobbing stopped.

"I'm sorry," she said. They were seated on the couch. His arm was around her shoulders and he was sitting forward, watching her with concern.

He said to her, "Remember a little while ago, when I said it would be easy?" and she nodded, afraid to speak, not trusting herself to. Things were happening inside her head that she couldn't stop, had no control over, and these things frightened her.

"Well, what I meant was, it's easy, because I could pay the bill off for you, give Brian his money, you're out of the woods."

She stared at him, trying to make his words make sense. Was he offering her three hundred thousand dollars? Just like that?

When she found her voice and trusted it enough to use it she said, "And what's in it for you? I mean, why would you do something like that?"

It was his turn to look away now, staring off, not being obstinate or anything, she could tell, but searching for an answer. Maybe trying to say what he wanted to without sounding corny. When at last he turned back to her they were no longer touching, but his eyes, God, they had the impact of a slap in the face, burning into her, hotly.

This Lano Branka guy said to her, "Maybe it's because I've never done anything nice for anyone before, all right?" with his voice breaking there on the last word, as if he was ashamed to admit it, and damnit to hell, there it was again, she was losing it, breaking down into sobs as he came to her, put his arms around her, and she hugged him hard, crying for him rather than for herself, surprised because in her ear she could hear the soft snuffling sounds he was making as he held her.

18

Percy Fincher sat in his mother's living room, watching her pour herself another stiff one. Lester's death was her excuse today, grief giving her the perfect justification for getting swacked. Before Lester's death, she'd managed to find other excuses on a daily basis.

Usually that excuse being a mixture of self-pity and pride. Nobody loved her, no one ever came to see her anymore. After all she'd done for them, all alone after the death of their father. Percy was old enough to remember his father, matching her drink for drink, sometimes giving her the back of his hand when she got too mouthy. He remembered after the man's death feeling a strange combination of grief and relief, glad that the man was gone and would no longer be around to beat him and his brothers. Then feeling guilty, too, right away behind the relief.

Percy sighed, squirmed in his chair, decided to give it one more shot. "That stuff's no good for you, Ma, you know that?"

"You gonna deny a woman a drink, her son not cold in

the ground, huh?" Her once-blond hair was colored now, thin, looking a little cheap there atop her head. Her eyes were bloodshot, and her hands shook. There were broken veins on her puffy cheeks, across the bridge of her nose, and crisscrossing her legs. A road map of alcoholism, Ma was.

"There's nothing worse than a reformed drinker," his mother said, then took a solid sip, closed her eyes as the straight cheap booze hit her innards. She took a deep breath. "Not everyone needs some sort of shitty self-help group to straighten themselves out, you know." Said with an accusing glare. His mother had never accepted the fact that one of her sons had slipped into the pit and had sought help. She probably believed that even if he was an alcoholic, he should be man enough to pull himself up by the boot-straps, get it together without sitting around tables, mouthing psycho-babble. She probably thought that what they discussed was their mothers' mistreatment of them.

He tried another tack.

"Did Lemuel call today?"

"Hmmf. Mr. Big Shot Coroner rich man. Too good to call his mother and see if she's bearing up. Hasn't set foot in this house in two years, did you know that?" Percy knew it and could understand it. He decided that his best move was to get the hell out of there, right now, before he got a glass and joined her on the binge.

"I gotta go, Ma."

"Yeah? Where you gotta go, eh? Off to one of those goddamn AA meetings? Too weak to make it without a bunch of sots, telling you about God?"

Percy didn't answer her, because he wasn't sure if he could and still show respect for her grief.

In his car, driving back to Longport, he came to believe that what he was doing was for the best, dogging Gaetano Biari, keeping an eye on who came and went. Eventually, if he could talk his brother into putting enough pressure on that on-the-take son of a bitch Daniels, one of the guys nailed for hanging out at the Biari mansion would maybe break, even if Gaetano didn't.

It wouldn't be too hard, getting Lemuel to keep the heat on. The boys, for some reason, had always stayed close. Even when Percy had moved to Akron, his brothers had written him, supported him. They saw things a bit differently than their mother did, maybe because they'd seen him drunk too often and Ma had as a rule been passed out by the time he came home.

He had to get his mind off his mother. He hadn't been to a meeting in the week he'd been back, and the thought of her, sitting there night after night pouring that cheap rotgut down her throat, man, it was killing him.

So think about something else. Like paybacks.

As a rule, the way the Biaris thought, so Atlantic City went, and that meant that no one would kill Lester without permission. The old man ran the city with an iron grip, no one could do anything without his okay, so even if he hadn't given the hit order himself he'd given it his blessing, which, in Percy's eyes, made him responsible.

The key to it, though, was the son, Gaetano. Gaetano had always been the weak link in the chain. The war or something had screwed him all up, made him lose his balls. Percy was twenty-six, sober three years. The war in Vietnam had ended when he was eleven. It was, to him, a distant memory, remembered only because the old man would watch the TV news at seven, eating his dinner on a tray in the tiny living room, grunting and saying, "Well, would you look at that?" when they showed the official body count for the week. The old man would say: "All the goddamn Veetnemeese we's killing, surprised they's any left to fight." To Percy, the war was experienced through the watching of movies in theaters, where you got up and walked out after it was over. He couldn't understand how anyone could have lifelong mental problems due to something that had happened to him maybe twenty years back.

He had been tailing Gaetano the night before, had

watched him go from his home to the house of his mistress, spend an hour there and then head out, driven in a Lincoln, to some cabarets to do some light drinking and some heavy business. Percy had used his telephoto lens and his Nikon to record the faces of all the parties Gaetano met with. He was a private citizen here in A.C., but he'd bet the FBI would be more than interested in the photos, when they got into the act.

Gaetano had been pulled out of the bar near four by his driver, who raced Biari to the car, handed him the cellular phone. Percy had watched as the man had sobered up right away, sat up in the front seat and talked in short sentences, mostly nodding, then had hung up and given an order to the driver. He'd followed them to the airport, and although he was dead tired, was intrigued enough by the sight of the tall young man they met there to stay on their tail.

Ange Biari was getting old, time being one enemy who always won the battle, if you were good enough to get past the lesser foes. He was, everyone knew, an early riser and one to take to his bed at a decent hour. So why was this guy being driven out to the mansion this late at night? He had to be someone important, maybe even the son of a bitch who'd pulled the trigger on Lester.

In Percy's mind, upon his arrival from Ohio for the funeral, there had been only a vague plan: follow Gaetano Biari, get enough on him to turn him over, squeal to the feds. If the younger Biari's mind was screwed up, Percy figured, maybe the thought of fifteen years or so in a federal prison under a RICO conviction would be enough to get him to drop the dime on whoever killed his brother. In any case, he couldn't go back to Akron, not when his mother was drinking herself to death and Lester was lying, unavenged, in a cold and lonely grave.

So maybe he'd blown it with the fellow last night, maybe that scumbag wasn't the guy who'd killed Lester. But he was up to no good, in any event, wasn't he? Shooting out to Ange Biari's house in the middle of the night, personally picked up by Biari's only son? And that prick, Daniels, he'd given him a lecture about harassing the honest citizens, come to gamble in their fair town. A light slap on the wrist, not harsh enough to make him suspect foul play within the department, nothing that would look bad before a jury, just a captain of homicide doing his job, trying to keep more bodies from turning up on his shores.

Well, the man, Pella, had seen him, made him, that was for sure. Percy had gone out of his way to let Pella know he was under surveillance. So okay, it had been a shot in the dark, following him instead of hanging around, following Gaetano back home. He knew where Gaetano lived, but if they'd taken this guy back to the airport, that would have been something, wouldn't it? Something the feds might be interested in, too. They were sure dragging their feet on this one. Well, he'd get enough evidence to make them come into it somehow. In some capacity. They might be slow to join the battle, but once they were in it, they were ruthless. Maybe he'd even have a talk with this Pella character, see where that led. He didn't look too tough before, especially when he'd spotted Percy inside in the unmarked squad behind him. Percy thought the man was going to pee himself.

The Biaris had to be involved. There was no way around that.

And the two of them would pay. Even if he had to kill them himself.

It was eight in the evening on a Saturday night and, sure enough, as he drove past the Biari estate he caught a glimpse of Gaetano's big car in the circular drive, the motor running. The driver was waiting inside the car, which meant that he wasn't going to be long.

No matter what happened, following him would be a better thing for Percy to do than sit around, watch his mother get blitzed. He checked his camera, laid it on the seat next to him, parked at the curb outside the main gates and settled in for the wait. Let them spot him. That might make things a little more interesting. Yeah, follow them close, see what comes of it.

Lano sat in the huge tub, soaking, a cold bottle of beer on the wide marble ledge leading all the way around it, like a swimming pool. There was a TV set into the far wall, and it was on to the casino station, Lano in a bathtub watching Brian O'Shea demonstrating the proper way to beat the house at blackjack. He was watching but paying it no mind. His thoughts were on Conway.

She was in one of the bedrooms, resting. She'd wanted to leave, after she'd stopped crying. Had tried to get up and he'd stopped her, hands on her shoulders, and had come dangerously close to making a move that might have led to disaster. He couldn't allow her to think that he was offering the money she needed to get free of O'Shea in return for sex. Although that would have to have been the world's most expensive piece of ass, three hundred dimes' worth. He'd held her by her shoulders and fought the urge to make the move, Conway not looking at him, her right hand on her brow. Her face was a mask of confusion and—what?—maybe fear.

She needed to be alone and he'd told her, gesturing at the penthouse suite, this joint, there's enough room for us both. He'd told her that she needed time away from O'Shea and the others, any high rollers who might take a liking to her, while she thought things over.

It was a funny thing for Lano, trying to convince someone to take his money. It left him feeling strange and a little weak. It was a good feeling, though.

He wondered now, why had he made the offer? It was a spur-of-the-moment thing, said and then already done, and he'd stick by it. Everyone should have a chance, their shot. He'd had his, and the money, even minus her three hundred, was a good sum. He would still be rich. Rich enough to do whatever he wanted. She'd asked him for help. He'd help her.

But was it that simple? Was anything that easy? He'd pulled her out of the ocean, felt a responsibility toward her, another new feeling. He'd never felt responsible for anyone in his life. It was a day for firsts. He knew, too, that if she didn't get out of town, eventually, when she was healthy again, O'Shea would have her doing business with guys who took a shine to her. The next time she did it, he wouldn't be there to pull her away.

But was it his problem? If she was a compulsive, she'd pay O'Shea back and it would be business as usual, Conway gambling then for a stake big enough to blow town in style, maybe pay for a classy gambling rehab clinic.

What it came down to was, how much did he want to help her? He didn't gamble for the money, you kept score with cash, that's all. So the gift of the three hundred wasn't that big a thing. He knew guys who owed Art three times that and still came into the casino back home every weekend, acting as if they had millions. No, money was for playing with, that's all. The time it would take to straighten her out, if she wanted help, that was another story.

A thought hit him with sudden clarity. It had been rolling around in his mind since the previous evening, back in the casino when his back was to the wall, there but as yet unformed, Lano too afraid then to confront it, carry it further. Now he was wondering, if he helped her out, maybe somewhere down the road it would rub off on him, he could get some help for himself.

He started in the tub, his elbow hitting the bottle and sending it rolling.

Am I a compulsive? The answer had always been there, no longer indistinct, not since last year when he'd near killed himself to pay back Tough Tony at six for five. He'd wondered then, about Gamblers Anonymous. Maybe dropping into a meeting, not telling anyone his real name, maybe even telling them he was there to see if the meetings could help his brother. The thought had passed through his mind and had been gone, quickly. As quickly as the promises about giving up the booze when in the throes of a hangover. Nothing of substance there. Just wind blowing.

But back then he'd had nothing to lose. Now, he was a millionaire.

No one knew the odds better than Lano. He knew that what was happening to him was something that happened once in a lifetime. He could, without half-trying, lose this million and a million more within a week or two of high-stakes gambling.

But God, it had been so good, winning it, knowing he was going to win it, the confidence, the crowd cheering him on. Could he give that up?

Yeah, and if he lost the million, how many of those happy gamblers would give a shit? He could hear them now, pointing to him as he left a casino, telling their companions, "There's the asshole, had a million bucks last week. Look at him now, stupid bastard."

And the feeling, what about that? The half a hard-on, was that normal?

Art had told him once that the difference between a compulsive and a regular joe was that they might both go a little wild with the fever, lose the house, the car, the family in a crap game, and the regular joe would go out there, build it all up anew, and never gamble again. Write it off to experience. The compulsive, well, he'd make promises. Try, too, to live up to them. As soon as there was a poke, though, man, he'd be off, losing it all again, over and over until he sought help or killed himself or wound up in the trunk of his car, stinking up the long-term parking lot at O'Hare Airport. Always trying to get even, to get all the way back. Never knowing that all he was getting was further and further into the hole, the hole then twice as big to crawl out of, then twice again, and again and again until it was a bottomless pit, swallowing you alive.

Lano had a chance now. He'd won big, against the odds. Maybe it was time to do something, before it was taken away from him. He thought of Conway and tried to remember when the last time was that he'd cried, and was surprised to think that it hadn't happened until after he'd won the money. Had he been crying due to his lifelong lack of feelings for others, or was there something else there? Wondering now if he had cried because he was indeed a compulsive, crying for the money that he already knew would be lost, crying because he knew up front that a life of happiness was not for him . . .

Unless he changed.

The beer had formed a foamy puddle on the floor tile, and Lano reached over, picked up the bottle and tilted it to his lips. Sleep on it, he decided, see if he still felt like changing in the morning. If his good intentions were still there he could get out of town in a hurry, with the woman and the bulk of the money. If not, if he reverted to type, then he'd tell the woman he had a change of heart, put her out. She wouldn't be his problem.

Even as he decided that he knew it wasn't to be, because the thought of doing it hurt him. Then knew it wasn't to be, because there she was, walking in hesitantly, wrapped in a Shamrock Casino terry-cloth bathrobe that came to her knees. She walked slowly but with determination to the television, snapped it off, then came to the edge of the tub, slowly, slowly, spread her arms and the robe dropped. Lano had to take a deep breath at the sight of her naked, then, slowly, she lifted her head until their eyes met, something there in hers telling him this was to be no simple piece of ass, something important was happening here, and then, without saying a word, she stepped down the three stairs and waded over to him.

19

She said to him, later, "I feel sorry for a lot of the guys that come here, you know? I mean, I know how it sounds, someone like me, in the hole as deep as I am, feeling sorry for some guy who owns junkyards or has a restaurant and makes a good dollar. But they're stuck and they don't know it. Maybe in a different way than me, but still stuck, aren't they?"

He asked her in what way they were stuck, if they were doing so good, not getting it. Getting her, though. Watching and listening as she spoke, naked and unashamed, speaking hesitantly at first then with conviction as she got into it, using little hand gestures to make a point. Lano wondered how long it had been since she'd had someone to open up with. Then wondered how long it had been since he'd had someone to do that with himself, becoming disappointed and a little disgusted with himself when the answer came to him: not since Millie.

It seemed so easy a thing to do, once you got going. It

THE PRIME ROLL · 203

started and as you spoke, the other one nodded, as if knowing what you meant, you gave each other the elbow from time to time, a little nudge as you kidded around and tried to ease the mood a little while discussing things of a serious nature. Then when one of you finished, the other changed the subject, spoke of something else. Or maybe you just held each other for a while, comfortable without words.

God, it was good, he'd almost forgotten how good.

"I mean, like, take the guys with all the heavy gold jewelry and the Rolex watches. They wear the stuff and play at the five-dollar tables and think they're successful because they got out of the Bronx. They don't understand, they've traded one kind of . . ." she paused to think of the proper word, "*desperation* for another." Conway nodding her head, confirming her choice. "Traded the desperation of the ghetto for the desperate search for acceptance, what they call class, telling everyone how hard it was growing up, sensitive when the dealers don't kiss their ass for them. Like they're special, coming here. It's all an act to them, a game. They want everyone to stand up and cheer them. Look at me, the big shot."

"Back home," Lano said, "on Rush Street, there're guys, hang around the bars, come in after getting off the night shift on the line at the Ford plant in Hegewisch, dressed to kill in silk suits. They get a few in them, tell the girls they're drug dealers. They get laid a lot, too. I used to watch them, wondering why anyone who had a good job would ever want to lie and have someone think they're scumbag drug pushers. When they couldn't get lucky, they'd flash their pay until someone like me conned them into a little game of craps in the alley. It was funny, they'd roll a six, I'd tell them, 'Even money you don't come right back' and they'd jump on it, like they were getting a deal, gonna double their money. The thing of it was, they never even knew they were losers. They walked into that alley thinking they were gonna make a killing off the rube had a few too many in him, drop all their dough, then couldn't wait until next week, come back and lose the next check to me."

"That's what I mean, what I was trying to say. They're losers and they don't even know it." Conway spoke the words and looked at him, her eyes wide, neither one of them wanting to carry it much further, to its logical conclusion, but Lano knew, and from the hurt look in Conway's eyes, could tell that she knew, too.

They, the two of them, were the real losers, because they knew it and did nothing about it. The Ford-plant guys, the guys who owned the junkyards, they played the game for a short time then went back to being who they really were. It was just that to them: a game.

Where is there, Lano wondered, for me to go when the game ends?

The old man was slipping and there wasn't a thing Gaetano could do about it. Whenever he brought it up, mentioned that maybe it was time to slow down a little, the old man would go berserk, act like he used to at fifty, when he could get away with smashing lamps and breaking sticks of furniture without having to worry about having a stroke. Finally, when he calmed down, he would tell Gaetano that as soon as Tomase raised the five million, things would be slower. He'd brought three already, and when the other two were here, he'd have his spot. Tomase would come in, take over the day-to-day operations, and Gaetano could be his good strong right arm, the old man himself a counselor to be turned to not out of respect but from need.

The stupid fucker thought he was going to live forever.

On top of that, he doesn't even hand the business over to his only son, but to some piece of shit gambler from Chicago who was buying his way in with money he'd robbed from his last boss. Was this a man to be trusted with the Biari millions?

Gaetano had to admit, five million was some serious money. It bought respect. He'd admit, too, that maybe he'd had some problems over the years, since the war. But he was getting better. At least he was off the maintenance doses of Thorazine the docs used to make him take to keep the demons away. He was going to be okay, would be able to handle things.

He'd tell the old man these things and his father would look at him, shake his head. Tell him that Tomase was a Sicilian and that Mad Mike character was from Naples, so it was okay to steal from him. Tell him that one Sicilian would never steal from another, ever. It was a matter of honor.

To Gaetano, this was a crock of shit.

Still, he was the boss, the man who'd carved a niche for them years ago and had fought tooth and nail to get the gambling referendum passed over a decade ago. So what if he was losing it a little? Any mistakes he made could be covered. There was a major one now, a gaffe the old man wasn't aware of and would go through the roof if he ever found out about. Well, Tomase had called from Philly, and was even now on his way here, ahead of schedule, but the way things were going he would be a welcome sight. If the old man didn't trust him, his only son, if the old man insisted on giving leadership to Tomase, then all he could do as a loyal son was to back the decision all the way.

Besides, he'd made millions here in Atlantic City, especially when the old man was away doing his three-year bit in Florida. There were millions more to be passed down to him with Tomase at the wheel, with little chance of doing time himself. The strike forces wanted the men at the top, not the middle men, and particularly not him. Hell, he was, in their eyes, a war hero. So what if the old man had pulled strings, gotten him medals he hadn't deserved? Hell, Army officers were no different than civilians, you waved money in their faces and they listened to you. No, it might not be a bad thing, staying where he was.

But he'd have to have a little talk with Tomase as soon as he could, tell him about the mistakes his father had been making, about the major mistake he'd made just last night, right here in this room.

There was Pop, behind the desk now, wearing a red-white-and-blue Nike jogging suit. Little hard-looking guy with the white hair, chomping a cigar. Fifty years ago he'd created a gangster persona for himself and since then had grown into it, in character around the clock, the old Ange who'd worked the docks in Bayonne a distant memory, probably even forgotten.

Gaetano felt a moment's shame because of his earlier disrespectful thoughts. The man knew what he was doing. If he thought Tomase was the best man for the job, then so be it. He'd back him up, bury the resentment, and make his money the way he always had, with little exposure and even less chance of getting popped.

One good thing about it, it got him out of the house. His wife, Belinda, was suddenly certain that he was having all these great love affairs because he was getting called out of the house so late at night by the old man. He was the only man he knew in their line of work who only had one mistress, for God's sake, but he'd gone home last night and had to listen to it, Belinda carrying on and crying, making a Bette Davis scene out of it. "Where did I go wrong?" holding the back of her hand to her forehead.

It would be a good thing for Tomase to get here and take the reins. He would want his own people around him, guys he'd known for years, and out of respect to the old man wouldn't dare cut Gaetano's piece of the pie. He could spend more time with Belinda and the kids, get to know the boys, hell, they were teenagers already and didn't want any part of him. Just wanted the season tickets to the Jets games and adios, and by the way, can we take the car? Yeah, it would be good, acting like a normal person again.

"Pop?"

"Goddamnit, can't you see I'm busy?" As usual, treating him like a little kid when they were alone. He had been about to ask if it would be all right to go on home for a couple of hours, come back when Tomase arrived. But now, he wouldn't dare.

The old man was muttering now. "Bother me, I'm trying to work. Shit, you fucked up enough."

Gaetano was hesitant to challenge him, because recently the man had a habit of reverting. He'd get upset and begin the hollering, mixing English with Sicilian dialect, calling him a "stupido cockasuck," or a "son-ah-me-beetch," throwing in a few threats, as if Gaetano were one of the help. But still, it hadn't been his fault . . .

"What was I supposed to do huh?" He stopped, listened to what he was saying. He'd sounded like a little kid, whining, while a bully rubbed his skull with his knuckles. He controlled himself, began again.

"Listen, it was a sound plan, Pop. Wally West just couldn't hit the guy with the cop following him."

"You was supposed to make sure you wasn't being followed, you stupe."

"Hey, the cop must have been here already, watching the place." Gaetano said it and watched his father stare at him with a mixture of contempt and pity.

"To think," the old man said, so softly that Gaetano decided he was talking to himself, "you come outta my balls." He shook his head and bent to his desk, returning to his work.

"Hey," Gaetano said, then rose. "Fuck this. I'm going over to the Palermo right now, settle this thing. Fuck it, and fuck *him*. Who's he, we gotta kiss his ass? The cop too, he don't know shit."

The old man looked up, mad. "Siddown, you stupe." There was a quiet, implied threat in his voice. Gaetano, in spite of his feelings, obeyed. His father sighed, shook his head. Man sitting there acting like he's talking to a retard.

"Gaetano, how you get this way? The war do this to you, eh? Listen to me, 'cause I ain't got the time, explain things all night.

"We got the FBI sniffing around, just waiting for the United States Attorney to get home from his weekend skiing trip to drop down on us like a swarm of flies. There's already a dead union leader can maybe be linked to me. We got a cop, probably seen this character Branka come outta my house at dawn. First thing he does, he hangs around, sees where the guy lives, goes to the cops. Now, I own half the cops, but the other half, they don't play with us. They know what this guy is saying and what he's doing. Hell, half of them grew up with him or with one of his brothers. So what happens if Branka gets whacked? What you think the cop tells the FBI then, huh? Now you get it?"

"Hey, the cop can go, too."

"Sure he can. Guy's got a badge, just whack him out, right?"

Gaetano took a deep breath. The old man was making fun of him, but he was used to that. There was no sense in getting all angry about it. What was important was that the family didn't fall apart, that he didn't have to go to prison again. Well, he wouldn't wait for Tomase. When he spoke now he spoke softly, slightly afraid of the effect his words would have.

"Pop, when you grabbed the gun from the guy last night, you gripped the smooth part, the barrel."

His father looked up, sharp-eyed and alert. There was no old man sitting in that chair now, there was a vulture, looking for a weakness.

"What did you say?" He spit the words out, disbelieving, Pop thinking Gaetano was putting him on, trying to hurt him back.

"You grabbed the gun by the *bar*rel, Pop. I told West after he killed the guy to wipe it clean. After the guy didn't get whacked, I didn't want to tell you until it was clear you didn't want him hit. If we were gonna do him, I'da just had the thing wiped clean, put in his hand."

"And you didn't say nothing?"

"I didn't want to get you going."

"Get me going?"

"Pop, it was supposed to be a simple hit . . ."

"You stupido cockasuck!" Ange Biari screamed, rising from the chair, "You dumb son-ah-me-beetch! Why you ignorant—"

The old man continued to rant and Gaetano held his tongue, unhappy, but knowing better than to say anything.

Art the Arm was tired, dead on his feet, but his mind was alert and racing. Had he gone too far with Lano? He'd tried, since he'd taken the kid in, to be a father to him without showing the memory of Lano Sr. disrespect. Maybe he should have been more affectionate to the boy. More understanding. Instead of always pushing, trying to make the kid into a spitting image of himself or his father. He should have let the boy just be himself.

It was very late, nearing dawn. But he couldn't sit back and allow this kid to get killed, out there in New Jersey, way in over his head, playing with guys who'd invented the rules, some of which Lano wasn't even aware existed.

He checked the dough, then locked it in the vault. Christ, if nothing else, he'd had the best weekend of his life. The weather had driven them all indoors this weekend. But now the place was almost dead. Art watched Elihue on the TV screen yawning in huge gasps, the pills the big black man had been sucking on the past two days wearing off now. He'd close up at six, pay Elihue and send him home to do whatever the guy did between Sunday morning and Friday evening, when he reported to work. A good hustler, Elihue. Pay him five bills a night and turn him loose, man watched the door like a hawk and guarded it with his life.

He tried to think of Elihue, of anything but Lano, but it wasn't working.

Lying to Lano years back about Millie Swan, what about that? He'd seen the look in the kid's eyes when he'd told him that Millie was working at O'Shea's Shamrock.

Had he been wrong? It had been a judgment call. Millie had come to him, pregnant with Lano's child, and he had told her what he felt to be true. Christ, he'd done the girl a *favor*. Both of them, when it came down to it. Shit, Lano would have been divorced in a month, or the woman would have killed him in his sleep, the first time she found lipstick on his shorts.

No, it wasn't easy, this father bullshit.

He'd made a vow, which he believed to be sacred, to the kid's old man. He'd raise him to manhood. Make him a man. The problem was, at this point in time, Lano was light-years away. Of age, legally, yeah, but far from a man. Old Uncle Art had always been there to pull his fat out of the fire, always there to keep him from having to grow up.

Well, not this time. He'd given the kid a dig, had first told him to come on home to give him the out if he wanted it and then swiped at his balls to make sure he didn't. The boy had to learn that this life was no fun, nothing to admire. The books and movies made it look good, but Art knew better. He'd sent a boy to Atlantic City, and if the boy survived, he would come back a man. He'd sent him with the best of intentions, not knowing about Tomase, but things happened, were destined, and now it was up to Lano.

Art wouldn't be able to sleep, would not be able to rest until the thing was resolved, one way or the other, and if it turned out for the worst, if Lano got killed, then nothing would stop him from going to Atlantic City and taking care of the Biaris and Tomase himself. But for now, it was up to Lano. Lano would survive by his wits or die due to his lack of them. In their world it was survival of the fittest, and he'd given the kid all the tools he'd need to survive.

Art hoped to hell the kid had enough sense to use them.

Art sighed, shook his head, and reached for the phone. It didn't surprise him to learn from the clerk at the Palermo that Lano hadn't been seen all night. He felt a little disappointment and a lot of relief. The kid had chickened out, was coming home. Thank Christ. There were better ways to teach him about the life. Maybe, if he asked Mike to, the Mad One would sit the kid down in his office, put the fear of God in him. Give him a look at the Chair. Art smiled, feeling a little refreshed, figuring it wouldn't take more than an hour or so for Lano's plane to land at O'Hare. He'd wait, give the kid some shit when he picked him up, just to keep him on his toes.

They would doze off for a while and after a time one of them would start in again. Sometimes they would make love, and sometimes they would just cling to each other, wordlessly. Lano lay in the dark with his hands behind his head, wondering about things. For instance, about what O'Shea had said to him. And about how foolish it would be to stay here in a town where he might well be heading for an early death, just to prove something to himself.

Things had changed here, that was for sure, and this woman beside him—now stirring and gently reaching out, touching his chest softly, as if reassuring herself that he was still there—was the reason.

Did he need false assurances of his manhood? Not likely. He'd felt more like a man after breaking down in her arms than he had in years, acting the part in dark alleys, hotel rooms and the back rooms of mob-controlled gin mills. Something had broken loose inside him, things he'd held back for years were right there, in his heart, waiting to be identified by an intellect to which they were foreign. Things he'd buried after Millie left him.

No, all of a sudden he didn't feel the need to prove anything to Art or the Biaris or even to himself. He had all of the proof he needed, where it counted. If they confronted him he would not back down, but he would not go looking for them, as he'd been planning, or make them come to him by blatantly disobeying their orders.

He knew, now, what he would have to do. Tonight, too, not wait until morning when the sun was shining and he could go down to the vault, take a look at his million and maybe change his mind, want to turn it into two million. No, act now, while the thought was fresh in his mind and the desire strong. He'd backslid too many times to trust himself. He would go get the money from the other casinos, then from the safe at the Palermo, then come back, collect Conway and get the hell out of town before he had a chance to think himself out of it. He'd thought himself into deep holes too many times before to want to take the chance of doing it again.

"Conway?"

"Mmmm?" There was a tiny smile touching her lips, her unlined forehead held a gentle sheen of sweat. The slight puffy spots under her eyes endeared her to him.

"Conway?" he said again, and this time she reached for him, anticipating his desires, and he had to shake her a couple of times to get her eyes open and focused on him.

When he was sure she was awake he asked her, "Is there a casino limo, a car I can get, with a security guy maybe to drive? Can I call O'Shea and get one?"

"What for?"

He told her what he was going to do and for a moment she stared at him, wide-eyed now, fully awake, the panic in her eyes evident and alive. It passed quickly, but it had been there and he had seen it.

She didn't want to leave and he knew it. Maybe it was that she just wasn't sure yet. He felt a knife thrust into his chest, insecurity gripping him, wondering if he'd made a mistake. Was she just playing with him, a woman looking for a way out only in some fantasy? Would she change her mind about him when the dawn broke and the fever returned?

"You don't have to call Brian. I have access to the car, and I think I know a security guard who'll get out of bed to guard you, you want. His wife's the dealer you handed that big tip to when you won."

"I'm gonna take a shower. Would you line it up? We've only got about an hour before the casinos close for the night."

She was sitting up now, Lano on the pillow at eye level with her small, round perfect breasts. He could see the soft blue lines and the freckles on the milky white skin. God, please let her come with me.

"On one condition," she said, and when he asked her what she said, "you have to take me with you."

Aloud, softly, Lano said, "Thank you," with feeling, not really speaking to Conway at all.

The guard's name was Edward Spencer and he carried a .38 Colt in a polished leather holster, low on the right hip. He drove them to each of the casinos in one of the house limos, waited right outside the casino doors with the car idling and the heater on and the snow drifting down, Conway in the backseat shooting the breeze with him because she was barred from all the casinos in town. They'd talk about Lano, what a good guy he was, Edward telling her over and over about the tip Lano'd left his wife, Donna, "Christ, all that money . . ." his voice revealing awe. Lano would walk into a casino and be back ten minutes later, the money in the deep pockets of his overcoat. At one of the places he was followed out by a couple of guys dressed only in business suits and Edward began to get out of the car, quickly, then got back in with a sigh of relief when he discovered that they were only executives, trying to talk Lano into staying at their hotel.

Conway said, "Look at him, he's enjoying this, he's making them stand out in the cold while he leads them on."

"Shit, check him out, the way he's winking at us," Edward said.

"Isn't he something?" Conway said.

She said it and then thought it: Isn't he something? Then decided that he surely was.

There had always been the thought, in the back of her mind, that someday she'd get out. She somehow knew that one day someone would come along, someone she cared about so very much that she would run away with him, change and become everything she and her mother had always hoped she would be. Maybe even an actress. God knew, she had enough experience with sorrow to carry any phony Hollywood movie scene off.

Was this the man, though? The thought bothered her. She'd never seen her Prince Charming as an Italian, nor as a gambler. My God, she was always reading about these people and their gang wars, winding up in the trunks of their Cadillacs and Lincolns, getting murdered in Italian restaurants. She'd never even dated an Italian, although she'd come close to working for one in the recent past, when her gambling debts were so high that this dago pit boss threatened to put her out on the streets hustling to pay them off. Just the thought of that experience was enough to make her shiver, even in the warmth of the luxury stretch vehicle.

She sat looking out at Lano, working a game on the casino executives, and she said to herself, Isn't he something? Wondering in her heart just exactly what he was.

At the Palermo, Lano said, "It'll take me a little longer, get my bags packed and the money out of the safe. Don't worry, all right?" and Edward told him to take his time, he was on the payroll and was enjoying this work, would work for nothing the rest of the week for him, shit.

Lano entered the hotel and told the clerk on duty to prepare his bill and get his cash out of the safe, the guy all fidgety, giving him funny furtive looks, reminding him of the two Biaris last night in the old man's mansion. He began to walk away, thinking about the clerk, wondering what was wrong . . .

Then turned right around again and said to the guy, "You touch that house phone, and I'll break your fingers, you got me?" Decided that wasn't enough, and dragged him around the desk by the scruff of his neck, pulling him outside with him.

Someone was in the room waiting for him, that was obvious. What wasn't so obvious to Lano was how he was supposed to react, what he was supposed to do. He could get his cash and leave, right now. What would he be out, some clothing?

Yeah, but it was *his* clothing.

The thought of some mob bums—who'd already set him up once—now sitting in his room waiting for him, like he was some goof conventioneer, outraged him. There were some things you had to put up with, some things you could swallow, and some things that you just didn't have to take. Having your home invaded was one of the things you didn't have to take. He'd made up his mind not to go looking for them, but now they had come looking for *him*, and there was a difference in the act that was not to be ignored.

His game plan was: get Edward and go on up, confront whoever was in the room, straighten them out, pack and then leave. By the time they untied themselves, he figured, he could have O'Shea paid off and be on a plane heading south and west. Then he wondered how close Edward was to any of these people, decided that even if *he* hated them, the man still had to live here among them. If Lano wanted to confront them, that was his business, his risk to take, but he couldn't ask Edward to risk his life to help him settle a score, no matter how much dough he'd given the man's wife.

Edward saw him dragging the guy out of the hotel and came right out of the car, his hand on the butt of his pistol, bringing it half out before Lano opened the car door, shoved the guy in, then called Edward around to the front of the car.

"Let me have your piece," Lano said, "then take the little guy, go in there and get my money bag out of the safe. He goes near the phone, break his leg."

"What's going on?"

"You don't want to know." Lano watched as Edward hesitated, thinking it over. He was glad that they'd been having a good time, that they had been hitting it off, because there was no law that said the guy had to give him the gun, it was strictly up to him, if he thought Lano was an asshole or someone not to be trusted with the piece then it was all over, because without the gun Lano wasn't about to go up there.

Edward shrugged and nodded his head, probably too cold to worry about it much. He handed Lano his piece and pulled open the door, said, "Come on, twinkletoes, let's go get Mr. Branka's money." Lano heard the man say, "Mr. *Who's* money?" and said over his shoulder, "Pella," as he pulled open the hotel door and entered the place.

20

Two things happened, one right after the other, that gave Percy pause for thought. The first thing was, some guy was pounding on the car window—he'd fallen asleep on the job. His first thought, before it dawned on him that he might be in trouble, was to thank God that he'd left the car running. Otherwise he might have frozen to death.

He opened his eyes and shook his head, trying to jar the sleep out of it, and saw a fat, ugly little guy—hell—standing out there without a hat on, acting oblivious to the cold.

"Get outta here, you cheap copper son of a bitch . . ." the guy shaking his fist and spraying spittle on the window.

Percy rolled the window down with his left hand, brought the camera up with his right, got it positioned, and click, snapped a quick one of the guy, then watched as the man threw a hand up to his eyes, the bright flash blinding him. That was good, as it gave Percy time to drop the camera into his lap and reach under his left armpit and pull out the piece.

The man was blinking at him, not looking so tough now.

Out of the corner of his eye Percy could see a big maroon, what was it? Yeah, a Lincoln Town Car, sitting there at the gate to the mansion, a blond floozy-looking broad sitting in the passenger seat looking scared. He swung his attention back to the little fat man, pointed the pistol directly at his oversize head and said, "This is a Beretta, seven in the clip, one up the pipe, the safety's off, it's cocked, and at this range I can't miss. You want to repeat what you were saying, asshole?" That tore it, the guy hesitated, looked about to say something, then spun on his heel and raced back to the car, not looking much like a tough guy at the moment.

Percy slipped the piece back into its holster, watched as the woman said something to the man, then saw him slap her once with the back of his hand. He looked at the license plate, saw it was a rental, and he wrote down the number in his notebook. As the man laid a patch of rubber onto the Biaris' driveway, Percy smiled and said, "When tires spin, Goodyear grins."

He turned his car around, drove down to the end of the block and parked behind a thick patch of trees, in the driveway of another big house that had only one light shining in a window. He hoped they wouldn't call the cops. He could just see Biari's driveway from here.

He sat there, the snow settling on the hood of his car, and wondered what to make of the newcomer to the game, the little fat guy with the big mouth and the yellow streak, when the second thing happened.

Gaetano's car came tearing up out of the driveway, two figures in the front seat, the car screeching to a halt at the gate and both men jumping out with pistols in their hands. One was Gaetano, the other was one of the bodyguards. Percy searched his mind for the man's name, then got it. Wally West. Did time in Attica for extortion, trying to milk money out of Brooklyn store owners to keep their windows and internal organs intact before coming down here, making good with the Biaris. They got back in the car and headed away from him, toward the bridge, and he waited awhile, let them get a good head start before starting the car up and following them with his lights off.

He lost them a couple of times on their way to Atlantic City, afraid of getting too close, knowing they'd be watching for him. He'd pop on his lights and speed up, slowing down when he saw their taillights, following for a time then falling back, switching off the lights when a stray car would come between them and give him cover.

When they turned off onto Illinois Avenue, he had a good idea where they were going, to the guy, Pella's hotel, and he dropped back, went around the block and left the car in the Sands' parking lot, walked back to the doorway and stared at the big round mirror there for maybe an hour until the limo from O'Shea's Shamrock pulled up.

He stood there, patiently, with his arms crossed, his shoulder against one of the green walls, inside the well-lighted parking garage, warm and cozy in here, ignoring the stares of the attendants. Hell, he was paying, wasn't he?

But he pushed off the wall and paid attention when Pella came out of the hotel dragging the shivering, terrified desk clerk. He took a step closer when the driver—Christ, was that Edward Spencer?—handed him a pistol.

When Edward and the clerk followed Pella inside, he made his move.

He walked into the hotel with his head down and his hands stuffed into his pockets, a big loser going in to get some sleep before coming back for more in the morning. He walked past the desk—there was no one there now, the only sounds coming from the bar; jukebox music and laughter. He went straight to the stairway. Only when he was inside and away from curious eyes did he begin running up the steps, two at a time.

Lano hid the pistol in the folds of his coat until he got in the elevator, then took it to the floor under his, got out and found the stairwell. He walked up the steps, quietly, listening at the fire door for any sounds, anyone talking. It was quiet. The gun was in his hand, up by his ear, the safety off and his finger resting lightly just inside the trigger guard. He opened the door and stepped through fast, bringing the gun down and pointing it to one side of the door and shifting quickly to the other, spotting no one. He breathed deeply, through his mouth. He didn't know his hands were shaking until he saw how the gun was jiggling at his ear.

He knew, though, that his bowels were in an uproar.

Christ, how did anyone ever go into armed robbery? Carrying a gun all the time with the intention of pointing it at another human being, maybe even kill them if they balked.

All right, enough of that. It was time to get on with it.

He walked quickly to his door, frightened that someone would come out of one of the other rooms, grateful that so far he hadn't seen anyone. What would he have done if he'd come out of the stairwell with the pistol pointed out and had aimed it at some couple heading in for the night or down to the bar for a nightcap?

He put his key in the door, thought briefly about trying to whistle, to appear casual, decided that he didn't have any spit in his mouth and probably couldn't purse his lips if his life depended on it. He could feel the muscles in his jaw jumping as he clenched his teeth.

He kicked the door open and entered the room, gun down now and pointed straight out, right at the chest of Gaetano Biari, who was sitting in the chair next to the bed. The other man in the room, the guy who'd driven him here last night from the airport, was perched on the bed, pointing a pistol at Lano.

"Tell him to drop it."

Gaetano said, "*You* better drop *yours*, Lano. Way you're shaking, you're liable to have an accident, shoot me. Then where'd you be?"

The other man giggled—a high-pitched little laugh, the son of a bitch was enjoying himself—and said, "Looks about to have an accident in his pants, Mr. Biari." Lano saw Gaetano give the man a deadly look—Lano's gun was pointed at Gaetano, not at the other guy, and Gaetano wasn't laughing, and Lano followed his gaze.

Seeing a guy with icy eyes staring at him, the .357 rock-steady in a calm dry hand. Lano, feeling the sweat dripping down his wrist and feeling the gun twitching crazily, did a quick assessment and wondered if he should feel proud or ashamed.

Gaetano said, "Shut up, Wally," and Wally snickered. Lano decided that he was pegging the boss's son for a coward.

"Drop the gun, Lano," Wally said, now taunting him, making fun of Gaetano, "before we both shit our die-dees."

Gaetano leaned forward violently, said, "I said shut *up*, Wally." And Lano had had enough.

"Sit the hell back," he said to Gaetano, then turned and put the gun squarely on Wally, edged forward until the barrel was between the man's eyes. "Go ahead and shoot, Wally. See what happens."

Wally stopped sniggering and a vein began to pulse in his throat. "Be careful now—shit, that thing's loaded."

"Got something to say now, Wally? Feeling cute?"

"Put it down, Lano." Gaetano now gently suggesting.

Lano's hand was shaking terribly; the pistol was bumping Wally's forehead in time with his heartbeat. He knew what he looked like, a madman shaking, both hands on a gun and still not able to keep it still. He felt saliva drooling down his chin, and he began to breathe deeply, heavily through his nose, expelling the air harshly the way a fighter does after throwing a punch.

"Drop the gun, Wally," Lano said.

"Drop the gun, Wally," Gaetano said, echoing him. Lano wondered if he was imagining it, or if there was an edge of humor in the man's voice.

Wally was perspiring now himself, shifting a little, his mouth open and his eyes up and crossed, trying to stare at the barrel of the gun. Slowly, he pulled the sights of his pistol away from Lano's chest, opened his hand and let the gun drop onto the bed.

Lano took two steps back, motioning with his gun. "Into the toilet." And Wally didn't hesitate, stood and walked stiff-backed into the bathroom, as if expecting a bullet to enter his lower back at any second. It was a temptation, but Lano passed. Gratefully, he dropped the pistol to his side, keeping one eye on Wally through the open bathroom door.

"He's got another one on him, starts walking through that door, I shoot you, you got it, Gaetano?"

"All I want's what's in your hand, Lano." Gaetano's hands were palm-up in a gesture of peace. "We just came for the gun."

"Two of you, with Wally's gun out, broke into my room to ask me for the gun?"

"You ought to be smart enough to know, we wouldn't do anything in our town. You don't shit where you eat."

"Yeah, well, Lester Fincher must have figured he was safe, too."

And Lano knew he'd scored. The man flinched before composing himself.

"Don't pay any attention to that cop, Lano. He's from *Akron*, for Christ's sake. He don't know nothing."

"Daniels couldn't wait to call you, could he?"

Gaetano shrugged. The man was in control again, speaking with quiet authority. He had what Art would call "olive-oil bullshit," his voice making you want to trust him. His smooth assurance cut through Lano's fear, made him realize that the man thought he was an easy mark, a sucker.

Gaetano said, "Among others. We got a few calls, the past twelve hours, people telling us about you. We hear you did pretty good over at O'Shea's tonight."

What was he saying?

"Gaetano, you break into my room, bring some badass with a gun with you, what am I supposed to think?"

The man shrugged. Mr. Cool there holding his camel's-hair coat over his lap, perfectly knotted silk tie tight against the collar of his white shirt. "I don't care what you think. My father made some calls today, found out that Art overreacted a little bit, Tomase ain't about to get himself whacked, messing with you out here. We decided we needed the gun back, get it from you before *you* overreacted, killed some nigger on the Boardwalk looked at you wrong, got yourself twenty-to-life in Rahway."

"I might overreact, huh?"

"Well, you didn't act very brave last night, truth be told, at my father's house. No disrespect intended, you're still holding the gun, but let's face it, you were shitting your pants last night when we gave you the gun, you didn't want it then. What, you grow attached to it all of a sudden?"

Lano said, "Out of a clear blue sky, I can see the real need for it." Then said, "So you came up here with Wally and his three-fifty-seven in my best interest, is that right?"

For the first time Biari looked a little unsure of himself, but there was something phony there behind the eyes that didn't ring true. It seemed to Lano as if the man was laughing at him and acting afraid at the same time, as if the insecurity was put on.

Biari said, "Well, to tell you the truth, Lano," phony little flash of grin, there and gone, Silly me!, "we were supposed to put a little scare into you for going into O'Shea's after you were warned away. Now you're gonna be in the paper, a celebrity won a million dollars, and that cop from Akron can put you with us. O'Shea turns up dead, who they come looking for?"

"What's that got to do with—?"

"Lano, just give up the gun, all right?"

Lano's mind was racing. The man thought this was the gun his father had given him last night. If he was telling the truth, there was no problem. Lano would hand this one over and by the time they found out it wasn't the right pistol, he'd be gone. He'd take Wally's and would hang on to it until he got onto the plane for home.

The problem was, he didn't believe the guy.

But did that make a difference? Either way, the Biari mob wouldn't have the pistol that most likely had put Lester Fincher to sleep for all time. No one would have it. It was buried out near the ocean, where no one would find it. Maybe he could make an anonymous phone call to the feds after he was back home, have Art or Elihue tell him how to do it so they couldn't trace the phone he was calling from, run him down and make him testify. No matter what happened, one thing was certain: they weren't going to get away with this.

"I give you the gun, it's all settled, right? I walk, do what I want?"

"I'd like to tell you that's how it is, Lano, I really would, but this ain't a dream world. This is real, and the fact is, you held me at gunpoint. My father, he isn't going to be happy when he hears about that. In fact, he's gonna want to eat your liver." Gaetano sighed, worked his hands into the coat on his lap. "Not to mention all the trouble you've caused us, doing what you wanted instead of what you were told. It's like you're two different guys. The scared little kid last night at the house, and the tough punk, gonna do what he wants after he's out of the sight of the grown-ups."

That stung. Maybe because it was so close to the truth. Lano walked backward, sat down on the bed, put his forearms on his knees. He'd never understood how heavy a gun was, how hard a pistol was to hold over an extended period of time. He was getting pushed into something here, maybe the same thing they were setting him up for last night. Only now the scenery had changed, they had a way in they hadn't expected would be there when they'd begun their manipulation last night.

He made a decision, quick and without guilt. Whatever the man wanted he'd agree to, then immediately put out his mind. Screw it. He wasn't bound to them by blood oaths or by honor.

"So what do we do now, Gaetano, to make things right?"

"Give me the gun, first off. Then take Wally's and go over to your friend O'Shea, you got an in there, you beat him out of a million, he'll do anything for you. Get him all alone somewhere nice and quiet, and blow his fucking head off." Gaetano Biari smiled. "That's all."

Lano knew he should keep his mouth shut, just agree and get the hell out, but he knew it would look bad, upon reflection, if he didn't ask the obvious question. So he said, "Why Wally's gun? I was supposed to blow Virgil's head off with this one here but it isn't good enough to shoot O'Shea?"

He knew right away he'd drawn blood. Knew, too, that Biari was winging it, hadn't thought of this. Which was a relief. That meant that Angelo wasn't aware of this conversation, of what his son was trying to pull. By the time Ange was informed it would be too late. Lano and Conway would be in the wind.

Gaetano covered up fast, and Lano wondered how a guy like this stayed out of the joint, ignorant son of a bitch thought he was wise because he was born a Biari. Lano felt more and more at ease, in control and command of his emotions, as the man shrugged and said, "Let me see it."

Lano laughed. "You think I'm nuts? I hand you the gun, Wally comes charging out of the toilet or you shoot me. No, I don't think so."

"Lano, if I wanted you dead, you'd be dead, believe me." Gaetano slowly lifted his coat off his lap and Lano saw the long barrel of a chrome-plated pistol pointed directly at him. "Forty-four Smith, got an eleven-inch barrel on it, ribbed sides, blow you away and go through the walls, down the hall, kill three or four people in the elevator. All I got to do is pull the trigger." He let the gun fall into his lap, raised his hands. "All I want to do is touch the thing, check it out. It's an old piece the old man keeps in the safe, ain't been fired in years. Tell you what, bring it over here, hold the grip, put your finger on the trigger it makes you less fearful. Just let me see the barrel for a second. Come on, don't be scared. I dropped my gun and Wally's in the shit-house."

Lano couldn't understand it, but didn't argue. He walked over to Gaetano, holding the pistol, and the man bent side-ways so the thing wasn't pointed right at him, some of his cockiness gone, then held the gun with the camel's-hair topcoat, rubbed it hard a few times up and down the barrel, leaned over and stared at it hard, as if checking the serial number or something. Lano knew he was bullshitting, put-ting on a show. The key had been his rubbing the barrel, as if wiping off fingerprints . . .

He thought of the night before, Ange grabbing the gun from his son and thrusting it at him, forcing him to take it. He fought to keep his expression blank, to keep the fear out of his voice as he said, "You don't want to look down the barrel, see if it's rusty?"

Gaetano said, "After we're gone, you do that. I'm worried about it, shaking the way you are." He stood up. "We got an agreement?"

"Yeah, sure, if it'll get me off the hook. The second it's done, though, I'm gone. How safe am I gonna be back home?"

Gaetano grinned. "Shit, you're with Art Pella, who's with Mad Mike Tile. You think we're crazy?" He said it and Lano didn't answer because that's exactly what he was thinking.

"Wally, let's go!" Lano watched the man sidle out of the bathroom, giving him a wide berth. He began to lift the gun. Gaetano's pistol had disappeared somewhere, the guy was putting on his coat, ignoring Lano now. Close to him, Lano could smell expensive after-shave and see just a dust-ing of barber powder on his shirt collar. Gaetano turned to him and said, "I'm picking up Wally's gun. Don't worry, I won't give it to him until we're in the car. All right?"

Lano couldn't help himself, he had to say, "I'm not worried," to which Gaetano immediately had to say, "Sure you're not."

They walked from the room without a backward glance or another word to him . . .

And weren't out the door two minutes before there was a knock at the door and Lano went to open it, throwing the gun on the bed, opened it up expecting to see Edward and there was the cop, Fincher, holding a pistol on him.

Well, hell, just when things had been going so well. Here he was, just having scammed a couple of hard-core mobsters, at least one of them a killer, and now this. He thought about what he'd done, decided that if there had ever been any doubt about his balls or manhood it had been laid to rest. Too, he was feeling so damn good about it. Then decided, shit, there was no use backing down now. He was on a roll.

Lano smiled and said, "Listen, Percy, I was only kidding about your mother . . ." then turned his back on him and walked into the room, figuring that if he didn't get shot then the guy had a sense of humor.

21

O'Shea stood in the middle of his casino, everyone gone now, staring at the empty glass box. His pride and joy, gone. He was ostensibly supervising the installation of the slot machines, but Malcolm was doing all right there; hell, the place had just closed and half the machines were already on their stands, bolted down and ready to go. O'Shea felt the need to gamble, for action, wanting it, tasting it, but afraid to leave, unable to leave the one thing in the world he'd considered to be his lucky charm. The million was only a short walk away, locked in the vault behind the cashier's counter. Even if he wanted to, though, he couldn't get in there and look at it. He owned the place, but it took two people, he and Malcolm both, to get in there. And that was only after the time lock cut loose, which wouldn't happen for another four hours. At ten Sunday morning, the two of them would open the vault the same way they did every day, the half-million that was their cushion inside, ready to be put to use. That was usually all they kept on the premises. They, like every other casino on the Boardwalk, and for that matter the ones on the Strip and in downtown Las Vegas, had a money room, where white-gloved workers wearing pocketless jumpsuits tossed the stacks of dollars into counting machines. There were coin counters there, too, ready to be put into use first thing tomorrow. From there the cash—which had been counted under the watchful eyes of IRS agents to curtail skimming—would be transferred to interest-bearing accounts across New Jersey by a swarm of armed guards, using a convoy of three unmarked but heavily armored vehicles, two of which would be decoys.

It sure wasn't like the good old days.

Still, even if he could get into the vault, it wouldn't do him a lot of good. It wasn't his million anymore. It belonged to the one guy he'd met in his life that he couldn't figure out.

What was Lano's game? He wondered this, watching Malcolm watching him, giving him furtive little glances, seeing if he was okay before returning to the army of installers. What did the man want? Or better yet, was the man aware of *what* he wanted?

This kid, he'd thrown himself into a near-frozen ocean to save a woman he didn't even know, then came back that night to—what?—win her love, or maybe save her from something? Was he one of those types who considered himself a knight in shining armor, put on earth to rescue women from themselves? Or maybe he was just complicating it too much. Maybe the guy was just horny.

No, if that was it, he wouldn't have faced death for a piece of ass. Not in this town, where otherwise happily married but compulsive broads had been known to roll over for strangers or give blow-jobs in the back alleys for a single green twenty-five dollar chip.

So what was it? He himself had nearly handed Conway over to him. Maybe he wanted her to go for the guy, leave with him. He sure didn't feel that they had much going for themselves anymore. For the longest time he'd felt in love, but, recently, he'd been cold, distant, wanting it to end but feeling somehow responsible for her. Shit, like an old married man working the mills, carping at the old lady. Treating her like dirt and talking down to her all the time. He figured she'd be better off elsewhere, but was unable to give her up for some reason which he still wasn't able to figure out. Although he'd tried to drive her off.

Usually, when it was over, he'd give the girl a couple of grand traveling money, to get her on her feet, suitcases as a going-away present to pack all the clothes he'd paid for. But he just hadn't been able to do this with Conway, picturing her in his mind, little frail Conway hurt and confused, out in the world all alone with no place to go. No, he just couldn't do it.

She'd changed, too. At his throat all the time, rubbing it in when she'd get a few bucks ahead. Maybe he wanted her to get fed up and leave him. Maybe that's why he'd told her to go up to the high roller's room and lay him. Hoping she wouldn't, that she'd yell and scream and tell him to go to hell, pack her bags and go and he'd be free of her. As if his recent acts, treating her like a whore, would be different than trying to make her one for real.

Also, he had to admit, when she'd tried to kill herself, he'd felt a moment's pride that she hadn't gone to the room and slept with the gambler. Proud that she'd rather choose death than whoredom.

Since then, though, he hadn't been able to face her. The doctor had given her some pills, and he'd tried to speak to her, but she wouldn't see him.

Was he in love, shit, for the first time in his entire life? Naw. If that was the case, he wouldn't have thrown her together with Pella or Branka or whatever the hell his real name was.

Now there was a cool head. O'Shea had been really happy for him, one gambler to another, when he'd won the money. For a second, he'd even forgotten that it was *his* money the guy was winning. His respect had deepened when the IRS and the gaming commission idiots had come along, the kid, all deadpan, seeing them coming and announcing in a loud voice: "My God, this'll almost cover the million and a half I've already lost this year!" Stopping the IRS dudes in their tracks. He'd filled out the form, but wrote it off as a loss already on another form, wouldn't even have to claim it on April fifteenth. Smart boy, there.

"Listen, it's not like it hasn't happened before," Malcolm said now. He hadn't even seen him walk up, he'd been staring at the empty glass box, daydreaming.

"It ain't the same, and you know it. The other two times we got hit, the guys were decent enough to take a check. This kid, he wants cash, *my* cash."

"It's his right. And by tomorrow, there'll be another million in there to take its place. These slots get to running, we'll be *swim*ming in millions."

O'Shea didn't answer him. Malcolm tried again, another tack. "Word got around already. We're up six-fifty-three and change for the night. Hell, Trump's, they might make a million a day, with the slots and everything. Tomorrow, we'll have the slots, and with the push from this kid's roll, I wouldn't be surprised if we went over two mill a day for a week or two."

"I'm going upstairs."

"To sleep?" There was more than a hint of hopefulness in Malcolm's voice.

"No, to gamble."

Malcolm didn't say anything, but O'Shea knew he was angry. He could feel his eyes boring into his own. He wondered if Malcolm was about to quit.

O'Shea said, "If the big winner comes looking, send him over. Maybe he'll lose the million back. A roll like that can't last forever." He shrugged, tried to get some of his cockiness back, to replenish the affinity they had once had but which he now felt slipping away, rapidly.

"You like him, don't you?" Malcolm said, surprise in his voice.

Looking at his reflection in the empty glass box, O'Shea said, "I'll be goddamned if I don't."

Millie was dealing craps tonight, upstairs in the needle-suite private game. She'd been almost afraid to punch in, half-expecting to see a pink slip and a final paycheck there in her slot where her time card was supposed to be because it was obvious she knew Lano well. Nothing was there, though, no bad news, at least.

And no one had said anything. Thank God for that. She'd had enough problems for one day.

All she could think about was Lano. About going to him, seeing what had changed, what was different about him. Tell him about Stevie, too, instead of acting like a child, going through relatives. It had been a mistake, that's all, the thing with Art.

But the man was so wise, knew so much . . .

She had been able to hide her confusion from her son, but still, she was relieved when it was time to go to work. She'd seen Lano enter the casino out of the corner of her eye and had had the time to talk to the pit boss, switch tables, to one far away from where he was gambling. Right away, she knew she was right in her decisions, because the first table he sat down at was the one where his latest girlfriend, Conway, was playing. So be it.

Millie would be off tomorrow night. She'd rent some children's videos, watch them with Stevie and by Monday, probably, Lano would be gone, with his million dollars, going off somewhere to give it right back to somebody else.

She watched Brian O'Shea enter the suite, all smiles and

nods and waves, the man who'd lost a million dollars acting as if it didn't matter. She called out hello as he passed the crap table. He said hello, snapped his fingers and reached into his jacket pocket, pulled out an envelope, handed it to the pit boss. "When you get your break, that letter's for you," O'Shea told her, and she smiled, feeling dread. But she had to hand it to the man, at least he had the balls to can her to her face instead of stuffing the pink slip into her time-card slot.

It must have worked, the guy must have a sense of humor, because he didn't get shot. Lano walked into the room, trying to act relaxed, trying not to hunch his shoulders. He heard the door shut behind him, turned, sat down in the chair. It was still warm from Gaetano; he could smell the man's cologne, a faint reminder of the recent past. The memory gave him courage. If he could back down two mafiosi, then this cop from Akron, Ohio, would be a piece of cake.

"You knocked out one of my teeth."

"You started it." Christ, wrong thing to say, sitting here acting like a couple of little kids after a schoolyard brawl.

Fincher must have felt it too because he smiled and shook his head. He walked over to the bed, picked up the pistol, turned it in his hand, shaking his head, the faint trace of a smile on his lips. Thick lips, too. Dark-featured man. He looked like a young, tanned Victor Mature.

"It doesn't make a lot of sense." He studied the gun. "I heard every word, standing in the hall. I scooted to the stairs as soon as I guessed you were wrapping it up, when he called his dog out of the toilet." He looked away from the pistol, at Lano. Piercing green eyes blazing, not smiling now.

"You almost blew it, didn't you? Almost killed them when you walked in."

"And you didn't come charging in, either. Not like the

cops usually would do. Guess it doesn't matter, I kill them, they kill me, just a few more guineas off the street, right?"

Fincher grunted. "You hit like an African friend of mine, guy I grew up with down the road a little bit. He had the same habit, twisting the punch for more power." Lano didn't say anything. "I saw you take the gun away from Spencer outside. Biari thought this was a gun he'd given you last night. What was that bit about checking it out? It didn't make sense."

"You couldn't see it from the hall. He wiped the barrel down."

"He gave you a gun last night, then came here tonight to give you a line of bullshit a two-year-old could see through, then wiped the barrel of the gun he thought he'd given you?" Fincher held the gun in his left hand, his own pistol in his right. He turned both pieces on Lano and said, "Where's the other gun?"

Just then there was a knock at the door. "Lano, you all right in there?" Edward.

Lano said, "You want to shoot me now, or let the guard in, have a witness?"

All four of them were in the room now, Lano and Conway perched on the bed, Edward in the chair, Fincher standing. Edward had walked into the room and had smiled, then stopped short, staring at the pistols in the man's hands, and had said, tentatively, "Percy? How you doing, man?"

They spoke to each other as if the one man wasn't holding a deadly firearm in each hand, as if Lano wasn't even in the room, Conway right outside the door. Like two old acquaintances running into each other on the street.

It turned out they'd grown up together right here in town. Although they'd been on the football team together in high school, they hadn't done much socializing. Edward had said it easily and without fear, the guns put away, in their respective holsters, Fincher standing awkwardly, remembering things that had been painful and perhaps still were.

"Wasn't your fault. You weren't allowed to hang out with Africans, no more than I was allowed to run with whites." He'd shrugged. "Rules of the street." He'd seen Lano's look of surprise and had changed the subject. When Edward told Percy that Lano was all right, a good gambler and a personal friend of the family, Lano wanted to kiss him.

Conway was staring at them now, eyes wide, her head swiveling from one to the other as they spoke amongst themselves, the men slightly more comfortable with each other.

"He wants you to kill Brian?" Edward was incredulous. "Hell, he's the most honest guy on the Boardwalk. Pays the best, too. Jesus, what are you into, Lano? First Gaetano and some punk come out of the hotel, now you tell me they were visiting you, telling you to kill my boss? Man, I thought I was just driving you, pick up some money and clothes."

"He says it'll make us even for my holding the gun on him."

"You believe him?"

"I believe I was supposed to have been killed last night, early this morning. I believe they began setting me up the minute Art called, that I fell right into their hands. They needed someone to get the heat off them about the murder of Lester Fincher, and I walked into town a gift-wrapped scapegoat. They were probably gonna have Wally kill me outside of town, with the gun in my pocket. That's why he was going on and on during the drive from Longport, keep me off balance, keep me from paying attention to where we were going. They knew I didn't know the town. He could drive me out somewhere dark and quiet, hit the brakes and turn and blast me out of the seat, I wouldn't even know what hit me, what with being so preoccupied, worried about the horror stories he was telling me." He looked at Percy. "About the wild Africans rule the Boardwalk after dark."

Edward said, "Well, why didn't he?"

"He spotted *me*," Percy said, and Lano nodded, picked up his thought and ran with it.

"Spotted you and kept up the patter, this time so I wouldn't notice you. But I did, watched you and felt your headlights on my neck all the way to the hotel."

"And today, why didn't they kill you today?" Edward seemed to be enjoying himself, working it out, and Lano didn't know how to take it. He didn't want the guy thinking he was expendable, there for his entertainment. But he was a big guy and wasn't shocked by discussions of death. Maybe he'd be a good man to have around.

"Me, again," Percy said. "I stuck around here for a while, and they knew it. West would have seen me, hell, I was *trying* to get spotted the last two nights. Almost caught my lunch, too, a little while ago watching Ange's place. Little fat swamp guinea in a rental car, not even wearing a hat, woke me up cussing and yelling. I drew down on him and got out of there, he went in and a couple minutes later Gaetano and West come out. I followed them here. Last night, I thought Lano was one of them.

"See, last night, though," Percy said, "and this morning, they didn't know if I was still hanging around or not. They couldn't take a chance on hitting—" He turned his head to Lano. "What the hell *is* your name, anyhow?"

"Lano Branka." He felt no twinge telling the cop who he was. Hell, the man had saved his life, twice. Besides that, he liked him. Shit, all of a sudden, he was a Leo Buscaglia, liking everyone.

But something the man had said stuck in his mind.

"Lano," Percy was saying, "they couldn't hit him thinking I'd be right here to grab them, get my hands on the pistol they'd planted." He turned to Lano. "Speaking of which, where is that pistol?"

Things fell into place. Lano snapped his fingers, and stood up, excited and a little scared. He said, "Wait, wait a minute, tell me what the little fat guy in the rental car looked like!"

22

"You're fucking short." They were sitting in the den, the fire blazing away. Ange Biari spoke with anger, staring with black dead eyes at a snookered Tough Tony Tomase.

Tomase had to think fast, and he knew it. As much as he wanted to, he couldn't climb over the desk, grab this skinny little prick by the throat and choke him. That would be more satisfying than pulling one of the pistols, blasting him into the middle of the next room. He wanted to but couldn't; the simple truth was, he had nowhere left to go.

But God, it was hard not to. The little old man was sitting there talking down to him, giving him a hard look. His piece-of-shit son standing behind him, chickenshit psycho couldn't hear a car backfire without jumping to the ground, standing back there like Don Hagen from *The Godfather*.

All right, calm down. Get control of yourself and make this bastard happy, satisfy him, or you won't get far. At the very least not out of Atlantic City. He needed these men, even the retarded son who had no balls.

One good thing though, he'd had the presence of mind not to tell them he'd brought the money. He'd told them he'd done it the same way he'd done it last time, express courier by bonded and armed guards. These guys understood such terms. They ran girls, drugs, all the other things, but they were, mostly, in the casino business. Money transfers, especially the types you didn't want the IRS to know about, could only be handled a couple of ways. He had time to think, as he stood there and listened to this idiot jagoff goof acting like a young man.

"First you come into my house, act like a badass, bring some *putana* with you to sleep under the same roof my dead wife used to sleep under, it ain't bad enough you insult me like this, but then you tell me you're short!"

Let him rant, get it out of his system. Tomase thought of Arliss, upstairs, sitting on the suitcase with the pistol in her hand. He'd told her that if he found her in any other position when he came back into the room, he'd use the gun on *her*. He hated having the money out of his sight, but this was an emergency and the woman was under his control.

"How you plan on making it up to me, this other half a million?"

Now they were getting down to the meat and potatoes of it. The guy, the skinny old little shit, he'd been running a game. Like Mad Mike ran on people with the chair there in his office, what did he call it, the Chair of Death or something. All along, Biari had been wanting something from him, had used his wrath and anger to get Tomase to do him a service. Shit, Tomase wasn't stupid. He was Sicilian, too, could see through this scam with his eyes closed. Well, the man was about to tell him what the scam was. If it wasn't too dangerous, he'd pull it off for him. There was too much at stake here to refuse. The top spot in Atlantic City didn't come easy, should, in fact, have been handed down to the retard son. He would do the service for the man, take over, and when the time was right, when he knew all there was to know and was wired in to all the coppers and politicians, well then he could arrange a little car accident for this son of a bitch. Over a cliff, wham, into the roaring surf. Maybe with the retard driving.

"You tell me, Don Biari. How can I make it up to you?"

As the man began to tell him, Tomase began to plot. It would be easy. A lot easier than he'd thought. The only thing he didn't understand, was, how did people this stupid get to the top of the heap?

From what they were telling him, they were not only stupid, but ignorant, too, didn't know how to handle things without ten subplots and all the Old Country bullshit. That was okay in Sicily, but here, in America, there was only one way.

Kill whoever got in your way and rob all of the rest.

How did they all get to be asshole buddies? That thought floated around Lano's mind as Edward drove them back to the Shamrock. One minute, Edward was a driver he'd barely met, and Fincher was a guy he'd tussled with in a police station. Edward knew Percy and had broken the ice in the hotel room, had lightened up a very tense situation, in fact, and suddenly they were all paisans, going to get the gun.

He'd decided, though, that he wouldn't show Percy where it was, would not let him get his hands on it until he and Conway were on a plane, heading for Chicago. Then the guy could dig it up, send for the FBI, anyone he wanted, but not before. He was grateful that there was someone he could count on, an ally to help him escape, but still, he wanted only to get out.

He had to be totally out of it. He'd tell Percy that and the man would nod his head over and over, saying sincerely, "No problem, hey, you're out of it, never were in it, shit, no problem." He'd say it just a little too quickly for Lano's taste, and besides, the guy was a cop; not to be totally trusted.

No, he wouldn't get his paws on the weapon until Lano and Conway were gone and Lano would not give him the directions to the pistol with Edward around. There would be no witnesses when he spoke, nothing that could come back to haunt him in a court.

Seeing that they were all of a sudden partners, wanting to divert Percy away from the constant discussion of the weapon, he asked him something that had been bothering him, and was amazed at the answer.

Conway felt left out. Left out, and a little frightened. It was hard, being scared with all these armed men around, men who were pretty much ignoring her, not letting her into the conversation, as if she wasn't important enough to even ask her opinion. That was bad enough, but to hear them talk, speaking of death and murder in everyday tones, like it happened all the time in their world . . .

She was having some doubts. Maybe she was better off, going back to Brian. Going anywhere, but without this man next to her.

It was so confusing, listening to him. Back in the hotel, at the casino, he'd been loving, kind, compassionate, a man who cared about her. In the Palermo, he'd been an entirely different person—cold, hard, tough, telling Percy at one point that he didn't care if he whacked out every Biari in the telephone book, as long as he did it after they got on a plane heading out.

Was this a man she wanted to be with? She'd ask herself the question and the answer would be . . . I don't know. Confusion and fear, back to haunt her again.

She remembered her earlier thoughts, about Italians and their bad habit of winding up dead in car trunks or in restaurants, blown away. She shivered.

Next to her, Lano said, "You cold?" Solicitous again,

caring. God, who was he; *what* was he? She shook her head and he said, "I can ask Edward to turn the heater up."

This time she didn't answer him.

It was funny, the things you found out. Last night he'd seen the guy for the first time, in the unmarked squad car behind the guy Wally's car in front of the Palermo, and he'd figured him for a Sicilian or something, dark-skinned, swarthy. If not Sicily, some other Mediterranean country, because he was definitely from the region, Portuguese or something.

Lano had said, "What was that you said about being African?" and Percy had said, "My father was African, light-skinned. My mother's Polish." And had left it at that.

Lano wondered how it had been growing up, half-black half-white, an outsider to each category, unwanted by the whites who wanted nothing to do with the Atlantic City ghetto blacks, an outcast to the blacks who hated the whites for keeping them down.

He thought about the man, a cop from Akron, Ohio. Man who'd grown up in the heart of the ghetto, with a couple of strikes against him at birth, growing up and turning into an alcoholic, as Daniels had told him. Getting his life turned around and coming home to avenge his brother's death.

He thought then about another black guy he knew, Elihue. Great big monster of a man who'd been born with all the advantages of middle-class life and who'd thrown them away. Hell, if the guy could have gotten his compulsions under control, he could still be playing in the NFL. He thought about the two men, compared them, the way he'd been compared to his father his entire life.

It was no contest. That made him feel a lot better about his decision.

The only thing that stuck in his mind, that bothered him, was that as long as he was comparing, he could see that he had a lot more in common with Elihue than he had with the cop. He wondered then if he had what it took to turn that around.

Tough Tony Tomase had gotten out of his trouble gracefully. He'd agreed to do the job for them, then had said, "And, Don Biari, please accept my apologies for bringing a woman of little virtue into your home. We shall leave immediately, and I will put her up in a hotel, while I take care of your business."

"*Our* business, Anthony," the little shit had said. "From now on, it's *our* business." Then he'd nodded, as if proving his point.

Christ, it was sickening. But he'd got through it. And was just about to leave when the retard cleared his throat and said, "Pop?" then waited until the old man looked at him.

"Pop," the retard said, "we got a little problem." Causing Tomase a major pain in the ass.

At last, he'd gotten away, collecting Arliss while the old man was still cursing away in dialect at the kid, calling him filthy names so bad that if the kid had any balls he'd kill him for saying them. He'd collected Arliss and had skipped, shutting her up when she started whining, "We gotta *leave*? Come *on*, Tony, I'm *tired*." One good thing, all he had to do now was look at her to shut her up. She was learning.

As was he. What a mess. First they kill a guy, president of some dipshit union, which they should have had in their pocket in the first place if they'd had any sense. Then the guy's brother, the cop, comes to town, trying to bring the Gee in to settle it. Then Art calls, of all people, wanting them to take care of Lano, hide him from the animal in Chicago, Tough Tony Tomase. He'd had to hide his anger when Biari had said the words, rubbing it in, knowing there was nothing Tomase could do about it. Yet. Hid, too, his glee, knowing that Branka was in town and part of the deal was to kill him. The cop, too, but the kid along with it as part of the bargain. It would be his pleasure.

He knew how to do it, had been killing guys and making them disappear since he was seventeen. First you get them in the trunk of your car, dead, go buy some steam irons and chains, a couple padlocks, take them out in a boat late at night and dump them over the side. Nothing to it. The fish ate everything that would rot and the chains would keep them down there forever if you applied them right. It would be easy. Two wet-behind-the-ears punks against Tough Tony Tomase? No odds-maker on earth would touch that bet.

Who was there to miss them? Art in Chicago, who wouldn't dare come here seeking vengeance; and the cop's mother, some drunk in the ghetto, a white broad drinking herself to death if the retard could be believed. No, he'd make them disappear, and make himself a hero to the Biaris in the process.

He gritted his teeth, fighting the resentment as he looked in the rearview mirror and saw the headlights behind him, the major pain in the ass he'd been given, the retard right on his ass. He'd asked the old man for a driver, someone to help him carry the stiffs back to the car, help bury them. The old man had given him Gaetano, as if he was doing him a favor, saddling him with the punk. Biari had told him that Gaetano was his right arm and it was all he could do not to say: "Shit, weak little fucker, ain't you?" But he'd bitten his tongue and had made good his escape, the retard probably being sent along as a punishment for fucking up, telling Lano to keep the gun and kill the casino owner. Taking his own car, too, arrogant son of a bitch, as if sitting in a car with Arliss would give him the AIDS.

Personally, Tomase didn't see what was wrong with what Gaetano had told Branka to do. At least they were sure where the kid was to be found.

He dropped Arliss off at the hotel the old man had said

he owned—*they* owned now—with a couple hundred bucks for check-in, and told her he'd be back in a couple of hours. He pulled to the curb, waited for Gaetano to get out of his car and get into the rental.

"You want to take my car?" Gaetano said. "It's one my man Wally picked up. It's not registered and can't be traced to us." Jesus, the idiot sounded like an anxious little kid, trying to make points with an angry parent.

Tomase, thinking of all of his money in the trunk, said, "Yeah, and with your prints and his all over it. No, we'll take mine. I ain't touched nothing but the door handle and the steering wheel, besides, I got one with an alarm on it, so no jigs can steal it, we're doing our thing."

Gaetano, taking his hand off the door quickly, staring at it then wiping the leather padding with his coat sleeve, said, "And the trunk. You touched the trunk when you put your suitcase in it."

"Oh, yeah, the trunk," Tomase said, then turned to the retard, smiling. "Good thinking, Gaetano," he said.

But he was thinking, You dumb shit. The smile, though, was genuine. Hell, what it came down to, he was being paid a half-million dollars, getting credit for it, for two murders.

That thought kept him smiling all the way to O'Shea's Shamrock Hotel and Casino.

23

"How you want to work it?" Percy sat with his arm across the seat, looking back at Lano, giving him the chance to make the rules.

Lano was grateful for the opportunity. Most cops he knew, they'd have taken charge by now, be giving the orders, and would screw everything up. This guy seemed all right, for a cop.

How did he want to work it? He wanted his money, that was one thing, and he had to tell O'Shea that Conway was coming with him. He wouldn't sneak out with her. He'd face it like a man, pay the guy off and they'd go, leave behind all the fancy gowns O'Shea had paid for.

God, though, it was quiet after hours. What, a mile from the other casinos, and it was like being in the middle of nowhere. Lights shone in windows high above them, but nothing here at ground level. Quiet darkness surrounded them, dangerous and maybe lethal. Lano was grateful there were two guys with guns close by who were on his side.

"I'll go in, tell O'Shea the score, get my money and then

you and Edward can take us to the airport. On the way, I'll tell you where the gun is."

As he said the last words Percy's face fell, and he was opening his mouth to speak when Conway said, "*We* go in," speaking for the first time in a while. "I've got to be there, Lano, when he finds out." All Lano could do was look at her, then nod.

To Percy, Lano said, "It's the way it's got to be."

Percy said, "You better tell him what the Biaris got planned for him," and Lano said, stepping from the car, just as he closed the door, "I got to ask him a question, first."

Percy watched them walk through the parking lot into the hotel, could even see them as they stopped and Conway picked up a house phone hanging on the scarlet-papered wall, tracking down O'Shea. He watched her hang up and say something to Lano, saw him nod, then watched him take her firmly by the elbow and head for the elevators. Soon, they were out of sight.

If the guy was running a scam, Percy would kill him. Which would be a shame, he was likable enough. He held no grudge about the punch in the face, because he believed this man would have labeled him whether the cops were holding Percy or not, it was the type of guy he seemed to be. It hadn't been a cheap shot. And from what the man had told him, he had no reason to be suspicious of him, as the Biaris had been setting him up since he'd got into town. He waited, time passing slowly, thinking.

It made sense, now. Lano was supposed to die at the hands of Wally West, who had most likely been given instructions from the Biaris to wipe down the gun and put it in Lano's hands, the gun that had been used on Lester. The cops would shake their heads and tell him, "Well, here's your man," and there wouldn't be a goddamned thing he'd be able to do about it.

Thank God he'd been following Gaetano.

But was this man to be trusted? Percy didn't see as he

had a choice. Either the man would level with him or he wouldn't. If he didn't, well, Chicago wasn't that big a town that he couldn't be found. He knew his name and figured he knew his line of work. He had friends in Chicago. For one brief moment, Percy wished that he could be able to trust someone without first knowing them for a lifetime.

When they got out of the car—what, twenty minutes ago—a blast of cold air had entered, chilling the interior, and Edward had turned the heater on high. They were sitting together in an awkward silence, and it was with a shock that Percy realized that it had been Lano who had kept the conversation going, kept things current, in the now, without time for thought of past affiliations or the lack of them. Now he felt as he had ten years back, in high school, on a bus with this same man, going to play against a rival school, teammates but separate, the two of them sitting across from each other, maybe wanting to talk to one another but forbidden by street protocol to do so.

Percy saw a pair of headlights coming down the street, something familiar about them, and suddenly he wasn't in high school anymore, he was a man, full grown and with life experience, cop's experience, nothing to be laughed at, not a man to be put down, either. He wasn't a half-breed now, or a nigger. Now he was a cop.

"Shut the car off and get down in the seat, Edward," Percy said softly as he slid down past the window, reaching inside his coat for his pistol. "That's the guy from Ange Biari's house coming."

Then not feeling so cocky, as a matter of fact feeling a little embarrassed as Edward said, "No need for that, man, the windows are tinted." He shut the car off, though.

Percy sat up and nodded, watched as the man drove around the lot, checking cars, watched as he pulled into the closest parking spot to the back of the hotel he could find, watched as Tony Tomase and Gaetano Biari got out of the car, checked the doors to make sure they were locked. He saw Tomase put a key in the car's front fender and turn it, setting an alarm. Then watched them walk, confidently, toward the front of the casino.

"They're going to the Boardwalk side." Edward sounded excited, maybe a little scared. "There's a door right here in back, why they want to go all the way out there?"

Percy got out of the car with his gun held at his side and began to jog silently after them. "Stay here," he said.

Every dealer got a break at the top of the hour, union rules, so you wouldn't break your back, being on your feet eight hours at a time. Up here in the suite the rule still stood, even though it was what you could call a nonunion shop. You had to go into another room, smoke your cigarette or drink your pop, take ten minutes then report back for another hour.

Millie took her break, trying hard not to give anyone the satisfaction of seeing her upset. She held her head high, walked into one of the other rooms, sat down in a chair and opened her letter.

They spoke first to Malcolm Lynch, Lano and Conway holding hands as he led them into his office, showed them to plush leather chairs. "He's in the needle," Malcolm told them, "gambling." He went to the bar, looking old and weary, someone who'd spent his entire adult life with a man he'd figured to be a winner, maybe having doubts now about his decisions; the choices he'd made. He poured Scotch and brought drinks to them without asking, the gracious host, the guy who'd spent thirty years pouring drinks for high rollers in offices like this one.

"I tell him, 'Quit the gambling, Brian,' and the man looks at me like I'm his old lady and he's thinking about divorce. All of a sudden, I wonder if I know the guy."

"Tell me about it," Conway said.

Lano was surprised at the change that had come over her

as they'd entered the place. As Malcolm led them through the silent casino, she'd become more sure of herself, the woman standing tall and stepping out, on her own turf and knowing it. Strutting, Lano'd thought.

He said, "Why take the risk, gambling after hours? Can't you lose your license?"

Conway sipped her drink. "They all do it. It's known and overlooked. A lot of things are overlooked here."

"It's done by the casinos that're locked in," Malcolm said. "We don't get our license until Tuesday. We've got enemies. He thinks if the troopers come raiding, he'll have time to clear the suite, get some champagne in there and say he's throwing a party. I tell you, he's giving me ulcers."

"The slots look good." Conway now, speaking in the voice of the expert. "That should put him over the top."

Malcolm stared at her solemnly. He said, "You're leaving him."

Lano looked at her, waiting, and it took her a while to nod her head.

"I better get you up there, break the news."

Tomase was in his element, planning all the way from the hotel, driving slowly, expertly, using his signal when he turned. "I hate this cowboy shit, you know it?" he'd said, but the excitement in his voice betrayed him; he was loving every minute of this. They'd checked the Palermo, had called from a pay phone outside one of the casinos, Tomase ordering Gaetano to go up and make the call; Mr. Pella, he'd been informed, had checked out. The clerk, Gaetano reported, sounded frightened.

Now, standing on the Boardwalk, staring up at the lights high atop the hotel, he said to Gaetano, "You're sure you had him good and scared, that he'd do what you told him?"

"He was shitting blood, Tony. He'll do it, think we're even."

"Okay, he's had time to get here, get to the man. He

ain't done it yet or the cops'd be swarming the joint. This kid knows nothing from hits. He'll whack the guy and panic, want to lose the gun, throw it in the ocean. You go around back and watch that door, just in case, I'll stay here, where he'll come out. You hear gunshots, come running, we ain't gonna have time to waste. I'll try to get the drop on him, get him to the car before we do the job. Give it a half-hour, the kid don't come running out, looking terrified, I'll eat the car."

"What if he did the job, got into a room and went to bed?"

"Not the type, not enough balls. We'll give it a half-hour, by then the sun'll be coming up. He ain't out by then, we'll make another plan for him, go right over to the cop's mother's house, take care of him."

"But how do you know he's still in town? How do you know he ain't on a plane, heading for home?"

Tomase looked at the man, standing there in about three grand worth of clothes, probably his first hit. The goof shivering, probably not from the cold, either, although it was cold as shit. He said, "Your dad said he won a million dollars, right?" then waited until Gaetano nodded.

"Let me tell you something, Gaetano," Tough Tony Tomase said. "This kid could whack O'Shea, me, you, your old man and four nuns, and have a posse of feds on his ass, he wouldn't leave town. Not till he loses every dime of that money back." Tomase turned his back then, dismissing the retard, and was grateful a minute later when he turned around and the dummy was gone.

"Hey, the big winner," O'Shea said. He was holding a drink in his hand, the liquid dark amber, barely diluted. It did not appear to be his first of the night. Lano was aware of the hush that had followed his entrance, it reminded him of the quiet that had followed his exit from Art's office, when the gamblers had all thought he was about to die. He heard the whispers and the mutterings, Here was the guy who'd won the money in the glass cage. He was aware, too, of Millie there working the crap table, staring at him. He didn't want to look her way, wasn't sure what might happen inside him. If he kept it all business and got out of there, he would be fine.

O'Shea was looking at Conway now, something there in his eyes, this man with the expressive face and the hearty bluff manner suddenly looking soft and old. "Conway." He said it softly, for her ears alone.

"Brian," Conway said, the same way.

"I want to ask you a question," Lano said, and O'Shea turned to him as if he'd been interrupted in the shower.

"What's that?" Glowering now.

"When I won the pot, you were cheering me on. Did you mean it?"

O'Shea grunted, as if it had been a dumb question. "Sure I meant it, what gambler in the room didn't mean it?"

"You were happy I won?"

"What is this, Twenty Questions?" O'Shea was looking from Conway to Lano, then back, his eyes seeming almost magnetically drawn. They'd go from soft to hard when he looked at Lano, then soft again as he gazed at Conway. Lano wondered if this was the same guy who wanted to rent her out the night before to some slob, took him for a bundle. " 'Course I was happy, till I realized it was my money you were winning." The bluff and bravado back now, the big-time casino owner and letting everyone know it.

Lano didn't like the way the two of them were looking at each other. She had let go of his hand in the elevator, and Malcolm had looked away as it had happened, as if he had known she was going to do it. Malcolm had gestured for O'Shea to come over to the corner, where they now stood, out of earshot of the rest of the gamblers. O'Shea had walked over, bowed and beaten, half in the bag, but was now getting it back, taking on the personality he'd lost, regaining it as he stood looking at Conway.

Behind him, Lano could hear the gamblers back at it, dice clicking and cards slapping felt; cheers and whoops from the winners, groans from the losers.

His mind made up, he said, "Gaetano Biari ordered me to kill you," and was happy, because that got the guy's attention, his eyes came off Conway's and bored into Lano's.

"When I got to town, the two of them were talking about giving you a heart attack or a stroke, so watch what you eat and drink. They must have someone in the kitchen on the payroll. Just now, a little while ago, I was told to come over here and shoot you."

"You gonna do it?" O'Shea wasn't challenging or even sounding amused; the man was just asking a question. Malcolm's face had become watchful. Lano shook his head.

"How about you?" he asked Conway. "You gonna shoot old Brian?"

Lano watched her take a quick hesitant step forward, as if about to step into O'Shea's arms, then she caught herself, stepped back to Lano's side, took his arm. She didn't answer O'Shea's question.

He wasn't giving up that easily. "You leaving me, Conway?" Now there was amusement in his voice, as if the act was unthinkable. "Going away with this fella here, to get straight? Taking off with a gambler who's gonna help you beat your problem, are you?"

Lano sensed her hesitation, her confusion, felt her hand come off his arm. She had to say it, confirm it. He wanted to jump in and take over but if he did she'd always wonder. He held his breath until she said, "Yes," softly, barely audible but still a yes, and he let his breath out with a sigh of relief.

"Well," O'Shea said, "I ain't gonna let you."

24

O'Shea said, "There's a little matter of a ton of dollars and change you owe me, Conway, and even if this stiff wanted to pay it for you, the money he insisted on having in cash is locked in the vault, we can't get at it till ten. By then, I can talk some sense into your head, tell you a few things about guinea gamblers with smooth lines of bullshit. He'll have you inna goddamn street in Chicago, leaning on a lamppost in six months when the odds catch up to him."

Lano looked at O'Shea, ready to attack, then controlled himself. This was not the time or place; if he attacked here, he'd get killed, all the gamblers up here were O'Shea's friends, not his.

Instead of swinging, he said, "I'll take a check."

"A check all of a sudden? After you made me take my money out of the glass?" There was contempt and amusement in O'Shea's voice. Lano ignored it, told himself to just get the check and get out, this was no time for pride.

O'Shea said, "Just pay me what she owes me and then walk out with my woman, right?"

"I'm not your woman," Conway said, and Lano thought, Good for you. He wanted to remind them that O'Shea the great lover had been the outside force that had pushed her into the ocean, but if she didn't know it, nobody did. He kept his mouth shut and waited for the hand to be played out.

"You said cash, I followed your wishes. You got to wait . . ." O'Shea's voice trailed off, his eyes slightly glazed over as he stared off into space, and suddenly Lano knew: it was a setup, had been all along. This son of a bitch had walked them into a trap he'd set in advance, knowing they'd be here and what they'd want, or he was playing it as he went along. Either way, he was getting cute, and Lano knew his way around cute.

"I'll tell you something," O'Shea said, softly but with feeling. "I've known about guys like Angelo Biari wanting to hit me since the day I broke ground here for the Shamrock. Him and others like him been threatening me, beating my people, sending me fucked-up slots since the day I got to town. It ain't stopped me yet, and it ain't gonna stop me now." He had pulled himself to his full height and he was staring intently at Lano as he spoke, and with each word his voice grew in power. Beside him, Lano could hear Malcolm breathing hard.

"Fuck 'em. I didn't last as long as I did in this business having a jelly spine, without knowing things, too."

His green eyes looked over Lano. "Like for instance, buddy, I know about you, too, guys like you. All you had to do was come in this morning, get your million, and you and this little card-whore here could have slipped away into the night, never to be seen again. But you didn't, and you're standing there wondering why I'm not grateful because you're offering me what she owes me. See, it's because I know you, how guys like you operate. For instance, you've paid your bookie before you paid your rent, haven't you? Before you put food on the table. You live by the gambler's code, same as me.

"Now, Conway here, she was starting to learn. But she was too cute right from the start. All she ever had to do was bat those green eyes at some asshole and *wham*, his heart's gone, wanting to protect her from whatever's bothering her, save her. She probably made you bring her in here with you, too, hoping I'd make a scene. Well, the only scene I want to make I already made, and did you see what happened? I say fifty words to her, she's ready to come into my arms, suck me off again for a few bucks off the bill, but you're standing there and it stopped her. The thought of you with your million cash, and your young stiff one down there in your pants, that stopped her, too.

"Until she gets bored, Lano, or you say the wrong thing, or the money runs out. Then she'll start looking around for some other young, handsome son of a bitch to take care of her. Christ, buddy, ain't you seen bitches like her before?"

Behind him, Malcolm grunted, a sound of pleasure. Lano didn't know what was going on, why they were acting this way. The man had spoken for two, three minutes, and he'd had his say. Now it was time to go. He'd either take the money or he wouldn't.

"Give me a check for seven hundred, O'Shea, and we're gone."

O'Shea was shaking his head, and Malcolm swaggered over and stood next to him—Christ, rubbing his hands.

"Welcome back, Brian," Malcolm said, "we've missed you."

"It ain't that simple," O'Shea said. In his eyes, there it was, that familiar twinkle, only stronger now, the wattage full up, a nuclear power plant running behind them. Feverish eyes staring at Lano, a smile on his lips, O'Shea said, "I took this bitch in, she owed a hundred-fifty out there to the casinos. Over two years, starting then—Malcolm, what'd the vig be, six for five weekly? Counting the dough she's lost to me? Seven, eight mill? And the suite in the needle, a grand a night for two years, there's another seven-thirty. The jewels, the gowns, the trips, the meals, all the things I paid for so she could adorn my arm and give me pussy. There's more there I've paid for than you'll ever see."

"Come on, Conway," Lano said.

"You think you can walk away, do you? Owing me ten mill, baby? *You know who I am?*" He'd raised his voice and now the gambling stopped, the other men in the room were staring at them, some smiling, others merely curious.

Brian O'Shea, speaking almost in a whisper, said, "I never broke my word in my life, it's one of the reasons I'm where I am. I give you my word now, what she owes me, it's forgotten about. She owes me nothing, we're even, if you do one thing for me."

"What?"

O'Shea smiled at him.

"Roll against me, one time, double or nothing for the million," O'Shea said.

Jesus Christ. One roll for a million. He'd come to town with a little under one-forty, he'd won—what—twenty-five, given ten away as a tip. All that money was wrapped in the money bag, inside his pants with his coat buttoned around it. That money and the million in the safe represented all he owned.

Lano knew about a gambler's honor, knew guys who didn't have it, too. He was one who did, a man who'd cut his kidney out and sell it before letting a gambling debt go bad. He owed O'Shea three hundred for Conway, who'd stayed when she had a chance to leave. A couple of times now. If he lost he'd still be ahead a good sum for a night's work.

If he won, he'd have over two million of his own.

Lano felt the tingling begin in his spine, work its way up to his neck and enter his head, buzzing now. The other gamblers were staring at him, waiting for his answer. Confidence filled him. He could roll eleven sevens in a row if he wanted to. One roll of the dice, what was that when he could feel the bulge down there between his legs as he stiffened up, because he was on the prime roll, the big one, the one he'd heard about all his life and was just now beginning to really believe was happening to him?

As he walked quickly to the crap table, he said over his shoulder to O'Shea: "You're on."

Millie held the crap stick and without thinking she pulled the dice to her, away from Lano. The other dealers were staring at her, the pit boss, too. O'Shea wasn't paying any attention, not yet, until she said, loudly, "Don't, Lano. Don't you do it." That got his attention.

"Give him the dice, Millie," O'Shea said, the threat in his tone.

"Give me the dice, Millie," Lano said.

Without another word, she angrily pushed them his way.

He held the dice in his hand, shook them around in there, feeling the signals they were sending down into his arm, into his shoulder, and he began to shake them fiercely, sending his own message, seven-come-eleven, nothing less would do, and he lifted his arm to the sky, shaking madly, laughing, shaking his head because he knew, he knew what was coming and he let the dice go, shouted, "Come to me!" and watched them hit the backboard and bounce back.

One, one. Snake eyes. He'd crapped out.

They were cheering, but for O'Shea this time. Malcolm was the loudest, clapping his hands together and whistling through his teeth, his face a mask of rapture.

Lano felt as if he'd been punched in the stomach, hard. By someone wearing a pair of brass knucks. Conway had her arm around his waist and was leading him to the door, away from them all, all of them who were ignoring them, all except for Millie. She had been staring at him with something akin to pity in her eyes, and that hurt almost as much as the lost million.

Everyone else, though, was ignoring them. They weren't worthy of acknowledgment. They were the losers.

He walked with Conway's help down to her room, and as she was packing the phone rang, O'Shea telling her, "Two suitcases, I'm not kidding, that's it, Conway," and she hung up on him, filled the two suitcases with all the jewelry and the glittering gowns as Lano sat on the bed, watching her, holding his stomach in both hands.

But he'd known. It was supposed to happen! And he'd lost.

Or had he? Conway was still here, beautiful, free and clear of her debt, but still with him, not with O'Shea down the hall, clapping for the big winner. That counted for something. She wasn't looking at him pityingly, either. And the hundred-sixty something in hundreds, pushed down his pants, there was that. He walked to the bar, poured himself a stiff Scotch and downed it, and it tasted so good he did it again. There, that was a little better.

"Win a few, lose a few," he said. His voice sounded shaky, but he could make an attempt at humor and that counted, too. It would be all right.

The money was down there, noticeable in his waistband, sweat forming around it. If he went back in there, laid it on the table . . .

"I'm ready," Conway said, and after a minute Lano hurried to her, picked up the bags.

Percy had come up slowly, around the far side, and had listened to Tomase tell Gaetano their half-assed plan. As soon as he heard him tell Gaetano to go around back, he'd made his break, run quickly around the building, covering the block in record time to the other side. He stood there breathing into his hand so the white breath wouldn't sneak around the corner, give away his position. When he had it under control, he snuck a peek around the side of the building.

Tomase was punching his bare right hand into his gloved left, keeping the circulation going. He was standing stock-still, his back to Percy, staring intently into the glass front of the hotel, a little to the left and behind the entrance, partially hidden by the big iron green shamrock.

Percy took stock. He was alone, that was for sure. The second he'd come around back he'd waved Edward off; this was not his fight. He'd heard the motor come to life and the limo pull away as he turned the far corner, before Gaetano even left the Boardwalk. So, he was alone as far as firepower was concerned, his pistol against whatever this mob punk was carrying, and what Gaetano would have. Although that shouldn't be a problem.

Christ, the wind was killing him. Still coming off the ocean, tearing into the corner and around it like a whirlwind. Tomase had the iron shamrock for a windbreak, but he was alone, exposed and vulnerable to the elements. He checked his watch; twenty-five minutes had passed since the two men had come onto the scene, nearly an hour though since Lano and Conway had gone inside.

What the hell was keeping them?

The sun was due up anytime, it was close to seven and the first streaks of false dawn were lighting the eastern sky. Percy slipped off his right glove, dug out his holstered pistol. He held it straight down his leg and it felt good.

He was standing there watching Tomase's back when he saw the man stiffen, reach his hand into his right coat pocket and pull out a hog-leg, a .44 it looked like, or a .357. Percy rounded the corner, bringing his gun up, when Tomase yelled, "Freeze!" at Lano and Conway coming through the glass doors and all hell broke loose.

* * *

By the time they got to the deserted lobby he felt a little better, good enough to ask if the security guys and the night clerk were maybe in the laundry room, having some fun. Conway, however, was not in the mood.

Since leaving the gambling suite, she'd been nearly silent. Lano wondered if she was having doubts, and found to his amazement that he didn't much care. She'd asked him to help her, as she stood dripping and freezing on the sand right out there ahead of them, and he'd done it, had helped her out.

The thought made him feel much better, lighter and clear of head. He'd done it. Had helped someone who had reached out to him. Maybe he had proved Art and Arliss and the rest of them wrong. Maybe he was growing up.

He didn't have time to dwell on it because as they walked through the doors—Lano sideways so both suitcases would make it through—Tough Tony stepped out from behind the shamrock on their right and pointed a pistol at them, was shouting for them to freeze when Lano made his move.

He shoved Conway hard as he pushed ahead, turning, dropping one suitcase and throwing the other at Tony, who swiped at it with the pistol butt, ducking and shutting his eyes, and Lano dug into his gut with a good one, a right, when he heard the boom behind Tomase and felt the sting in his neck, high, right under his ear.

He shouted, "Run, Conway!" and took four steps, five, and was over the railing, landing hard on the packed cold sand, then up and running, the wind lashing at him, eyes searching, one post, two, three, right there, he dropped to his knees and began to dig in the dirt, needing the piece, because he knew he was bleeding to death, could see the drops of blood hitting the sand, feel it soaking the collar of his overcoat and Tomase had brought friends, shit, it was probably Virgil up there who'd shot him.

The sounds of two pistol shots, different guns each firing a single time, drifted to him, the pounding surf drowning the noise out as he dug, twisted his fingers down in there good, then heard footsteps on the wooden stairs, then another shot, close, but not hitting him, then heard Tomase's voice telling him to turn around, now, slow.

Lano began to do it, rising and feeling faint, seeing Tomase looking up, staring at the stairway, trying to see to the Boardwalk. "Who you got up there?" Tomase's voice held a tone Lano hadn't heard before; fear—no, terror—was in it. His face was sweat-covered, twisted in a mask of pain.

"I thought he was with you."

"You wiseass son of a bitch!" Tomase swung around, turned to him, took his eyes off the stairway, and raised the gun. Lano looked down what looked like a cannon bore, then saw a blur as something fell past him, falling from above, a form, a man, then it took shape as it rolled on the sand and Tomase fired at it, three times, and the blur that was Percy Fincher came up to one knee, fired once, twice, hitting Tomase in the chest and driving him against the stairs, firing again as he rose to his feet, firing until the weapon in his hands was empty.

Lano fell to his knees in the sand and dug again—yeah—there it was, the gun wrapped in the plastic bag. It seemed like a good idea to give it to Percy now, let him have it. He believed he was bleeding to death. It would be, he thought with a shock, a kindly last gesture.

Percy was walking toward him, a little shakily, slapping another magazine into the pistol with his palm, saying something that Lano couldn't hear because all of his attention was on the stairway now, at the figure slithering down the stairs, seeing that it was Gaetano, with a gun in his hand and drawing a bead on Percy's back, and he stuck his finger in through the plastic, stuck it in hard, and it broke through and it was on the trigger guard, then inside it.

Lano fired past Percy, pointing the gun with both hands,

felt it buck in his hands and saw Gaetano jump with each of the three shots he fired, finally falling to the stairs, his hand caught on the wooden banister, holding him on a slant.

Lano leaned against the post, staring at Percy. He felt weak, light-headed. "Conway?"

"Christ!" Percy was racing for the stairway but she was there, calling Lano tentatively, revulsion on her face. Back-lit by the garish neon of the Shamrock, she looked almost surreal, frightening. Or maybe it was him. He watched Percy guide her past Gaetano's body, taking charge now, going to Tomase's body and digging around in the pockets, coming up with keys.

"Take these, shut off the alarm, there's a Lincoln out back, parked three rows from the rear entrance. Take off, go to . . . the Palermo and check in under Lano's name— no, under Pella. Wait for us there."

She was almost running, heels catching in sand, when Lano became aware of the weight in the front of his pants, then cursed because there was no way he could escape, he didn't have the strength, and he'd be damned if he'd pass out and let some crooked Atlantic City copper take his bankroll. He said, "Conway," surprised at the strength in his voice, and she stopped, turned, began to walk toward him, her hand to her mouth. He transferred the pistol to his left hand, dug into his pants with his right, gave her the bank bag. "Take this, put it in the hotel safe."

"My God, you're bleeding."

"I'm all right, just *go!*" He wanted her out of there because there was a vague idea floating around on the edge of his mind and he didn't want her to see him do what he was thinking about doing.

He waited until she was on the stairs, then gone, and he said to the cop, "Get away, call the feds. Right now. You weren't here, you didn't see anything, you don't know anything, get the feds and fade, come see me if I make it."

Percy was staring at him. "You need an ambulance."

Lano walked on unsteady legs to the body of Tough Tom

Tomase. "You weren't here," he said to Percy, his voice now sounding as if it was coming out of a wind tunnel. He lifted the gun, pointed it at Tomase's body, then pulled the trigger, pumped the last three shells into Tomase's chest. "You weren't here," he said again, then slowly sank to the sand, crumpled, feeling warm.

"The bullets, Lano, shit, you need an ambulance, I can't leave you." In the distance there was the sound of sirens coming this way. "I shot the guy, what, eight times."

"Seven, you load eight. You shot *me* once." The thought was amusing. He held his hand to his neck, took it away and showed the bloody palm to Percy. He was grinning. "See?"

"Yeah, but I shot *him*, too."

Lano looked at him, still grinning foolishly. The man looked rooted to the spot, too scared to move. Dummy.

"My bullets are in there, how you gonna explain that?"

"You dumb shit," Lano said. "Old man Biari's prints are all over the barrel of this gun, and your brother's the fucking coroner."

He laughed weakly, this was a good one, having to tell the man who his own brother was, what he did for a living. "Now fade, man, before they get here." He watched as Percy finally caught on, got it, turned and ran for the stairway. He looked at the body there beside him, Tough Tony not looking so tough now, looking deader than shit, truth be told. He giggled at that one, too. Deader than shit.

"See you in hell, Tony," Lano said, "but not this time, maybe. Maybe not just yet . . ." and slowly, conserving his strength so he could get the job done, he began to dig a hole in the sand.

25

Conway Mallory had run into the casino and had called the police immediately, had reported a shooting under the Boardwalk in front of O'Shea's Shamrock Hotel and Casino. She declined the offer to leave her name. She walked around the outside of the building because the casino was closed and there was no through access now to the back door. The wind tore at her, at her hair and at the light hose on her legs, trying to rip them from her, expose her naked skin to the elements.

Lano'd been shot. Lano had risked his life for her, twice. First, swimming into the ocean after her, that had taken courage. She'd thought about it later, about what he'd done, and she'd felt what she'd believed to be true love. It had been the first time in her life that she'd truly wanted to throw in the towel, and then, when she'd tried to, it had been just like in the fairy-tale books, a prince had come to save her. The only problem was, her Prince Charming was a compulsive. He'd saved her, then won and lost a million dollars, all within twenty-four hours. She looked at the money bag in her hand and became a schemer.

That was Brian's word, schemer. He'd call her that when he was angry with her. She wondered if he'd ordered his men to call her bluff that night, to wait until her hair was floating before going in after her. Well, it didn't matter now. What was done was done, and if that had been his order she just would have died.

The guy, Lano, he'd risked his life again just now, using precious seconds pushing her out of the way before flipping the suitcase at the man with the big gun. God, she'd watched the man and Percy shoot at each other, Percy hiding behind the corner and sticking his gun out first, then his head, then firing before the man took flight, headed down the stairs after Lano.

But he was shot, Lano was shot.

Yeah, and he was broke, too. She'd got hip to the game upstairs in the needle, could feel the tide turning against her when Malcolm had smiled like an asshole as she'd let loose of Lano's hand, and she'd almost blown it, had almost gone to Brian when he'd spoken kindly to her. Fortunately, she'd spent two years with the man, knew his ways, could tell when he was setting her up for the kill. Telling her he owned her, the son of a bitch. Calling her a card-whore.

Lano, too, what was he trying to pull, gambling everything on one roll of the dice? Was that dumb, or what? Then getting shot. She felt sorry for him, but it was his own fault, losing everything at once. If she'd had a gun, she might have shot him herself.

Now he'd handed her a bunch of money in a bank bag and Percy had given her the keys to a brand-new Lincoln, look at it shining there under the parking-lot lights. Carefully, she shut down the alarm, then unlocked the door, got in. A brand-new Lincoln and a bunch of money . . . And a schemer. She'd bet that if she left right now, she could be in Philly before the sun came up, it was only sixty miles away. Maybe she could even get back to the West Coast before anyone got concerned about the car.

She was about to start the car when she had second thoughts about it. She pushed them out of her mind. She had to think of herself first. If she became weak now, gave in to her feelings for Lano, she might give in to Brian or some other hustler here again, too, when they came calling, which they surely would if she stayed.

Another thought came to mind, jolting her. The car had been owned by a dago, from what Lano had told Percy and Edward, a dago in the mob. And how did they dispose of each other? In Italian restaurants or by leaving the bodies in the trunks of their cars.

My God, where was Edward?

Slowly, Conway took the keys out of the ignition and got out of the car. She left the bank bag on the seat. Her clothing and jewelry were all over the Boardwalk, where Lano had thrown the suitcases, and suddenly she felt no guilt about taking his money to replace them. She walked around the car, inserted the key in the trunk, popped it.

She let her breath out in a rush because there was nothing in there but a little suitcase. In the distance, she could hear sirens, the ambulance coming and the law. She closed the trunk, got back into the car and started it, drove away. She would check the suitcase as soon as she got to Philadelphia, see if there was anything in there she could use.

As she drove, she began to hum, then sing aloud. She was still young. Maybe there was still a chance she could make it as an actress. This time, she'd roll her eyes at some director, turning on the charm, open those green suckers wide and say, "Help me . . ." or "Please . . ." wistfully. So far, it had worked every time. And if she had to, there were other things she could roll for the producers, too, things she'd been keen on hanging on to years ago but which didn't make that much difference to her now. She began now to think about taking the scenic route out to L.A. Through

Nevada. She patted the bank bag and drove slowly, carefully, obeying all the traffic laws.

She was smiling as she drove out of Atlantic City.

Lano opened his eyes and *wham*, the bright light assaulted his left one. "What the fuck?" he said. Someone had a grip on his eyelid, was holding it open. The doctor grabbed the other eyelid, popped it wide, shone the little penlight at the right orb. "You want me to say ahh?"

"I want you to say a prayer, mister. A fraction of an inch to the left and you'd be gone, the artery would have been torn to hell." The doctor was young and bald, had grown the hair on the sides and back long to compensate. He wore round glasses.

"How come there're no cuffs on me?"

"Cuffs?" The doctor looked surprised. "What for? Crime victims don't get the cuffs, the criminals do." He studied Lano with a professional gaze. "What's your name?" he said, and Lano asked him how the hell he'd got in there, then noticed that it wasn't a hospital at all, as he'd expected.

He was lying in a king-size bed in a suite in the needle of the Shamrock Hotel and Casino.

"So the security guard heard the shots, was coming to investigate when Conway came running in, called the cops. He called O'Shea to cover the casino's ass, get the game closed down, all the time I'm on one of the other lobby phones, talking to the FBI."

Lano could not believe his ears. When Percy'd come in he'd craned his neck—hadn't that hurt like hell—looked out the door, expecting to see someone wearing a uniform standing guard.

"O'Shea comes down and I put it to him, help me out or I swear to God, my brother will put a stiff in his refrigerator, swear he was using them in his restaurant spaghetti sauce."

"You didn't."

Percy smiled, remembering. "Words to that effect. Afterwards, though, once he got you in here with the hotel doctor patching your neck, he told me he didn't need the threats, he'd have done it for the sake of helping another true gambler."

"He's full of shit."

"Yeah, but I bet it's fun for him to believe he's not."

"The feds come?"

Percy nodded. "They're searching for the guy whose blood is all over the sand under the Boardwalk, doesn't match up to the two stiffs. Lemuel took charge of both bodies, dug the bullets out. His report states that the two died from severe internal trauma caused by injection of lead bullets fired from a thirty-eight revolver."

Lano smiled back. "Or words to that effect."

"You were pretty cool down there last night, you know it?"

"I was light-headed."

"Yeah, but you had the presence of mind to shoot the fat little bastard with the gun killed my brother and Gaetano."

"They pull Ange in?"

"Not yet. They're talking to him, though. I haven't even spoken to the locals yet, but the feds are ready to charge him, soon as they get the gun."

"The gun's in a shallow hole, right next to where Tomase was lying. Where I was sitting."

"I was with them all night, answering questions. Christ, they're putting a task force together, everything."

"How'd you get them out here?"

"I told them I witnessed Ange kill his son and some other mobster, under the Boardwalk. That I was staking out Gaetano. That's no secret, hell, even Daniels will have to testify to that."

"They ask you why you didn't stop them?"

"Not once. They didn't seem too concerned about that. Probably happy to have them off the street."

"Just another couple of dead guineas."

"Mobsters, man, not guineas."

"It'll work out all right, you know it? You saw Ange pull the trigger, then you went to call the feds, tell them the target of three federal grand juries was killing people, Ange buries the gun and runs. They'll have him after all this time, put him away for something he didn't do."

"It only seems fitting."

Lano looked off, then back to Percy. "Do me a favor, call Conway, tell her to come and get me, I got to get out of this place. Shit, before the feds see me looking out the window with a patch on my neck or something."

"Uh, Lano?" Percy said slowly, then said, "There's a little problem there with that. . . ."

So she was gone. With his money. He thought about the fact that he'd almost decked O'Shea last night for insulting her honor and his mouth twitched, came close to a smile, but he wasn't ready for that yet. Then he thought of something else, and reached for the phone.

"Art?" Shit, he'd got him out of bed.

"Christ Almighty, where you at, are you okay?!"

"Art, calm down, I been shot, but I'll be all right."

It was the right thing to say. He had the man's attention now and when Art spoke again his voice was filled with a concern Lano had never heard before. "You gonna make it?"

"I'm fine, but I got to ask you a question."

"Shoot."

"How'd Bucking Bronco N. do over at Balmoral Friday night?"

There was a hesitation, and for a second he thought Art had hung up on him. He'd probably only been thinking about it, though, because a couple of seconds later Art said, "He's still running. Came in last."

"Thanks, Art."

"I read the papers about that other thing. Your name wasn't mentioned. Your problem has to do with that?"

"Yeah, I'll tell you about it when I get back."

"You need anything?"

Well, he'd asked. "Could you wire me a grand, Art? At the Palermo? I'll get it back to you as soon as I land."

"What happened to all that—?" Art cut the question off, remembering where Lano was. "It wasn't the prime roll after all, was it, Lano?"

Lano didn't answer.

Art hesitated, as if making a decision. Lano heard him blow his breath out hard, then he heard Art say, "Millie Swan's called here four times in the last twelve hours. Look her up before you leave, Lano." Then he heard the phone click in his ear.

Lano didn't call Millie, because he wasn't quite sure if he could face her. Instead, he walked the streets of Atlantic City, the grand in his pocket, half-hoping someone would try and take it away from him. It was broad daylight and he didn't think that would happen. Although the time of day didn't seem to stop the drug pushers or the hookers: they were out in force. They called Atlantic City "Beirut by the Boardwalk," and now he knew why. On every block there were storefront voodoo shops where you could go in and get a lucky spell cast for ten bucks, other stores where they sold books on how to break the bank. There were fast-food joints and a couple of Italian restaurants, soul-food places but mostly there were burnt-out shells of what had once been homes. The crackheads and the heroin addicts and the tapped-out compulsives lived there now, without running water or heat.

The weather had broken, the sun shining and the wind

dead, it was maybe forty degrees, cold still but the Bahamas compared to the past few weeks.

Lano's bag was locked in a locker at the bus depot. He'd catch a bus at three, take him to Philly where he'd get on an Amtrak train to Chicago's Union Station. He didn't feel like flying, not the way his luck had been. Too, he was in no hurry to face Art.

He walked the streets with his hands in his pockets, aimlessly, heading in a roundabout way for the Boardwalk but in no hurry to reach it. He felt no desire to gamble. He had a thousand in his pocket, borrowed, all he had to show for twenty-eight years of life.

He didn't know what he wanted to do now, but had the strong suspicion that whatever happened from here on out he was through with the gambling. There were other ways to make a buck.

He'd be all right.

The thought of Conway bothered him, but not much. He'd made his choices, his decisions, and he'd live with them. She'd have to do the same. If he ran into her on the street, he'd say something, but he wasn't about to go looking.

He reached the Boardwalk, mounted the steps, and there he was, facing the ocean again. The casinos behind him held no interest for him. He crossed the Boardwalk, noticing the strollers out for a walk in the fresh salt air. A lot of them were smiling. He smiled back.

There was a woman out along the water's edge, vaguely familiar from behind, looking out to sea. There was another woman, too, this one a little farther down the beach, wearing a scarf over her head, throwing shells into the ocean, skipping them for a small child. Feeling a strong sadness, Lano turned and walked in the other direction, to the next stairway down, got out onto the sand and kept his eyes straight ahead, looking at the water.

Behind him, the casino neon glittered. Ahead, infinity stretched, as it had since time began.

Lano felt almost good.

There was more to it than he could think about right now, a lot more, and when the time was right he would see it as it was, for what it was, take it out and look at it and try to make some sense out of it all, but for now it was okay to just stare off into the waves, relaxing and feeling almost good. Sometimes it was better not to be able to figure out everything, just to roll with the punches.

"Lano?" A female voice, soft and surprised. He turned, faced Arliss Owen. The side of her face was swollen a little bit, multicolored but healing. That son of a bitch, Tomase. He smiled at her, gently.

"Hello, Arliss."

"My *God*, what are you *doing* here? Am I happy to see you. What happened, do you know what *happened*, did you hear about Tony? He stranded me in a hotel and disappeared . . ."

"I'll tell you all about it later, on the bus."

"Bus?"

"The three-o'clock to Philly. We're going home."

"On a *bus*?"

"Arliss, I'm tapped out."

"You're *what*?"

"But I got enough, get us both back to Chicago."

"On a *bus*?"

Lano was still smiling faintly, gently, seeing her as she was, this woman who'd told his recording machine that he had to grow up, that he had no character. He'd give her the chance though, and if she passed, he'd understand.

Arliss was backing away now, embarrassed, muttering that she'd see him later, telling him how sorry she was.

Terrific.

He didn't say anything, but followed her with his eyes, watching Arliss back away until finally she turned and hurried away from him.

He figured she'd be all right. After all, she was in a town filled with high rollers.

He turned his back to her again, on her and on Atlantic City, the man who'd lost a million dollars on one roll of the dice, standing staring off to sea, and when he heard a woman's voice softly speak his name he thought it was Arliss and didn't turn around.

Until Millie touched his arm.

He stared at her, at her and at the little boy at her side. He didn't trust himself to speak at first, there was a lump in his throat and a great heaviness in his chest. Tears filled his eyes.

"Are you all right?"

He nodded.

She smiled sheepishly, shrugged. "He fired me, you know, Brian did, for trying to get you not to roll."

"I should have listened to you."

"First, though, he gave me your letter."

Lano nodded again.

"There's a lot to talk about, Lano."

He was thinking, thinking and remembering. About how he used to love this woman, still did, if he wanted to be honest. The wind picked up, pulling at her scarf, and he had to look away from her. He looked down at the child and froze.

He was staring down at himself twenty-five years ago.

Oh, dear God.

"Lano?" Millie said.

Softly, so softly that he wasn't even sure that he was speaking the words, Lano said, "Come to me," and she did, moving into his arms, and he turned, put one arm around her waist and leaned down, lifted the child up with his other arm, and began to cry.

"Don't," Millie said.

"I'll be all right," Lano said.

"You sure?" the child said, with concern.

Millie told her son, her own voice breaking, "He's sure, Stevie, we'll make him sure."

The three of them stood that way for a long time, silently,

and when Lano had control of himself, all he could think of to say was, "It's a good thing I lost, Millie."

"Lano, have *you* changed."

"Wait'll you hear about it."

Changed, and maybe along the way gained some character.

He hugged her to him, Stevie, too, who wasn't complaining, and he smiled, then laughed, looking out at forever with his back turned on a shallow, shabby little town.

ABOUT THE AUTHOR

Eugene Izzi has lived in and around Chicago all his life. He is the author of five previous novels: BAD GUYS, THE EIGHTH VICTIM, THE BOOSTER, THE TAKE and KING OF THE HUSTLERS. He is currently at work on his seventh novel, INVASIONS.

Here is a special advance preview of IN-VASIONS, the newest title from Eugene Izzi, available as a Bantam hardcover in April 1990.

If you walk north on State Street in the city of Chicago you will see some sights. The State Street Mall in itself is something to see, the wide sidewalks and the vendors and the stores being only a part of the strange beauty. Mostly, it's the people who make the show worthwhile.

Depending on the weather, you can see breakdancers, singers, guitar players, sidewalk-corner preachers, bag ladies, winos, yuppies, ghetto gangbangers, tourists, suburban shoppers, cops, robbers, hustlers, hookers, pimps, grifters, and, to top it all off, resentful union bus drivers blocking the streets to all of the above.

The farther north you get, the stranger things seem.

This year, the rage is Cajun food and fly fishing.

Everywhere you look, you will see restaurants catering to the yuppies, their neon signs proclaiming their food to be authentic Cajun, implying that all the other restaurants—and there are plenty of them—serve some sort of *counterfeit* Cajun. Every other store, it seems, caters to fly fishermen, or some other specialized branch of sport.

On North State, there are no gyms or ginmills. You can find health centers and health clubs, and workout worlds, but no gyms. There are places called saloons, and clubs, and a couple even dare to call themselves taverns, but there are no real taverns on North State, and absolutely no gin-mills.

Where State meets Rush at Cedar, things get hot. There's some serious money in this area, and the only thing that a Southsider would recognize is the Walgreen's drugstore on the corner. And he'd only recognize it until he got inside. On the South Side, you don't take ugly and yapping little doggies into your corner drugstore and expect people to walk around them as they search for their Anacin.

At the next block State Street stops being State Street and turns into North State Parkway. Hefner used to live on North State Parkway before heading for L.A. His mansion is still there, the biggest on the block, surrounded by a high iron gate, the gate mostly always unlocked nowadays. Hef had his own private drive and courtyard. A brass plaque, proclaiming the place to be Hefner Hall, is attached to the vine-covered stone wall of the mansion's facade.

At Division you take a quick right and head east, and as you pass the streets named after trees, Oak, Cedar, Maple, etc., a strange thing happens.

Money grows on these streets.

Many of the homes and mansions and estates in the area are now for sale. The stock market crash has taken its toll. Real estate signs are in the windows of more homes than usual, the homes done up nice and pretty, having age and architecture on their side but not taste. Some of these grand old places have been painted lime green and bright yellow, trimmed with red. One, in fact, is pink. With black lacquered window frames. Still, you smell money, and the rich, after all, *are* different than you and me.

The last street you come to before hitting Michigan and Lake Shore Drive is Astor Street.

All of the residents of Astor Street live on North Astor Street, as there *is* no South Astor Street. North Astor Street runs from Division down to North Street, covering a total of five blocks. The cross streets on North Astor are, in order: Scott, Goethe, East Banks Street, Schiller, and West Burton Place, some serious names indeed. On any of these streets, there is the smell of money. There are gorgeous homes on these cross streets, mansions and apartments, condos and high rises. They are the setting, the semi-precious stones surrounding the flawless D diamond that is North Astor Street.

There are no yellow, green, black, orange, or pink facades on North Astor. To be sure, some of the mansions have been cut up into condos, and some soulless, godless, money-grubbing capitalists have torn down some of the mansions and built high rises, but they are few and in themselves are soulless.

Even the penthouses in these high rises, with breathtaking views of Lake Michigan right across the boulevard, are, when you come right down to it, really just good addresses and nothing more.

The mansions, the ones that haven't been cut up into condos and apartments, have ghosts, and that is something no modern high rise can claim.

Ghosts of people named Worthington and Field, Pennington and DuPont. Ghosts of men with first names like Hoddington and Jameson, their wives named Ashley and Clayton. The ghosts of old money walk in the halls of the mansions, and their power is still felt in dark rooms. Power of people who had Lord and Lady in front of their names.

The farther north you get on Astor, the better. The last real street is the fourth, the fifth actually being more or less high rises and condos until you get to North Street.

On this last block, money talks and bullshit walks, particularly in the last five mansions on the east side of the street.

Four of them are for sale. A sign in one of them lets you know that it has already undergone over $2.5 million in renovations. You have to put up a $25,000 bond assuring your good intentions to be allowed a walk-through. This serves to keep the merely curious away. These last five homes are not and will not be cut up into condos. The owners won't allow it. It is all or nothing in these homes.

The fifth house is the largest mansion on North Astor Street.

Most of the others are butted right up against one another, side by side with no breathing room. There are no gangways on North Astor. There are, however, private drives, private alleys, private courtyards, and even a private park. The park these days is populated mostly by black women wearing white, nannying the children of the rich Astor Street residents. Most of the black people you see, for that matter, are wearing white jackets and work here. The fifth mansion on North Astor was butted up against nothing. Its address was 5258 Astor, and it had land.

Two acres of it, in fact. Surrounded by a nine-foot stone privacy fence. At the front entrance by the sidewalk there was an eight-foot iron gate, electronically controlled from the inside or from the street if you had the right coded magnetic card. There was an intercom grille attached to the stone pillar that held one of the gate hinges, so the owner could screen his visitors.

The other residents of North Astor, the homeowners as well as the renters, would never say anything right out, but you could figure from five minutes of general conversation with them that they were green with jealousy of the guy who owned the mansion, right down to their black silk Calvin Klein underwear.

* * *

The muscular tall guy was holding a wee little Mexican chihuahua on a slim leather leash, the leash attached to a leather collar studded with blue, green, and red rhinestones. It was early October, and there was a chill in the air, but the character wore a purple silk ribbed tank top that ended just above his navel, showing washboard abs. His hair was obviously dyed, bright yellow, combed straight back in a sweeping style. It hung to his shoulders, brushed them as he tossed his head to get the few wisps that fell forward onto his forehead out of hs eyes. He had on black spandex pants with the name of a race car written down each leg. He had something stuffed down the front of his pants, making his groin area appear massive, but the casual passerby couldn't make out what it was without being too obvious, and the big guy ignored the few men who did try to see what was down there. He minced as he walked slowly forward on his Air Jordans. He passed a couple of black nannies dressed in their nurses' uniforms, watched with a bemused and frank expression as they tried to keep from cracking up as they approached, made it, then laughed aloud the second they passed, kidding each other. One of them said, "Lord, what a waste of a fine-bodied man . . ." and the guy smiled.

He passed the big house, stopped so the dog could relieve itself in the gutter. As it squatted, he said, "Really, Foo-foo, couldn't you have waited until we got to the alley?" Giving the house a quick once-over, seeing nothing out of the ordinary. The stop-sign-shaped red sign attached to one of the gate halves said in bold white letters: PREMISES PROTECTED BY ADT TRIPLE-ALARM SYSTEM! TRESPASSERS WILL BE PROSECUTED TO THE FULLEST EXTENT OF THE LAW! The man looked around the property through the gates, his eyes wide, Foo-foo pulling at the leash. He felt the urge to boot it in the ass, but that would be out of character. After a short time, he gave in, walked with the dog to the end of the block, around the corner, and into the alley.

Here Astor Street looked a lot like Beirut. There was gang graffiti sprayed on the tall privacy fences, most of them topped with barbed wire, curling three or four feet into the air all the way around the edge of the properties. The stone fence surrounding 5258 North Astor didn't have the wire, but had razor sharp arrowheads sticking out of the thing at one-foot intervals. The man knew that broken glass was embedded between the iron heads. Someone had posted a bill to the middle of the wall, the little poster mimeographed, hung crookedly. It had a picture of a rat in a circle, with a line drawn through the rodent. It said, TO CONTROL PESTS, PLEASE SECURE THE LID ON YOUR GARBAGE CANS! To Foo-foo, the man said, "Quaint," then minced out of the alley, setting his face in a mask of open invitation, ready to take the ridicule he would have to face farther south, down State, as he headed back to the parking lot where he'd left the stolen car.

The mob guy's name was Tonce DiLeonardo, and they called him the Lion. He had a full head of hair that he dyed black and had styled every week at a place called The Gentleman's Shoppe. He liked the Shoppe part, it showed that the fuckers who owned the joint had class. He was sitting across the desk from a guy he considered to be a punk, but a guy he needed right now, so he fought the urge to climb over the desk and slap the son of a bitch, the way he was sitting there grinning at him. He'd be giving up maybe twenty-five years, the punk was maybe thirty, thirty-one, but they were both big and weighed about the same and the Lion figured that experience was on his side.

They sat in the office of the Lion's South Side home, in

what he called the Lion's Den. There were bodyguards outside in the hall and in the living room, the muscle belonging to both of them. He didn't like the fact that this kid had brought in some of his toughs, like they had a chance against his men if he decided to get hard. Still, he didn't say anything. Yet. He'd poured the kid a drink personally, watched him sip it, saw the surprise on the kid's face because this was seventy-five-year-old Royal Salute, top-shelf stuff, better than anything the kid had ever put down his throat before. Tonce figured if this guy had ever had a shot of this stuff before, it was after stealing it in a liquor store robbery; he pictured this slob behind an alley somewhere, drinking Royal Salute out of the bottle, maybe after mixing it with Kool Aid or Boone's Farm. The kid made a face, lifted the glass in a mock salute, then drank the rest of the scotch down in one gulp, with a flick of his wrist. He slapped the glass down on the desk, burped, and said, "Good shit, Mr. D," smirking still.

"Thank you, Tommy," the Lion said, then made up his mind. The second the deal was done, he'd suffocate the life out of this kid, teach him a lesson.

But for now he smiled, sipped his own whiskey, placed the glass right in the middle of the coaster in front of him, and said, "Tommy, tell me a little about one of your boys, a fella named Jimmy Vale."

"Good man, one of the best the Brotherhood got. Tough, takes no shit from the niggers inside. Why, he do something? This what this sitdown's all about?" The Lion just looked at him.

"Mr. D," the cocky little shit said, "maybe you ought to tell me what this is about."

The tall, muscular man had pulled off the wig as soon as he got the car out of the garage, had pulled into an alley and removed the thing, tossed it on the seat. He pulled a bag off the floor of the passenger side, got jeans and a sweatshirt out of it, and pulled them over the fag clothes, leaving on the Air Jordans. He liked those Air Jordans. He shoved the wig into the bag, fought the urge to shove the dog down in there, too. Shit, they'd done a job on it, had put little pink bows on the sucker's ears and one on its little rat tail. He pictured the chihuahua's picture on a poster, with a line drawn through it. Little rat-looking ugly thing. Even now—you'd think the dog would know better—it was standing up on the stolen Chevy's seat, barking its little ass off when he needed a little privacy. He shushed it—it was too little to hurt—put the car in gear, and drove slowly out of the alley, heading for home.

Manny Aeilo stood on the front terrace of the Winnetka mansion his boss owned, surveying the grounds and the surrounding estates with a pair of 10×50 power binoculars, the kind with the wide-angle lenses. Slowly, he'd pan right, then left, looking for signs from New York. He did this three or four times every day, never at the same time, staggering the hours to throw off anyone who might be watching him.

Like the guys late this past summer. They'd been slick, he'd give them that, but he was slicker. You didn't last thirty-seven years in his business being second best.

Those guys had been thorough. At any given time, day and night, there were four guards on duty, protecting Mad Mike Tile from his enemies. Thirty-two guys in Manny's crew, none of them weak, although lately, some of them were going soft. He'd call one of them to him, late last August, early September, hand them the binocs, say to them "Take a look, tell me what you see," and none of them ever saw anything.

The guys doing the surveillance work had been that good.

They'd dress like typical Winnetka residents, in jogging clothes or bathing suits, all the time wearing the radios attached to their heads, but Manny could tell: from the look in their eyes; the way they looked a little too closely at the mansion; hung around the park across the street trying to look casual, that they were checking the place out.

He'd go to the boss, to Mike, tell him his suspicions and what would the man say? Manny's paranoid, seeing dragons in his old age. Mike would tell him that his underlings in the Chicago outfit loved him, revered him, the great Mike Tile who'd brought dope into the city, after years of stringent rules against the white powder. Everyone was making money, tons of the stuff, Mike would tell him. Why would anyone want Mike Tile dead? Manny didn't know, didn't have an answer for him. Sometimes it would take him an hour just to get in and talk to the man, having to wait until he was through with the young girls he'd taken such a shine to since his wife's death.

Mike would talk to him and be rubbing his nose, shaking his full head of long white hair, running his fingers through it. Sniffing. Mike, what, sixty-four or -five now, and in the last two years he'd started with the young chicks and the sampling of his own wares. Rich enough to snort all he wanted and never even tap the main source.

Manny remembered the good old days, when it was gambling and broads that brought in the money. Plenty to go around, too, with the old man in charge, the Swordfish, ready to go to war and chop the hands off anyone who dared to venture into drug dealing.

Manny had been good, rising through the ranks of Mike's crew until he was the chief, second in command. They would sit down and between the two of them devise a way to defeat their enemies, those who wanted what Mike Tile had.

They'd done that recently, too, three years back when Mike had taken over and decided to give the dying outfit a cash transfusion, drugs being their plasma. It had been fun, the three of them—Mike, Manny, and Manny's right hand, Louis Bamonti—putting their heads together to find a way to destroy the black and Hispanic gangs that had total control of the drug dealing in the city back then. Louis had claimed it was impossible, and Manny had just looked at him.

These gangs, these young, stupid kids who'd filled their heads with dumb ideas, running around wearing gold chains as heavy as hemp, driving their black muscle-cars, had been easy. The ones who wouldn't negotiate had been killed in the style they themselves had immortalized, the cops had gone looking for other gangs, when all the time it was the Tile outfit that had done the killings, using the unfamiliar Uzis and MAC-10s to do the job, throwing the cops off their scent.

What it came down to, in Manny's mind, was leadership, generalship. Now that his own wife had died and his three children were grown, he had taken a room in the mansion, the walls filled with bookcases, every book having to do with war, with warriors, with killing. Manny could name every shogun who ever existed, every Roman emperor. Early on, he'd known that it wasn't in him to lead, to be the head of his own family. But he could be the best mob crew chief who'd ever lived, the greatest gladiator. He had no patience for the politics involved in being on top, the ass-kissing and speaking in riddles symbolically. He said what he had to say, the only way he knew how, straight and to the point, without bullshit or any extra words. Patton was the best general who'd ever lived, in Manny's opinion, but he would have made a terrible president.

He believed that he was Mike Tile's Patton.

A bunch of disorganized blacks and Hispanics, punks who

worshipped money, were no match for him. He'd taken them over and had been greatly rewarded for doing so.

As had Mike Tile. The millions poured in, tens of millions, and Tile's national esteem with it. Everyone loved him, Mike would say. Men, women, children, even his own bodyguards, see how they admired him, partied with him? Found him new untouched young girls who wanted to go somewhere in life?

If everyone loved Mike Tile, Manny wondered, then why was somebody setting him up?

Frank Vale was pushing thirty-five and had never done a day in the penitentiary, though he'd spent a night or two in the can over the years, usually for some bullshit in a bar late at night, having to teach some wise guy a lesson. He figured by his own count that he'd pulled maybe three hundred burglaries, so the fact that he'd never been pinched for one carried a lot of weight.

He saw himself as a perfectionist with a tight lip, and that made him maybe the best thief in the city. Only one man had ever done time because of a score he'd set up, and that made him one of the most sought-after thieves in the city. But he was careful, chose only the best he could find to work with, guys he knew he could trust and who would die before giving him up if for some reason they got put in the trick bag. He didn't deal in egos, never had a problem giving orders and could take them, too, if the guy giving them knew what he was talking about.

He figured it beat punching a time clock.

He'd been married once, briefly, to a girl who'd changed in days from a sweet young kid into a nag, bringing her entire zoo into his house the day after the wedding. Two fifty-five-gallon glass tanks filled with freshwater fish, a mixed-breed mutt dog, a calico cat, and a parrot. The bird's name was Gonzo, which she thought was cute, and the ugly, green son of a bitch would actually take seed out of her mouth, then coo at her, peck gently at her nose. He'd try to touch it, stick his finger in the cage to pet its head, and it would bite him, drawing blood a couple of times before he decided that it would never like him. His wife would bill and coo at the bird, "Gonzo loves only his mommy, isn't that right little baby?" like he was supposed to be jealous of it or something. When he started thinking about making soup out of the thing or pissing in the fish tanks, he figured the marriage was in trouble. He'd gotten a no-fault divorce and had bought her off with a hundred grand cash for six months of her time, and packed her off with his best wishes. He'd kept the dog, and found that he liked it better than he ever had the wife.

He stood six feet three inches tall and in the summer got down to two-ten, would bloat up to maybe two-twenty in the winter but would never lose his hardness, the well-defined muscles kept tight and strong through daily workouts. He didn't do it because he was vain, but because he thought of his body as a machine that had to be kept tuned. He wasn't just playing with his own life here, there were other men to consider. He had to be in top shape, sharp and ready with good reflexes, and they would all get out alive and prosper after a score. He demanded this of himself and of the men he worked with. Behind his back, he knew, they called him the Iceman.

He kind of liked it, being called that, because it fit his image of himself. There was only one man alive he would ever really open up to, tell things to, and that man was his brother who was now in the joint, wrapping up a nine-year sentence for home invasion. Thinking of his brother made him smile. Christ, he missed that kid. It would be good to see him.

He pulled the car to the curb about two blocks from his

house, shoved the dog under his sweatshirt, the little mutt nipping at him and fidgeting, shit, and jogged home, where the two men he'd picked for the job would be waiting in his basement, studying the floor plans and the alarm systems for tonight's score, the big mansion at 5258 North Astor Street. He would be happy to tell them that it looked like a go.

He turned the corner onto Sheridan and spotted the two cops at the same time they saw him, knew they spotted him and so fought the urge to just turn around and walk away. He walked, casually, toward them, bending down and letting Foo-foo loose, holding the leash, putting a curious look on his face as he pretended to spot the guys. The first one he knew, it was that prick, Gunon. The second one was new, probably just came into the unit, was learning the ropes. The new kid was holding his own, giving him the insolent stare that was the trademark of the elite Police Reconnaissance and Intelligence for Crime Control unit, called PRICC by the thieves of Chicago.

"There a problem, officers?"

Gunon answered, grinning. "Problem, Frank? Now when did we ever have a problem with you, huh?" Frank said nothing. This was a part of the life he'd chosen and he'd learned to accept it.

"Nice dog you got there," the new kid said, and Gunon giggled. "I read a study once, said all a you tough guys was undercover faggots."

Frank took a deep breath, let it out. He said, "Tell you what, there's a way to check it out. Why don't you kiss my ass, and if I get stiff, you win." He dropped the leash when the young cop started coming at him, put his hands up, then dropped them because Gunon had his hand on his piece there at the front of his waistband, ready.

"Go ahead, badass, add assaulting an officer to the charges."

"What *are* the charges?" Frank said. The kid had stopped advancing, was standing there letting Gunon handle things. He was breathing hard though, and Frank wasn't looking forward to the visit to the basement of the precinct house. Gunon had lightened the grip on his pistol, in control and showing it. He was grinning in the oily way he had, like a pimp does, pretending to be friends with someone he was trying to beat out of some money.

"Planning a score and not telling your partners about it. That's a serious offense in this town, you know." Gunon laughed, he had a habit of cracking himself up, and his partner smirked.

"Gonna bust you up, Mr. Big Time. Mr. Big-Time Thief. And I can't wait."

Gunon said, "Giraldi, cuff this asshole and put him in the car."

(Now read the complete INVASIONS, on sale in April 1990 whatever Bantam hardcovers are sold.)

Praise for Joseph Wambaugh

"Joseph Wambaugh's characters have altered America's view of police." —*Time*

"Wambaugh is a master artist of the street scene."
—*Publishers Weekly*

"Wambaugh is a writer of genuine power."
—*New York Times Book Review*

"Perhaps better than any other contemporary writer, Wambaugh is able to convey just what it is that makes cops different from the rest of us and, more important, why."
—*Library Journal*

Nobody Writes About Cops Better Than Wambaugh
Don't Miss Any Of These Bantam Bestsellers

☐	27386	DELTA STAR	$4.95
☐	27259	GLITTER DOME	$4.95
☐	27148	LINES AND SHADOWS	$4.95
☐	27430	SECRETS OF HARRY BRIGHT	$4.95
☐	26932	ECHOES IN THE DARKNESS	$4.95
☐	28281	THE BLOODING	$5.95

Look for the above books at your local bookstore or use this page to order.

— — — — — — — — — — — — — — — —

Bantam Books, Dept. JW3, 414 East Golf Road, Des Plaines, IL 60016

Please send me the items I have checked above. I am enclosing $_____
(please add $2.00 to cover postage and handling). Send check or money order, no cash or C.O.D.s please. (Tape offer good in USA only.)

Mr/Ms _____

Address _____

City/State _____ Zip_____

JW3-12/89

Please allow four to six weeks for delivery.
Prices and availability subject to change without notice.

Now there are two great ways to catch up with your favorite thrillers

Audio:

Kinsey Millhone is...

"The best new private eye."   *—The Detroit News*

"A tough-cookie with a soft center."   *—Newsweek*

"A stand-out specimen of the new female operatives."
                                    —Philadelphia Inquirer

Sue Grafton is...

The Shamus and Anthony Award winning creator of
Kinsey Millhone and quite simply one of the hottest
new mystery writers around.

Bantam is...

The proud publisher of Sue Grafton's Kinsey Millhone
mysteries:

☐	27991	"A" IS FOR ALIBI	$3.95
☐	28034	"B" IS FOR BURGLAR	$3.95
☐	28036	"C" IS FOR CORPSE	$3.95
☐	27163	"D" IS FOR DEADBEAT	$3.95
☐	27955	"E" IS FOR EVIDENCE	$3.95